UNHOLY FIRE

ALSO BY ROBERT J. MRAZEK

Stonewall's Gold

Love to
Dick & Gerry —
Happy New Home

Unholy
Fire

A Novel of the Civil War

Robert J. Mrazek

THOMAS DUNNE BOOKS
ST. MARTIN'S PRESS ⚏ NEW YORK

THOMAS DUNNE BOOKS.
An imprint of St. Martin's Press.

www.stmartins.com

Library of Congress Cataloging-in-Publication Data

Mrazek, Robert J.
    Unholy fire : a novel of the Civil War / Robert J. Mrazek.—1st ed.
      p. cm.
    ISBN 0-312-30673-3
    1. United States—History—Civil War, 1861–1865—Fiction. 2. Courts-martial
and courts of inquiry—Fiction. 3. Hooker, Joseph, 1814–1879—Fiction.
4. Washington (D.C.)—Fiction. 5. Conspiracies—Fiction. I. Title.

PS3563.R39 U54 2003
813'.54—dc21   2002032512

First Edition: April 2003

10 9 8 7 6 5 4 3 2 1

For my parents, Bill and Blanche,

the source of any and all inspiration

The aim of war is murder; the methods of war are spying, treachery, and their encouragement, the ruin of a country's inhabitants, robbing them or stealing to provision the army, and fraud and falsehood termed military craft. The habits of the military class are the absence of freedom, that is, discipline, idleness, ignorance, cruelty, debauchery and drunkenness. And in spite of all this it is the highest class, respected by everyone. All the kings, except the Chinese, wear military uniforms, and he who kills the most people, receives the highest awards.

—Prince Andrew Bolkonski, in
War and Peace
Tolstoy

During the winter (1862–63) when Gen. Joseph Hooker was in command, I can say from personal knowledge and experience that the headquarters of the Army of the Potomac was a place to which no self-respecting man liked to go, and no decent woman would go. It was a combination of barroom and brothel.

—Capt. Charles Francis Adams Jr.
(grandson of Pres. John Quincy Adams)
First Massachusetts Cavalry

Author's Note

In the winter of 1862 Pres. Abraham Lincoln was desperate to find a successful commanding general for his ill-fated Army of the Potomac. As the second year of the war drew to a close, many considered his previous selections of field commanders to be scandalously, if not criminally, deficient.

The Union had begun the Civil War with high hopes for a quick victory. The army's commanding general was Winfield Scott, the valiant warrior who had helped defeat the British fifty years earlier in the War of 1812, and then gone on to glory as the hero of Chapultepec in the war against Mexico.

At seventy-five, Winfield Scott was still an imposing six feet, five inches tall, but there were few traces left of the powerful warrior. His weight had ballooned to more than four hundred pounds, and he spent most of each day preparing himself for supper, when he would mount a huge throne chair and typically consume four dozen oysters, a brace of snipe, a leg of lamb, a joint of beef, and a full platter of pastries, all topped off with his favorite wines and brandies. No horse was large enough to carry him into battle. He could barely fit inside a carriage.

Clearly, Lincoln needed to find a more active field commander. He settled on Gen. Irvin McDowell. It was an unfortunate choice. A man of peculiar contrasts, the teetotaling McDowell viewed even tea and coffee as dangerously stimulating to the brain. Yet his gluttony rivaled Winfield

Scott's. One of his favorite culinary practices after consuming a gargantuan meal was to eat an entire watermelon, including the rind. When it came to fighting battles, however, Lincoln had to push him hard to use the army. McDowell was reluctant to move against the Confederates even though their forces were considerably smaller than his own. Under pressure, he finally headed south into Virginia.

On the night before the first great battle of the Civil War, McDowell collapsed at his headquarters after an intestinal attack caused by a bad section of watermelon. The next day, the Union army was routed at Manassas, Virginia, its remnants retreating in complete panic back to Washington that same night. Rumors immediately began circulating through the capital that General McDowell was a traitor. The morning after the battle, Lincoln dismissed him as commander.

President Lincoln's next choice was the diminutive Gen. George Brinton McClellan. Just thirty-four, "Little Mac" patterned himself after Napoleon. He was the first American general to understand the art of public relations. The victor of a small skirmish in the mountains of West Virginia, McClellan and his supporters had embroidered the tiny engagement into the greatest victory since Yorktown. However, he proved to be an expert at reorganizing an army shattered by its humiliation at Manassas. His problems only began when Lincoln asked him to use it. If McDowell had been reluctant to fight, McClellan made avoiding battle an art form.

By November of 1861, his army numbered more than 120,000 men, while the Confederates could muster only 45,000 to repel him. Yet McClellan managed to convince himself that the enemy force was four times the size of his own and demanded more troops. Lincoln became increasingly impatient.

In the spring of 1862, McClellan decided to ferry his vast army by ship to the southeastern tip of the Virginia Peninsula. He then slowly moved north toward the Confederate capital of Richmond. After a long, unsuccessful attempt to lay siege to the city, he retreated back down the Peninsula. When McClellan began whining for more troops, Lincoln decided to bring in Gen. John Pope, who had recently won a successful engagement in the Western Theater of the war.

Unfortunately, Pope was incompetent, as well as a blowhard. After publicly denigrating the troops he was about to command, he stated that henceforth, "My headquarters will be in the saddle," which led one irreverent observer to declare, "The dumb son of a bitch doesn't even know his headquarters from his hindquarters."

This proved to be exactly the case. Outmaneuvered at every step by Gen. Robert E. Lee, he suffered another disastrous defeat near Manassas, in virtually the same place where McDowell had been routed a year earlier. With the Union army in a state of near chaos, Lee now led his forces into Maryland in the first invasion of the North. The prime minister of England, Viscount Palmerston, was fully prepared to recommend that the Confederacy be recognized as an independent nation after Lee's next anticipated success. Lincoln was forced to call McClellan back to try to save the day.

Fate now presented "Little Mac" with a golden opportunity that remains unparalleled in American military history. By chance, a written copy of Lee's complete plan of operations was found by two Union soldiers and taken to the commanding general. It revealed that Lee had split his army into four separate parts. If McClellan moved quickly, he had a chance to annihilate Lee's forces before they could reunite, thus ending the war.

McClellan squandered three days moving his army just thirty miles to the village of Sharpsburg, Maryland. There, Lee, with a force only one-third the size of McClellan's, audaciously decided to stand and fight. McClellan, instead of using his overwhelming advantage to attack along the whole battle line, sent his men into the battle piecemeal. When the carnage at Antietam was over, the two armies had simply fought to a bloody standstill.

President Lincoln was finished with McClellan. Who would be his next choice? The decision was complicated by the fact that Lincoln's popularity had sunk to its lowest ebb in the war. In addition to having selected a parade of losing generals to command the Union army, he had shown a terrible penchant for appointing militarily incompetent political friends like Sen. Edward Baker to important army commands. Their failures had led to the unnecessary deaths of thousands of brave Union soldiers. Further, his appointment of corrupt politicians like Simon Cameron to the highest posts in the War Department had resulted in the theft of public funds on a monumental and unprecedented scale. Even worse, war profiteers were delivering military equipment to the army that was often shoddy and defective.

Understandably, many of the army's career officers had come to revile the president. As the military defeats piled up, their anger became increasingly palpable. It was shared by the public at large. In the national election that took place just a few weeks after the Antietam battle, Lincoln's Republican Party lost thirty-four congressional seats.

President Lincoln narrowed his next choice of army commander to two senior generals, Ambrose Burnside and Joseph Hooker.

Like McClellan, Burnside had achieved a small success early in the war. Lincoln had taken notice of it and promoted him. Although his performance thereafter was undistinguished, few others in Lincoln's army had excelled either. It was said of Burnside that he not only knew he was incompetent but was the first to admit it. This self-deprecating geniality appealed to Lincoln, as it did to many of Burnside's fellow officers. Early in his career, he had been an ardent poker player, once losing six months' pay in a single game. He fell in love with a girl from Kentucky and proposed marriage. As they stood together at the altar, the minister asked if she would take him to be her husband. "No," she exclaimed. Burnside, who also suffered from chronic diarrhea, handled all his disappointments with manly dignity. At Antietam, he came up woefully short again. As usual, he was the first to admit it.

Joe Hooker had different problems. Often called the most handsome officer in the Union army, he was an unrelenting critic of his superior officers, who naturally despised him. He had also earned a reputation as a hard drinker and a libertine. At the same time, Hooker had achieved the best combat record of any senior officer in the Union army. Almost rashly brave, he usually rode a white horse into battle, which made him as conspicuous a target as any general could be. A brilliant brigade commander, he had proven similarly successful when promoted to division and then corps command. Hooker fought his troops with a drive that bordered on recklessness. At Antietam, he sustained a serious wound while personally leading his men into the battle.

As history records, Lincoln chose Burnside, the man he personally liked, to command the army. By mid-November, 1862, the Army of the Potomac, 115,000 strong, and the largest military force then assembled on the planet, was on the move again.

Ambrose Burnside had a plan, and it reflected the simplicity of a man devoid of imagination. He proposed to push his whole army across the Rappahannock River near Fredericksburg, Virginia, and then head straight for Richmond, just fifty miles farther south. By capturing the Confederate capital, he could end the war.

The truth be told, if Burnside had carried out his plan with dispatch, American schoolchildren might today be laying flowers at Ambrose Burnside's tomb, not Ulysses S. Grant's. For when Joe Hooker, commanding the Center Grand Division, arrived at the Rappahannock River on November 19, 1862, he was amazed to discover that Lee had been caught by surprise. The enemy force facing him consisted of two batteries of field artillery, one regiment of cavalry, and three hundred infantrymen.

From his advance headquarters at Falmouth, Virginia, Hooker immediately requested permission to move his forty thousand men across the river, it then being shin-deep in places, and to take the high ground above the city of Fredericksburg. Burnside considered the request and promptly rejected it. Instead, he ordered Hooker to remain at Falmouth and wait for his engineers to bring up pontoon bridges that would make it easier for the rest of the army to cross.

So Hooker and his men sat down to wait.

UNHOLY FIRE

CHAPTER ONE

Camp Benton, Maryland
Along the Potomac River
October 1861

ON THE MORNING before my first battle, I awoke to find a rime of frost on the moss-covered ground under my tent. Although it was only mid-October, the weather had grown markedly colder every day.

At around eight o'clock, a Rebel sharpshooter shot and killed one of our pickets down at the river. It was the first death in the regiment, and I wondered how many more there would be before the war was over.

We had spent five weeks trying to turn the six hundred men of the Twentieth Massachusetts into fighting soldiers. The regimental drummers would beat reveille every morning at six. After the first roll call there were squad drills, then breakfast, followed by sick call. We had company drill until dinner, followed by combat drill, dress parade, roll call, supper, and, finally, tattoo at nine o'clock. Along with the other officers, I would then work until one or two in the morning to prepare for the next day.

Our camp was situated on a low mountaintop near Poolesville, Maryland. At night the sky was so clear that we could actually see the signal fires in the Blue Ridge Mountains nearly fifty miles to the west where Confederate scouts were monitoring the movements of our army in the Shenandoah Valley. Just across the Potomac, the landscape was lit by the gleaming campfires of the Confederate brigade bivouacked around Leesburg, Virginia.

Every Saturday, we joined our sister regiments in Colonel Baker's new brigade for parade drills. They were the Nineteenth Massachusetts, the

Seventh Michigan, and the Forty-second New York, also known as the Tammany Regiment. Those men impressed me as the toughest group in the bunch. Based on the number of brawls they kept getting into, it seemed they were definitely spoiling for a fight.

On the night before the battle, Major Fred Wheelock strode briskly into my tent right after tattoo sounded. He had been at brigade headquarters all evening and could barely suppress his excitement.

At thirty, Major Wheelock was much older than the other junior officers, but like me he had no prior military experience. On the day Fort Sumter fell, I was in the middle of my last term at Harvard. Major Wheelock was then a Massachusetts state senator. Like thousands of others, we had both enlisted as soon as we learned the news.

"The Twentieth is going into action tomorrow, Lieutenant McKittredge," he said. "General Stone has ordered our brigade to cross the Potomac into Virginia. Colonel Baker has given us the honor of going in first, ahead of the main force."

I was thrilled that we were finally moving into action. Major Wheelock unfolded a map and spread it on the camp table. His index finger went directly to a spot on the Virginia side of the Potomac River.

"This will be our point of attack. It's called Ball's Bluff," he said. "They say the river is fairly wide there . . . well over a man's head most of the way. Between the Maryland shore and the Virginia side there is a small island."

I could see the island on the map. Someone had scribbled the name Harrison's on it.

"How high is Ball's Bluff?" I asked Major Wheelock.

"Close to two hundred feet, I understand," he said.

Just the thought of it took me aback.

"But why there?" I blurted.

The hard stare Major Wheelock gave me reflected his obvious exasperation at the idea that a twenty-year-old lieutenant was questioning important military strategy.

"Colonel Baker is confident that the Rebels will never expect a force of this size to attack there," he said coldly. "He told us to think of this movement like the gambler who stakes his whole fortune on one bet."

"How are we getting over?" I asked in a chastened voice.

"They are sending a small fleet of barges up the river to us," he said. "Because you were once an island lad yourself, I thought you might want to lead the first element across tomorrow night."

I immediately volunteered for the job. Major Wheelock showed his approval with a terse smile. In spite of the chill, he was sweating profusely, and I wondered whether he was ill.

"After making sure there are no Rebels on Harrison's Island, you will lead the advance element across to the Virginia side, there to secure the high ground above the bluff for the main force that will follow you in the morning," he said. "Colonel Baker will be in tactical command of the whole operation."

I had met Colonel Edward Baker just once on the parade ground, although I had read about him since I was a boy. One of the great men of the Republic, he had enjoyed a brilliant political career before the war and been elected as a U.S. Senator from two different states. Many men claimed to be a friend of Abraham Lincoln, but the president had actually named one of his sons after Baker. Although he had no more military experience than Major Wheelock or me, he certainly looked the part of a fine military leader.

"Well, you have a lot to do," said Major Wheelock, folding up his map and placing it inside his uniform coat. "Don't let me down, Kit."

"I won't, sir," I replied.

As soon as he left, I went straight to the tent of my first sergeant, Harlan Colfax. He was a bull-necked farrier from western Massachusetts and knew more about soldiering than any man in the regiment. In the Mexican War, he had fought as a private and come back with two promotions for gallantry under fire.

Sergeant Colfax was forty-six years old, with the weathered face of a downeast lobsterman. Although his manner toward most junior officers was as rough as a December cob, he had seemed to take a liking to me from the first day I had been assigned to the company. Maybe it was because I was the same age as his youngest son. Whatever the reason, his adroit handling of the men, in spite of my own ineptitude, had turned our company into the best in the regiment.

I told him the details of Colonel Baker's plan for the attack and repeated Colonel Baker's words about the gambler who was willing to stake his whole fortune on one bet. Harlan removed his battered pipe from his mouth and spat tobacco juice on the ground.

"It may be his bet," he said, clearly unimpressed, "but it's our lives."

We spent the rest of that night as well as the next morning preparing and equipping the men I would be leading over. Our advance group moved out late in the afternoon, arriving at the Maryland side of the Potomac River with two hours of daylight left.

Ball's Bluff was visible through the haze across the river, and I took a moment to examine the terrain through my binoculars. It was very imposing; but unlike the rocky cliffs of Maine, the bluff was completely covered by trees and vegetation. I couldn't even tell if there was a path leading to the top. In the setting sun, the opposite shore was on fire with red-and-gold foliage.

Sergeant Colfax, who had gone ahead to meet the unit that was bringing the barges up from Washington, came toward me waving his arms in disbelief.

"No boats, no barges," he said.

The thought that we would have no means of crossing the river had never occurred to me, and I silently berated myself for not having considered the possibility. At the same time, I tried not to show my misgivings to the men who were crowded around me.

"Well, we had better find some," I said, trying to keep my voice even. "Take ten men upriver and come back with anything that floats. I'll take another group downriver with me."

"Goddamn it, sir, the whole brigade has to get across that river tomorrow," growled Harlan.

"Don't worry, Sergeant," I replied in front of the men. "I'm sure the barges will be here in time for the main force."

DARKNESS HAD FALLEN by the time I returned from the foraging expedition. We had found two small rowboats, neither bigger than a Maine dory. Harlan arrived back ten minutes later. He had enjoyed better luck, finding a large rowboat that could carry ten men. Unfortunately, it had been out of the water for some time, and the seams leaked so badly that constant bailing was required just to keep it afloat.

I went across with the first group to make sure that Harrison's Island wasn't occupied by Confederate pickets. We found a small, abandoned farmhouse there, and I ordered the men to secure it as a command post for Colonel Baker. By then the main attack force was starting to come across from the Maryland side. As they arrived, each regiment was deployed in one of the pastures that covered most of the island.

The barges had still not come, and it took six more hours for the main body to be rowed over in the three boats. Shortly after midnight, Colonel Baker came across with the last of his troops and immediately went to the farmhouse. There were four tiny rooms inside, and each one was packed with officers straining to listen to the colonel as he made his final disposi- tions. In the reflected glow of the oil lamps on the kitchen table, his smil- ing, handsome face exuded total confidence.

"Believe me, gentlemen, we will enjoy a glorious victory tomorrow," he said in a deep baritone voice. "This brigade is ready to fight."

A robust man of around fifty, Colonel Baker was tall and well formed, with a prominent nose and a firm, clean-shaven jaw. He had removed his hat, and the ring of silver hair crowning his shiny head gleamed in the lamplight. He slowly pivoted in a full circle to face all the officers who were peering at him through the doors of the three other rooms. A cloud of moths swarmed above his head.

"Tomorrow we have a chance to square the books on Bull Run and strike an important blow for freedom," he went on, as if orating on the floor of the Senate. "I expect us to emulate Caesar's Tenth Legion . . . to smite them a real lightning blow!"

With those words, his right fist slammed down on the kitchen table. There was a pause, and then another voice rose from the back parlor.

"What about those barges, Colonel?" asked one of the regimental commanders, with sarcasm in his voice. "At dawn, we've got to ferry more than two thousand men over there to the cliffs of Dover. We'll need to move fast if we're to have any chance of surprising them."

A look of minor annoyance came over Colonel Baker's face, as if someone had complained about one of the men's shoelaces being untied. He waved a hand at the host of moths hovering around his head.

"That's a very good point," he replied, with an elegant smile. "But why don't we just leave that to General McClellan. He has all the resources of the United States at his disposal. I'm sure they are on their way as we speak."

At three o'clock that morning, my advance group was ready to cross over to Ball's Bluff. I had ordered Sergeant Colfax to have the three boats carried over to the Virginia side of the island for us to use in the next crossing. Just before we moved out, Colonel Baker came down to the shoreline to see us off.

"I understand they call you Kit," he said, shaking my hand and patting me on the back as if I was a favored constituent. In the darkness I could only see the outline of his massive head.

"That's right, sir," I said.

"So you have the honor of going in first," he said next, his voice filled with confidence. "I'm told you grew up on an island off the coast of Maine."

"Yes, sir."

"Well then, I'm sure you are not intimidated by that little beak over there."

Actually, Ball's Bluff was about the same height as the tallest cliff I knew in Maine. I had tried to imagine two thousand soldiers attempting to climb it as part of a full-scale attack. It would have been impossible.

"No, sir. I will do my best."

"Yes, of course you will," he said.

My small force set off into the black, starry night. Aside from the boat poles swishing in the water, there was no sound of movement from any of us. Of course, there could have been a thousand rebels waiting for us on the bluff, and we never would have known. I just stared forward into the void until the bow of the boat scraped up on the Virginia shore.

The riverbank was as slippery as axle grease. Mature trees grew right down to the edge of the water. The current was stronger than on the Maryland side, and it was hard for the men to find their footing. As one of the boats swung away from the bank, it struck a man who then fell back into the river with a loud splash. I nervously awaited the shout from a Confederate picket on the bluff, but the only sound I heard came from the branches swaying above us in the wind.

Using a masked lantern, I finally found an opening in the trees that disappeared into the darkness and sent Sergeant Colfax up to reconnoiter. He returned ten minutes later, out of breath and excited.

"The path leads to the top, but it's no wider than a horse's ass, Lieutenant. We'll have to go up single file."

After sending the boats back for the next load of men, we started toward the top. It soon became obvious that the path curled back and forth like a coiled snake from one end of the bluff to the other as it wound its way upward. With no break for a rest, it took us twenty minutes to get to the summit. There was another short rise at the top of the bluff, and then the ground leveled off into what appeared to be an open field. I immediately put out scouts in every direction and ordered the rest of the advance group to come up.

The scouts reported back that the field ran for more than two hundred yards toward a tree stand that ringed the far end of the field. There was no sign of the enemy. As the rest of my men came across from Harrison's, I deployed them in a line along the near edge of the field.

As dawn paled the sky, I could make out a wagon lane that led inland through the trees on the left. Straight ahead of us and to the right was the large field. I sent four scouts to again reconnoiter the woods beyond it.

While I waited for them to return, the first elements of Colonel Baker's main attack force began coming over the summit of the bluff shortly after daylight. They were from the Fifteenth Massachusetts, and after forming up, they headed off down the wagon lane. Their officers were taking very few precautions about keeping the men quiet any longer. We could hear their nervous chatter a long way down the road. It was no more than ten minutes later that scattered musket fire broke out from the direction they had taken.

"I'd say someone knows we're here," growled Sergeant Colfax, spitting out a dark glob of tobacco juice.

I sent word back to the command post on Harrison's that the Fifteenth had made contact with the enemy. Then we sat down to wait for the rest of the main body to come over. I watched as two wounded men from the Fifteenth were carried back on litters to the crest of the bluff. By then there was no way for them to get back down the path because it was choked with men working their way to the top.

I continued to scan the tree line in front of us with binoculars until the scouts came back. Johnny Harpswell was the first one to report in. He said that Confederate troops were moving into the big patch of woods opposite our position, although he didn't know whether they were militia or regular combat units.

Johnny had been in my class at Harvard, and like me he had enlisted right after Fort Sumter. The captain of the heavyweight crew team, he was six and a half feet tall, with slablike shoulders and incredible strength. However, his boyishly handsome face was covered with freckles, which made him look about sixteen. Although he had been offered a commission after he volunteered, he turned it down, saying he preferred the simpler life of a private soldier.

"Well, Kit, I think this is going to be interesting," Johnny said, as if the two of us were about to visit the Acropolis on a college jaunt to Europe.

By eleven o'clock in the morning, the rest of the Fifteenth Massachusetts had finally made it to the top of the bluff. They formed up and moved inland to join their advance detachment farther up the wagon lane. Shortly after that, Sergeant Colfax pointed out to me that the flow of men coming up from the river had completely stopped. We went back to the crest of the bluff to see what was happening.

The reason for the breakdown was apparent as soon as I looked down the slope. About halfway down the circuitous path, a large bronze cannon was lodged on the narrow trail like a cork in a bottle. Several ropes were tied to the gun carriage, and a group of soldiers was straining at the lines to manhandle the cannon up the narrow track. Ahead of the soldiers manning the ropes, four men with axes were laboriously chopping down trees to widen the trail. They were cursing a blue streak and loudly demanding to be relieved.

Another officer joined us at the crest, and I recognized him as a member of Colonel Baker's staff. He was a former congressman from Philadelphia.

"The colonel's favorite cannon," he said, smiling broadly. "It was a gift from the people of Oregon, and he is very fond of it. It's his good luck charm."

Behind the cannon, hundreds of soldiers stood bottlenecked along the entire length of the winding path. Dozens more were standing with their muskets resting on their shoulders in the shallow water down at the river-bank, prevented from even starting up the path. I looked through the tops of the trees toward Harrison's Island. At least a thousand more were still waiting to come over, most of them just milling about or sitting on their packs. The only craft being used to ferry the attack force were the same three rowboats my men had found the previous night.

"Don't look so grim, Lieutenant," said the staff officer. "It's going to be a great day for the Union. I can smell victory in the air."

"Yeah . . . they're gonna kill us all," muttered Sergeant Colfax, as we walked back to our position. Harlan had already survived the disaster at Bull Run back in July.

None of us had eaten anything since we'd had supper the night before. Some of the men still had food in their knapsacks, and they shared it around as far as it lasted. Fortunately, we had all filled our canteens in the river, and there was plenty of drinking water. The sun had started its downward journey when the colonel's bronze cannon finally came over the crest.

"Three hours to drag up one lousy piece," said Harlan Colfax. "The goddamn Rebs have probably got a whole battery over in those trees by now."

Colonel Baker came across from Harrison's early in the afternoon. Apparently, someone had finally located a barge, because the colonel's big white horse was led over the crest right behind him. His cannon was already deployed out to the left of us.

He ordered our regiment to form the middle of the line facing the woods across the pasture. Then he ordered the New York Tammany Regiment to move forward in a rank up ahead of ours and to the right. I heard a good deal of grumbling from them as they came through our position. They no longer seemed to be spoiling for a fight.

It was well after three o'clock by the time the last of the men from

Harrison's were finally fed into the ranks, and the sun was dipping down toward the tree line. Off to the left, I heard the confident tattoo of a long drum roll followed by the bark of a crisp order to dress one of the lines.

"Well, General McKittredge, what happens now?" said Johnny Harpswell, with an impish grin.

Down on one knee, I remember looking up toward the heavens and mouthing a silent prayer. "Please, God," I prayed fervently, "don't let me die until I have made love to a beautiful woman."

As if in answer to my prayer, the Confederates chose that moment to open up on us. The entire tree line at the other end of the pasture belched out a tremendous plume of smoke, and a split second later, the balls from their first volley of musket fire came whistling past. One tore through the sleeve of my uniform coat and another ricocheted off the scabbard of my cheap presentation sword.

Almost in concert, the Tammany Regiment, which was in the rank up ahead of us to the right, turned as one and ran back through our positions. Their embarrassed officers followed behind, frantically waving their swords and bellowing for their men to rally. Now we were out in front by ourselves.

Another coordinated volley of fire erupted out of the tree line. Men were being hit all around me. Although the Confederates were still completely invisible to us, our troops began firing blindly into the woods. The reek of powder smoke filled my nose.

"Stand fast, men!" I heard one of the company commanders shout, his powerful voice loud and clear over the din. I remember thinking that it was a poor choice of words, since by then most of the men had wisely dropped to the ground. The ones who had been hit were the fellows who had raised their heads or gotten up to shoot on one knee.

Over on the left, Colonel Baker's bronze cannon began to return the Confederate fire. His artillerymen were well trained, and the first round they fired exploded to good effect in the distant tree line. The Rebel officers must have targeted them then because, after the next enemy volley, none of the gunners were left standing.

Colonel Baker coolly went forward and encouraged some men from the ranks to take over the job. They were more than willing and rushed to load the cannon, firing it as soon as the shell was in place. Unfortunately, they were not prepared for the recoil, and the gun carriage careened backward straight down the rise, crushing several wounded men who were lying in its path before disappearing into the ravine below.

I began walking along the line, making stupid jokes and encouraging the men. As each second went by, I wondered when I would be hit.

"Lord, don't take me now," I remember praying over and over, "not until I've at least kissed a woman in passion."

"They're firing beautifully," called out Johnny Harpswell, as if we were watching a hockey game against Princeton.

Major Wheelock was shot twice in immediate succession, both balls ripping through his chest. The second one flipped him over on his back. With each heartbeat, his lifeblood poured forth and soaked the earth beside him.

The man lying directly in front of me raised his head to call encouragement to his younger brother, who was farther down the line. An instant later his warm brains were blasted into my eyes. I wiped them away in order to see. That was when the Confederate infantry began moving out of the trees and into the field opposite our position.

"It's the whole goddamn Reb army," yelled someone standing behind me.

As they began to come on, I could hear the swelling roar of the Rebel yell for the first time. It slowly grew to a crescendo of noise that drowned out even the noise of the firing. The war cry reminded me of a huge wave about to break on a rocky shore.

On either side of us, men from the other regiments began to melt away. Glancing back down the rise to the bluff, I saw soldiers who were not wounded running toward the path that led to the river.

Colonel Baker was killed a few minutes later. He was out in front of the men on the left, exhorting them to hold on, when he was hit by a hail of fire that slammed him to the ground like a hammer blow. I learned later that he had been struck by eight balls. After he was carried to the rear, no one else took command.

Although I know it was just an illusion, it seemed then as if the ground caught fire, with acrid, foul-smelling smoke billowing up all around us. To my left and right, men were writhing in their death struggles like huge demented worms.

The Confederate attack had driven the surviving pockets of resistance back closer and closer to the edge of the bluff. We were no more than fifty feet away from it when I felt a wave of uncontrollable anger sweep over me. It was like nothing I had ever experienced before. For the first time in my life I wanted to kill someone with my bare hands. Black rage filled my brain, crowding out all conscious thought except the compulsion to destroy the men who were massacring us.

"Let's be shot advancing instead of being slaughtered here like sheep!" I shouted to the men standing around me. "We're going forward!"

This may sound strange, but it was without fear and filled with elation that I began to charge back up the slope, waving my sword above my head. Never in my life had I felt anything so intensely. Glancing behind me I saw that more than a score of men had followed my lead, including a fiercely grinning Sergeant Colfax. Close to the top of the rise there was a wall of dense powder smoke. As it broke up, I could see a mass of Confederates advancing toward us. Above them waved a huge battle flag, blood red against the setting sun. The surprise of seeing us charging toward them when the battle was so obviously lost caused them to pull up short.

I waded into the first line, slashing madly with my sword as I went. A man toppled to my left, his eyes going vacant as he fell to his knees. Another figure, nothing more than a blur off to the right, fired at me with his pistol before the razor-sharp edge of my sword caught him on the side of the head and he went down, too.

Unlike most men who are shot in battle, I actually saw the soldier who tried to murder me. Although my revolver was already empty, I was still holding it in my right hand when my eyes were drawn to the sight of what appeared to be a comical stage figure towering over the other men. His white-maned head was crowned by a top hat that must have made him nearly seven feet tall.

With his rutted, cadaverous face, he may have been the oldest man on the battlefield. Seventy would be my best guess, although he stood ramrod straight. Even for a Rebel, his choice of uniform was distinctly odd. It consisted of a double-breasted blue frock coat that had matching rows of large gilt buttons running down the chest. He wore white breeches and had on black riding boots that came all the way up to his thighs. The way the tails of his frock coat were billowing out behind him on that windswept plain, he looked like nothing so much as a gigantic old blue jay.

As we glared at each other, he raised a smoothbore musket to his right shoulder and aimed it straight at me. I am going to die now, I remember thinking. That certainty brought with it an odd sense of calm. I became convinced that some conscious part of me would actually watch me die and then go on.

In the vain hope that there was one cartridge left in the cylinder, I aimed my revolver at him and fired. The hammer fell on a spent chamber. A split-second later, his musket exploded in flame.

I felt myself being lifted bodily in the air before coming to rest on my back. At first, I had no idea where the ball had taken me. However, my roving fingers quickly found the wet warmth covering my abdomen. My uniform was perforated in several places, and it struck me that he must have been firing buck and ball.

I had no time to ponder the question as two hands seized me by the shoulders, and someone started dragging me back down the rise. I was still conscious when we reached the edge of the path that led down to the river. It was clogged with men, and the Samaritan laid me down on the ground nearby. As he headed back up the rise, I saw that my rescuer was Harlan Colfax.

Colonel Baker's riderless white horse walked slowly toward me and stood by my side, calmly munching grass a few inches from my head. As I looked into his placid eyes, an insane thought ran through my mind. It was the notion that since I had yet to kiss a woman in passion, God would not take me.

Turning my head, I could see dozens of men still standing or kneeling along the edge of the bluff, firing up the rise into the smoke, then stopping to reload their muskets. The Confederates were pouring down a deadly fire from the field and opening up more gaps in this last Union line with each volley. I saw one man throw down his musket and leap out over the edge of the bluff, dropping into the trees far below.

That was my last conscious recollection until the face of Johnny Harpswell swam into focus above me. He appeared to be overcome with emotion, and tears were flowing down his freckled cheeks.

"I'm sorry, Kit," he said, and then repeated it again.

"It doesn't hurt so bad," I said, as the sound of firing continued unabated.

"It's torn open your stomach wall . . . I've tried . . . to put it all back inside."

I believed then that the wound was mortal.

"I'll get you back, Kit, I promise," he said.

A moment later, I felt myself being lifted up again, this time enveloped in his powerful arms. I passed out once more as he began carrying me down the path.

I awoke to find myself lying propped up against the gunwale of the same rowboat I had come over on the night before. There were no longer any oars in it, and the soldiers were using their arms and muskets to paddle back toward Harrison's Island.

It had also started raining very hard. The drops were roiling the water around the boat like a summer storm lashing the surface of a pond. I remember being puzzled not to feel any moisture on my face. Then I realized it wasn't rain.

I looked back toward the top of the bluff. All the brilliant red-and-gold foliage was gone, destroyed by the musket fire. Confederate soldiers stood several rows deep along the crest and were firing down at the men still trying to get away. For the Southern boys, it was nothing more than a grand turkey shoot.

For those of us down below, it became a desperate race for survival. Many of the men had shed their equipment and were trying to swim for it. They were shot as they struggled in the water, trying to make headway against the strong current. A hundred others who couldn't swim, or were afraid to try, just huddled along the riverbank as volley after volley of murderous fire poured down on them.

Johnny Harpswell was beside me in the skiff, his boyish face streaked with dirt and blackened powder. He was churning the water with the butt of his rifle in a fine, fast, rhythmic cadence.

"So this is your reward for being the stroke of the Harvard crew," I said.

Grinning, he was about to give me a proper retort when his head jerked to the side and a fountain of blood, bone, and teeth burst from his open mouth. A ball had struck him in the lower jaw, carrying most of it away. The exposed muscles in his upper jaw were still expanding and contracting as the force of the ball took him over the side.

I must have fallen unconscious again because when I next opened my eyes I was lying on the ground and a large, hairy, sad-eyed man was leaning over me, examining my wound.

"So . . . thirsty," I whispered.

"I cannot let you drink, Lieutenant," he said in a shaking voice. "But I must do something with your vitals. They are covered with hen grass and dirt."

I was fully awake now and the pain was coming in stabbing waves. Oddly, it seemed to be centered in my groin at first, although I was not wounded there. As I turned away from the obscenity of my exposed viscera, he gently rinsed them using an oaken bucket filled with river water. After repacking the entrails into my stomach cavity, he covered my abdomen with a strip of clean cheesecloth.

Tears were streaming silently down his face as he finished the job. Before moving on, the great hairy beast knelt on the ground next to me, just staring into my face and mouthing what might have been a prayer. Then his face drew closer and closer to my own until I felt the pressure of his lips on mine. It was only for a second, and then he was gone.

God knows what possessed him to do it. Perhaps, he was overcome with emotion. I'll never know. It was certainly not the kiss I had been longing for. As the pain grew to raw torture, I concluded it was God's way of mocking my lustful prayer before the battle.

I raised my head high enough to see that I was lying in one of the pastures around the old farmhouse on Harrison's Island. Hundreds of wounded men were scattered along the ground in every direction. One day earlier we had all been full of confidence, standing proud with our shiny muskets and handsome uniforms, part of a seemingly unstoppable force. God help the Rebels I had thought then. Now we were just individual mounds of filthy rags, stinking from sweat and urine, and dying in agony.

An elderly surgeon came along as night descended. He briefly examined each man, after which he pinned a colored card on the man's chest. The cards were red and blue. When he came to me, he leaned over, raised the edge of the now blood-soaked cheesecloth from my stomach, and without any expression in his face pinned a red card on my chest. Then he poured some amber liquid into a tin cup and helped me to swallow it.

"This is laudanum," he said, "it will ease the pain."

It did. When I next awoke it was to darkness. A sliver of moon had risen in the east, and I was very cold. Closing my eyes, I prayed that I would survive. When I opened them again, two men were kneeling on the ground beside me. One of them held a lantern over my face.

"Another for the dead pile," he said, reaching down to grab my legs.

My mouth was so dry I could not speak.

"Aww, he's shit hisself. I can see his guts, too," said the other one.

They picked up the man next to me, placed him on a litter, and left.

A harsh wind came up that made the suffering doubly hard for the men still lying in the fields with no blankets. A few well-intentioned soldiers cut up raw pine boughs and lit several small bonfires. Unfortunately, the swirling wind whipped the burning embers and smoke in every direction, just adding to the misery.

A few yards away from me, an officer babbled on endlessly about the plans he wanted his wife to make for their five children. He must have been very wealthy because the dispositions kept coming for more than an hour until he died.

As the balm of laudanum began to wear off, we all began to groan and wail in an unholy chorus, our torn bodies each moving to an individual ballet dictated by the spasms of pain. The wailing was punctuated by howling shrieks, as tortured nerve endings came back to life. My own screams lasted as long as my strength held out. Eventually, they subsided down to pathetic moans, and I rolled back and forth from side to side, clutching the purplish bloody mass inside me as if there was something I could do to put things back together the way they had been.

It was after I had already given up against the enormity of the pain and was praying for God to take me that I felt a sharp, painful sensation under my neck. Reaching up, I discovered that the locket my mother had given me the day I left our island was gone, ripped free by someone who thought he was robbing the dead. I felt him go through my pockets, but could do nothing to stop him.

Finding it impossible even to die, I cursed God and cursed my fate. By the time I regained my senses again, the bonfires had gone out and there was no longer any movement around me. Then I thought I heard someone calling my name. Another cruel illusion, I decided.

"John McKittredge," I heard someone shout again, and knew it could not be a dream. I could see the glare of a torch moving slowly through the darkness forty or fifty feet away from me.

"Call out if you can," came back the same voice, which I now recognized as that of Harlan Colfax.

"Here, Sergeant," I shouted, but the words came out like the bark of a small dog.

The light came closer as he went from body to body.

"Here," I called out once more, and then he was at my side, his rough, homely face reflected in the torchlight like a treasured heirloom.

"I only got across an hour ago, Lieutenant. I've been looking for you ever since."

His eyes closed for several seconds after he pulled my bloody hands away from my stomach and saw what was there. It was his only visible reaction before he said, "I've seen worse today, believe me," and ripped the red card away from my chest.

There were two men from the regiment with him. They placed me on a litter and carried me to the farmhouse, which had been turned into a surgical hospital. In the courtyard, corpses lay everywhere, covered with canvas shrouds. I was carried inside.

In the light of the oil lamps, I could see hideous shadows playing on the whitewashed walls as a surgeon cut and sawed away at a man lying on the kitchen table. It reminded me of paintings I had seen of the Spanish inquisition.

"Doctor, this officer is still alive," said Sergeant Colfax to a surgeon who was standing in the hallway smoking a cigar.

The doctor stepped back into the kitchen and raised a lamp over me. I saw that his arms and hands were smeared with blood. With his soiled white apron, he looked like one of our island fishermen after they had finished gutting a day's catch.

"I do not mean to sound harsh," he said, wearily shaking his head, "but this man may just as well be dead. In fact, it would be a blessing for him. His stomach was raked with buck and ball. The wound is mortal. I might add that he is also exsanguinated. Look at his skin."

"He is what?" said Sergeant Colfax.

"Exsanguinated . . . drained of blood," the surgeon said.

I felt another feeble wave of anger course through me. It gave me just enough strength to say, "I'm still alive, damn you, and if you would help me instead of talking and shaking your head, I might survive."

A sardonic smile creased his weary face as he stared down at me on the litter. Glancing at the gore covering my stomach, he said, "You have more than one kind of grit inside you, I think."

"That he does," said Harlan Colfax, his voice husky.

"I will clean the wound and stitch it up. The rest is up to a higher power than mine."

They placed me on one of the tables in the kitchen. It was the same one that Colonel Baker had pounded his fist on the night before when he had called on us to deliver our lightning blow for freedom.

As a surgeon's assistant began to cut my uniform away, I looked over at the soldier who was lying on the other table. A doctor had been sawing at his leg a few minutes earlier, but now they had left him in peace. He was no more than a boy, and he had a sweet, puzzled grin on his face. His eyes were fixed on something I could not see. Then the surgeon was standing over me again. He held a moist sponge close to my nose that was soaked in ether.

"I don't know whether you will thank me or curse me for what I am about to do," he said.

A few moments later, I didn't care.

CHAPTER TWO

I CAME BACK into the world to find myself on a wooden pallet in the back of a quartermaster's freight wagon. The teamsters would slap the reins, we would roll along for a minute or so, and then the wagon would come to a jolting stop. With each dip and furrow in the road surface, a new chorus of pitiful moans would issue from the wounded men crammed in alongside me. Our combined stench floated around me like a miasma.

I heard someone yell an order, and the canvas flap covering the back of the wagon was suddenly pulled away. My eyes recoiled at the blinding sunlight. Two men scrambled up onto the freight bed and gently lifted up the man on the pallet beside me. He was handed down to two more men standing at the rear of the wagon. Then the first two came back for me.

As they transferred me to a canvas litter, I could see a long stream of wagons stretching far down the road behind us, all waiting to deposit the same horrendous cargo. They carried me toward the double-door entrance of what appeared to be a massive livestock barn. A sign was stenciled above the doors. It read: U.S. SANITARY COMMISSION—FIELD HOSPITAL TWELVE.

One of the wounded men began screaming at the elderly doctor who was supervising the arrival of new patients. The doctor's face was weary and haggard, and he was clearly overwhelmed by the number of men arriving all at once. The wounded man was wearing lieutenant's bars just like mine. He was missing his right arm.

"This isn't a hospital!" he shouted. "Take me to a hospital!"

"I'm sorry," the doctor kept repeating. "I'm very sorry."

"I gave my arm for this country," the lieutenant shouted back, his voice breaking into a sob.

The man on the gurney next to me had been shot through both legs. He gazed toward the surrounding buildings with a calm, appraising eye. "Poultry farm from the look of it," he said, in a philosophical tone. "Big one, too."

Mercifully, I faded out again.

"Lieutenant McKittredge?"

I was lying on a straw-filled canvas mattress in the lower bunk of a two-tiered bed constructed of rough pine boards. A spectacled man was standing over me. He was middle-aged and slender, with fine blond hair.

"Lieutenant McKittredge," the man repeated. "I'm Dr. Bolger, and I will be providing your care. Please forgive the state of this . . . facility, but with all the casualties since Bull Run, there simply aren't enough hospitals. At least here you will enjoy the country air."

The shed we were in was about one hundred feet long and fifteen feet wide, with a slanted tin roof. The walls consisted of overlapping pine boards nailed to support studs. At the far end of the shed, laborers were tearing out the remaining chicken roosts of the building's former occupants. Army carpenters came right behind them, erecting more bunk beds.

"I'm . . ."

"Yes?" Dr. Bolger's kindly face leant closer.

". . . in pain . . . terrible pain," I whispered.

"Yes, I know, and I have something for you right here. It is a strong opiate dissolved in alcohol."

"Laudanum?"

"Yes, laudanum. It will deaden the pain considerably and help you sleep during these next difficult days."

He removed the cork from a brown glass bottle and poured several drams into a small glass. He gently lifted my head and held the glass to my lips until it was finished. The alcohol seared my throat as it went down. He put the cork back in the bottle and laid it down on the blanket by my side.

"You are going to need this, Lieutenant," he said. Behind the thick lenses of his spectacles, the doctor's eyes were filled with sadness. "And many more, I'm afraid, over the next few days."

"Where am I?" I asked.

"In Maryland . . . a few miles out of Washington," he said. "It is called Glen Echo."

I watched as a wounded man was carried into the shed and placed in one of the bunks along the far wall. Dr. Bolger brought over a small camp stool and sat down at the edge of my bed.

"I deeply regret having to be the one to tell you this, Lieutenant McKittredge, but it is ordained by medical science that you will die from this . . . grievous injury. I have never seen a man with your type of wound survive."

"Why must I die?" I asked. The laudanum was already deadening the fire in my belly.

"I have examined the stitches and the dressing. So far there appears to be no evidence of infection. However, I am far more worried about the perforation of your peritoneum . . . that is the serous membrane that lines the cavity of the abdomen. When that membrane is torn, it invariably leads to peritonitis. This condition is always fatal, particularly when the viscera have been . . . disturbed. I also fear that you will contract erysipelas, which is an acute febrile disease associated with intense edematous . . ."

"I think I understand," I said. "How long do I have to live?"

"That is very hard to say. I would expect to see the onset of peritonitis fairly quickly, but it is impossible to predict exactly when. When it does happen, you will know it. The pain will be excruciating, I'm afraid."

"What is your best guess?" I said, feeling a sudden sensation of euphoria from the opiate. My voice sounded strange to me, foreign and spectral.

"As quickly as a few days from now, although you may survive a week or more. You appear to have a sound constitution."

As he spoke, I felt as if I was being carried away on a pink cloud. It was like nothing I had ever experienced before.

"I have implanted a drain in your wound to carry away the by-product of infection," Dr. Bolger went on. "It is connected by a copper tube to the receptacle beneath your bed."

"Thank you, Doctor."

"Is there anyone you wish us to notify that you are here?"

I thought of my parents on their remote island off the coast of Maine but concluded that the news would only cause them greater anguish. There was the headmaster of my boarding school, but I had not corresponded with him in over four years. I had made one good friend in college, Frank Bartlett. He was in the army. I knew of no one else who cared whether I lived or died.

"No, Doctor," I said, soaring toward the pink clouds.

I awoke to the putrid smell of rotting flesh. The blistered, suppurating feet of the soldier in the bunk ahead of mine were squirming back and forth two inches from my nose.

I was very thirsty and called out for water. An orderly filled a mug from the barrel next to the door and brought it to me. It had the odor of spoiled eggs, and the smell of it made me so nauseous I couldn't finish it. Instead, I took several more swallows from the bottle of laudanum that Dr. Bolger had given me.

For the next few days, I floated in and out of consciousness. At one point I recall a young man waking me to say that he understood I wanted to dictate a letter. He was holding a writing tablet and pencil. I remembered then that I wanted to send a letter to someone but couldn't remember who it was. I desperately fought to clear my brain, but to no avail.

My body had become a stranger to me, and I was no longer in control of its functions. Some days I would sweat from every pore until my bedclothes were drenched. At other times the chills shook me so hard that it seemed I was coming apart. I felt total disgust at the trembling creature I had become.

Weeks passed. There appeared to be an endless supply of laudanum, and the orderlies provided me with a new bottle as soon as the old one was consumed. In late fall, rain became a constant, and its hammering on the tin roof of the chicken shed was usually sufficient to bring me back from the mellower world where I had gone. It also drowned out the lamentations of the others.

The boy in the bunk above me was dying from multiple gunshot wounds, and early each morning he would begin to make the same low, groaning sounds. They would slowly build to a long, keening wail, shivering and desolate.

"Fix it. Oh, please fix it," he would repeat over and over. The night orderly finally cured his disruptions with laudanum. He was dead a few days later.

There were more empty beds each morning. As men died, they were carried to the dead house for shipment home. The ones who recovered were sent back to their units or released as unfit for further active service.

I spent every coherent hour thinking that it might well be my last on earth. I lived without hope in that hazy, opium-induced state, knowing where I was, but oblivious to what was happening beyond my fetid bunk. My wound emitted a stench all its own, along with a greasy yellow pus that was supposed to be carried through the copper tube into a receptacle beneath my bunk. Usually, I would find it pooled in my crotch when I came awake in the morning.

I remembered Dr. Bolger once commending the fact that we were at least enjoying good country air. Certainly, there was wildlife. My body became covered with fleabites, my hair lousy with lice. The shed was overrun with field mice, and even the onset of winter failed to diminish the legion of flies that bombarded us. One of the boys joked, "Ever'time I kill one, another forty come to his funeral."

Prior to Ball's Bluff, I had stood six feet, two inches' tall and weighed 187 pounds. I lost a third of it during those first weeks. Looking back, I don't know how I held onto life. Part of it stemmed from the insistence of Dr. Bolger that I consume small amounts of beef broth each day. The hospital also had a bakery in one of the farm buildings, and I occasionally enjoyed a soft roll with butter.

I was mildly encouraged to discover that my internal plumbing continued to function, although I would usually have no control over when and in what form the end product would be delivered. Since I could not stir from the bed, I did my best to capture the contents in a bedpan.

A slim sense of hope began to stir in my mind when I observed the reaction of Dr. Bolger each time he passed me on his daily rounds. As the weeks went by, his manner seemed to change from one of pity to questioning surprise.

Then I looked up one morning to find Harlan Colfax standing at the side of my bed. His sergeant's stripes shined bright gold on the arm of his new blue uniform. I couldn't find the words to tell him how glad I was to see him. It must have been plain on my face.

"Sorry to tell you this, Lieutenant, but I think there is an overheated horse under your bed," he said, with the crooked grin of old. I couldn't help but smile back at him.

"Something infinitely worse, I'm afraid."

He pulled a stool next to my bunk and sat down.

"Well," he said, "you're a hero, Lieutenant McKittredge."

"Don't be ridiculous," I said harshly.

"You were mentioned in dispatches," he said. "This was written by the little big man himself, George Brinton McClellan . . . General Order from Army Headquarters."

He unfolded a copy of the orders. "I wish to particularly commend Lt. John McKittredge of the Twentieth Massachusetts Infantry for his bravery in leading a valiant counterattack on the enemy position at Ball's Bluff. He has gained lasting honor in this army for his courageous action in the face of an overwhelming enemy force. By order of, et cetera, et cetera . . . ," Sergeant Colfax concluded, handing me the paper. "Well, what do you think of that?"

"Not much," I said.

"I also have an article here that my wife sent me from one of the Boston newspapers," he said, removing another folded page from his tunic. "It compares you to Hercules, the young lion of Troy."

I pushed it back at him, unread.

"How many did we lose?" I said, and his eyes became grave.

"Thirteen of the twenty-two officers in the Twentieth. Two-thirds of the regiment was killed, wounded, or went missing."

"What about Johnny Harpswell?"

"He's on the missing list," said Sergeant Colfax.

"Then he's dead," I said, shaking my head. I told him what had happened to Johnny in the skiff.

"If I've learned one thing about war, it is that there is nothing fair about who lives and who dies on a battlefield, Lieutenant . . . just as there is no reason to feel guilty about surviving," said Harlan.

"I will not survive . . . at least that's what the doctors have told me."

"Well, you'd better ask them for another opinion. I did, and they started hemming and hawing. Hell, they are probably too embarrassed to admit they might have been wrong. Whatever it is you're doing, just keep it up."

"The laudanum cure . . . That's what I'll call it if I ever get out of here," I said, with a grin.

His face remained grave.

"That stuff will kill you, Lieutenant," he said, sternly. "You should start cutting back on it right now."

Harlan stayed with me for more than an hour, telling me everything that had happened since the battle. There were rumors, he said, that General McClellan was planning to take the whole army in ships down to Yorktown, where it would attack up the Peninsula, capture Richmond, and end the war. After the victory, all of us were to come together for a great homecoming celebration in Boston, he said. But the look in his eyes told me that he didn't believe a word of it.

The last thing he said to me was, "I'll tell you this, Lieutenant. From everything I've seen, the real problem is our generals. If we could just swap ours for the Rebel generals, I think this war would be over in a month."

The following weeks went by interminably slowly. Occasionally, a well-intentioned Washington society matron would bring some religious tracts and pamphlets through the hospital wards, but the women rarely stayed very long, driven off by the smell of bodily corruption. Since few of them were under the age of fifty, the men made no effort to retain their company.

One young man from Indiana proved to be a remarkable animal trainer. His name was Walter Clapp, and he had been shot through the lung at Bull Run. In the hospital he had developed the nervous habit of blinking his eyes uncontrollably whenever someone was talking to him.

A few weeks after his arrival, Walter captured two of the field mice that lived under the hospital sheds and then bribed the orderlies with tobacco to allow him to breed them in a copper boiler stored under his bunk. He began training the mice to do various tricks by rewarding them each time they performed one correctly. It took months, but he eventually had them performing a macabre little dance on their hind legs, while another soldier played the "Wedding of Figaro" on his hornpipe. Figaro was also the name of Walter's finest performer, the Edwin Booth of his mouse company.

I celebrated my twenty-first birthday by leaving my bed for the first time. By then, Dr. Bolger was already convinced that I was the beneficiary of a major medical miracle, and that my case deserved a place of honor in the annals of medical science.

With the help of an orderly, I lurched on my atrophied legs to the opposite wall, where I stood for all of ten seconds before nausea caused me to beat a hasty retreat to my bunk. It became a challenge to spend a little more time on my feet each day. Soon I could stand unaided for almost five minutes before returning to my bed. On Christmas Day, I walked to the washroom all by myself. There was a cracked section of mirror fastened to the wall over one of the sinks. I cautiously sidled up to it, actually afraid of what I was going to see. It was far worse than I imagined possible.

The whites of my eyes were a muddy yellow, and jaundice had turned my skin the color of ripe squash. My eyes had retreated deep in their sockets, and my cheekbones stood out starkly against the jagged edges of my face. My brown hair was streaked with gray.

Defeated, I went back to my bunk, lay down, and spent Christmas Day watching a winter squall deposit three inches of snow on the sill. The other men celebrated Christmas that night by singing hymns while they stood around a small evergreen tree lit with tiny candles. My own celebration consisted of a full pint of laudanum. When it was finished, I asked one of the orderlies for another.

"Merry Christmas, Lieutenant," he said, handing me the bottle.

One brutally cold morning in February, I awoke to discover that the raw, pasty skin over my stomach wall no longer leaked yellow pussy fluid. The bad smell was suddenly gone, too. I knew then that I was physically getting better and celebrated by paying an orderly to heat me enough water for a hot bath. For an hour I soaked my body up to the neck in its restorative warmth. For the first time since I was wounded, I actually felt clean.

It was only when Dr. Bolger decided that I no longer required the use of laudanum as a painkiller that I discovered the depth of my dependency on it. Although the orderlies would no longer give it to me, the opiate was easy enough to acquire elsewhere. The supply seemed endless, and it could be purchased for little more than the cost of a few ounces of tobacco.

It was so plentiful in the wards that there was no way to control it. For men who had lost their faces or their legs or whose wounds were judged to be mortal, the overworked doctors had no other means of comforting them. It became as easy to purchase as coffee. That same day I acquired another bottle, this time a full quart. I can't recall exactly how long I nursed it, but at some point, many hours later, the thought came to my addled brain that I needed to destroy the evidence of my illegal action. The obvious means of doing that was to finish the bottle. It put me into a comatose state.

I regained consciousness to find Dr. Bolger roughly shaking me by the shoulders. From the look on his normally kindly face, I could see that he was outraged at my descent. Perhaps it was because he felt he had played a small part in my miraculous recovery. Perhaps he just liked me and didn't want me to die. I don't know.

"You are throwing God's gift away," he said, with deep emotion. Seeing the empty bottle of laudanum next to my hand on the bunk, he picked it up and smashed it on the floor.

"Lieutenant McKittredge is to receive no more pain medication of any kind," he said angrily. "Notify everyone on the ward that this is an order."

"Yes, sir," said the orderly.

Dr. Bolger stood up and slowly shook his head in frustration and disappointment.

"This is blasphemy," he said.

In spite of his orders and my own self-loathing, I had no intention of eliminating the one thing in my life that provided solace and escape. Now that I was ambulatory, it was easy for me to purchase the opiate in one of the other wards. My solution to the problem at hand was simply to hide it elsewhere on the hospital grounds. Meanwhile, I found my appetite slowly returning and began to regain a little of the weight I had lost, along with a small measure of my former strength.

As my physical condition slowly improved, I worried that Dr. Bolger would order me released from the hospital. The thought that I would be permanently severed from my connection to an inexhaustible laudanum supply became a frightening concern. I began to feign symptoms that were designed to arouse his sympathy during morning rounds. However, I could tell from his manner that he wasn't deceived.

One morning in early April, I was dozing in my bunk when I smelled the odor of a strong cigar. Opening my eyes, I took in the form of a man so massive that he actually blocked out the light from the window.

Unshaven and dirty, he was wearing the most disreputable uniform I had ever seen on a colonel in the federal army. Two of the buttons on the uniform coat were missing, and his linen was seedy and frayed.

He had a thick mane of unruly hair the color of furnace ashes, and he was staring down at me out of enormous slate gray eyes that looked like huge nail heads. Taking the heavily chewed end of a large cigar out of his mouth, he said in a deep, gravelly voice, "I know exactly what you're thinking."

The whole effect of him was so ludicrous that I said, "What is that?"

"He stood before me like Polyphemus, shapeless and horrible," said the behemoth.

"Virgil?" I found myself replying foggily, as if performing for a professor back in Cambridge.

"Excellent. You have a brain," he said.

I closed my eyes, already tired of his game.

"Are you ready to report for duty?" he said.

"No," I said, eyes shut.

"As the bard once wrote, you smell to heaven."

"No worse than your cigar," I replied, looking up at him once more.

"You are talking to a senior officer, Lieutenant. I could have you court-martialed for your insolence," he said gruffly.

At the same time, there was a mocking grin below his unshaven red cheeks. I again surveyed his unkempt appearance before deciding to say nothing further.

"Beauty and wisdom are rarely conjoined," he said, as if again divining my thoughts.

"You have my invitation to leave," I said.

"I'll be leaving soon enough," he said, puffing on his cigar and blowing the smoke in my direction. "And you're coming with me."

I laughed in his face.

"You should be ashamed of yourself, slacking here while boys with serious wounds are lying in dog beds," were his next words.

"You have no right!" I blazed back at him.

"So you had a small intestinal complaint," he said, without a hint of humor. "Is the army supposed to beg for forgiveness before you to return to duty like a man?"

I saw that he was trying to bait me and held my tongue.

"I have an honest job for you," he said.

"I'm not looking for a job," I said, sitting up to see him in better light.

"The choice is yours," he replied. "You can also be arrested for dereliction of duty"—his eyes bored into my mine—"among other charges."

In spite of his Falstaffian bulk, I saw now that he was neither fat nor dissolute. Deep-chested and broadly built, his gigantic head had an air of distinction to it, and his restless gray eyes glinted with intelligence. There was an air of authority to him, perhaps a faint echo of ruling blood.

"Who are you?" I said.

"Ahh . . . you would pluck out the heart of my mystery," he responded.

"Then go to hell," I growled, regardless of the consequences.

"My name is Valentine Burdette," he said, suddenly serious. "I work for General Marsena Patrick, the provost marshal general of the Army of the Potomac. We deal with thieves, murderers, and deserters."

"You've finally caught up with me then," I said, sarcastically.

He grinned once more, and deeply furrowed lines etched the corners of his eyes and mouth. I noticed that his long, high-bridged nose was canted over to one side as if someone had hit it repeatedly. With his personality, it wasn't difficult to imagine why.

"There are men seeking to profit from the Union and to destroy it by their actions. It is our job to make sure they are not successful. We also investigate corruption in the delivery to the army of substandard military stores and equipment that has already cost many soldiers their lives."

"Why me?" I said.

"Why not you?"

I shook my head in disbelief. None of it made sense, at least as far as it affected me.

"The army takes care of its heroes," he said then.

"I'm no hero," I said.

"Some others think differently. Let's just leave it at that."

"And what do you do, Colonel?" I said.

"Thank you for the military courtesy. You can see how important military etiquette is to me," he replied.

"Yes," I said, glancing once more at his atrocious uniform.

"I, Lieutenant McKittredge, am a trial lawyer, and a very good one," he added in a resonant voice that he probably used to good effect on juries. "I know you've been through a lot . . . but no more than thousands of other unlucky men in this war. Now I have need of someone like you for an important job. You'll just have to trust me on that."

"I have no qualifications for an important job," I said.

"Yes, you do," he came right back.

"What are my qualifications?"

"Before I tell you, I have a question. Are you addicted to opium?"

"No," I said, looking straight into his eyes and lying.

"All right," he answered, after a moment's pause. "Now, let's discuss your qualifications. Are you honest?"

"In most things."

"Do you have common sense?"

"Sometimes."

"Are you able to write a declarative sentence?"

"Yes," I said, suppressing a grin.

"You have all the qualifications I'm looking for. Now I have no more time to waste. Are you coming with me?"

I found myself nodding at him.

"What do they call you?"

"Kit," I said.

"You can call me Val," he said, as I began gathering up my few belongings in a paper sack. I thought about the pint of laudanum that I had hidden the night before behind the ward privy and immediately regretted my decision. My mind started racing to figure out some reason to explain why I couldn't leave after all.

"You have everything you need in here," he said, picking up my sack and waiting for me to move past him. As I walked out of the chicken roost for the last time, I saw Walter Clapp preparing his mice troupe for its matinee performance.

"Good luck, Kit," he called out.

"Good luck to you, too, Walter," I said.

Outside, Colonel Burdette motioned to two soldiers who were sitting on the driver's box of a small hansom carriage that was waiting near the door. A moment later we were seated in the back of it.

"To the asylum!" shouted Burdette.

I assumed he was making a joke.

CHAPTER THREE

THE CARRIAGE CAME OUT of dense woods and emerged onto the Maryland heights above Washington City. Below us, military encampments covered the landscape to the east as far as the eye could see. There were a dozen fortified redoubts, each sprouting scores of cannons. An intricate network of trenches and elevated rifle pits connected all the forts together. To the south, a great stone bridge spanned the Potomac River.

After spending the entire winter in hospital, it was exciting to see that spring had actually arrived. On both sides of the road, wild dogwoods were alive with white blossoms, and the bright pink redbuds dazzled the eye.

In the distance, there were several massive buildings. I recognized the highest one as the Capitol Building, its dome still only half complete. Then the carriage descended from the heights, coming out on a road that ran alongside a shallow, marshy canal. The canal meandered eastward, and we followed it into the city.

The first thing that struck me about our capital was the smell. One source of the stink became evident when we rode by the carcasses of several horribly bloated horses floating on the surface of the canal. They looked like they had been there for some time and were covered by a horde of flies and insects.

"Behold, our Athens along the Potomac," said Valentine Burdette.

The smell got worse as we went along. At times the color of the canal was actually yellow, like a gigantic flow of infected mucous. It was as wide as a small river, maybe sixty yards across. Along the opposite bank, we began to pass makeshift tent camps interspersed with roadhouses, saloons, sawmills, warehouses, and towering mounds of coal and firewood.

A monstrous mechanical contraption on wheels came groaning toward us from one of the wooden bridges that spanned the canal. Pulled along by a tired, sway-backed mule, its cargo was another dead horse. The animal was riding on its back with its legs extended upward in the air, suspended by a block and tackle from the timber framework above the cart.

"Twenty dollars says I know exactly where that horse is going," said Colonel Burdette, and I had no doubt he was right.

We rode past the president's mansion, where a dozen sentries lounged at their posts. The grounds of the mansion seemed more befitting a prison yard than the home of the president. Unlike the carefully trimmed parks in Cambridge, the grass was as high as my ankle, and the flowerbeds were choked with weeds. The mansion itself was badly in need of a coat of paint.

Then we turned onto a broad avenue, and suddenly the Capitol Building loomed up ahead of us, high on the far hill, completely dominating the landscape. Traffic now came toward us in a constant stream of drays, farm carts, hansom cabs, and military traffic. An artillery battery roared past along the cobbled section of the roadway, creating a formidable din. Behind it came a horse-drawn omnibus. In addition to the passengers inside, there were another dozen people lying or sitting on the roof, most of them clinging to a low railing that ran around the edge. They were all black.

"So much for the equality of the races," said Colonel Burdette, caustically.

The north side of the avenue was filled with important brick buildings, including hotels, restaurants, and fine shops. The other side boasted an unbroken vista of dingy saloons, weed-filled open lots, and decrepit rooming houses. Street peddlers shouted their wares on every corner. A large sow lay sprawled in one of the doorways.

The carriage turned into one of the side streets, and we rode north for another mile or so, passing wood-framed row houses, small shops, and livery stables, until the buildings thinned out and gave way to patches of open land where cattle stood munching at hayracks.

Just when I was beginning to wonder if the whole strange journey wasn't part of an opium-inspired dream, I spied another massive building ahead of us. It was located in a tree park and surrounded by an eight-foot-high brick wall. Armed sentries stood guard at the iron-gated entrance.

We came to a stop long enough for one of the sentries to glance inside the coach. Upon seeing Colonel Burdette, he saluted and waved us forward. As we rolled past the iron gates, I noticed a sign engraved in the high brick wall that read: WASHINGTON ASYLUM FOR THE MENTALLY AFFLICTED.

"So this is where you're taking me," I said, downcast at the thought that I was to be finally committed because of my addiction. I looked up to see Colonel Burdette grinning at me.

"Space in the nation's capital is at a premium, Lieutenant McKit-tredge," he said, as we arrived at a brick-sided entrance portico. "This is the headquarters of the provost marshal general of the Army of the Potomac."

It was a forbidding fortress of a place with iron bars covering all the windows on the first and second floors. There were three separate wings to the main building. One wing still served its intended purpose as a hospital for the insane. The others had been converted into office space for the Provost Marshal General Department. Part of our wing also contained several convalescent suites for wounded, high-ranking officers.

The dark, cavernous halls were filled with soldiers rushing in all directions, their boot heels clattering on the polished oak floors. Hand-lettered signs were tacked onto the door of each office identifying the activities being conducted inside. Colonel Burdette escorted me to a small room in the middle of a long corridor on the second floor. The barred windows let in very little natural light. The principal illumination came from a gas lamp mounted below the ceiling.

There were two desks in the room. A lawyer assigned to the Judge Advocate General's Office occupied the first one. His name turned out to be named Harold Tubshawe, and he was very stout, with a ruddy cherubic face. Perhaps to compensate for the fact that he was prematurely bald, he had cultivated a luxuriant beard.

It then being Saturday, Colonel Burdette informed me that on Monday morning, I would begin conducting background investigations into pending court-martial cases to determine which ones warranted prosecution by the judge advocate general. Only the most serious cases required trained lawyers, he said. The rest were dealt with in trials presided over by regular officers who served on rotating adjudication boards.

"I'm assigning you five cases to start with," said Colonel Burdette, handing me a batch of file folders. I scanned the cover sheets. Four of them involved enlisted men who had left their military units without proper authorization. In the fifth case, a federal paymaster was suspected of embezzling two hundred dollars. None of them seemed remotely important.

"Take the files home with you," he said, after providing me with a set of keys for the doors and file cupboards. "Be prepared to act on them as I direct you on Monday."

I remembered then that I did not have a home.

"I've taken the liberty of securing a room for you at Mrs. Warden's," he said, as if again divining my thoughts. "It is a pestilential hole by official Washington standards, but a definite step up from your chicken shed in Glen Echo."

Mrs. Warden's turned out to be an old, sagging frame house in a small mew near Lafayette Square. Colonel Burdette accompanied me there in his carriage, alighting just long enough to escort me inside and introduce me to Mrs. Warden, the proprietor. It was obvious from his greeting that they were well acquainted, but neither made mention of how or why. She was about sixty years old, with mocking eyes and a sturdy frame.

"Well, I'm glad to see a young officer who doesn't favor mutton chops and chin whiskers," were her first words. "Give me a clean-shaven man every time to see if he has character in his face."

"I believe he will benefit from your ministering soul, as black as it is,

Ella," said Colonel Burdette, turning to leave, "that and your prowess with butter and chocolate."

His parting words to me were, "She was born in the garret, but to the kitchen bred."

I understood his import after sitting down to supper an hour later. First, however, she showed me to my room, which was on the top floor of the house and looked out onto the roof of a small livery stable. It was very close in the room, and when I raised the window to let in some fresh air, I could hear voices coming from the room directly below mine. A man and woman were arguing, their words indistinct. Mrs. Warden heard them as well.

"The Masseys," she said. "Mrs. Massey is twenty-three; her husband is fifty-one. She is in love with Captain Spellman, who lives on the first floor. She doesn't think anyone else knows. Of course, everyone in the house knows, with the exception of Mr. Massey."

I agreed to pay her four dollars per week for the room and an additional fifty cents per day for my morning and evening meals. That proved to be a sound investment. Mrs. Warden and a hired girl served the meals family-style around a large dining table in the front parlor. That first night the main course consisted of an Irish stew served from an enormous tureen. She had eight boarders aside from me, including two aging civil servants, an Italian vegetable grocer, and a blind man with shoulder-length silver hair. I sat between Mr. Bliss, a linguistics expert at the Library of Congress, and a lovely young woman with a French accent who turned out to be the notorious Mrs. Massey.

Certainly, she did not look the part of a wayward wife. There was innocence in her smile, and she seemed completely unspoiled. Her husband, a priggish-looking man with poached eyes and a receding chin, was sitting on the other side of her. Next to him was the only other man in uniform. He introduced himself as William Spellman.

Mr. Bliss asked me where I had gone to college, and I told him.

"Have you knowledge of syntactics?" he asked hopefully, after I had shaken his clammy palm.

I had no idea what he was talking about

"The signs and symbols in both natural and artificially constructed languages," he said tartly. "And semiotics?"

When I shook my head in confusion, his lips curled downward, and he didn't say another word.

Mrs. Warden removed the lid of the tureen, and a fragrance rose toward me that smelled almost spiritually rewarding. Soft chunks of lamb and beef were submerged in a good, brown gravy and surrounded with mushrooms caps, carrots, turnips, onions, and potatoes. Platters of hot sour cream biscuits and bowls of creamed spinach rounded out the simple fare, and I found myself falling to the meal with genuine relish.

The discussion at dinner centered on several of the new generals who were now making their mark on the war, including Philip Kearny and John Reynolds. Captain Spellman was particularly excited about the rise of General Joseph Hooker.

"There was an account in the *Journal* today that recounted how he won the sobriquet of 'Fighting Joe' at the Battle of Williamsburg," he said, his voice marked by the Beacon Hill cadence of the Boston aristocracy. "Basically, he attacked their whole army with just his one division and might have won the day, too, if General McClellan had supported him. Instead, he lost 20 percent of his division in the attack."

"I happen to believe that General McClellan is the greatest soldier of the age," said Mr. Massey.

"Then why don't you tell us why the greatest soldier of the age chose to put his headquarters fourteen miles behind the battle line?" said the silver-haired blind man at the far end of the table. "McClellan had no idea what was even happening."

The man's chin and mouth bore terrible marks of disfigurement, although a full beard covered much of it. In spite of his infirmities, he ate his meal without difficulty in precise, economical movements.

"From what I have read about General Hooker," continued Mr. Massey, "he seems to reserve all of his fighting ability for drunken brawls in this city's worst dens of iniquity. You should be reading the *Sentinel.*"

"I wouldn't wrap a fish in that newspaper," said Captain Spellman.

Mr. Massey was undeterred.

"The man was a hellion at West Point," he went on in a superior tone, "and in the Mexican War he apparently spent most of his time in houses of ill-repute."

"Lies," said the silver-haired man, harshly. "He is the finest fighting general we have. Loyal to his men, personally brave, and he never asks them to go where he won't lead. If McClellan had supported him at Williamsburg, we would be celebrating the end of the war in Richmond right now."

"And how would you know?" retorted Mr. Massey, with sarcasm.

The blind man carefully folded his napkin and put it down in front of him.

"Because I was with him in the class of '37 at the Point. . . . And because I was with the army in Mexico when he led the attack of Hamer's Brigade through the Mexican artillery fire at Monterey," he said without pause, "and because I was with him when the Voltigeurs went over the barricades at Chapultepec and ended the war."

He stood up from the table, and replaced his chair in its proper place.

"Joe Hooker was the only first lieutenant in the whole army to be brevettted three grades up to lieutenant colonel for his gallantry in the three major battles of that war," he said, staring fiercely through his sightless eyes at Mr. Massey. "Since I am leaving on the morrow, let me say it now. You, sir, are an ass."

As he slowly made his way out of the dining room, Mrs. Warden's servant girl passed him on her way in bearing the dessert, which consisted of an apple crisp, warm from the oven, and topped with clotted cream.

As I stared down at my portion, I thought of what it might have been like to serve under a fighting general like Joe Hooker, a man who led from up front and knew how to fight a battle, instead of under a vainglorious fool like Edward Baker.

Although I tried to do justice to my dessert, the craving for laudanum began to take possession of me before the rest of the dishes were even cleared. I realized it was the first full day since I had entered the hospital more than six months earlier that I had not consumed my regular dosings.

The temperature of my skin seemed to be rising by the minute. Perspiration began to form at the roots of my hair. A few moments later, it was soaking the scalp and dripping down the back of my neck. Looking up from my plate, I realized that Mrs. Massey was trying to gain my attention.

"Your color is quite alarming, Lieutenant. Have you been ill?" she asked, with genuine concern in her eyes.

"Yes. I just came from the hospital," I said.

She nodded knowingly. By then there were thousands of us wandering the city.

"Is there an apothecary nearby?" I whispered to her.

"Yes, but I doubt it would be open at this hour. What do you need? Perhaps, I can lend you something," she said. "Is it for pain?"

Even as I nodded, I regretted it. If everyone in the house already knew she was in love with another boarder, how could she be counted on to keep my secret? Farther down the table, I heard raised voices. Her husband was now in a heated discussion with Captain Spellman.

"I believe in the cause of freedom for the colored as much as the next man," said Mr. Massey, his adam's apple bobbing up and down. "Nevertheless, the Greeks cherished slavery. In fact, Plato and Aristotle believed it was vital to an ordered society."

"But we have made two thousand years of human progress since then," asserted Captain Spellman.

"Perhaps," responded Mr. Massey, "but in their infinite wisdom, our own Founding Fathers decided to guarantee slavery in the Constitution. I refer you to Article one, sections two and nine. The Southern states are only demanding their rights under the Constitution."

I felt my nerves beginning to give way, and it was all I could do not to bolt from the table. Mrs. Warden was eyeing me closely from the kitchen door.

"I don't think an issue like slavery can ever be compromised when one side views the Negro as a human being and the other sees him as a good head of livestock," said Captain Spellman, his cheeks turning red with anger.

"You see the colored man as a human being, then," Mr. Massey replied.

My head felt as if it was going to explode, and I knew that if I didn't leave the table at that moment, I would break down in front of everyone.

"Please excuse me," I mumbled, almost reeling as I headed for the back staircase. I barely made it to the door of my room, fumbling for the key and then staggering inside. Something behind me momentarily blocked out the lamplight from the hall, and then I heard her lilting voice behind me. She must have come up the front staircase right after I left the dining room.

"It will be all right, Lieutenant," said Mrs. Massey. "Lie down now. I will bring you something for the pain."

As soon as I was on the bed, my body began to shudder, just as it had during those first long nights in the hospital. The tremors started in my hands, rapidly moving up my arms to the rest of my body, coming in short, staccato bursts until I thought I would split apart.

The door to the hallway opened, and she was back again.

"Here," she said, raising my head and putting a spoon to my lips. "This will help you."

I didn't need her to tell me what it was. I recognized the earthy fragrance of the opium and felt the raw authority of the alcohol as it coursed down my throat. But of what value was a spoonful, my demented brain cried out. She was holding the bottle in her other hand. I seized it from her grasp and tilted it to my mouth, gulping the mixture down as greedily as a man dying of thirst. There was less than a pint left in the bottle, and it was gone in a few seconds.

"Oh, you poor soul, you poor soul," she murmured, stroking my forehead.

The shuddering finally subsided, and I was still again.

"I must go," she said gently.

"You have saved me, Mrs. Massey," I said. "I am in your debt."

"My name is Adele," she said, softly closing the door behind her.

I lay awake all that night facing the enormity of what I had become. As the gray dawn crept slowly into my room, I silently swore that I would never again be without the one thing I needed to survive, which was a steady source of laudanum.

My first foray into the netherworld of an addict produced a satisfactory result. One didn't have to be an investigator for the provost marshal to know that the easiest place to find laudanum would be at a hospital. There was a new one just ten minutes on foot from Mrs. Warden's. Formerly a government office building, it took up a whole city block on Seventh Street and was already brimming with hundreds of army casualties.

The morning after my breakdown, I found the man I was looking for in a saloon on Sixth Street that was frequented by the hospital staff. For agreeing to supply me with two quarts of laudanum, I promised to pay the young attendant ten dollars. Two hours later, I was on my way home with the hoard that he had brazenly stolen from the dispensary. I tried not to think about the men who might be suffering without it, and vowed that I would find another source as soon as possible.

ON MONDAY MORNING I started my job at the Provost Marshal General's Department. Mrs. Warden informed me that a military van regularly traversed the route from the War Office on Seventeenth Street to the asylum. I rarely had to wait more than fifteen minutes for transportation to and from work.

On my first morning, Val Burdette explained the procedures he wanted me to follow in reviewing court-martial cases. It was my job to confirm the factual basis for the pending charges that had been brought. The first step was to interview the accused. If the person admitted guilt, I was to try to ascertain whether or not there were extenuating circumstances in the matter. If the accused claimed innocence, I was to use my initiative in determining whether the evidence was sufficient to bring the matter forward to a military tribunal. My legal colleague in the office, Harold Tubshawe, was available for consultation.

As it turned out, the overwhelming number of those accused were clearly guilty of the crimes they were charged with. Occasionally, I would conclude that there was an extenuating reason for what they had done. Val Burdette would take my findings and recommendations into account before deciding whether to turn the case over to the Judge Advocate General's Office for prosecution.

In that first month, I handled twenty-seven investigations, most of them involving the court-martials of soldiers accused of desertion, cowardice, theft, bounty jumping, embezzlement, sexual deviancy, drunken-

ness, and assault. I also investigated the dealings of two small contractors
who were accused of selling shoddy equipment to the army and one case
of bed-wetting.

I awoke each morning to the aromatic splendor of Mrs. Warden's
freshly baked breads and pastries as the smell drifted up the back staircase
and slowly filled my room. My appetite returned like a lost muse, and by
August, I had gained back much of the weight I had lost in the hospital.
My cheeks filled out, and my eyes emerged again from their sockets. In
fact, it would have been hard for a stranger to look at me and know that I
had ever been wounded. There were only two constant reminders of what
had happened to me on the windswept plain above Ball's Bluff.

The first was revealed each time I disrobed and saw the intricate network of jagged lines that were etched in livid red across my abdomen. The
second was the fact that I was consuming a steady flow of opiates laced
with grain alcohol every twenty-four hours. Although I was always under
the influence of opium, it did not prevent me from functioning in the job
I was assigned to do.

My routine did not vary in any material way from one day to the next.
While shaving each morning in my room, I consumed the first cup of
laudanum in the collapsible tin mug my mother had sent me upon my
enlistment in the army. After going downstairs to breakfast, I would
return to my room for a second measure. Then I would go to my office in
the asylum.

At work, I would wait until shortly before my lunch break at 11:30,
and then adjourn to the washroom down the hall from my office. There I
would remove the bottle labeled "disinfectant" that I regularly replenished
and kept hidden in a crevice behind the corner sink, fill one of the paper
cups next to the water crock, and then go to one of the thunderboxes to
consume the laudanum in relative safety. At around three every afternoon,
I would go back to the washroom for another cup.

Upon returning to Mrs. Warden's in the military van, I would avail
myself of another mug in my room before going down to supper. Back
upstairs, I would have a final measure at around eight o'clock. On those
long, sweltering summer evenings, the sun would still be streaming in the
windows when I stripped off my uniform, closed the curtains, and fell

naked across the bed. On rare occasions, if the black hole of opium-induced oblivion proved elusive, I would supplement the usual ration until I finally passed out.

During that time I never went to a play or concert, never read a book or newspaper, never attended church, and never took part in exercise or joined friends for a meal at a restaurant. I had no friends. I saw no one outside my office or the rooming house. My only knowledge of what was happening in the world came from conversations I overheard at work or around the dining room table at Mrs. Warden's.

I knew that General McClellan had failed in his attempt to lay siege to Richmond in June and had been replaced by Pope, who suffered another great defeat near Manassas in August. A few days later, the flood of wounded came streaming back into the hospitals around Washington like a bloody tide. The slaughter was so great that the Sanitary Commission ended up pitching a hospital tent on the grounds of the asylum. The familiar stench of physical corruption assaulted my nostrils every time I left the building for the next two weeks.

My life was one of complete subterfuge and concealment. Every Saturday night I would leave the house by the backstairs dressed in an old slouch hat, a patched workman's coat, and denim overalls. By then, I had made contact with an army quartermaster named Spangler, who operated his private affairs out of a row house in the notorious area known as Swampoodle. Among the range of army goods he peddled, Spangler had crate upon crate of laudanum for sale.

I paid him four dollars a bottle, which was a small fraction of the money I had saved during all the months I had spent in the hospital. My monthly pay as a lieutenant, including the bonus I received for my wound, was just over a hundred dollars. Laudanum was my only personal indulgence.

Spangler had no idea that I was an army officer. If I had truly cared about my responsibilities as an investigator for the provost marshal general, I could have had him put in prison for twenty years. He was a far bigger thief than anyone I had investigated up to that time. Consumed with self-loathing every time I transacted business with him, I would ride back to Mrs. Warden's in a hansom, and carefully conceal the bottles behind the hay bales in the small livery stable that faced onto the alley behind her house.

Of course, I wondered whether Val Burdette knew of my condition. I also wondered why he had salvaged me from all the human detritus at the field hospital. Did some fellow officer of mine bring me to his attention? Did a surgeon of his acquaintance hear of my case and mention it to him?

He seemed to have the prescient ability to divine almost everything; but after getting me started in my job, I rarely saw him. He was in charge of prosecuting major fraud cases involving military procurement contracts, and the work often kept him traveling for days and even weeks at a time.

Being emotionally cauterized, it never occurred to me that he might also be concealing mysteries of his own until I overheard Tubshawe talking with one of the lawyers in the next office about him one day. I knew it was Val they were talking about since Harold had come to refer to him as Colonel Vagrant, due to the perpetually sad state of his uniform.

"I tell you he was absent without leave for more than a week," said the other lawyer. "At first, General Patrick thought he might be the victim of foul play from someone he'd prosecuted. But then he just turned up again at his office. Everyone is talking about it."

"He should be court-martialed," pronounced Tubshawe, his cherubic face contorted in anger. "The man is a disgrace to the legal profession."

"And to the army," added the other lawyer.

They noticed me staring at them and went back to their work.

CHAPTER FOUR

ONE STORMY NIGHT in mid-September, I was having supper with the other boarders when Captain Spellman came rushing in from his staff job at the War Office, his uniform cape streaming water.

"A great battle is taking place in Maryland," he announced excitedly. "The armies have collided near some little village called Sharpsburg."

Mr. Massey was still an unrequited believer in General McClellan, and he loudly proclaimed to us that this time Little Mac would completely annihilate Lee's invading force.

"Isn't it grand?" he said, with a triumphant smile. "This battle will surely end the war."

"In that case, Captain Spellman, your wife will certainly be glad to have you back in Boston, won't she?" asked one of the civil servants, with a leering glance at Mrs. Massey.

The captain's smile disappeared as his eyes moved in her direction, too.

"Well, I won't be discharged right away, of course," he said lamely.

At the asylum the following morning, the same air of excitement and anticipation filled the corridors. Every time another military van arrived from the War Office, a new rumor would sweep through the building. It was reported at around nine that Lee had been killed and Jackson was now in command of the Rebel army. Our boys had won a crushing victory, was the next one, and General McClellan was on his way back to Washington to claim the presidency by popular acclamation.

Considering the number of times our army had been defeated, the pendulum of emotion was capable of swinging from euphoria to panic in a heartbeat. As the day wore on, the tenor of the rumors began to change. By noon a report swept the corridors that General Hooker had been killed, and that the army was in flight toward Washington again. Tubshawe, who had never seen active service, left the asylum at around two o'clock to warn his family of the possible need to evacuate the city.

I happened to be looking out the window of my office late that afternoon when I heard the sound of galloping horses. As I watched, a troop of cavalry came pounding up to the entrance portico of our wing. In their wake came a large black brougham drawn by four white horses.

As if they had been waiting at the door, three white-jacketed orderlies came rushing out as the carriage pulled to a stop. The coach door opened, and two soldiers in the brougham gently lowered a sedan chair to the men waiting on the ground. Strapped to the chair was an inert form wrapped in hospital blankets. The orderlies carried the sedan chair inside. A minute or so later, I heard them coming down the hall toward the convalescent suites at the end of our corridor. Silence returned and I thought nothing further about it.

When I arrived for work the next morning, unofficial reports from General McClellan's headquarters near Sharpsburg, Maryland, had finally reached Washington. The general was claiming a great victory. Based on similar inflated press accounts in the past, I remained skeptical.

"As I recall John Pope claimed victory last month," I said to Harold Tubshawe. He had taken the precaution that day to wear a large pistol on his belt, as if the Rebels might storm the asylum at any moment.

"There is no way those barefoot vagabonds can defeat us again," said Tubshawe fiercely.

That morning, General Patrick, the provost marshal general, had called an emergency meeting to address the rash of desertions that had recently beset the army. The desertion rate usually increased fivefold or more just before a major battle, particularly in the units that had a high percentage of bounty men. All of us were ordered to attend the meeting.

Ordinarily, I would already have consumed at least two cups of laudanum by then and been ready to go for several hours without replenishment. However, while shaving that morning, I had discovered to my chagrin that the new bottle I had brought from the livery stable was mislabeled and contained only castor oil. By then it was too late to replace it with one of the others.

Upon arriving at work, I went directly to the washroom down the hall from my office. Unfortunately, an officer was washing at the sink, and I left without gaining access to the bottle hidden there.

General Patrick's staff meeting dragged on all morning. At around eleven I excused myself and made another foray to the washroom. This time a cleaning attendant was mopping the floor, and I was forced to abandon that attempt as well. When the meeting finally adjourned for lunch, I rushed back to the washroom only to find a group of men attending to their ablutions. In my increasingly demented state, I was almost convinced that some maniacal force was at work.

It was two o'clock when the staff meeting finally ended, and I had another chance to try for the laudanum. By then my uniform was soaked with sweat, and I could feel the onset of another bout of the tremors coming on. I hastened down the dark corridor to the washroom. There was no noise behind the door, and I silently prayed that the room would be empty.

I swung open the heavy door. There was no one at the dripping sinks, and I went straight to my hiding place. Without pause, I removed the bottle from its crevice. Normally, I would have transferred it to a cup and then headed for one of the thunderboxes. In my haste I just removed the cork, tilted it to my mouth, and swallowed. When the grain alcohol began to sear my throat, I paused for a few seconds, and then tipped the bottle again.

"Is there enough for everyone?" came a loud voice behind me. It so startled me that I almost dropped the bottle as I turned around. A tall man was standing in front of the door to one of the thunderboxes.

He was wearing a purple silk bathrobe that had gilt dragons sewn all over it. Beneath the robe he wore white silk pajamas. His shoulders were resting on a pair of padded wooden crutches, and I could see that his right leg was wrapped in linen bandages. I immediately knew that he must have come from one of the convalescent suites farther down the hall and was therefore a senior officer.

"What is your pleasure?" he asked pleasantly.

Handling the crutches as if they were new to him, he came slowly forward until we were four feet apart. The man was as tall as I, but with a more strapping build. Clean shaven, he appeared to be about forty, and had thick, flaxen hair, a sharp pointed nose, and a dimpled chin.

"I'm sorry?" I responded.

He must have read the guilty look on my flushed and sweaty face.

"What are you drinking, Lieutenant?" he asked, his voice taking on a harder edge.

"Medicine," I said.

"Medicine," he repeated, with a lazy-eyed grin, "from a bottle that says disinfectant?"

"May I ask whom I am addressing?" I responded with spirit, having learned during my last months in the hospital how to avoid direct questions about my drug use.

"You're addressing someone who outranks you," he said, with a sudden haughtiness. His eyes were a remarkable purplish blue, but they were anything but soft.

"You are out of uniform, sir," I said next.

"I am out of uniform after sustaining an honorable wound, Lieutenant. But, of course, you have probably never gotten close enough to a battlefield to see one," he said, his voice now filled with contempt. "What are you . . . a clerk? No, even worse . . . you're probably an army lawyer from down the hall. Am I right?"

"I've seen my share of honorable wounds," I said.

"Really," he came back, "and where would that have been?"

"At Ball's Bluff."

He held my eyes for a moment, as if trying to decide whether or not I was a liar.

"What is your name, Lieutenant?"

"John McKittredge," I said.

He nodded, once.

"I am currently residing in the third suite down the hall, Lieutenant McKittredge," he said. "Report to me there at five o'clock this evening."

"Yes, sir," I said, and turned to leave.

"Leave the bottle on the sink," he added.

I went back to my office, and sat down at my desk to await my fate. I had managed to finish only a few swallows of laudanum before he interrupted me, but it was enough for the temperature of my skin to cool and for the shaking in my hands to stop. I asked Tubshawe if he knew who was occupying the convalescent suites.

"I heard General Martindale was recuperating in there last week for his piles," he said.

For the next hour, I tried to think through all the possibilities of what could happen to me. There was no doubt the man was a senior officer. Since he had been wounded, he was obviously in a field command. Based on my own experience with line officers, he would probably have little or no tolerance for a clerk who was addicted to opium, and it would be easy to confirm what the bottle contained. If I was also accused of stealing it from a military hospital, a long term in a military prison could be in store. At around four I felt the tremors begin again and wandered over to the hospital wing of the asylum.

It was at exactly five o'clock when I arrived at the door of the third convalescent suite. There were two sentries posted on either side of it. A burly major with the shoulder straps of a general staff officer was smoking a cigar in the hallway in front of the door. He looked up as I approached.

In all my twenty-one years of life, he was the first human being I had ever taken an active dislike to from the first moment I saw him. Perhaps it was the arrogance in his eyes or the barely controlled hostility in his manner. I had had my fill of staff officers in the first year of the war, but it was more than that.

"What do you want?" he demanded curtly. The man had a well-sculpted face with wavy black hair. His unnaturally long eyelashes gave his eyes a feminine cast. His lips were shaped in a Cupid's bow.

"I was told to be here at five o'clock," I said.

He stared at me for several seconds and said, "This corridor is off-limits, Lieutenant. Now turn around and get moving."

"I was told to be here at five o'clock," I repeated.

The major stepped close enough for me to smell the cigar on his breath. He was three or four inches shorter than me but much broader in the chest and arms. His uniform looked freshly pressed, and the tan leather gauntlets tucked behind his sword belt appeared new.

Looking over his shoulder, I saw that one of the sentries by the door was staring at me. As I watched his eyes widened as if he was trying to communicate something. The next thing I felt was the major's hand on my wrist. Like a coiled spring, he spun me around, pinning my right arm behind my back, and then shoving me forward. At the same time, he extended his boot in front of mine, causing me to trip and pitch headlong to the floor.

"You're not very good at following orders, are you?" he said.

I regained my feet and slowly began walking back toward him, only wanting to wipe the arrogance off his face. He must have seen the murderous look in my eyes.

"You keep coming and I'll have you arrested, Lieutenant."

"I was ordered to be here at five o'clock, Major. That's how good I am at following orders," I said, halting in front of him.

I saw the first hint of doubt come into his eyes.

"Who ordered you to be here?" he said.

"A blond-headed man on crutches wearing a bathrobe with gold dragons all over it," I said.

He stepped backward as if I had pushed him.

"Wait here," he said. He went to the door, knocked twice, opened it without acknowledgment, and disappeared inside. The same sentry who had earlier tried to signal me whispered, "Major Bannister's mean as a scorpion, sir."

"Thanks for trying to warn me," I said.

Then Major Bannister was back.

"You can go in," he said, holding the door open for me. As I passed him, he said, "How do you know General Hooker?"

"I don't know him," I responded, as he closed the door behind me.

No one was in the first room, which was set like a parlor, with a walnut drop-leaf table, a horsehair leather couch, and numerous side chairs. There was a desk by the window. It was covered with military documents, maps, and newspapers.

"Come in," said the voice I remembered from the washroom. The second chamber was smaller than the first and furnished with a walnut bed-stead, a chest of drawers, and two comfortable leather chairs.

He was still wearing the silk pajamas. The Chinese bathrobe lay next to him on the bed. His handsome face was bathed in a warm pool of light from a standing lamp behind the chair in which he was sitting. His ban-daged leg lay outstretched in front of him on a small ottoman.

I came to attention.

"Major Bannister has informed me that he may have acted somewhat harshly with you," he said. "It's entirely my fault. I gave him rather strict orders that I wasn't to be disturbed this evening."

"Yes, sir," I said, wondering why he would bother to apologize, consid-ering the punishment I assumed was coming.

"Simply put, my only reason for secrecy is that I don't want official Washington to know I'm here just yet. There will be no peace if they find out, and I haven't had a night to myself in weeks. I think I've earned one."

He must have seen the confusion on my face, because he stopped then, smiled, and said, "Do you know who I am, Lieutenant?"

"I do now, sir."

"Well, the provost sent over your records, and I first want to apologize for calling you a clerk."

"There is no need to apologize, General Hooker. I'm no more than that."

"Very few lieutenants are mentioned in dispatches by the commanding general. In your case the deed fully warranted it."

He tried to move his bandaged leg on the ottoman, and his face sud-denly went pale. Smiling wanly, he motioned me to sit down.

"Never hide your light under a bushel basket," he said next. "Not after an exploit like that one . . . Just look at McClellan. He's never gotten closer to a bullet than Harriet Beecher Stowe, and one would think from the press reports that he is the reincarnation of Achilles."

I laughed out loud, and he joined me.

"Personally, I have a fondness for good whiskey," he said, when I was settled in the chair facing him. "Perhaps you would care to join me for a glass. . . . Of course, I also have your bottle of disinfectant here if you would prefer that."

"Whiskey is fine, sir," I said, not choosing to tell him that I had already purchased and consumed a pint of laudanum from the janitor in the hospital wing. Desperation drives one to do things that are usually better left unsaid. He poured an inch of the smoky liquid into two small tumblers.

"I have a warm spot for officers like you," he said, taking his first swallow with a satisfied grin. "I've fought the enemy at close quarters, too . . . down in Old Mexico, but I won't bore you with ancient history. I have a question for you."

"Yes, sir."

"What was going through your mind just before you led that extraordinary charge . . . after you already knew all was lost?" he asked.

I thought back to that moment at Ball's Bluff. In my mind's eye, I stood again below the crest, watching the men falling around me.

"Anger," I said.

"Exactly," he responded.

"Mindless rage . . . and something else . . . It was as if God had just whispered in my ear that I wouldn't be killed that day."

"Yes, just so," he agreed. "I know the feeling well."

Smiling, he took another pull of whiskey.

"Was it laudanum you were imbibing in the washroom?"

I looked at him and nodded.

"One of the dirty secrets of this war," he said, "but in your case, certainly justified. My surgeon took a look at your hospital records. He says your case is destined for the medical textbooks."

"I would rather not have had the honor," I said, and he chuckled.

"Don't worry about my reporting you, son," he said. "I don't ride with God's cavalry."

His glass was already empty, and he poured himself another drink. I shook my head when he held out the bottle to me.

"I am probably the last one who should be dispensing advice on this subject," he went on, "but I would advise you to try to cut back on the opiates. You should find another interest to replace it."

"Yes, sir. That would probably be a good idea."

"Are you married?" he asked next.

"No, sir," I said, finishing the whiskey.

"Not a sound idea, at least in my case," he came back. His cheeks were getting rosier by the minute. "I have learned much in this life about the appetites of the female of the species. Enough to decide not to marry and enough not to let the sanctimonious mob nail me to the cross of so-called respectable behavior. Another short one?"

"No thank you, sir," I said, my voice thickening.

He poured another inch into his glass.

"So how do you think this war is being fought?" he asked.

The image of Johnny Harpswell's face exploding in the rowboat filled my mind, and I started telling him what I had witnessed at Ball's Bluff.

"Moronic stupidity," he said, when I was finished. "And I'm afraid it won't be the last before we're through. Did you know that General McClellan was provided with a complete set of Lee's operational plans just before the battle at Antietam?"

"No, sir."

"Well, through a remarkable piece of luck, he was. And Mac still wet his pants at the thought of facing that old man, even after learning that Lee had divided his army into four parts. Of course, that's how much Lee respected the young Napoleon . . . Lord . . . if Mac had moved faster than a centipede just that once, the war would be over right now."

He took another pull on his whiskey.

"Forgive me. I have a tendency to be indiscreet," he said. From the look on his face, he didn't look all that happy at the thought of the war being over.

"I'll say this," he pronounced, his voice rising again, "Lee . . . that magnificent old bastard . . . what balls. Outnumbered three to one and he stood there with his back to the Potomac and just dared us to come against him!"

The general's resolute blue eyes were alive with excitement. At that moment he reminded me of one of those flaxen-haired Norse gods of old that I had only seen in picture books. Then the light in his eyes momentarily faded.

"Now, McClellan," he said, "*his* balls are about the size of bird shot."

I heard someone knocking on the outer door.

"Here, have another," said the general, refilling my glass. A moment later Major Bannister appeared in the doorway and said, "Will you be having your supper now, General?"

"Yes, of course . . . serve it right there in the sitting room, Bannister. And Lieutenant McKittredge will be joining me. He looks like he has been on mean rations for a while."

From the look Major Bannister gave me, I could see he wasn't thrilled that I was still occupying the general's attention. Staff officers tend to be jealous about such things, particularly if their competition is junior in rank. He supervised the setting of the table with a white cloth, formal silver and china, before going out again.

That's when General Hooker said, "So what about the ladies? I'm sure that someone with your Lochinvar looks has had ample opportunities in that department."

I found myself telling him that growing up on an island with a population of sixty people did not lend itself to learning some of the important social graces. Although he was staring at me in rapt attention, his eyes were now moving in and out of focus.

"Are you telling me you have never had a woman?" he asked.

I felt my face get hot. He laughed out loud.

"I thought so. *Virgo intactis,* as the ancients would say."

I was about to respond when I again heard voices in the outer room. Major Bannister appeared in the doorway.

"May I assist you to the table, General?" he said, almost obsequiously; but by then General Hooker was already mounted on his crutches and heading out of the bedroom. When Bannister turned to look at me, there was anger in his eyes.

The meal had been ordered from Crouchard's and was served from metal warming ovens. The first course was a wine-based mushroom soup followed by Maryland soft-shell crabs and then a joint of lamb. There was a dark burgundy wine and a dry white wine. At some point I realized that all the dishes had been removed from the table and we were alone again. By then, he was calling me Kit.

The general began talking about his life out in California before the war. He had resigned from the army and at one point was living in a driftwood shack right on the ocean, he said, enjoying a variety of women of all ages and backgrounds. He even fell in love with a young Mexican girl, he said; but her parents disapproved, and he was forced to leave that part of California. It must have been around one in the morning when he asked, "Have you ever been in love, Kit?"

"No," I said, my brain now little more than suet.

"When you fall in love with a woman, you will know it, my boy. I have fallen in love many times. Each time it happens, you will have the responsibility of a . . . a Michelangelo setting something magnificent to canvas . . . or moulding it with clay . . . the challenge of a . . ." He stopped at that point to drain the whiskey in his glass. "No time for love now . . . Just balling . . . more's the pity."

I could hear a faint knocking on the outer door to the suite. A few moments later the sound came again, this time a bit louder. The general took notice of it, too.

"Who the hell is it?" he demanded, as I got up and went to the door.

I opened it to find a young woman standing in the hallway. Not more than twenty, she was dressed in a low-cut emerald green gown that exposed her ample bosom. Although the night was cold, she wore no wrap, and I wondered how she had gotten there without a coat.

"Well, you look a little young to be a general, honey, but I'm not complaining," she said, smiling up at me.

Her hair was tawny blonde, and she was very pretty in a lush-figured way. Even drunk, I knew why she was there.

The sentries were no longer at their posts by the door, and I leaned past her to look down the hall. They were standing with their backs to us at the entrance of the corridor.

"Another member of Hooker's staff," I heard one of them leer to the other, before they both laughed.

"My word, I didn't know they made them like you anymore," said the young woman. "I just wish I'd met you back in Moline."

"Who is it, Kit?" General Hooker called out from the other room.

"Tell him it is Leonora," she said, glancing into a pocket mirror she had removed from her small purse.

"It's Leonora," I called out dumbly.

There was a pause before he said, "Yes, the enchanting Leonora. Well, send her in here," called back General Hooker.

"Where are you from?" she whispered, as we headed toward the bedroom, her skirts rustling with each step.

"Maine," I said.

"Well, you can find me at the Carroll Arms," she said.

There was one awkward moment when General Hooker looked appraisingly at his new visitor, and then his eyes swung back to mine. For a second I thought he was going to invite me to stay. I'm not sure what I would have done if he had.

"I will see you in the morning, Lieutenant," he said, with a parting handshake.

CHAPTER FIVE

I DIDN'T SEE THE GENERAL the next morning, and I never made it back to Mrs. Warden's that night. In fact I barely made it down the corridor to my office. After lurching inside the pitch-black room, I found my greatcoat and managed to spread it on the floor before collapsing in a heap. I slept like the dead until a man came through in the morning to light the office gas lamps. I went to my desk and cleared my head with a cup of laudanum.

Harold Tubshawe came waddling in a half hour later carrying a satchel of legal files he had taken home with him. I saw that he was no longer wearing the heavy pistol at his waist and assumed correctly that he knew the latest military crisis was over.

"Did you hear the news?" he cried. "Fighting Joe Hooker himself is right down the hall in one of the convalescent suites . . . the greatest hero of the greatest victory the world has ever seen. Shot off his horse while personally leading his men into the bloody cornfield. The account is right here in the paper. And McClellan reports that Lee had two hundred thousand men with him . . . yet Mac still whipped him, by God."

"Quite astounding," I said, and headed out into the corridor.

In spite of the general's precautions, the whole world seemed to have suddenly discovered his hiding place. Men in tailored suits and women in taffeta gowns were bustling up and down the corridor like a school of sharks. Tubshawe joined me in the hallway.

"Well, you look a sight," he said, disapprovingly. "You might at least have the discipline to shave and comb your hair before reporting for duty. Why, General Hooker himself might come right by here this morning."

"I'd be very surprised," I said, wondering if Leonora was still in residence. Smiling, I went back into our office.

"I wonder if we'll get a glimpse of him," said Tubshawe. "That would be something to tell my grandchildren about someday."

He kept pacing to the doorway and then peering around the corner. By nine o'clock, a seemingly endless stream of admirers filled the corridor. At one point they were backed up all the way down to the entrance to the building on the first floor. Tubshawe squealed with delight each time a famous senator or congressman passed by on his way to General Hooker's suite.

"There goes Laird Hawkinshield," he said, with awe in his voice. "He was my congressman in Ohio. There is talk he will run for president after the gorilla is gone."

I ARRIVED THE next morning to learn that the general had left the hospital. A hand-written note from him was lying on my desk.

"There is a place on my staff for you whenever you want it," was the first line. The postscript read, "As far as your personal tastes, I would strongly urge you to find another mistress."

I considered his offer of the new job only long enough to realize that acquiring laudanum in the field was by no means a certain proposition. The thought of working under Major Bannister did not appeal to me either. I destroyed the note.

The excitement of General Hooker's visit was quickly supplanted by the arrival of another horde of wounded into the city. Antietam was the greatest slaughter ground of the war up to that point, and another temporary hospital was set up on the grounds of the asylum to treat a small fraction of the bloody host. Every morning for three weeks, I could see orderlies feeding arms and legs into the incinerator behind our wing of the building.

One unseasonably cold afternoon in October, I returned to Mrs. Warden's to find two policemen standing on the front porch. Between them stood Mr. Massey, who was gazing down at his hands with a puzzled expression on his face. Passing him on the porch, I saw that his wrists were confined by heavy iron manacles. His shirt and suit coat were heavily spattered with red stains. Inside, Mrs. Warden was sitting on a couch in the front parlor, staring straight ahead and struggling to control her emotions.

"That pathetic little man went and did it," she said, her voice barely audible. "He actually did it."

I heard a noise behind me, and turned to see two men in white uniforms carrying a wooden stretcher down the backstairs. Underneath a blood-stained sheet, a human figure was strapped to the frame.

"He waited until she was asleep and cut her throat," said Mrs. Warden.

I held the front door open for them as they took her outside and put her body in the back of a covered lorry. Watching her go, Mr. Massey turned to the policeman next to him and smiled.

"She never should have told me she was leaving me, you see," he said in the same insufferable tone that he employed while lecturing us at the dinner table. "What else could I do?"

Captain Spellman was inconsolable when he returned from his staff duties at the War Office to discover what Mr. Massey had done. The following day he resigned his commission and returned home to Boston. It was a sign of the times that within an hour of their departure, a line of people was waiting outside the front door to rent their rooms.

I do not know why Adele's death seemed more important to me than all the men whose names I read each morning on the Antietam death list. Perhaps it was because she had been so kind to me on that first night. Whatever the reason, my anger at the waste of it was only dissipated by greater draughts of laudanum.

IT WAS A SATURDAY NIGHT in early November, and I had just returned to the small livery stable behind Mrs. Warden's house after buying another week's supply from Spangler, the crooked army quartermaster.

The faint light of a street lamp leaked through the window above my head as I knelt down on the dirt floor and began concealing the bottles inside the mound of hay bales at the rear of the feed shed.

"'What potions have I drunk of Siren tears,'" came a disembodied voice from the shadows. I stared into the darkness but saw nothing. From inside Mrs. Warden's, I could hear the sound of the piano in the front parlor, accompanied by the lilting tones of a woman singing, "Barbara Allen."

"'Affliction is enamour'd of thy parts,'" said the familiar baritone, "'and thou art wedded to calamity.'"

The titanic form of Val Burdette separated itself from the massive pegged beam that held up the stable roof and came slowly toward me.

"This will not do, Kit," he said. "It is time."

"Time for what," I replied, already knowing the import of his words.

"It is time to deal with it. Opium will rot your brain."

"It is none of your affair," I said hotly.

"Pour it out," he said, "all four bottles. . . . I've already taken care of the one in your room."

The very thought of destroying the new supply seemed like a sacrilege. At that moment I would have sooner cut off my hand, for I was already feeling the first desperate urges. As usual, he seemed to be reading my thoughts.

"When did you have your last draught?"

"Around six," I said, truthfully.

"Well, I cannot do this for you," he said. "You must take the first step. After that, I promise to help."

"How can you help?" I asked derisively.

"I've had some experience in these matters," he said.

I was still kneeling on the dirt floor with the open rucksack in front of me.

"Start with the first bottle," he said, as if it were the simplest thing in the world. "That will still leave you three."

Looking to buy time, I picked up one of the brown bottles from the bag and removed the cork. As its earthy fragrance rose toward me, it was all I could do not to tip it to my mouth.

"Pour it out," he demanded harshly, and I did, watching the laudanum soak into the loose hay at my feet.

"Now the next one," he said, when the bottle was empty.

As I glared up at him with undisguised loathing, an idea suddenly struck me, brilliant in its simplicity. I would accede to his demands, but as soon as he was gone, I would head right back to Spangler's.

I quickly poured the second and third bottles into the hay, grinning in the darkness at the thought of what would happen when Mrs. Warden's cow ate the opium-laced fodder. As the remains of the last bottle gurgled out of the stem, I again looked up at him.

"Satisfied?" I asked.

There was a look of amusement on his ugly face.

"I am," he responded. "Let's go."

"Go where?" I blurted.

"You don't think I've done this just so you can go back to Spangler, do you?"

I was stunned that he knew him by name.

"Anyway, your conniving quartermaster is no longer in business," he said, pulling out his watch. "By now he is behind bars at the Capitol Prison."

"I'm starting to feel sick," I said, slowly standing up.

"You will feel far sicker in another hour," he responded. "In the meantime we must reach our destination."

He led me outside. A coach was waiting in the alley. We were no sooner inside than the driver lashed the horses and we were off.

A dense fog lay close against the city, and the street lamps were but smudges of pale yellow against the rimy night. The gloomy weather only made me more jaded at the thought of what awaited me when we reached our unknown destination.

As we turned onto Pennsylvania Avenue, the orange brilliance of the shop windows cut through the murk, and I could see people moving along the sidewalk, their spectral shapes outlined against the light. Then the coach was climbing the steep grade that led up Capitol Hill. I began to hear a series of clanking sounds, as if men were pounding massive bells with a dull gong. Cloaked by the fog, the noise would stop for a moment and then resume with another series of sharp retorts.

A horse car passed us on its way down the hill. In the hazy gleam of its interior lamps, I saw a full cargo of boisterous young soldiers, their faces wreathed in smiles. I remembered feeling that same innocent excitement when our regiment had arrived at the Capitol Building during the first summer of the war.

The fog thinned a bit as we reached the brow of the hill, and the riddle of the metallic noises was solved. Lit up in the glow of hundreds of firepots, I could see men scrambling like monkeys across the unfinished dome of the Capitol. High above us, workmen were pounding bolts into the iron framework on which the outer skin of the dome was being constructed. The stanchions looked like the ribs of some gigantic beast, as the Capitol Building disappeared into the mist.

We rode on for another mile or more along an unlit thoroughfare lined with wood-framed row houses. Then we were out of the city and on a deserted country lane. The driver finally reined the horses to a halt in front of a small brick farmhouse. A faint light came from behind the shuttered windows.

Val stepped down from the coach without a word, waiting for me to follow him before he approached the front door. I turned to see the carriage disappearing in the direction we had come.

Someone was obviously expecting us. As Val raised his hand to the iron knocker, it swung open. A short, stocky man filled the doorway, an oil lamp in his right hand. His small head was covered by a grotesque red wig.

"I'm ready for you, Colonel," he said, stepping back to let us pass.

I saw that the man's right foot was missing. In its place was an iron bar connected to a carved block of wood. We headed down a set of stairs that led below ground. At the foot of the stairs, we arrived at a heavy oak door that was anchored with iron straps to the mortared stone foundation wall.

Val opened it and then waited for me to go through before closing the door behind him. The brick-walled chamber smelled of wood smoke and fermenting apples. It was about twelve feet square, with a floor of loose cobblestones. There were no windows.

A log fire burned brightly in a grate that was set into the left wall. Two chairs sat in front of the hearth and an iron bed along the right wall. In the center of the room was a round, drop-leaf walnut table, from which two guttering candles flickered in the dank air.

"I would advise you to lie down and try to build up your strength for the contest ahead," said Val, removing a book from his coat pocket and sitting down in one of the chairs next to the fire.

I walked over to the bed. It was covered with a thin, straw-filled mattress and a single pillow. Two woolen blankets were rolled up at the foot. I sat down on the edge of the bed.

Thus began the longest night I have spent on this earth.

Less than an hour later, the perspiration was pouring from my body and soaking the bedclothes. Val poured a large glass of water from a pitcher on the table and brought it over to me.

"You are becoming dehydrated," he said, with almost clinical indifference. "Drink as much water as you can."

The tremors began in my hands a few minutes later.

"The first twenty-four hours will be the worst," said Val, as my body began to shudder uncontrollably. A white stabbing pain exploded behind my eyes, followed by a headache so intense that I passed out. Sometime later I awoke to find that the shaking had subsided.

"You should try to sleep," he said from the chair as I waited for the next round of tremors.

They came on slowly, finally taking hold of my body until a racking pain swept back and forth through all my muscles and joints. Then they would ebb away again, leaving me spent on the mattress. Each new wave was more painful than the last. Through it all, Val sat calmly reading his book.

I realized how much I hated him.

"Get out . . . get the hell out!" I cawed, my voice just a hoarse whisper.

He didn't look up from his book.

A spasm of nausea came on with no warning, and my stomach began heaving up an odiferous green fluid. By the time Val had moved to put a pan under my chin, much of it had spewed through my nose and mouth to soak the bedclothes. The uncontrollable retching continued unabated until I passed out again, desperately trying to take air into my tortured lungs.

I dreamed then that I was lying in the dead house at the hospital at Glen Echo, surrounded by stacks of maimed and bloated corpses. It was terribly cold, but the frigid air did nothing to diminish the stink of effluvium that hung over me. Johnny Harpswell appeared at my side, grinning down at me out of his ruined face. Colonel Baker, his toga-clad body riddled with bullet wounds, was standing next to him, complaining in a querulous voice about the lack of support we had given him during the battle.

I briefly came back into the world to find something weighing me down with the force of an apple press. It was Val, holding my shaking body in a rough embrace. Although he had covered me with blankets, I was shivering from a cold that I had never experienced before. All the warmth in my body seemed to be escaping through the skin. When the spasms stopped, he helped me to drink a mug of water. It came right back up with more putrid bile. I drifted away again.

When I next awoke, it was very dark. For a moment I thought I was looking across the sea at a distant ship's lamp. Then I realized that my eyelashes were crusted over with a gluelike film. I used my filthy knuckles to wipe them clear. In the faint glimmer from the coals in the grate, I could see Val's massive form, now slumped in the chair.

Time passed. I have no idea how long I lay there, drifting in and out of consciousness. At some point Val covered me with still another blanket. The next time I came back to life, it was to the stillness of an empty room. The fire in the grate had burned down to embers. Val was no longer there. My body was covered with sweat. I threw off the blankets.

The craving for laudanum was still as elemental to me as thirst or starvation. We must escape, my brain whispered to me. I forced myself to sit up, dropping my legs to the floor one at a time. Once we are free of this house, the voice murmured inside me, we will find a Samaritan to take us to a hospital. There we will find what we need, the voice assured me.

Trying to stand up, I swayed back and forth, finally grasping at the corner post of the bed to steady myself. I made it as far as the chair where Val had been sitting and rested a minute. The next leg of the journey took me to the door.

It was locked from the outside. In a futile rage, I feebly hammered against it. A minute or two later, a key began moving in the lock. The door swung open, revealing the crippled man. He had left his red wig upstairs. The crown of his head bore witness to a horrible scalping wound.

"Must leave now," I said.

"You need to go back to your bed," he said, taking my arm and propelling me across the room like a helpless invalid. I sagged down on the bed, drained of energy, and began shivering again.

"Must have laudanum," I gasped, as he covered me again with the blankets. "I will pay you."

Ignoring my plea, he went instead to the pitcher and bowl, wetting a rag and bathing my face with it. He built up the fire and left the room. I finally slept again. The next time I awoke it was to find Val back in his chair, reading. In the firelight his vast hairy head looked like a mass of knotted gray thongs. He glanced up and saw me watching him.

"What time is it?" I asked.

He removed his watch from his waistcoat.

"About three," he said.

I had lost track of whether it was night or day.

"In the morning," he said, sensing my confusion.

My mouth was very dry, and I had trouble swallowing. Val went to the table and poured me another glass of water from the pitcher. Sitting on the edge of the bed, he raised my head and put the glass to my lips. It was very cold. I had never tasted anything so good. When I finished it, he poured me another. I finished that one, too.

"Let's see if it stays down this time," he said, returning to his chair.

It did.

"Well done," he said a few minutes later, as if I was becoming a prize pupil. "It should become easier now."

"How do you know so much about all this?" I asked.

He paused for a time, as if undecided on whether to tell me.

"Two reasons," he said finally. "The first is that I once studied medicine. My father was a doctor, and . . . very strong willed. He expected me to follow in his path."

It was hard for me to imagine someone more strong willed than Val.

"My father died when I was in my last year of medical college," he went on. "I saw no reason to pursue it further. The law was always my true passion."

"And the second reason?"

He stared back at me for several seconds again before he spoke.

"Because I was like you," he said.

"I don't believe you," I said. "I've never even seen you drink a glass of wine."

"How do you think I got this?" he said, pointing to his off-kilter nose. "I had my demons, and they led me to where you are now."

"What kind of demons?" I asked, still skeptical.

He stared into the fire.

"There was a time when I was known in the Springfield, Illinois, courts as the mastodon," he said, with a taut smile. "Aside from obvious physical similarities, it was principally because I regularly enjoyed trampling my opponents in the courtroom. I never let up. My favorite targets were the railroads. Very difficult adversaries . . . several of them were represented by the best lawyer I ever met."

"Who was that?" I asked.

"Abraham Lincoln."

"He represented the railroad interests?"

"Very ably. It made him one of the wealthiest lawyers in Springfield. And he needed every penny to pay the bills Mary ran up each month."

"Who won?"

"Who won what?"

"The cases in which you were adversaries," I said.

"Who do you think?"

I was still pondering the question, when he said, "Abe is the one who started calling me 'the mastodon.'"

I smiled at the thought of it.

"And then?"

"And then I took an important case in the Colorado Territory representing several Indian tribes. The federal government had appropriated their land on behalf of the Western Pacific Railroad Company. It was typical of those times. No compensation. I was there for several months before the case was settled."

Standing up, he walked over to the fireplace and added another log to the grate. When he turned toward me again, his face was veiled in darkness.

"It was two weeks before Christmas, and I was preparing to return home," he said. "A wire arrived from my brother stating that my wife was very ill. Of course, I left immediately."

I waited for the words I already sensed were coming.

"She died the day before I arrived."

"I'm sorry," I said, knowing that words could give no comfort.

He nodded and said, "She had succumbed to scarlet fever. . . . Highly contagious, as you probably know. We had three children . . . two girls and a boy. They contracted it as well."

The only sound in the room came from the flames licking the new log.

"I was unable to do anything to ease their suffering. It took them all."

The enormity of his loss took my breath away.

"The rest is predictable, I suppose. . . . Whiskey was the easiest path to oblivion. I went on a bat that lasted two years. I stayed drunk . . . mostly fighting drunk. . . . I tried many times to die."

"Will the craving ever go away?"

He shook his head and said, "If you are like me, you will be cursed to spend part of every day thinking about the next draught . . . It is not an easy road."

"Have you ever lost control of it?" I asked.

"Not yet," he replied.

I drifted away again. When I came back, he was standing by the bed with a steaming mug in his hand.

"Do you think you could keep down some broth?"

"Yes," I said.

I tried gripping the mug with both hands, but was wracked by another bout of shaking, and he had to feed me like a child, one spoonful at a time. The broth remained in my stomach less than five minutes before it was gushing into the tin wash pan.

"We'll try again in an hour," he said. An hour later, it stayed down.

Afterward, I fell into a deep sleep. I found myself dreaming again. This time the dreams were not about Ball's Bluff or Johnny Harpswell. They were of my island home off the coast of Maine, just as it had been when I was a boy.

Bathed in a radiant summer sun, I saw our fleet of two-masted schooners swinging gently at anchor in the harbor. There was a fresh catch, and the fishermen were standing in their aprons beside the wood plank tables in the flake yard, gutting and cleaning the cod with razor-sharp knives. The beach was covered in scaly flakes.

Great flocks of gulls swooped overhead, their shrill cries interrupted by sudden attacks to pounce on the entrails, heads, and tails. I could smell the reek of salted fish curing in the sun.

Then, suddenly, it was winter, and cold rain was leaking down from the slate shingles under the roof in the attic and soaking my pillow. I opened my eyes to the pressure of a cold wet rag on my forehead.

"How do you feel?" he asked.

The craving was no longer there. I was sure that it had not gone far, but the desperate need to have the opiate inside me was gone. I told him so.

"You might not believe it yet, but this is the beginning of a new life for you," he said.

"How long have we been here?" I asked.

"Three days and nights."

"No . . . that's impossible."

"It's true. I secured a week's leave for you. The next step is to regain your strength. Are you ready to go back?"

"Yes," I said weakly, and meant it.

As we came to the top of the stairs, Val introduced me to the man in the red wig. His name was Crisp, and he was originally from Springfield, having once served as Val's law clerk. His wounds were suffered during the Seven Days.

Less than an hour later, we were back at Mrs. Warden's.

The following day I began my new life. Upon rising, I took a long hot bath, had breakfast, and then ambled slowly around Lafayette Square, stopping several times to rest along the way. Within a week I was walking all the way to the Capitol, eating my packed lunch in the park beyond it, and walking back without a pause. My appetite was such that Mrs. Warden threatened to charge twice the fee for my weekly board. I cheerfully volunteered to split the new pile of firewood in her yard, and she readily accepted the offer.

As each day passed, I grew steadier in my resolve that I could tame the beast inside my brain. For that was where it lived and still lurked. I went back to work the following Monday.

Chapter Six

Through much of that November I was primarily occupied with desertion cases, although I did handle the court-martial investigation of a soldier who was accused of stealing laudanum from a field hospital. He had become addicted to it after the amputation of his leg following Malvern Hill. I was able to get the charges against him dismissed.

One morning I arrived at the office to find a large envelope on my desk. It was addressed from the Adjutant General, U.S. Army. Inside was a parchment document that read: "Know ye, that reposing special trust and confidence in the patriotism, fidelity, and abilities of John McKittredge, I have nominated and with the advice and consent of the Senate do appoint him Captain in the army of the United States."

It was signed by Abraham Lincoln.

My first reaction was to send it to my parents because I knew it would make them proud. Upon closer inspection, I saw that my name and new rank were filled in with ink, while the rest was printed on the vellum stock, along with the presidential seal. Although it looked like Lincoln's signature at the bottom, there were far too many captains in the army for him personally to have signed all our promotion papers.

My colleague Harold Tubshawe was duly impressed. However, it was obvious from the disgusted look on his face that he had seen nothing in my performance at the Provost Marshal's Office to warrant a promotion of any kind.

In mid-November, I became embroiled in the military trial of one Simon Silbernagel. At first the case did not appear at all different from dozens of others I had already handled in my job, although it was on a much bigger scale. Simon Silbernagel was then the largest contractor supplying fresh beef to the army commissariats in Washington and Maryland.

The charges against him were detailed in a docket folder that landed on my desk one morning along with three others. I noted on the cover page that Tubshawe had been assigned to prosecute the case. The top of the first page read:

CHARGES: FRAUD AND MURDER

It is charged that said contractor, Simon Silbernagel, contracted to deliver to the Subsistence Department of the U.S. Army, fresh beef in equal proportion of fore and hindquarters meat (necks, shanks, and kidney tallow to be excluded) from steers of four years of age or older.

And that said Simon Silbernagel did willfully, corruptly, and knowingly deliver large quantities of beef from bulls and cows, as well as large quantities of diseased, ulcerated, and decaying beef, when he knew the true quality and condition of said meat.

And that said Simon Silbernagel did therefore willfully cause the death of Pvt. Ratliff Boone, a cook in the Subsistence Department who consumed such meat and thereafter died.

"This is a murder case," I said to Harold. "I'm not qualified to look into it."

"You would be wasting your time anyway, McKittredge. There is nothing to investigate," he said. "The man is guilty."

I might never have done anything further with it if he had not then added, "Silbernagel is a Jew."

"That is not evidence," I said.

"They are by nature parasites. Perhaps you read the newspaper of General Grant's recent order in his own military jurisdiction."

"Ulysses Grant?"

"The same. He has ordered all the Jews out of the Western Theatre of Operations. I only wish President Lincoln would do the same here. Obviously, this man Silbernagel didn't count on his diseased meat killing someone, but I will make him pay for it."

"What penalty will you seek if he is convicted?" I asked.

"Death by firing squad," said Harold. "I would prefer to see him drawn and quartered, but shooting him will serve as an example to the rest of the tribe."

It seemed to me that if bigotry was the underlying reason Tubshawe had already decided he was guilty, then prejudice might have also factored into the inquiry that led up to Silbernagel's indictment. That was the sole reason I decided to look into it.

I spent the next four days interviewing everyone whose name appeared in the docket folder, starting with Mr. Silbernagel. He was about sixty, with dark, liquid eyes and a well-cropped silver beard.

"I swear to you, Lieutenant," he said, with great emotion, "I have never sold diseased beef to the army. It's true I do not always supply steers, but a fat heifer provides better meat than an old steer. Ask anyone in the business."

I did ask, and every contractor I spoke to, including several of Mr. Silbernagel's competitors, took the same position he did.

"I probably shouldn't be saying this," one of them told me, "but he could have gotten a much higher price for his meat from private buyers than from the Subsistence Department. The bid he made to the army was so low there was no way he could make a profit on it. I remember asking him why he would want to lose money, and he told me he did it because he believed in President Lincoln and wanted to do his part to help win the war."

After talking to many people Mr. Silbernagel had done business with in the previous year, I became convinced that he was not a fraudulent contractor. Of course, that didn't mean he wasn't guilty on this one occasion.

It was clear from reviewing the army documents that an inspector from the Quartermaster Corps named Major Dana Pease was the pivotal witness in the case. He was in charge of the office responsible for inspecting meat delivered through the Subsistence Department to all the military camps in the district. On the day the ulcerated meat was delivered to the camp in question, he happened to be there on an inspection tour. Coincidentally, it was the same day Private Ratliff Boone, an army cook who was apparently fond of eating raw beef, died from food poisoning after consuming a portion of it. Major Pease had personally inspected the remainder of the suspect beef after Private Boone died and declared it to be diseased. He had ordered Silbernagel arrested and placed in confinement, pending the charges that were ultimately brought against him.

At the War Department on Seventeenth Street, I found a copy of Major Pease's military records in the Adjutant General's Office. He was thirty-six years old, and had served in the army less than a year. A letter in his file indicated that a colonel in the Quartermaster General's Corps had offered him a captain's commission based on his professional experience as a food wholesaler in Philadelphia. After receiving his commission, Pease had been placed in command of the meat-inspection department of the Quartermaster Corps for the Washington District. His promotion to major was accompanied by a commendation letter from the quartermaster general himself, praising his steadfast devotion to duty.

As the date of the trial approached, I could find no hard evidence to support my belief that Mr. Silbernagel was innocent. The day before the trial began, however, I did learn one piece of information that possibly suggested a more sinister reason for Private Boone's death.

It occurred to me that since Mr. Silbernagel had been confined at Fort Marcy since his arrest four months earlier, someone else was supplying fresh beef to the camps in the district. I found myself wondering who it was. Those records were on file at the Quartermaster General's Office.

What I discovered was that a week after Mr. Silbernagel's imprisonment, his contract had been summarily canceled. A day later, an "emergency" contract was entered into with a company named Consolidated Supply and Manufacturing, which was based in Philadelphia. Under the emergency contract, which had not been competitively bid, the new price for freshly slaughtered beef was more than three times what Mr. Silbernagel had been charging. The signature of Major Pease appeared at the bottom of the new contract.

I remembered that he had been a food wholesaler in Philadelphia prior to his commissioning. Back at my office, I wired the Provost Marshal General's Office in Philadelphia to provide me with information about the Consolidated Supply and Manufacturing Company, as well as a list of all the principals in the firm.

That afternoon I was briefing Val on everything I had learned in the case when an enlisted man burst through the closed door.

"Sorry to interrupt you, Colonel, but it's the gun carriages again," he said, out of breath. "This time at Fort Ward about thirty minutes ago."

Val stormed out into the corridor, bellowing for his coach to be brought around to the asylum entrance. A few minutes later, we were tearing across the city at breakneck speed, narrowly averting disaster at several intersections because Val could not refrain from craning his head out the window to yell at the driver to go faster.

We crossed the Potomac River at the Long Bridge and thundered down the Columbia Turnpike through the city of Alexandria. At Bailey's Crossroads, we turned east onto the Leesburg Pike and ran on for another mile or so until we reached the southernmost fortifications in the capital's defense ring.

At Fort Ward a sentry waved us through the sally port, and we rumbled across a narrow wooden bridge that spanned a moat leading into the interior defenses. There was no evidence that anyone was on high alert. Off to the left, a soldier was hanging laundry on a clothesline he had stretched between two timbers that formed part of the inner revetments of the massive earthen walls. We pulled to a halt at the foot of a path that led up to the outer parapet of the fort.

An artillery major was waiting for us when we leapt from the coach.

"It happened again, Colonel Burdette, just as you anticipated," he said, as we followed him up the corduroyed path. "As soon as I received word of the accident, I sent for you."

The earthen-filled fortification wall rose fully twenty-five feet above the plain and was topped with a wide parapet. Beyond the fortress walls, the flat Virginia countryside stretched for miles into the distance. Every fifty feet along the parapet, cannons faced south to thwart any possible enemy attack.

The two closest gun emplacements looked like they had taken direct hits from enemy artillery. Each had held a twelve-pound bronze Napoleon capable of firing a shell nearly a mile. Both cannons were now lying in the debris of their smashed gun carriages.

"I ordered the men not to touch anything," said the artillery major.

One of the guns lay canted over to one side, parallel to the fortification wall. The other was still in its embrasure, but pointing straight up in the air. The carriages that had supported them had been reduced to shattered timbers. An artillery sergeant who had been conducting the firing exercise stood waiting for us on the wooden platform that extended along the inner span of the parapet.

"What happened here, Sergeant?" asked Val, without any preliminaries.

"God help me, Colonel, I didn't mean to kill those men," he said, his voice almost breaking. "We had cleared the range of fire for the training exercise, and I . . ."

"It wasn't your fault, Sergeant. Just tell us what happened."

"I don't know, sir. First we had problems with these friction primers," he said, holding up a thin copper tube no larger than my little finger. "They're supposed to ignite the powder bag inside the barrel, but there was something wrong with the fulminate of mercury in the ones we were using. None of these are any good."

He threw the primer in disgust toward an open wooden crate. Dozens of the copper tubes were scattered on the ground around it.

"I ordered one of the men to get another crate of them, and those worked all right," he went on. "That's when we started the exercise."

I walked over to the wooden packing crate that had held the defective friction primers. Bending down to examine them, I was surprised to see that there were no markings on the crate to identify the name of the manufacturer.

"We had fired four rounds," the sergeant went on. "There was no warning . . . both guns were firing fine . . . but on the fifth salvo, the gun carriages just collapsed . . . both of them. They just seemed to disintegrate . . . splinters flying in every direction."

His eyes roved back toward the gun emplacement.

"The barrel of my own piece pitched hard left as the powder charge exploded, and the shell went about 30 degrees off in that direction," he said, pointing toward a tree-covered knoll several hundred yards beyond the fortifications. The hill was dotted with white Sibley tents. "That's when it hit those men over there."

In the middle of the encampment, one small cluster of tents appeared to have been leveled as if by a windstorm. As we watched, men bearing stretchers were heading down the knoll toward the fort.

Val walked over to the pile of debris behind the first gun emplacement and began to examine the shattered timbers of the gun carriage. He spent almost thirty minutes combing through the wreckage before conducting a similar examination of the second one. Picking up one of the defective friction primers from the ground, he put it in his pocket, and said, "I can learn nothing more here."

Before leaving the fort, we rode over to the encampment where the errant cannon shell had exploded. The bodies of three dead infantrymen lay side by side, covered with blankets. From inside one of the nearby tents, I could hear the same demented moaning that I remembered so well from Harrison's Island.

"This is an obscenity," said Val, staring at the carnage around us.

Having served in an infantry unit, I was well aware that powder sometimes didn't explode and that artillery pieces sometimes malfunctioned. But what we saw that day drove home to me just how deadly to an army's success defective equipment could be.

The trial of Simon Silbernagel began a few days later. Up to that time, I had never seen a court-martial case take more than three days from opening arguments until a final verdict from the military court. Yet three days into the trial, Harold Tubshawe had not even finished presenting his so-called evidence.

At one point he spent twenty minutes reading from a breeder's manual on the genetic differences between a steer and a heifer. Witnessing his methodical attack, I became convinced that there was an underlying motive for his overzealous prosecution of the case. I went home beginning to think that an innocent man might be shot for a crime he almost certainly did not commit.

That same evening I learned at Mrs. Warden's dinner table that President Lincoln had chosen General Burnside to replace McClellan as the commanding general of the Army of the Potomac, and that General Hooker was now leading two full corps of more than forty thousand men. According to the latest rumors, our army was preparing to launch a new attack from its base near Fredericksburg, Virginia.

As I listened to the other boarders fatuously offering their opinions of the latest war news, it almost seemed as if my night with General Hooker had been nothing more than the product of one of my fevered dreams. I found myself hoping that he would soon have a chance to add to the success he had earned at Antietam.

After finishing dinner, I went upstairs to my room, hoping to read a book until sleep finally overtook my agitated mind. Without laudanum, I had found it almost impossible to sleep more than a few hours at a time.

Lighting the lamp next to my bed, I crawled under the covers with a volume of Dickens, which soon carried me away to a different world. Eventually, rain began spattering the panes of the window, and its rhythmic beat eventually caused me to doze off.

The book still lay propped open on my chest when I was awakened by the sound of someone persistently knocking on my bedroom door. Picking up my watch, I saw that it was almost midnight. I got up and opened the door to find a soldier standing in the corridor, his India rubber cape dripping water onto the hall carpet.

"Colonel Burdette is outside in his coach," he said. "He asks that you join him there as quickly as possible."

I put on my uniform and greatcoat and went downstairs. The house was completely dark except for the lamp that Mrs. Warden always left burning in the front parlor window.

Val was waiting for me in the coach.

"I just returned to Washington this afternoon," he said, "and I read your memorandum on the Silbernagel case. It's time you understood the dimensions of what we are up against."

The muddy, rain-swept streets were empty of people, except for the poor unfortunates who had no place else to go in the overcrowded city and were forced to find lodging in doorways or under the raised wooden sidewalks.

We had traveled no more than five blocks before turning into a narrow, cobblestoned alley off Pennsylvania Avenue. To the left I could see the west wing of the Treasury Building through the coach window, and then we rolled through a small copse of trees. A large brick stable loomed up on the right, and the carriage swung toward it onto a rutted gravel path. Up ahead I saw two sentries standing by an opening in a high, iron rail fence.

Beyond them sprawled a vast unlit building. Even through the pouring rain, I recognized it immediately as the east wing of the president's mansion. The carriage pulled to a stop at the edge of the path, and we alighted. At the guard post we presented our identification papers to the sentries, one of whom held a lantern in our faces while the other found Val's name on a printed document that he was trying to protect from the rain under his cape.

"You're expected, Colonel," said the second sentry. He escorted us along a footpath that led around the southeast corner of the mansion. Suddenly, from the dense plantings off to my left, I thought I heard a woman's cry. Something bounded across the path, causing me to stumble into the sentry.

"What was that?" I called out, as the apparition darted into the thicket on the other side of the path.

"Tad's goddamn goat," the sentry muttered sourly.

He brought us to an unguarded door at the base of the southeast corner of the mansion. A small portico provided us temporary shelter from the driving rain.

"Thank you, Corporal. I know the way from here," said Val.

"Yes, sir," said the sentry, heading back to his post.

We went in through a small vestibule and down a dark, silent hallway. Val opened a door at the other end. Behind it was a narrow wooden staircase, and we followed it up to the next floor, coming out in a much wider corridor that was lit every twenty feet by copper-clad oil lamps set into the walls.

A threadbare Oriental carpet covered the floor, and numerous sets of muddy footprints attested to the fact that it had been well traveled that same evening. I was beginning to doubt that anyone was still awake in the mansion when we passed the first brightly lit room. Under a crystal chandelier, a young man with a black beard was working at a small mahogany desk, furiously writing in a large letter book.

We climbed yet another flight of stairs and found ourselves in a corridor that ran parallel to the one we had just traversed. A soldier stood at attention next to the big rosewood door on the right. It was open, and we went on through. There were three men in the room, one standing with his back to us, the second seated behind him, and the third sitting at a long library table. Val headed directly toward the second man. Suddenly nervous, I followed slowly behind him.

"Ahhh . . . the great mastodon," came a reedy voice.

I couldn't see his face because an elderly black man was blocking his body. The black man wore a starched white jacket and was cutting the seated man's hair with a pair of shiny scissors. As I crossed in front of him, the enormous head of Abraham Lincoln came into view.

"Speaking as your commander-in-chief," he said, staring up in mock distaste at Val, "let me say that your uniform is a gross insult to the military profession."

In fact, I was surprised to note that Val had actually made an effort to improve his normally disheveled appearance. He had combed his hair and buttoned his uniform. Unfortunately, this sartorial splendor was undercut by a matting of orange cat hair that covered the front of his coat.

"I will continue this level of dedication to military decorum until you make me a civilian again," replied Val.

Two gnarled hands emerged from under the white sheet that covered Mr. Lincoln up to his neck. He grasped Val's right hand with both of his own.

"I would rather make you a general, old friend, but then you would be bound to fail like the others."

"Then I'll stay a colonel," said Val, as the barber continued to snip the edges of the president's thick, unruly hair.

"This is the first chance I've had to get a haircut since the newspapers started comparing me unfavorably to a gorilla again," said the president. His skin was almost the color of saffron.

"You're the most comely gorilla I've ever known, Abe," said Val.

President Lincoln's haggard eyes moved to take me in.

"This is one of my officers . . . John McKittredge," said Val. The president gave me an appraising glance as he shook my hand.

"It's my sad duty to report that the war has finally come home to roost," said Val. "Captain McKittredge and I were just attacked out on the lawn by Tadpole's goat."

"He's a seasoned warrior that one. I would have assigned him to McClellan long ago, but of course the general already had a convenient scapegoat in me," said President Lincoln, as the barber finished his work and gently removed the sheet.

The president's private office was as large as a farm kitchen. There was a massive round oak table in the middle of it with a base carved into gigantic lion's paws. Horsehair chairs were scattered around the room. On the far wall, two leather-covered sofas faced each other under the two draped windows. A slant-front desk stood in the corner, its pigeon holes stuffed with documents.

President Lincoln uncoiled his long legs and stood up from the chair, wincing as he did so. He was wearing old carpet slippers on his feet.

"John, it's time for you to go home," he said to the clean-shaven young man who was writing at the oak table. Turning to Val, he said, "This is John Hay, the man responsible for everything that turns out right around here. John, meet the great mastodon of Springfield."

"I've heard the president speak of you," Hay said. " 'The best courtroom lawyer I've ever known,' were his exact words."

"And he doesn't exaggerate," said Val, with a grin.

"I began calling him the mastodon thirty years ago. It was because, like the great wooly mammoths of the Ice Age, he seemed a gentle soul until he got his Irish up, after which he ran amok in front of a jury, trampling those of us unlucky enough to be opposing counsel. He flattened me on more than one occasion," President Lincoln added with a rueful smile.

"I think I'll run over to see Brooks, and then come back in case anything breaks," said John Hay.

"No. I don't want to see you until tomorrow morning," replied the president in an admonishing tone.

The young man nodded, giving me a lingering glance as he went out the door.

"Mary had some food sent up a little while ago," the president said, pointing to a platter of cold meat, pickles, and sliced bread on the round oak table. "Please, help yourselves."

A large silver pot of coffee rested on a separate tray, its rich aroma filling the room. While Val and the president went over to pour themselves a cup, I watched as the barber knelt down on the floor and carefully swept up the president's hair with a small hand broom. He put the trimmings in the pocket of his jacket.

"You treat those clippings like they were gold bullion," I whispered.

The man seemed to swell up with pride.

"To some people they are, sir."

He gathered up his tools in a small leather bag and started to leave.

"Thank you, Henry," said President Lincoln.

"May God keep you safe, suh," said the old man.

Val went over and closed the door behind him as the president crossed over to the leather sofas under the windows. He walked as if his feet hurt, his legs bent at the knees, his feet barely lifting off the carpet. Dropping to the sofa, he curled his right leg over one of the arms and let himself fall backward.

"It's still hard for me to believe," said Val, "that in this whole vast nation, the people turned for their president to a one-horse lawyer from a one-horse town."

"For me, too," said President Lincoln. "But it happened at a time when a man with a policy would have been fatal to the country. I have never had a policy."

As I watched, his left eyelid began to droop down. Oddly, the right one stayed fully open.

"Well, you look even more worn out than the last time I saw you, Abe," said Val. "And that was when the doctors mistakenly thought you had smallpox."

The president nodded.

"Have you ever seen a nestful of just-hatched baby birds, Val?" he asked. "All of them beseeching their mother to find enough worms to feed their ever-demanding beaks?"

Val nodded and said, "Sure."

"Well, it is my unpleasant duty to have to feed that horde of baby birds every morning. They line up downstairs by the dozens . . . connivers who want to be postmasters, incompetent officers demanding promotions, shipowners who want my permission to buy Southern cotton, crack-brained inventors with the plans for secret weapons that will end the war, devious salesmen begging for a sutler's license or a government contract . . . all of them beseeching me to anoint them with their life's desires."

The melancholy eyes focused for a moment on me.

"As if that isn't usually enough to wear me down, tonight I was blessed with the opportunity to preside over another harmonious cabinet session. If only the people of this land could see my cabinet team working in harness. You know, of course, that they all hate each other. Every one of them. In fact, to my knowledge, they only agree on one thing."

"What is that?" asked Val.

"That each and every one of them would have made a better president than me," said the president with a mordant grin.

Seated just a few feet away from him, I realized that the deeply furrowed creases around his eyes and mouth were actually laugh lines. They completely disappeared each time he smiled.

"There are just too many jealous pigs for the teat," he said next.

" 'But jealous souls will not be answered so,' " said Val in what I knew had to be one of his arcane Shakespearean references. " 'They are not ever jealous for the cause . . . ' "

President Lincoln's eyes glimmered with recognition as Val paused in midsentence.

" 'But jealous for they'ar jealous. It is a monster begot upon itself, born on itself,' " the president continued.

"Precisely," said Val, and they both chuckled together.

President Lincoln pulled a gold watch out of his vest pocket and quickly glanced at it.

"How goes your investigation?"

Val's smile disappeared.

"First, and most important, let me say that I believe there are several plots being hatched to kill you, Abe. . . . It's hard to separate the rumors from fact. . . . Mostly, the rumors involve Confederates; but as you know, there are a lot of people right here in the capital who . . ."

The president held up his right hand in a motion to stop.

"A handful of people know what I am about to tell you," he said, with a glance toward me.

"Kit can be trusted," said Val.

"Do you know where Mary and I occasionally go to get away from the stench of that canal out there?" he said.

"The Soldier's Home near the hospital?"

"Yes. Well, it was in September . . . a few nights after the Antietam battle, I was working late in this office. Mary and the boys were already there waiting on me for dinner. The military escort I was expecting to accompany me had not arrived, so I decided to ride over alone. I was going north on Sixteenth Street no more than a mile from here when my horse suddenly shied. As I leaned forward to calm him, I heard a shot ring out, and the horse took off, thankfully with me still on board. When I got to the Soldier's Home, I told Ward Lamon what had happened. He asked me where my top hat was, and I told him that it must have blown off when the horse got spooked. Later that evening Lamon pulled me aside and showed me the hat. He had gone back and found it lying by the edge of the road. There was a bullet hole through it."

"My God," said Val.

"So I know you are right. But I have come to the realization that if someone wants to kill me badly enough he will find a way to do it. If I wore a coat of chain mail and surrounded myself with a praetorian guard, it would be of no import in the long run. And I cannot be held captive to those fears and still do this job, as frustrating as it sometimes is. I must try to do the best I can with each day that I'm given. . . . Maybe God will grant me the chance to make up for some of the mistakes I've made. Now tell me about your investigation while I am still reasonably coherent."

He winced again as he got up to pour himself another cup of coffee.

"You brought me here to try to get a handle on the pervasive corruption," said Val, "and I can tell you now that it will be almost impossible to

stem the tide. The corruption is systemic. It began with your appointment
of Simon Cameron as secretary of war. He put up the for sale signs to all
the predators."

President Lincoln came back and sat down opposite us again.

"Whatever understanding I have developed in this life about the pecu-
liarities of human nature, it was inconceivable to me that a man of
Cameron's position could be a thief of such monumental proportions. I
remember asking Thad Stevens about it when the rumors first began coming back to me. He has known Cameron for the last thirty years. Tell me
the truth, I asked him, would Cameron really steal? 'No, Mr. President,'
Thad told me. . . . I don't think Cameron would steal a red hot stove . . .
at least not if it was bolted to the floor.'"

I couldn't help grinning. Val, too.

"Well, Thad Stevens wasn't exaggerating," the president went on,
"which is why I finally made Cameron ambassador to Russia. I figured
that was far enough away to keep him out of mischief, although I was
tempted to write to the czar to warn him to bring his things in at night."

Val didn't smile this time.

"I wish the corruption ended with Cameron," he said, "but it has only
gotten worse, Abe. What he started has become an epidemic of greed,
profiteering, and criminal misconduct. Two years ago Washington was a
sleepy Southern town of thirty thousand souls, most of them God-fearing
civil servants. Now there are almost two hundred thousand soldiers based
in and around the capital. The city is filled with thieves, deserters, pick-
pockets, flimflam artists, cutthroats, and spies. Hell, there are more
whores in this city right now than Baptists, and the police receive payoffs
to protect the whorehouses, as well as every other form of criminal activity. On top of that, you have a military establishment that is up to its ears
in graft. The War Department is corrupt at every level . . . from the commissary butchers to the most senior officers in the Quartermaster Corps. I
have gathered substantial evidence that a number of senators and congressmen are involved, including members of the Committee on the Conduct of the War."

"I am not surprised," said the president, wearily shaking his head. The left eyelid began to droop again. His right eye remained on Val, who pulled a document out of his breast pocket and handed it to the president.

"Here is my report," he said. "I can already prove that many of the bids for military equipment and supplies are systematically rigged for favored contractors who have paid large bribes. And it is not at the margins, Abe. Millions are being stolen from the Treasury every month. A lot of the defective equipment is what you would expect . . . boots that separate from their soles . . . shovel blades with the tensile strength of eggshells. But now we are seeing disablements that have not only cost men their lives but could well cost us a major battle."

"A battle? How is that possible?" asked President Lincoln in a skeptical tone.

"The most deadly peril involves our heavy artillery. It ranges from faulty primers to gun carriages that actually disintegrate, in some cases after only a dozen firings. The first one self-destructed about a month ago, shortly after the Ordnance Bureau began replacing all the carriages for our guns. Since then there have been more than twenty similar incidents. You can imagine the impact if these failures were to occur in the middle of an opening barrage or while providing fire support during a major attack."

"Why can't you just remove the ones that fall to pieces?" demanded President Lincoln. "The impact of this could be devastating."

"It's not that simple. Although they were fabricated by a number of different manufacturers, the carriages are identical in specifications. Unfortunately, none of them carry markings that identify the individual manufacturer, so there is no easy way to identify which ones are defective. That was probably done intentionally by Cameron's people."

"Well, you don't have much time," said the president. "Burnside is planning to launch his attack against General Lee. It is of vital importance that all his ordnance function properly."

"I have issued a request for the names of all the manufacturers of the carriages, as well as the friction primers. Tomorrow morning I am heading down to Falmouth to try to locate and question the individual inspectors who passed muster on the defective ordnance. There is no way these things could have passed proper inspection."

"Is it sabotage?" asked President Lincoln.

"No, I don't think so," said Val, "but I believe it is just as insidious. There are those who would be quite happy to see this war go on for years . . . the longer it lasts, the greater their profits. Have you ever heard of a company called Consolidated Supply and Manufacturing based in Philadelphia?"

"No," said the president, wearily shaking his head as the clock on the mantle chimed twice.

"The company appears to have won procurement contracts in a number of different supply areas, including the gun carriages. Kit is currently involved in a case in which they may have illegally conspired to win a large commissary contract. Hopefully, we will soon learn the names of the principals and how they are connected."

"What would you have me do at this point, Val?" asked the president, laying the pages of the report on his lap and rubbing one of his bony ankles.

"As we unmask the men responsible for the most serious crimes, you must get rid of them, no matter how powerful they are. That is the only way to control the epidemic."

"If they work for the War Department, it will be a relatively simple matter," said President Lincoln. "And I will do it. However, I don't have the power to get rid of corrupt senators and congressmen."

"We have our friends in the press to expose them," said Val. "Then it's up to the people."

"Yes, of course," President Lincoln responded. "Well, one burning house at a time. Since the Peloponnesian Wars, men have preyed on others like this in times of war. I'm just glad you're here to help, old friend."

The president shifted his careworn gaze to me again.

"Well, Captain McKittredge, you have been conspicuously silent. What do you think of the way we are prosecuting this war?"

I imagined Johnny Harpswell standing in the room with me—and Harlan Colfax.

"Since you ask," I said, "with all respect, sir . . . from what I have seen, the war is being run by idiots . . . particularly the generals you have appointed."

President Lincoln canted his head to the side as if he wasn't sure he had heard me correctly; then he laughed out loud, the heartiest one he had yet enjoyed.

Val shot a hard glance at me.

"No, our young Apollo is right," said the president.

"I am no Apollo," I said, in hot anger.

His cavernous eyes became gentle.

"I meant no disrespect, Captain."

"When I was with the Twentieth Massachusetts, Mr. President, I had a first sergeant by the name of Harlan Colfax. I owe him my life. The last thing I remember him saying to me was that if we could just swap generals with the Rebels, this war would be over in a month."

He smiled, and the lines in his face disappeared again.

"A wise fellow," he responded. "In fact, when the war started, I offered command of our army to General Lee. He turned me down."

When his eyelid began to droop again, Val stood up.

"You know, we have a good one in the West," went on President Lincoln, also getting to his feet, "General Grant. He reminds me of the mastodon here . . . Once engaged he never lets up."

As we were heading toward the door, President Lincoln took Val's arm and gently stopped him in the middle of the room. I probably wasn't supposed to hear what he said next.

"Well, I have come to understand what you endured when you lost your family," he said softly. "Willie was my favorite."

"I knew," said Val. "He is in my prayers, Abe."

"I've never joined a church," said the president. "I guess my philosophy was like my old friend's in Indiana. . . . When I do good, I feel good . . . when I do bad, I feel bad. That was my religion . . . but I've sure thought long and hard about it since Willie died. It was so hard to lose him after Eddy. I can't think of any greater pain I have ever endured. But with each passing day, he becomes an ever sweeter ache in my heart. It has become . . . bearable."

"Yes," said Val, "bearable."

They shook hands again, and Val came toward the door.

When I looked back for the last time, the president was gazing at us with his mouth turned up in a doleful smile.

We slowly retraced our steps down the dark, silent corridors. Outside, the rain came unabated. We were in the coach and riding back to Mrs. Warden's when Val asked, "Where is your friend Sergeant Colfax now?"

"Harlan is lying in a soldier's grave somewhere along the Chicka-hominy River," I said. "He was killed while leading his men through the swamps near Fair Oaks during the Seven Days. His body was never recovered."

"I see," he said, with resignation in his voice. "Well, I'm glad you didn't mention that to him."

Chapter Seven

The trial of Simon Silbernagel resumed the next morning. Major Pease was called as the first witness of the day. He seemed close to tears when he talked about the death of Pvt. Ratliff Boone and stated repeatedly that he only wished he had come a day earlier to inspect the meat.

At the conclusion of his testimony, Mr. Silbernagel's lawyer had a chance to cross-examine him. After receiving the court's approval to produce an exhibit, he had two hindquarters of newly slaughtered beef brought into the courtroom on a trolley. One of them, he told the military judges, had been determined by army inspectors to be ulcerated in several places, while the other was merely bruised, and, therefore, still suitable for human consumption.

He then asked Major Pease to look at the two samples and identify which one was ulcerated. Harold Tubshawe immediately objected, but since Major Pease had made the determination that Mr. Silbernagel's beef was ulcerated, the presiding officer of the tribunal allowed the question to stand.

After examining the hindquarters for almost ten minutes, the major mistakenly identified the ulcerated hindquarter as the bruised one. Following the ensuing silence, Harold pointed out to the court that Private Boone had died from eating the beef, and that there could be no refutation of that truth. On that note the presiding officer of the tribunal declared that the court would recess for lunch.

In spite of the fact that I had not tasted either laudanum or alcohol for nearly a month, my brain had found a number of ways to signal me of its continual craving for both. Without warning, I often broke into a cold sweat, and my hands would begin to shake. Thankfully, it rarely led to uncontrollable tremors.

After fortifying myself with a bowl of soup in a nearby restaurant, I went back to the court. No one else had yet returned, so I stretched out on one of the benches in the empty chamber and promptly fell asleep. It may have been the product of my troubled mind, but I dreamed that I was again in the blood-soaked pasture back at Harrison's Island. I lay on the ground in the darkness, surrounded by shapes that were once rational men but now just members of our hideous wailing chorus. Over their cries, I thought I heard Sergeant Colfax calling my name.

"John McKittredge," I heard him call out, and I came tearing up from the depths of my haunted soul, the dream still clinging to the outer reaches of my mind. I opened my eyes to the sight of a man standing by the bench next to my head staring down at me. Startled, I sat up and looked around. We were alone in the court chamber.

Still unnerved from my dream, I could feel the sweat running down my face and into my eyes. Pulling out a handkerchief, I dried myself. The man took off his hat and sat down on the bench next to me. His curious languid eyes slowly traveled down my rumpled uniform to my unpolished boots. There was a stillness about him, no excess movement of any kind.

"Captain McKittredge," he said calmly, "do you have any idea what you are doing?"

Although his voice was very subdued, there was something in it that made me strain to listen. I knew he wasn't one of the participants in the Silbernagel trial. By then, I had seen them all.

The man was wearing a beautifully tailored gray pinstripe suit with starched white linen and looked like he had just come from the boardroom of a bank or a brokerage house. A heavy gold watch chain connected the pockets of his matching vest.

"Do you have any idea what you are doing?" he repeated, his lips barely moving.

Perhaps forty, his thickly pomaded salt-and-pepper hair was brushed straight back over a broad, leonine forehead. His eyes were almost color-less, of the palest amber. He was powerfully built, with the rugged physique of a blacksmith.

"What does it look like I'm doing?" I replied, with sarcasm in my voice.

The man's skin was even paler than his eyes, as if he had never been exposed to the sun.

"I think you are a sick man," he said. His amber eyes were now focused on mine. They were no longer languid. "I think you should immediately take leave until you are well."

"Who are you?" I said.

"I am someone who is fully aware of your meddling in this matter," he said next. Without ever raising his voice, the menace behind his words was clear. "And I can assure you that it has not gone unnoticed at the highest military levels."

Even to my laudanum-craving brain, it was obvious he was somehow involved in the official corruption that Val was secretly investigating on behalf of President Lincoln.

"You mean the Silbernagel case," I said.

"If you proceed in your efforts, you do so at your own peril."

"Who are you?" I asked.

"I am just an interested citizen who is trying to do you a favor, Cap-tain," he said, with a taut smile. "You are about to enter a maze from which it will be impossible to extricate yourself."

"I'm not frightened of you," I said.

At that moment my hands began to shake, and I moved to clasp them together. From the disdain in his eyes, I knew that he had seen my weakness.

"Then you must do what you must, Captain McKittredge," he said, standing up. "Perhaps we will meet again."

He began walking toward a door that led to the side entrance of the court chamber. Determined to find out who he was, I stood up and fol-lowed him across the room, arriving at the door a few moments after he went out. Incredibly, the corridor beyond the chamber was empty. Five offices opened onto the hallway, each one belonging to a senior officer of the court. Their names were posted on cards affixed to the doors. The first four were all locked. The last was empty. I went back to the court chamber.

While waiting for the trial to reconvene, I considered the recent chain of events and began to pose a set of questions to myself. What if Major Pease had used his supposed inspection tour to substitute ulcerated meat for Mr. Silbernagel's beef in order to justify canceling his contract? And what if Private Boone had been an unfortunate casualty of his plan, solely because he had a fondness for raw steak? Upon his death those involved in the criminal conspiracy would have had no choice but to bring murder charges against Silbernagel. Based on the facts, the idea seemed plausible.

If my hypothesis was true, there was probably a connection between Major Pease and Consolidated Supply and Manufacturing. I hoped that the report from the Provost Marshal's Office in Philadelphia would provide the information I needed to pursue this important link in the possible conspiracy.

When the court resumed its deliberations, Harold continued his questioning of Major Pease, which lasted through the remainder of the afternoon. That night I wrote up a summary of the day's events for Val, including a full description of the man who had threatened me. Knowing that Val must already be down in Falmouth, I put it on a packet boat the next morning.

The trial continued at a snail's pace for the next two days. The stranger did not reappear. Neither did I receive my report from the Provost Marshal's Office in Philadelphia. I sent another wire to the colonel in charge of that office asking where their inquiry stood.

It was late on a Friday when Harold produced a witness who had seen one of Mr. Silbernagel's drovers deliver a heifer to the slaughterhouse along with a shipment of steers. I nodded off as his testimony dragged on, only waking again to hear Harold's loud, exasperated voice saying, "I am asking you again Mr. Dobkin . . . did you see Mr. Silbernagel's drover butcher that heifer?"

"No, sir," said the witness. "I seen a heifer hanging from one of the hooks in the slaughterhouse, but I don't know whether it went to the army or to a private customer."

At that moment, someone tapped me on the shoulder. I turned to see a private soldier standing behind me.

"Captain McKittredge?" he whispered.

"Yes," I said.

"Could you follow me, please?"

When we reached the hallway, he removed an envelope from his tunic and handed it to me. I opened the envelope to find a message from Val Burdette.

"Urgent you join me at Army Headquarters in Falmouth," it read. "Have arranged transportation for you at Washington Navy Yard via Aquia Creek. Come as soon as you receive this. Val."

"I have a carriage waiting outside," said the private. "I am instructed to escort you to the Washington Navy Yard by five o'clock. Is this the address of your billet?"

He handed me a sheet of paper that had the address of Mrs. Warden's on it.

"Yes," I said.

"Then there is sufficient time for you to go there first to pack any items you might need for the trip."

A few minutes later, we were racing pell-mell across the city as if the fate of the nation rested on my new mission.

CHAPTER EIGHT

AT MRS. WARDEN'S, I packed a satchel bag with extra linen, under-clothes, and a spare uniform. I was no sooner in the coach than the driver whipped the reins over the horses' backs, and we were on our way again. It was a few minutes past five o'clock and the sky was already dark when the carriage rolled up to the docks of the Washington Navy Yard. The shore-line was shrouded in mist, but I could see the twinkle of oil lamps on several naval vessels as they rode at anchor in the Potomac Basin.

A naval officer even younger than me was waiting on the wharf when the carriage pulled to a stop. Introducing himself as Captain DeVries, he led me to a long jetty, where a side-wheeler named *Phalarope* was standing ready with a full head of steam. I was obviously the only passenger he was expecting because, as soon as I was aboard, the gangplank was removed and the boat immediately headed out into the basin. We were soon producing an impressive wake as the speedy craft headed down the Potomac River.

I stood at the stern, enjoying a last view of the lights of Washington as the city disappeared into the mist. Then the wind came up and the cold began to make my wound ache. Captain DeVries invited me to join him in the wheelhouse, where a small coal stove provided welcome warmth. Through the course of that night, we made our way steadily down the Potomac, rarely seeing another vessel. As the Virginia coastline sped by in the darkness, I could occasionally spy a flickering light from some lonely outpost along the shoreline.

At around two in the morning, it began snowing so hard that Captain DeVries decided to anchor until daylight. For the remainder of that night, we were no more than twenty feet from the Rebel shoreline, and I didn't sleep well at the thought that we might be boarded in that lonely roadstead and taken prisoner.

It was still snowing as we continued the journey the next morning. When we arrived at Aquia Creek, it was to a sight that filled me with astonishment. Next to the newly constructed wharf, which was fully one hundred yards long, we cruised past more than twenty large transport vessels, all waiting in the channel for a place to unload their cargoes. Captain DeVries joined me at the rail as I gazed at a scene of total pandemonium on the wharf.

There were six large steamers already tied to the pilings, and hundreds of stevedores were surging in and out of them in a steady stream. A line of empty wagons stretched off to the left, their teamsters slowly inching toward the wharf as space became available. Another long line of wagons, already loaded, was winding its way toward a phalanx of newly built warehouses that covered the high ground above the wharf as far as I could see. From a cleared space off to the right, a mountain of forage rose forty feet into the air.

"We have already shipped fifty thousand horses and mules down here," said the young captain, as I shook my head in wonder.

A hard-faced corporal from the Provost Marshal's Office met me at the wharf. The snow was showing no sign of waning, and I was glad to see he had commandeered a coach rather than an open wagon.

We waited more than fifteen minutes to enter the stream of transport vehicles heading down to Falmouth. There was a long train of artillery units, with siege guns, cannons, and wagons full of gunpowder and shells. Behind them came freight schooners, their massive wheels sunk almost a foot into the road mire, carrying barrels of flour, crates of hardtack, and other necessary staples.

When an opening finally appeared in the line of traffic, we started south. Along both sides of the road for the first mile were successions of open horse pens, each holding hundreds of animals. Then came fields dotted with crude log huts that had been dug into the ground and covered with canvas sheets.

"Those are for the teamsters. They have it good compared to us," said the corporal disgustedly. "If we don't break through at Fredericksburg, the army will probably be here all winter."

We passed into open country. It was mostly flat, with low melancholy hills in the distance. The landscape had been stripped of trees, fences, even saplings and brush. It reminded me of mange on a dog's back.

The road stretched ahead of us across the plain as straight as a spear. We passed men unstringing telegraph wire from huge wooden spools, and up ahead of them, a team of laborers who were erecting the poles to carry the wire. The corporal pointed across the road to where other laborers were laying track for a new railroad line that was being constructed to expedite the movement of supplies down to Falmouth.

Perhaps it was the rawness of the day, or more likely the fact that my brain was still craving its merciless mistress, but I began shivering against my will. The tremors continued for what seemed like an eternity. Finally, the shaking and quivering ended, leaving me feeling weak and defeated.

Out of the corner of my eye, I saw the corporal staring at me before he turned away. I knew the look on his face without actually seeing it. I had seen it often enough in the hospital, the look that said I was already used up at the age of twenty-one.

As we continued south, the terrain became even more desolate. In the distance I could see a stately mansion house on the brow of a hill. When we came closer, I saw that it was merely a shell, a burned-out ruin. One of the gigantic chimneys stood in solitary splendor, but it was no longer connected to anything. Two enterprising soldiers had built a fire in the open hearth and were sitting on a sprung couch in front of it, frying their salt pork at the end of long sticks under a canvas shelter.

"That was Senator Randolph's home," said the corporal, with a satisfied smile.

It was after four by then, and the light was already fading in the west when we finally arrived at the military camps near Falmouth.

"You'll be seeing our boys now, Captain," said the corporal, "a hundred and thirty thousand strong."

As he spoke, the first bivouacs of the Army of the Potomac came into view ahead of us. They filled the snowy plain in every direction, a seemingly endless landscape filled with Sibley tents, artillery parks, army wagons, cavalry units, log huts, ammunition piles, and thousands of cook fires. A thick smoke haze hung everywhere low to the ground, and soldiers would suddenly materialize out of the vaporous fog only to disappear again like ghostly spirits.

The regimental camps went on for mile after mile, instilling me with a level of confidence that an army of this strength and magnitude was unstoppable. But then I remembered feeling similar thoughts before Ball's Bluff.

The rattle of the coach wheels subsided as we entered the broad gravel drive of a country estate. It wound its way through a park of sycamore trees. Soldiers' tents were pitched right up to the edge of formal gardens. On the crest of a rise stood an impressive redbrick manor house built in the colonial style, with tall, white-trimmed windows and black shutters.

Officers and couriers were streaming in and out of the entrance as we came to a stop. Off to the right, I spied a line of thunderboxes that had been erected over a latrine pit. I told the corporal that I needed to avail myself and headed over to them. As I grasped the handle of the last one in the row, it turned in my hand, and a young man stepped out of the foul chamber in front of me.

He had flaming red hair and bright blue eyes. I knew his broad fleshy face instantly. It was Philip Larrabee, one of my classmates from Cambridge. I had not seen him in two years.

"Kit," he said, in an excited voice, "what are you doing here? Are you in a field command?"

"Just a policeman," I said.

"Hardly," he came back. "The *Harvard Crimson* had a whole page on your exploits at Ball's Bluff: 'the young lion of Troy.'"

"That was from war dispatches. They are always embroidered to the hilt. What about you, Phil?"

"I'm writing war dispatches," he said, with a grin. "And the Boston *Examiner* sent me down to do some portraits of the Massachusetts boys at the front."

I remembered then his skill as an artist. He showed me a tablet that contained some of his latest studies of men in camp. They were dead-on accurate.

"The rumor is that we are going to drive the Rebels off those heights within the next few days and then push on to take Richmond."

"I wouldn't know," I said. "Really, I'm just a policeman."

"Yes," he said, with obvious disappointment. "Well . . . see you then."

"See you," I responded.

After successfully moving my bowels, I rejoined the dour corporal, and he showed me to the tent that had been assigned to me within the grouping allotted to the Provost Marshal's Department. I left my satchel bag under the cot and followed him to the front entrance of the mansion. Inside, a wide oak-floored hallway ran the whole length of the house. We followed it to a room near the far end. Next to the open door was a hand-lettered sign that read: GENERAL HATHAWAY, PROVOST MARSHAL'S DEPARTMENT.

It had once been the family library, but the dark cherry bookcases were now bare. Inside the room I could see the colossal bulk of Val Burdette ensconced in a large leather chair in front of a snapping fire. There were two others with him. One was sitting down and facing Val next to the fire. He wore no insignia of rank, and the collar of his tunic was unbuttoned.

The other man wore sergeant's stripes on his immaculate uniform and was standing behind him. As I crossed the room, I realized that the man closest to Val was actually seated in a wooden wheelchair. He was holding a sheaf of papers in his right hand. A red woolen blanket covered his legs.

"Captain McKittredge, I don't believe you have met Brigadier Hathaway," said Val, without getting up.

"No, sir," I said.

"Please call me Sam," said the general, extending his hand. "And you go by?"

"Kit," I responded.

It was hard for me to believe he was really a general. Although his tousled black hair was going gray, he could not have been more than thirty-five years old. With his thin, youthful face and the rimless spectacles that were dangling from the end of his nose, he looked more like a young professor than a brigadier general. Above the glasses, though, his eyes were steely and uncompromising.

"This is my aide, Billy Osceola," he said. Short and wiry, the sergeant was about my age, with a rugged bronzed face and deep-set black eyes. When he shook my hand, I saw that two of the fingers on his right hand were missing.

"I'm sorry to have ordered you to come down here so precipitously, Kit," said Val, "but we have a major problem on our hands. Burnside's attack against Lee is no more than a few days away, and we are no closer to determining which gun carriages are defective. Thankfully, Sam and a young officer in the Ordnance Bureau solved the riddle of the friction primers. They came up with a simple test to gauge the efficacy of the fulminate of mercury in each tube. It means checking every one of them, but that process is already underway. As far as the gun carriages, though, there is still no foolproof way to determine which ones are suspect."

Sam Hathaway took off his glasses and placed them in his breast pocket. He suddenly looked more like a general.

"We need to secure the cooperation of at least one of the federal inspectors who were bribed to approve the defective carriages in the first place," he said. "If we can get one to talk, we'll hopefully learn which manufacturers are involved and which carriages have to be replaced."

"Two of the inspectors slipped through our grasp last night and are presumably on their way back to Washington," said Val. "The other one, a Major Duval, is still here, although he is being carefully safeguarded by his superiors. They are almost certainly aware of his perfidy and very likely complicit."

General Hathaway wheeled himself away from the fire.

"You've come a long way, Kit," he said. "You could probably use some coffee."

"Thank you, sir," I said, as he poured me a cup and refilled his own from a pot on the desk. Standing close by him, I saw there was an unhealthy pallor to his skin, as if he had recently been sick.

"Sam has been leading a one-man crusade against corruption down here," said Val.

"A thousand men wouldn't be enough," said the general, with bitterness in his voice.

A courier entered the room, went straight to the wheelchair, and handed him a dispatch. General Hathaway glanced at it for several seconds, initialed the document, and handed it back.

"Why does President Lincoln keep making these decisions, Val?" he asked, as soon as the courier was out the door. "Appointing corrupt men, incompetent men, one after another, to positions of the highest responsibility just because they have the right political connections. Cameron was the worst, but there are so many others. These bloody gun carriages are just one example of the iniquities they are responsible for."

I wondered then whether Val had confided in him about his relationship with the president.

"At first I thought he was simply misled," went on General Hathaway, "but it is endemic, Val, and it goes beyond corrupt profiteers. How could he commission someone with no military experience, like Congressman Banks, to be a major general and then allow him to be put in command of thousands of men? Do you know how many boys died because of his incompetence at Winchester? It was criminal."

Banks had been speaker of the House of Representatives prior to the war. At Winchester, he had suffered a disastrous defeat at the hands of Stonewall Jackson.

I waited for Val to come to President Lincoln's defense, but he remained silent.

"And Edward Baker at Ball's Bluff," he said, the passion rising in his voice. "The man had no idea what he was doing. Like Banks, another vainglorious fool. . . . His dead were floating up like cordwood to the docks of Georgetown for two weeks after that slaughter."

I found myself nodding in agreement with him.

"You left out Pope," said Val, finally.

"Yes," he said, staring down at his ruined legs, "Pope."

General Hathaway slowly wheeled his chair back to the desk.

"And now he gives us Burnside," he said, wearily shaking his head.

"Almost three weeks ago, Joe Hooker got here with forty thousand men. He could have waded his boys across the Rappahannock and pushed straight on toward Richmond if Burnside had just allowed him to cross. Now we have a hundred and thirty thousand, and I fear it won't be enough."

He pointed to a pair of binoculars on the desk and said, "Just take those glasses, Kit, and see for yourself."

I picked them up and walked over to the window.

"You can see them digging in across the river on the heights above Fredericksburg," he said. "Lee must have fifty thousand men waiting for us already, and the number is growing every day. Every Rebel in Virginia old enough to aim a rifle will be over there waiting for us."

The house we were in sat on a bluff above the northern bank of the Rappahannock. The southern bank swept up toward an ancient town of narrow cobbled streets. With the naked eye, I could see a mass of brick homes, church spires, and commercial buildings. Beyond the town, an open plain rose up a long wide hill. I put the binoculars to my eyes and focused them on the heights above it.

In the waning light, I could see the Confederate battle flag flying from a mansion on the crest. As I watched through the glasses, a battery of guns was wheeled along the ridgeline and moved into position facing down the slope. I couldn't imagine ever seeing better defensive ground.

"They are wasting their time digging in up there," I said, putting down the glasses. "No one in his right mind would try to attack that position."

"Well, that's Burnside's plan," said General Hathaway, his voice now drained of emotion. "As soon as his pontoon bridges arrive, the army will be sent across to attack those heights."

"Why did it take so long to get the bridges here?" I asked dumbly.

"Ask the Quartermaster Corps," said Val, "the same department that inspected the gun carriages."

I heard the muffled stamp of men's boots farther down the corridor.

"It's time to prepare for the party," said Val, breaking the silence. "All of our adversaries will undoubtedly be there, including General Nevins and Major Duval."

"What party?" I said.

"Joe Hooker's forty-eighth birthday party," he replied. "Dan Sickles decided to organize it. He loves giving parties, and this one is required attendance for every senior officer down here."

I knew who Sickles was; every citizen in the country did. A congress-man before the war, he had cold-bloodedly murdered his wife's lover, who was the son of Francis Scott Key. Sickles had somehow won acquittal for the crime on the basis of temporary insanity. After the war began, Lincoln had made him a general, and he was now commanding a division.

"Last week Sickles wired a ten-page list of required delicacies to Del-monico's restaurant," said Val. "Yesterday, a train of thirty-two Pittsburgh wagons rolled into camp, having come all the way from New York under full military escort. I'm told that one of them had an insulated metal com-partment containing two thousand pounds of chocolate ice cream."

"Why didn't they put the pontoon bridges on that train?" I blurted without thinking. Even General Hathaway laughed at that.

"You're learning, Kit," he said.

"Who is General Nevins?" I asked.

"Nevins is in charge of military procurement at the War Department, and he is Major Duval's commanding officer," said Val. "Before the war he was an intimate of Simon Cameron and one of the biggest campaign con-tributors to the Republican Party in Pennsylvania. He is financially con-nected to several influential members of Congress, so we must move carefully. These are some of the most powerful men in the Union, and they will stop at nothing to protect themselves. For tonight, our sole task is to discover any scrap of information that can help us identify the defective carriages."

Val and I left the library together, slowly working our way through the crowd of officers choking the corridor.

"I only wish we had more men like Sam Hathaway in the depart-ment," said Val. "He is the most dedicated and effective officer I have yet worked with in the army. Not only is he honest, but he is totally unafraid of taking on the high and the mighty . . . As you saw for yourself."

"You never defended the president," I said.

"For one thing, Sam was right about those decisions. Aside from that,

I cannot afford to let anyone know about what we are doing for the president, even Sam. Secrecy is vital."

"How were his legs paralyzed?"

"Wounded at Second Bull Run, I believe. He is to receive a presidential commendation from Father Abraham himself in a few weeks for what he did during the Seven Days."

Outside, night had fallen, and across the river I saw the distant fires of the Confederate army. As we passed a row of stables, I could hear the sound of a hammer clanging against an anvil.

Val turned and said, "'Piercing the night's dull ear; and from the tents, The armourers accomplishing the knights, With busy hammers closing rivets up, Give dreadful note of preparation.'"

"Henry the Fifth," I said, grinning. "Funny, looking at all those Rebel fires across the river, I was thinking of a line, too," I said.

"Let's hear it."

"'I wandered lonely as a cloud . . . When all at once I saw a crowd, A host, of golden daffodils,'" I said.

"A true warrior's refrain," said Val.

CHAPTER NINE

I WENT BACK to the tent and pulled out my satchel bag. The frigid air had begun to make my wound ache again, and I did not tarry in my ablutions. Cracking the ice in the pitcher, I poured a few inches of water into the bowl, washed my face with lye soap, and combed my hair. Although I had lost a great deal of weight since the start of the war, my spare uniform coat was still fairly presentable, and the pants were of good broadcloth. I buttoned my greatcoat over the uniform and headed for General Hooker's party.

Fog had settled near the ground, creating strange ghostly halos around the soldiers' fires and muffling the usual noises of camp. The raw air was keeping most of the army inside their tents and shelters.

Suddenly I heard the strains of what sounded like a full orchestra, and a moment later, a canvas wall materialized out of the fog ahead of me. It was like no tent wall I had ever seen before, stretching fully twelve feet into the air. It took several minutes of walking around the perimeter before I came to an opening in the wall. Sentries were posted on either side of it. Neither of them asked me for an invitation, and I stepped through the opening.

The first thing that struck me was the blessed warmth. An odd assortment of wood-burning stoves, probably stripped from homes in the surrounding countryside, dotted the perimeter of the vast canvas hall, conveying light and heat toward the crowd of pressing figures. A newly constructed hardwood floor provided further insulation from the cold. The word HOSPITAL was stenciled into many of the canvas panels, and I surmised that the party hall had been constructed by lashing together dozens of huge hospital tents. Army engineers must have spent a week constructing it.

The walls and support beams were decorated with Chinese lanterns, regimental battle flags, boughs of evergreens, and gaily colored bunting. More than two hundred officers congregated near the plank bars in each corner. There were kegs of whiskey and brandy stacked behind the bars, along with crates of French wines and champagne. Enlisted men in white cavalry-length tunics were making and serving the drinks.

Scanning the crowd, I recognized some of the most senior generals in the Army of the Potomac, including several I had heard General Hooker refer to as morons and cowardly imbeciles. There were famous senators and congressmen there, too. More than a hundred gaily dressed women, officers' wives and daughters, were gathered in the center of the pavilion. No one was dancing yet, but the orchestra was playing quadrilles from an elevated stand along one of the walls.

A line of plantation tables, each covered by a starched white table-cloth, was heaped with Delmonico's fare, all of it giving off a heavenly aroma. Engraved cards identified the lobster bisque, scallops bouillabaisse, Normandy-style fish stew, coq au vin, lamb en croute, suckling pig stuffed with apricots and sausage, and a selection of roast meats including beef, duckling, goose, and pork. Two men wearing rubber aprons were expertly shucking large oysters and laying them down in half shells on a vast bed of chipped ice.

As I stood staring at the opulent buffet, an officer strode briskly up to me. He was barely over five feet tall, with thin brown hair and close-together eyes.

"I tell you, Kit, it's sordid," he said, in a tremolo voice.

For a moment, I didn't recognize him.

"Charles?" I said uncertainly.

"Of course, it is I," he responded.

Charles Francis Adams Jr. had been another one of my classmates in Cambridge. He was the grandson of former-president John Quincy Adams.

"What are you doing here?" I said.

"I'm posted with the First Massachusetts Cavalry," he said. "It's disgusting."

"The cavalry?" I asked.

"Not the cavalry," he exclaimed. "Him!"

He pointed across the planked floor, and I looked up to see General Hooker making his entrance across the hall, surrounded by a dozen staff aides.

"The man of the hour," said Charles, his voice laden with sarcasm. "Look at him swaggering in front of the ladies with that priapic strut."

A burst of spontaneous applause erupted from the women in the center of the pavilion as he went by. The tailored uniform he was wearing seemed sculpted to his powerful body. Towering over the men around him, he looked more than ever to me like one of the warrior gods of old.

"He is a satyr, a debauched womanizer. . . . everyone in Washington knows it," Charles declared, rocking rhythmically up and down in his tiny cavalry boots.

A soldier with sweat running down his corpulent face came by with a tray of drinks, and I took a glass of what looked like new cider. Charles was drinking from a pewter mug with his family crest engraved on it. I was confident it also contained no alcohol. At Harvard, Charles had been the head of the campus temperance society.

"I'm reliably informed Hooker is already belittling the ability of General Burnside to command the army," he said in a confidential tone.

"That wouldn't be difficult," I said.

Val Burdette came up to us, his mammoth form blocking out the light from the Chinese lanterns. As Charles turned to face him, his jaw dropped. Although in honor of the occasion Val had attempted to shave, he had apparently lost patience with the effort, and the left side of his face retained several days' growth. His thick gray hair spilled out well below the edge of the collar of his seedy uniform coat. He was holding a foul-smelling cheroot in the fingers of his right hand.

"Captain Adams, I would like you to meet Colonel Burdette," I said by way of introduction. The top of Charles's head barely came to the height of Val's chest, and his open-mouthed stare suggested a man gazing up at a reptilian monster.

"Charles Francis Adams Junior," said Charles, carefully enunciating each syllable. When he was nervous, he trotted out the mantle of his family's famous name like a gold-hilted sword.

"Charles," I said, "Colonel Burdette is in charge of investigating serious contracting fraud on behalf of the army."

I'm not sure the words registered. Val took a deep drag on his cigar and said, "Do you want to hear the latest rumors? I picked up several good ones at the bar."

"Jeff Davis is about to sue for peace?" I suggested.

"To the contrary. The Confederate navy is secretly constructing a fleet of ironclads down in Cuba. They are all more powerful than the *Merrimack*, and the Rebs are planning to send them up the Chesapeake to attack Washington as soon as they are ready."

He took another puff of his cigar before adding, "Of course, that one happens to come from the biggest shipbuilder in the North."

"I assume he is offering to construct enough federal ironclads to meet the threat," I said.

"Precisely," he said, his dark gray eyes glinting with humor.

"But it sounds exactly like something the rebels would do," protested Charles.

"The second is far more troubling," went on Val, his face now serious. "It's another plot to assassinate Lincoln, this one involving disgruntled officers who are afraid that some of his blunders will kill most of the army before he's through. I have heard it now from two different sources, both of them unimpeachable."

"And the third rumor?" I asked.

"That's the best one of all," he said, with a ferocious grin. "Jeff Davis has personally hatched a plan to burn the capital to the ground using Japanese mercenaries."

"Well, at least they should be easy to spot," I said.

"Speaking of plots, our Major Duval has arrived. He is currently indulging his fondness for seafood over there at the buffet table," said Val, moving off in that direction.

I looked over at the crowd in front of the seafood bar. An officer with imperial moustaches that curled up at each end of his mouth was sucking down a raw oyster. With dramatic flourish, he tossed the empty shell over his shoulder and reached down to pick up another. Charles began rocking up and down in his boots again as a great round of applause burst forth from the ladies in the center of the pavilion.

"Here comes the other disciple of debauchery," he said, glaring over my shoulder.

General Dan Sickles was striding across the floor toward the guest of honor with the springy step of a bantam rooster. Joining the group of officers surrounding General Hooker, he stopped and waved to the cheering crowd. As General Hooker turned to greet him, he glanced momentarily in the direction where Charles and I were standing. Less than a minute later, I saw Major Bannister coming toward us through the crowd.

"I'm extending General Hooker's compliments," he said, with a formal bow. "He was hoping you would join him for a libation."

Charles began staring at me as if I had somehow betrayed the honor of the Republic. I knew it would have been impossible to explain it all to him right then. I didn't bother to try. As he pivoted on his heel and stalked away, I followed Major Bannister across the floor.

"I'm surprised to see you again," Bannister said coldly. "Perhaps, it will not be the last."

General Hooker was standing in a circle of other officers. Aside from Dan Sickles, there were two other generals in the group whom I didn't recognize. It wasn't until one of them briefly stepped back that I saw General Hathaway seated in the middle of the group in his wheelchair. Sergeant Osceola was standing just beyond the generals at the edge of the circle.

"I thought I saw you over there, Lieutenant," said General Hooker, greeting me with a warm handshake. Then he noticed the captain's bars on my tunic and added, "A promotion, I see. Congratulations."

"Thank you, sir," I said.

"Allow me to introduce General Sickles, General Couch, General

Nevins, and General Hathaway," he said, gesturing at each of them in turn. "Gentlemen," he said with a grin, "I was privileged to meet Captain McKittredge when we were both confined to the Washington Insane Asylum."

Seeing the expected befuddlement on their faces, he laughed out loud. From the rosiness in his cheeks, it was obvious he had been indulging his fondness for whiskey. General Sickles gave me a curt smile. Of medium height, he had restless brown eyes and a blunt face adorned by a Roman nose and a drooping black mustache.

"I'm sure there is a point to this story somewhere," he said.

"It isn't what you might think," said General Hooker, and he began to explain why we had both been there. He left out the part about our meeting by the thunderboxes.

"Kit has seen me at my worst, I'm afraid," he concluded, with another grin in my direction. "Thankfully, he is the only officer with a Harvard degree who knows how to keep a confidence."

"You hope," interjected Sickles, glancing sharply at me.

"He is a young Homer with innocence in his nature," said General Hooker, "although he has some dark secrets of his own."

General Nevins was whispering in the ear of General Couch. From what I could see, there wasn't a hint of avarice or deceit in his highbrowed, distinguished face. He had the same mournful eyes and benign countenance of the Presbyterian minister who used to come across from the mainland to preach at our island church over Christmas week.

Looking down at General Hathaway, General Hooker said, "Are you getting any closer to identifying the men responsible for supplying us with those collapsing gun carriages, Sam? As far as I'm concerned, they should be lashed to the barrels of our siege guns and fired off at the Rebels."

I was still looking at General Nevins. The benign expression never left his face.

"Yes," said General Hathaway. "Actually, Captain McKittredge is down here to help us with our investigation."

"Excellent," said General Hooker, as Nevins's eyes connected with mine. When I smiled pleasantly at him, he turned away.

"The miscreants are probably right here lapping up your whiskey," said

General Couch, speaking for the first time. His head was shaped like a giant acorn.

A waiter came up, balancing a platter of drinks on his hand.

"Gentlemen, I would like to propose a toast," said General Hooker, picking up a glass of whiskey from the tray. "You must all try this single malt . . . sent all the way from Scotland for me."

Not having had a drop of alcohol since my time in the cellar, I refrained from picking up a glass. As he was raising his own, the general noticed me without one.

"Surely you will join me in my birthday toast, Kit," he said, with a friendly grin.

Sensing all their faces on me, I picked up a glass from the tray and raised it with the others.

"To the honor and glory of noble warriors," said General Hooker.

Like the others, I drank it down in one swallow, almost instantly feeling its burning comfort speeding through my system and straight to my brain.

To my utter astonishment, the general then stared down at Sam Hathaway and said, "To you, Sam."

General Hathaway turned his head away as if struck. He was wearing his spectacles again, and with his professorial air, it was hard to believe that he had ever seen combat.

"Before he was consigned to a desk, Sam Hathaway was the best regimental commander in my division," said General Hooker. "I hope he won't mind my telling some brother officers about his exploits on the Peninsula."

"That was another man, General," said Sam.

"It was you, my friend."

Looking back to us, he said, "During the fighting at Fort Magruder, we were being raked by Confederate artillery and in danger of being driven. I even had to post a line of cavalry across the road just to cut down the deserters as they tried to run. On his own initiative, Sam led a counterattack against the batteries that were murdering us. I watched it all through my binoculars. Damnedest thing I ever saw on a battlefield."

General Hathaway was looking ever more uncomfortable. His fingers moved toward the wheels of his chair.

"Sam was calmly strolling out ahead of his men carrying a furled umbrella under his arm . . . just as if he were on his way to the library."

He turned to look down at him again and smiled.

"When he was within a hundred yards of the Confederate position, an artillery shell exploded at ground level just behind him at the edge of a shallow ravine. Naturally, a few of his men decided to take advantage of the situation and dove straight into the cover. The rest of the regiment halted as one right behind them. That's when Sam walked back there with the shells exploding all around him."

I tried to imagine him when his legs still worked, tall and fearless.

"According to a subaltern who saw the whole thing, Sam just spread his umbrella over the men in the draw and declared, "Come along, boys, we need you up ahead."

General Sickles was nodding his head in approval.

"Isn't that what you did, Sam?" asked General Hooker.

General Hathaway didn't acknowledge him. He was staring straight ahead, his fingers now gripping the wheels of his chair.

"That's exactly what he did. But that wasn't the best part," said General Hooker. "When they stayed glued to the ground, Sam reassured them by saying, 'Don't worry, boys, I've got an umbrella.'"

All of us laughed together.

"Shamed into action, his regiment returned to the attack and drove the battery from the field. You saved more than my reputation that day, Sam."

General Hooker removed a thin leather case from his uniform coat and opened it in front of us. Inside, resting on a bed of white silk, was a red enamel-and-gold medal. He leaned down and pinned it on General Hathaway's chest.

"The president authorized me to have this struck for you personally, Sam."

A feeling of profound sadness came over me just then, looking down at him as he tried hard to control his emotions. I knew what he was going through, all that he had lost.

"As I said, General . . . that was another man," Sam Hathaway declared grimly. "Thank you for the generous words, but I need to return to my office now."

We watched as he navigated his chair through the crowd. Sergeant Osceola followed him across the floor.

"When did his luck run out?" asked General Sickles.

"Second Manassas," said General Hooker. "He was shot in the spine after doing his best to carry out one of Pope's harebrained orders. That young aide of his, Osceola—full-blooded Seminole I believe—saved his life . . . was shot several times doing it."

"Bad luck," said General Couch. "Sam had a brilliant future."

"By your leave, Joe," said General Nevins, giving him a formal salute before heading across the floor. I watched as he disappeared into the crowd at the buffet tables. A few moments later, the crush parted long enough for me to see him talking animatedly to Major Duval. Some distance behind them, Val's familiar bulk loomed above the rest of the celebrants.

The military orchestra struck up a Strauss waltz, and the romantic music quickly drew scores of couples to the dance floor. General Hooker handed me another glass of whiskey. I reluctantly took it, telling myself it would be my last.

"There's a rumor going around that McClellan will soon be restored to command," said General Couch, his acorn head now swaying back and forth to the music.

"The gravedigger of the Chickahominy back again? Where did you hear that?" demanded General Sickles.

"From Ben Wade," said Couch. "He said a group of senators are actively working on Little Mac's behalf."

"The nation's capital," said Sickles in disgust. "Built by giants; inhabited by pygmies. I can tell you this . . . the cock will crow three times before Abe Lincoln puts that pigeon-livered bastard back in command."

"Well, at least Burnside is loyal to the cause," said General Couch. "I've always had my doubts about McClellan."

"Burnside is loyal all right," said General Hooker, "but one only has to look into those Guernsey eyes to realize he is a complete imbecile. If his current battle plan is allowed to stand, he will go down as the greatest corpse maker of the war."

I happened to be looking toward the dance floor when my eyes were drawn to a small group of people standing to the side. Something about one of them jarred my memory, but at first I couldn't place what it was. Continuing to stare at them, I suddenly recognized the debonair man with the leonine head and pale eyes who had threatened me at the Silbernagel trial.

"Pardon me, sir. But do you know who that man is?" I asked General Couch, who was standing next to me. As I pointed toward him, my quarry smiled back at me and gave a jaunty wave. He was the only man in the group not wearing a uniform.

"Which one?" asked General Couch, but as I looked again, he had disappeared. I immediately started walking toward the place where I had last seen him. General Hooker's voice brought me up short.

"Kit," he said, motioning me to his side, "when the business with the gun carriages is concluded, I want you to join my staff. I need a younger officer who has seen real action. There are too many armchair warriors as it is."

"Thank you, General," I said, continuing to stare at the spot where I had seen the stranger last.

"It's agreed then," he responded. "We'll drink to it."

I knew it was a mistake but was no longer thinking clearly, and I consumed the drink in two swallows. It followed the first two down my throat with the old familiar ease. I remained at the general's side, joining him in another glass of whiskey when the waiter came through again. The stranger did not reappear.

I was about to take my leave when the music suddenly stopped and I heard an angry yell, followed by the loud smack of a physical blow. As the crowd parted on the dance floor, I could see an officer lying spread-eagled on his back. Another officer was standing over him with his fists raised. I recognized him from the shoulder straps. It was Major Bannister. A woman in a red satin dress was standing next to him.

In the ensuing silence, Major Bannister's next words carried across the floor to us.

"Stay away from her or I'll kill you," he said.

General Hooker motioned to another staff officer standing near us, and he immediately came to his side. "Have Bannister sent back to his tent under guard," he said, as the man on the floor struggled to regain his feet.

The staff officer moved off to carry out the order. I was standing close enough to hear General Hooker's next words when he turned to General Sickles and whispered, "You need to talk to Mavis right away."

Sickles nodded. A second later, the orchestra resumed playing a gay waltz, and couples began dancing again as if nothing had happened. General Hooker's cheeks were as fresh as cherries.

"The truth be told, Kit," he said, shaking his head in world-weary fashion, "if you look down through the wars in history, most of them were fought over women."

He must have interpreted the boozy look on my face as one of condemnation, for with genuine affection in his voice, he added, "Try not to be too judgmental, my boy. You're going to be forty-eight yourself someday."

With that, he handed me another round of single malt.

The woman in the red dress had remained standing in the same place where the two officers had been fighting. No one made a move to comfort or assist her. She slowly walked to the edge of the dance floor, pretending to examine her dance card.

At the same time, a large group of officers and their wives began forming at a respectful distance from General Hooker in order to extend their birthday greetings.

"Well," he said, "I suppose I must attend to my well-wishers."

As he left us to receive them, I turned to say good night to General Sickles.

"You will remain here for a moment, Captain," he said, in a peremptory tone.

"Yes, sir," I said.

General Sickles was gazing steadily in the direction of the woman in the red dress. When she finally happened to look in our direction, I saw him nod, almost imperceptibly. She walked straight toward us.

"Good evening, Mrs. Bannister," he said, as she came up.

"It's good to see you again, General," she responded.

"I would like to present Captain McKittredge, a friend of General Hooker's," he said next.

From her dazzling smile, it did not appear that she drew any distinction between a general and a mere captain. I took in the fragrance of lilacs.

"It must be wonderful to be so tall," she said.

"Not when you're in the line of fire," Sickles came right back.

"No, I suppose not," she said.

She had pale gray eyes and dark russet hair that fell in natural ringlets down to her bare shoulders. Her pretty oval face was marred only by a tiny field of smallpox scars on her cheeks that she had artfully concealed with paint and powder.

She turned back to face General Sickles.

"On behalf of my husband, I deeply regret what just happened," she said, her breasts swelling the low-cut gown with each breath she took. "I was simply dancing with Lieutenant Mitchell, and the next thing I knew. . . ."

"Please don't give it a moment's concern, Mrs. Bannister," replied General Sickles. "These things always happen as battles loom close. Right now, the men's emotions are on a razor's edge."

"Thank you for your understanding," she said. "I didn't want anything to spoil General Hooker's party."

"It would be impossible for you to do that, Mrs. Bannister."

As they looked at one another, silent messages seemed to be passing between them. Then General Sickles turned to me and declared, "Captain McKittredge, I would like you to escort Mrs. Bannister to her lodgings. After that, you are free to return to the party."

"Yes, sir," I said, although at that point I wanted nothing more than to return to my tent.

"Where are you staying, Mrs. Bannister?" asked the general.

"I'm at the Fitzgerald estate with some of the other army wives. It is very crowded there, as you can well imagine."

"Yes," said General Sickles, "we all must make sacrifices. Perhaps we will meet again soon."

She smiled back at him.

"I understand," she replied.

"My personal carriage will be brought around for you," he said.

Demurely taking his hand in her own gloved one, she made a deep curtsy.

"Thank you for your kindness, General Sickles," she said. He bowed his head for a moment and then walked toward another group of officers.

"Are you ready to leave?" I asked.

"Yes, I am, Captain McKittredge," she said. "If you will give me a few moments to put on my boots and coat, I will meet you at the entrance to the pavilion."

She began walking toward the section of the tent where the guests had left their winter garments. As I slowly made my way through the crowd toward the entrance, I saw Sergeant Osceola heading straight toward me. His golden bronze skin and rough cast face set him apart dramatically from the other guests.

"I've just come from Colonel Burdette," he said. "He told me to tell you that Major Duval is on the run, and there is nothing more that can be done here tonight. We will meet in General Hathaway's office tomorrow morning at six."

"Thank you, Sergeant," I replied. "I'm afraid I must leave now anyway."

"Yes, sir," he said.

That was when I saw them. They were standing together about fifteen feet away. Physically, the two young women were complete opposites. The first one was dark complected, the other very fair. I assumed that they were probably the daughters of officers attending the party.

In spite of the whiskey, my mind was suddenly alive.

Unlike the other women there, they were not dressed in formal evening gowns. The dark one was wearing a simple, cream-colored linen dress trimmed in white lace. The blonde girl wore a dress in cobalt blue.

The raven haired girl was strikingly lovely, with a slim, tapered face, luminous brown eyes, and a delicate figure. The mass of her black hair was combed up above her head and in the lantern lights gave off the blue-black luster of raw silk. It dramatically highlighted her exquisite cheekbones and finely shaped nose.

There was a sadness in her eyes, as if she had experienced a recent loss or bereavement. Unlike the blonde girl, whose brittle laugh carried shrilly across the floor, she seemed downcast. It may sound strange or even adolescent, but at that moment I felt as if my heart had suddenly been awakened to the essence of beauty and desire.

As she looked in our direction, the hint of a wistful smile came to her full lips, and I saw that one of her front upper teeth was charmingly crooked. It made her otherwise flawless face somehow more real and beautiful to me. She turned to address the blonde girl, who was several inches shorter, and had the angelic look of a Botticelli nymph. Her hair was swept up in the same fashionable manner as the other girl's and was held in place with a lacquered, black barrette.

"They seem to know you," said Sergeant Osceola, and I laughed out loud.

"I think I would remember, Sergeant," I said, unable to stop staring at the young woman with the sad eyes. "However, I wouldn't mind introducing myself."

The blonde girl was swaying in time to the music, her teeth white in another burst of laughter. I was feeling Dutch courage from the whiskey and was about to suggest that we go over to meet them, when I suddenly remembered Mrs. Bannister. Torn between my obligation to General Sickles and my desire to meet the young woman, I reluctantly opted for duty, consoling myself that she would still be there when I returned.

"I must go," I said, already moving toward the entrance.

"Yes, sir," he said.

From some distance off, I could see the anger on Mrs. Bannister's face.

"Please forgive me," I said, reaching her side, "but I just met someone who had an important message for me."

I could tell she was about to convey her displeasure, but then her face softened and she said gently, "Well, I hope she was worth it."

"There is no she," I said, but recalling the sad-eyed girl, I hoped there would be an opportunity to find out.

We went out into the night to discover it was snowing again. The wind was coming in great gusty blasts, driving the small, hard flakes into our eyes.

General Sickle's black carriage was waiting for us. The snow-covered coachman urged his team of four matched horses toward the entrance as we came out, and I helped Mrs. Bannister into the carriage. A moment later I was beside her on the cushioned seat, and we were on our way. It was bitterly cold in the coach, but a down-filled quilt was lying on the front seat, and I spread it over her lap.

"We will share it," she said, leaning forward to arrange the quilt over my lap as well. As the coach rolled past the soldiers' camps heading north, it struck me that just twelve hours earlier I had been sitting in a court chamber on Pennsylvania Avenue listening to Harold Tubshawe drone on about the dangers of kidney tallow.

I felt bone weary from everything that had happened since. In spite of my best intentions not to fall asleep until I saw her safely home, my head slowly fell back against the headrest, and I dozed off to the rhythmic beat of the horses' hooves on the hard-packed road.

It was the scent of lilacs that brought me awake again. Slowly regaining my senses, I realized that the constant beat of the horses' hooves had not changed. But when I opened my eyes, Mrs. Bannister's face was no more than a few inches from my own.

"You know, you are a very beautiful young man," she murmured.

I felt her hand moving under the lap blanket. It rose up alongside my left leg and stopped.

"Mrs. Bannister . . ." I began.

"My name is Mavis," she whispered, "and I'm not going to devour you."

Her hand began to move again, coming to rest between my thighs. As we sat close together in that freezing carriage, it suddenly seemed as if every nerve ending in my body was alive with sensation, little pinpricks of pleasure that charged every pore of my skin.

"How old are you?" she asked.

"Twenty-one," I said.

Her eyes expressed surprise.

"How is it that someone of your . . . relative youth . . . became a friend of General Hooker's?" she asked, her eyes still just inches from my own.

"I met him after he was wounded," I said. "I guess we shared that experience in common."

Her lips gently touched mine and then drew away.

"Will I see you at the party?" she asked then.

I thought she was confused. We had just come from the party.

"I understand," she said. "One must be very discreet."

The carriage began to slow as the driver on the box reined in the horses. A few moments later it came to a stop, and her hand slid away from my thighs.

"I am not entirely wicked," she said, raising the cowl of her cape over her head. "I just married the wrong man."

The carriage tilted to the right as one of the soldiers on the box jumped down to the ground and came around to open the door. In the moment before he did, Mrs. Bannister whispered, "I hope to see you very soon, Captain McKittredge."

The door opened and a wind-driven gust of snow swirled into our faces. She gave the young private her gloved hand, and he helped her down from the carriage. I saw that we were under the covered portico of a large country house. She looked back up at me once more and smiled before the soldier opened the front door for her and she disappeared inside.

Then the carriage was on its way again. As we rode south, my mind kept returning to the sad-eyed girl I had seen at the party and whether she would still be there when I got back. The snow began coming harder, and the carriage slowed to a crawl when we got behind a convoy of freight wagons.

It was well past midnight when we arrived back at the party tent. My heart sank when I saw that all the other carriages had already departed. Through the open tent flaps at the entrance, I could see two men clearing the banquet tables. Otherwise, the hall was empty. Riding back to camp, I felt a profound sense of loss, as if something infinitely precious had passed out of my life before I even had a chance to sample its measure.

Aside from a few sentries, no one was stirring at the encampment near Sam's headquarters. Going straight to my tent, I removed my greatcoat and uniform. When I went to pour some water for a wash, it was frozen solid in the pitcher on the camp table. Instead, I drew on my long flannel underwear, put the greatcoat back on, and burrowed down into the blankets on my cot. The image of the raven-haired girl was still in my mind when I blew out the oil lamp and fell into a black sleep.

CHAPTER TEN

I FELT SOMEONE shaking my arm as if he was trying to tear it out of the socket. For a few moments I thought I was again back at Ball's Bluff, lying in the blood-soaked pasture on Harrison's Island.

"You must wake up, Captain," said a voice tinged with desperation. I remembered where I was and opened my eyes to discover it was still pitch dark outside the field tent. A hissing lantern was suspended above my face. Beyond its harsh yellow glare, I could see the outline of someone standing next to my cot.

"What is it?" I groaned at the form above me.

"You must come, Captain McKittredge," came back the voice, which I now recognized as belonging to a member of General Hathaway's staff. It was still bitterly cold, and as I tossed off the covers, the freezing air literally stung my face. That did nothing to stop the vicious pounding inside my head. I had the strange sensation that my body was about to split open. I even knew exactly where it would start, at the top of my head, then rend down through the middle of my back.

"Colonel Burdette ordered me to find you, sir, and bring you to him."

"Where is he?" I asked, still waiting for my head to come apart.

"A few miles from here," he said, "right near those nigger shanties."

I took off the greatcoat I had worn to bed over my long underwear, put my uniform back on, and finally the greatcoat again. As I was drawing on my boots, I noticed that the direction of the wind had changed in the night. It was coming from the north now and whipping the front flaps of my tent back and forth with loud snaps.

"What time is it?" I asked him, wrapping the greatcoat close.

"Just after four," said the soldier.

Outside, the wind was still coming in heavy gusts, driving the snow into my eyes and making me turn my back to it. In spite of all the alcohol I had consumed at the party, the frigid air began to restore clarity to my brain.

The wagon commandeered by the young soldier was completely open to the elements. Both of us rode on the box, and it made for a very unpleasant journey. Another two inches of new snow had fallen since I had gone to bed, although it had now turned to driving sleet. The wind blew it directly into our faces as we headed north on the highway.

We slowly passed through the thousands of soldiers' tents and log huts that now covered the ground for miles around Falmouth. A handful of sentries were about, and they stared at us with forlorn expressions as we went by. On the northern edge of the military encampment, we came to the place where the Negro contrabands had made temporary shelters in the previous weeks. There were hundreds of them, most containing runaway slaves who had drifted North seeking the protection of the army. Others were living under scraps of canvas or out in the open.

A hundred yards farther on, the soldier turned the wagon off the main road, and we began following a narrow, snow-covered gravel road that cut through a small stand of piney woods. Up ahead there was a small clearing in the forest, and I could see lights waving slowly back and forth. In their pale reflection, the snow was a pure ice blue.

Small clusters of Negroes lined both sides of the lane as we rode toward the lights. Drawing closer I saw that the illumination came from railroad lanterns that were being carried to and from a single cross path. At least fifty soldiers were milling about in a rough circle near the moving lamps.

At the center of the circle, standing hatless in the freezing rain, was the massive figure of Val Burdette. He was still wearing the decrepit uniform I had seen him in at the party, but it was now covered with a canvas ground sheet. Someone had chopped a hole in the middle of it for his head. His hair was frozen into a monumental crown. A dead cigar was clamped in his mouth.

"Move everyone out of here!" I heard him shouting. Under the prodding of the guards, the crowd of soldiers slowly began to move back until there was a cleared space around him.

My headache was still raging as I drew up beside him. "Is it Major Duval? Have you run him down?"

He shook his head no.

"Sam's men were still tracking him when I left to come out here," he said, morosely. "This is something infinitely more sad . . . a dead girl. She was discovered about an hour ago. Unfortunately, the whole area around the body has been disturbed."

I now saw that a blanket covered a form on the ground in the middle of the rough circle. For thirty feet in every direction, it looked like a herd of cattle had been grazing. Beyond the edge of the little clearing, a belt of tall evergreens swayed and moaned with every gust of wind. Even with a hundred thousand soldiers encamped within a few miles of the spot, it was a lonely and dismal place.

From a wagon near the tree line, men began unloading canvas and lumber. Val called out to a sergeant who was standing nearby.

"I will also need eight fully charged lanterns," he said.

As we waited, Val led me over to a small group of men who were standing near the wagons. Two of them were Negroes. One looked to be about Val's age. He was tall and stocky, with carefully trimmed gray hair, and intelligent black eyes. Dressed in a well-worn black suit, he stood with his arms protectively wrapped around the shoulders of the shorter Negro, who I now saw was a teenage boy.

"This man and his son found her while they were out searching for firewood," said Val. The Negro looked straight ahead, his face expressionless. One of the soldiers guarding him began to shake his head in disgust. I thought he was about to say something, but instead he just spat in the snow.

"We're ready, Colonel," someone called out. I turned to see that the soldiers near the girl's body had finished nailing together four crude wooden frames, and were lashing them together in a rough rectangle around her. They then stretched canvas across the frame, completely covering the sides.

As soon as they had finished, Val pulled one edge of it aside for us to enter. Once inside the enclosure, he carefully placed the eight lanterns around the edge of the blanket. Kneeling down, he uncovered the body.

The girl was lying on her back in the snow, and she was as naked as the moment she had entered the world. The truth be told, she was the first naked woman I had ever seen. It was a moment that I had often dreamed about, and I imagined that it would be both exciting and profoundly erotic. That was hardly the case. Her face was childlike, almost angelic. If the body had not been that of a mature woman, I would have thought she was no more than fourteen.

Her bewildered eyes were wide open, and they stared up at the universe far above us. The pitiless sleet had kept them filled to overflowing, giving the impression that she was still silently weeping at what had been done to her. In the glare of the lanterns, her body seemed more like a marble statue than a person who had lived and breathed. The color of her skin was ethereally white.

"The word of her discovery must have spread quickly through the regimental camp just south of here," said Val. "They all came to have a look at the dead snow angel."

Unless one of the soldiers had shifted her body, it appeared that whoever had left her there had arranged the corpse in a respectful, almost ritualistic way. Both hands were folded over her chest, not quite covering the tips of the woman's conical breasts. Her long golden hair had been carefully arranged around the head like a regal crown.

I could now hear a growing tumult in the ranks of the soldiers who remained at the edge of the perimeter near the Negro man and his son. There were several inarticulate shouts, followed by a low keening rumble of angry voices.

"Keep order there!" Val yelled out to the provost's guards, and the voices subsided.

"I fear that things could get out of hand if the soldiers conclude that the contraband and his son were responsible for this."

Val removed the layer of hair covering the girl's shoulders and brought one of the lanterns closer. I could now see an inch-wide band of ugly bruises around her neck.

"Thanks to the natural curiosity of the soldiers, any important information about the murderer or his vehicle has been trampled out of existence," he said.

Removing a small magnifying glass from his coat pocket, he gently pried her mouth open and peered inside the oral cavity. Then he proceeded to study virtually every inch of her body. For several minutes he inspected her toes and the soles of her feet. I turned away when he began to make a close examination of her genital area.

"She was murdered elsewhere, of course," he said, "but the fact that the snow melted and then refroze directly beneath her suggests that she was still warm when placed here. Whoever left the body obviously wanted to leave no trace of her identity. The only thing I can state with any certainty is that she is of foreign origin, probably German, and made her living as a prostitute. From the traces of chronic inflammation around the pelvis, I would also be willing to wager that she was in the early stages of a serious venereal disease, possibly syphilis. An autopsy should confirm it."

He asked for my help in turning the body over, and we did so together, carefully placing her on an army blanket adjacent to the place she had been lying. I saw then that the area between her narrow shoulder blades was covered with a pattern of livid weals. Val used his glass to examine them more closely. Then he conducted a thorough examination of the back of her head, legs, and feet.

That was when I happened to look over at the frozen outline in the snow where her body had lain. My eyes were immediately drawn to an object that was glistening brightly in the reflected glare of the lanterns. Crouching down next to the spot, I could see a shiny black object protruding from the snow where her head had lain. I cracked the thin film of ice that surrounded it with my fingers.

The object was no sooner in my hands than the words were forming on my lips.

"I know who she is, Val," I said.

"You knew her?" he asked, incredulous at the prospect.

"I didn't know her, but I saw her. She was one of the guests at General Hooker's party last night."

I held the lacquered black object up to the light. It was six inches long and emblazoned with tiny gold dragons.

"The girl was wearing this barrette in her hair when I first saw her. She was talking with another girl. I thought they were probably the daughters of officers."

"This one was no vestal virgin. She played in the sacred fire," he said, covering her body with another blanket. "And I'm sorry to add that she was probably pregnant."

He gently closed her eyes with two fingers.

"At least we know why she was in Falmouth. The far more difficult question is who brought her down here for the assignation."

At that moment I heard angry shouts from outside the enclosure.

Regaining his feet, Val stepped outside and ordered that a wagon be immediately brought to us. Perhaps, a hundred soldiers were now clustered around the Negro man and his young son. The soldiers were being held back at the point of bayonets by the men Val had assigned to stand guard.

Someone in the mob yelled, "Did these two niggers kill her, Colonel?"

"There is no reason to believe they are responsible!" Val shouted back as he strode toward them. He didn't stop until he reached the Negro contraband, whose arms were still wrapped protectively around his son.

"For your own protection, sir, I am having you and your son taken into custody," he said quietly. "I will see you in the morning and arrange for your release."

There was a hint of fear in the Negro's eyes as he stared silently back at us. I wondered then if it was because he had something to hide or was understandably worried about the safety of himself and the boy. He nodded once, and we moved off.

A raw gray dawn was breaking when we finally left that desolate place and headed back to Falmouth. The sleet had stopped and even the blustery wind had died down by the time we deposited the young woman's body in the icehouse of the estate where General Hathaway's office was located. Val ordered that a guard be kept at the door to the icehouse until further notice.

Chapter Eleven

"Who are you, sir?" I asked.

"My name is Thomas Beecham," the black man replied in a low voice. "This is my son, Daniel."

It was almost nine on that same morning. Val and I were sitting in the kitchen of a large, two-story brick building that had once served as the overseer's house on the country estate where General Hathaway had established his headquarters. It was located about a mile from the mansion house at the end of a shallow valley. Sam had promised to notify us as soon as his men had captured Major Duval.

Opposite us were our only witnesses in the murder of the young prostitute. In the light of day, the man looked much older to me than the night before. Of course, he might very well have thought the same thing about me. I had gotten barely two hours' sleep, and even less the previous night aboard the *Phalarope*. That combined with the whiskey I had stupidly drunk at General Hooker's party had left me completely jaded. Fortunately, one of the provost's guards had brought us a small pot of coffee.

Although he had been up all night, Val seemed immune to exhaustion.

"Don't you ever get tired?" I asked him as we arrived at the overseer's house.

"Fatigue is almost entirely mental," he said, striding through the door. "You should learn to control it."

I thought that twelve hours' sleep would be a better way to control it, but didn't bother to tell him so. He sat down at the kitchen table and began writing case notes into the small, leather-bound notebook that he always carried in his coat. Mr. Beecham and his son were brought in a few minutes later.

While waiting for him to finish his notes, I attempted to employ one of his investigative methods, which was to closely observe every important detail about a witness who might have a bearing on the case.

I started with Mr. Beecham, observing that although his skin color was of the blackest ebony, he also had a thin, sharply pointed nose that suggested mixed blood. Daniel Beecham was much lighter skinned than his father. He was also of slighter build, but he had the same intelligent black eyes.

Mr. Beecham's suit and matching waistcoat were made of fine wool, but the style was very much out of date. The material was worn to shininess at the elbows and knees, although the numerous tears in it had been carefully mended. The boy's clothes looked like castoffs, but they had been brushed clean.

Beyond that, I could discern nothing of import or interest.

Val finished writing in his notebook and put down the pen. Looking up, his eyes focused for a moment on the boy and then his father.

"I'm surprised that a trained medical practitioner would have been subjected to such extensive physical abuse," he said.

A look of astonishment transformed Mr. Beecham's impassive face.

"I am at a loss to know how . . ."

"Forgive me," said Val, as if he had simply indulged in a cheap parlor trick. "After observing the tincture of mercury stains on your thumbs and the corked scalpel blade in the breast pocket of your waistcoat, I concluded that you were obviously versed in the medical arts. Then I happened to notice the scars you still bear from the iron betsy."

As he spoke, my eyes were drawn to the collar of the man's white linen shirt. Just above the neckline, I could see the upper edge of a band of livid pink tissue.

"The betsy was riveted around my neck until the day we escaped," he said, glancing at his son. "I was also hobbled with leg manacles."

"It seems incongruous that a man of letters would be subjected to the collar and chain."

"The answer is this, Colonel," he said. "My first master was a cultivated man, an English-trained doctor who maintained a large farm in Calvert County, Maryland. That is where I grew up and was fortunate to be granted an education, including his teaching me the rudiments of medicine. After my training, I became responsible for the care of all his slaves. When he died many years later, I, along with my wife and children, was sold to a tobacco planter named Gisbourne in Port Royal, Virginia. . . . He was not a cultivated man."

"When was that?" asked Val.

"In 1859."

Through the window I could see that a small crowd of soldiers had gathered alongside the road that ran past the front of the overseer's cottage. There were no more than twenty of them, but their angry voices carried into the room where we were sitting.

"And then?" said Val.

"Two years ago, my wife and daughter were sold to a planter in Mississippi," he said. "It was then that I . . . I attempted to go after them. I was overtaken by slave catchers a week later in the Carolinas and have worn the collar and manacles ever since. That is, until a week ago," he said.

I wondered how he had effected his most recent escape, but Val did not pursue it.

"Where is your wife now?" he asked instead.

"I do not know," he replied, his black eyes expressionless.

"How long have you been at the contraband camp?"

"We arrived there late last night. After warming ourselves near one of the fires, I saw the stand of coniferous trees just off to the west of the camp. Daniel and I went there to cut boughs for a temporary shelter."

"Tell me how you discovered the body of the young woman," said Val.

"She was brought to that spot in a carriage while we were gathering boughs inside the wood stand," he replied.

"Did you see who left her there?"

He paused for a second and then nodded.

"How many of them were there?"

"Just one. He was driving a coach. The lamps were unlit. It made no noise in the snow."

"You have excellent powers of observation," said Val, at which the boy looked up at his father with obvious pride.

"How many horses?" I asked.

"Two," he said. "After coming to that place, the man stepped down from the box and removed the young woman from the coach . . . although I did not then know it was a woman. She was wrapped in a blanket. He put the blanket down on the ground and unfolded it. Then he lifted her in his arms and laid her on her back in the snow."

Mr. Beecham stopped for a moment and shook his head.

"It was very strange," he went on. "That man stood for almost a minute looking down at the body. Then he knelt down next to her, pressing his palms together as if in prayer. After a few moments, he stood up again, went back to the coach, and drove away."

"How far away from him were you?" I asked.

"About twenty yards," he said. "Close enough to see that he was wearing the uniform of a Union soldier."

Val nodded approvingly.

"An officer or an enlisted man?" I said.

"I could not tell."

"What did you do after he left?" asked Val.

"I did not know then whether the woman was still alive. I went to her. She was dead."

"And then you sought help," said Val. "Leaving the cut fir boughs at the edge of the lane."

"Yes. Daniel and I walked all the way to the sentry post at the military encampment down the road."

"That was a very brave thing to do. You could have just walked away," said Val.

"I have a daughter, too," said Mr. Beecham.

"Do you think you could identify the soldier?" I asked.

"I never saw his face clearly," he said. "I did see his outline against the snow. I can describe his size . . . his walk, if that would be helpful. And there are one or two other points."

There was a knock on the kitchen door. One of the provost's guards entered the room and handed Val a message. After reading it, he leaned toward me and whispered excitedly, "It's from Sam. They have taken Major Duval. He is in Sam's office right now."

Standing up, Val said, "I'm sorry to interrupt our talk, Mr. Beecham. You have been very helpful, but there is another matter that we must address immediately."

I followed Mr. Beecham's eyes as he glanced toward the window. The crowd of angry soldiers beyond the post-and-rail fence had doubled in the time since I had last looked. I mentioned it to Val as we headed outside.

The day was raw and bleak, with ominous black clouds racing across the sky. Just above the horizon, I could see the hazy outline of the previous night's sliver of moon. As we walked toward our coach, one of the men in the crowd yelled, "Give us them bastuds, Colonel! We know what to do with them!"

"They are not guilty of any crime," called out Val. "They simply discovered the body."

"So *you* say," came back the same voice.

Val looked hard at the man, and then went straight to the sergeant in command of the sentries around the building.

"I'm ordering you to find your lieutenant. Tell him that I want a full squad to be posted around this building," he said, "armed and with bayonets. Do you understand me?"

"Yes, sir."

"The two Negroes inside are very important witnesses, and I don't want these idiots trying to take matters into their own hands."

"Yes, sir," said the sergeant. "I understand."

Val took a moment to examine the door at the front entrance. It looked stout and solid.

"See what you can find to reinforce the downstairs windows," he said. "We will be back in less than an hour."

"It will be done, Colonel," said the sergeant, saluting him as we boarded the coach.

"Bigotry is by far the ugliest of man's sins," Val said, as we rode in the open coach to General Hathaway's headquarters.

The captured inspector was already sitting in General Hathaway's office when we arrived at the mansion house. Sam was seated behind his desk, drumming his fingers in obvious frustration. Billy Osceola was standing at the window, looking across the river at the Confederate positions on the heights above Fredericksburg.

"Meet Major Duval of the War Department's Inspection Bureau," said Sam.

He was no longer wearing his gold-braided uniform, and his carefully cultivated imperial moustache drooped forlornly below his chin. The brown civilian suit he had on was heavily spattered with dried mud.

"He was taken while trying to board a supply ship at Aquia Creek," said Sam. "After he gave our men a false name, they were smart enough to search him and found his real papers inside his boot. At that point he asked to be taken to General Nevins's headquarters."

The man glanced up at Val and me and gave us an obsequious smile.

"I have been trying to tell the general that I was ordered to report back to Washington right away," he said, in a pronounced French accent.

"Major Duval has refused to answer any of my questions about the defective gun carriages," said Sam.

"I must again ask you to send me to General Nevins," repeated Major Duval. "He will vouchsafe my honor in every way."

"I don't care if Montgomery Meigs vouches for you," said Sam, with rising anger in his voice. "I am ordering you to tell me who paid you to pass muster on those gun carriages."

Major Duval gave him another shrug.

Val and Sam took turns asking him questions that would help us to identify the defective gun carriages. In response, Major Duval kept replying that he didn't know. Every few minutes, he asked for a message to be sent to General Nevins.

Behind his wire-rimmed spectacles, Sam's eyes had narrowed to steely slits. Val stood up from his chair near the fire and stretched his massive frame.

"Frankly, I'm not sure if Major Duval understands his position," he said, grinning pleasantly. "Sam, you say that when he was taken at Aquia Creek, he gave a false name before his identity papers were found in his boot. What are we to conclude from those actions?"

"That he was obviously deserting his post," I said.

"I had no intention of deserting," Major Duval came right back. "I was reporting back to headquarters in Washington."

"What is the penalty for desertion?" asked Val casually.

Sam slowly opened the drawer of his desk and removed a Colt revolver.

"By the powers vested in me by the provost marshal general," he said, placing it on his lap, "I find that you are guilty of the charge of desertion in the face of the enemy."

"You cannot be serious," cried the inspector, as Sam began rolling his wheelchair toward him. Billy Osceola moved up behind the French officer's chair and placed his hands on the man's shoulders.

"You cannot do this," cried Major Duval. "I demand that you take me to General Nevins."

"You've had your chance," responded Sam, as the wheelchair drew closer.

"You cannot do this," he shouted again, as Billy gripped his arms more tightly.

"The punishment is death," said Sam, with glacial calm. "My sentence will be carried out immediately."

As Sam reached the inspector's chair, he lifted the Colt from his lap. From the look on his face, I fully believed that he was going to execute the man on the spot. Seeing the grin on Val's face, I relaxed.

"Mon Dieu . . . non," cried the Frenchman, sending a spray of spittle into the air.

His eyes darted from Val to Sam and back again.

Sam placed the barrel of the revolver against Major Duval's temple.

"Tell us what we need to know, and you will live," said Val. He stood up and took several paces away from the chair.

From the corner of his eye, Major Duval saw him moving out of the line of fire.

"I would be forfeiting my life!" he suddenly cried out.

"Your life is already forfeit," said Sam, thumbing back the hammer with a loud click.

Major Duval rocked forward, dragging Billy with him.

"Wait . . . please wait . . . I tell you," he cried out, his English no longer faultless. "Is in shipping documents. They show you where bad carriages were sent."

"We already surmised that," said Val dismissively. "Unfortunately, the ones we have are forgeries."

"But I know where real ones are!" he shrieked, the gun still at his head.

"Where?" demanded Val.

"At the Quartermaster General's Office in Washington."

"No, they're not," said Val. "We've already checked those records."

"You see false ones," cried Major Duval. "The real ones in different place. I can show you where."

"It is too late for that, we need the information now," said Val, his voice devoid of pity.

"You can wire Washington," he begged. "I'll tell you where to find them."

Sam eased back the hammer and lay the revolver down on his lap again.

"You are a fortunate man, Major Duval," he said. "You had better not test my patience a second time."

As Billy released his arms, Major Duval sank forward and vomited on the floor. Sam summoned two guards, who raised him to his feet, and escorted him out of the room. He staggered out as if drunk.

"Well done, Sam," said Val.

General Hathaway grinned back at us.

"I suppose it helps if one has reached a level of anger where it actually becomes conceivable to pull the trigger," he said with relief. After putting his glasses back on, he looked professorial again.

Val went to the desk and began writing in one of Sam's order books.

"After Major Duval gives you what we need, I would suggest that you send this wire to Ted Connell in my Washington office along with the instructions of where to find the shipping files," said Val. "Connell is completely trustworthy. Once he has the documents in his possession, he should immediately head down here with them. There will be far too many routing manifests and bills of lading for him to wire them all. Once we have them here, we can match the shipping dates with the dates that each artillery unit received its carriages."

Sam nodded and said, "I will order a packet boat to be waiting for him at the navy yard. With luck, we will have everything we need by late tonight."

Val looked at his watch.

"In the meantime Kit and I have found an important witness to the murder of that young woman last night. We need to go back and interview him as quickly as possible."

"Go on," said Sam. "I'll take care of things here."

The low dark clouds above us looked heavy with snow as we emerged from the mansion house and headed back in the open coach to the overseer's cottage. The ruts and fissures in the ancient farm lane were glazed with new ice, and the coach wheels made sounds like pistol shots as we cracked through them.

"Wake me up when we get there," said Val, laying his head back against the rear cushion.

I gazed across the pure white landscape, thinking of the dead girl lying in the icehouse, and then of her sad-eyed companion at the party. Could she be a prostitute, too? It seemed impossible.

We overtook a cluster of soldiers who were striding quickly along at the edge of the lane. Oddly, none of them were carrying their rifles, which didn't make sense if they were on their way to sentry duty or to take part in a drill or exercise. Farther down the road, we passed another group of men headed in the same direction.

As the coach emerged from a stand of hardwoods into open country, I thought I heard the staccato sound of a full battle cry. Startled, I looked over at Val, but he was fast asleep, the collar of his greatcoat turned up against the biting wind.

Then we came over the brow of a hill and the entire vista opened up below us. In the distance I could see the roof of the overseer's cottage about a quarter of a mile away. But it was what lay between our coach and the cottage that caused me to bolt upright in amazement.

An ocean of blue uniforms filled the small valley ahead of us, turning the pristine, snow-covered fields on both sides of the lane into a vast landscape of slush and mud. Perhaps two thousand soldiers were already there, with more arriving every minute. The undulating mass nearest the cottage seemed to sway in the distance like a living thing. Val came awake beside me on the seat as a low roar that sounded like sea surf came back toward us on the wind.

He rubbed his sleepless, bloodshot eyes as he surveyed the scene in front of us.

"I have badly misjudged the speed at which those ugly rumors travel," he said. "We must act quickly to avert a tragedy."

Up ahead of us, the lane was completely choked with soldiers. The teamster reined his horses to a stop.

"We need to get through there, Corporal," Val called up to him.

The teamster spit a slug of tobacco juice into the snow.

"Can't see how, Colonel," he said, turning to face us. "Not without runnin' those men down in the road."

For the first time since I had met him, Val looked at me with indecision in his eyes. The soldiers just ahead of us were acting like spectators who had arrived too late to buy tickets to a sporting event. Most were aimlessly milling about at the edge of the throng, while others cavorted among themselves, obviously enjoying the break from camp routine. Two bare-chested men were engaged in a good-natured wrestling match in the snow.

"I have an idea," I said. "At least it's worth a try."

I told the teamster to change places with me, and I took his place on the box. Grabbing the reins in my left hand, I removed my revolver from its holster and fired twice into the air. The men standing in the road all spun toward the sound. That's when I whipped the horses forward.

Seeing the coach rumbling toward them, they frantically scattered to each side of the roadway, leaving a narrow path for us to navigate through. Their shouts drew the attention of the men in front of them and we were soon moving at a slow trot down the lane. A little farther on, it was necessary for me to fire another round to set off the same reaction. I was glad to see that very few of the men in the crowd were armed.

It was while driving through that sea of tightly packed bodies that I saw the ugly truth at the heart of a mob. The faces of the men were flashing past me, each registering for an instant as we hurtled by. At first they were basically good faces, some curious and some angry, but open and honest. As we drew closer to the front of the throng, however, they became contorted masks, their eyes like livid gashes, one face after another transfigured with hate and loathing. Above the indecipherable din, one shriek rose toward me.

"I seen what they done to her!" he was screaming.

At the end of the lane, we broke through the last crush of men and into a large patch of open ground near the overseer's cottage. The sturdy post-and-rail fence that bordered the front yard of the property was the only physical barrier holding back the mob.

On the other side of the fence, a single rank of twenty armed guards from the Provost Marshal's Office stood shoulder to shoulder facing the massive throng, their bayonets fixed in front of them. A few feet behind them, a young lieutenant stood by himself in the yard, coolly smoking a cigarette. He held his presentation sword loosely in his right hand, its tip resting against his right shoulder.

Stepping down from the coach, Val turned to the teamster and said, "Take it around to the back of the house."

The teamster was looking back at the mass of men we had just come through, his face a pasty yellow. I saw his lips moving, but no sound came out as he urged the horses into motion. The young lieutenant stepped forward, giving us an offhand salute. He was about my age, with corn-colored hair and startlingly blue eyes.

"Lieutenant Hanks . . . temporarily assigned to the provost marshal," he said. "These were all the men I could scare up on short notice. I have another ten inside covering the doors and windows."

"You did well, Lieutenant," said Val.

"Give 'em up, you nigger-lovin' sons a bitches!" shouted one of the men behind the post-and-rail fence. The soldiers around him took up the same call. I watched as one of them, bolder than the rest, began climbing over the top rail.

"Two steps forward!" shouted Lieutenant Hanks, and the single rank of guards advanced, their bayonets extended at chest height. The man quickly crawled back behind the fence.

"I will need ten minutes, Lieutenant," said Val.

The blond officer tossed his cigarette to the ground and carefully crushed it with his boot.

"I just hope it's important, Colonel," he said with a lazy grin. "A man could get his pants mussed here."

"One of the Negroes inside is our only witness to a murder last night," said Val. "He and his son are innocent of any wrongdoing."

Lieutenant Hanks stared at him earnestly for a moment. Then he said, "Well . . . don't much like a mob anyway."

"Can we get them out from the other side of the house?" asked Val. With his back to the mob, the lieutenant gestured toward a thick line of six-foot-high boxwood shrubbery that extended out from each wing of the overseer's cottage. From the left end, it ran about fifty feet to a brick carriage shed and a large woodpile. The section on the other side connected the cottage to a small brick summer kitchen.

"Those boxwoods effectively divide the mob," he said, "but the last time I looked, there were already a hundred men gathered at the back of the house."

Out of the corner of my eye, I saw a large rock come sailing toward us through the air like a mortar shell. It fell harmlessly to the ground, but another quickly followed, smashing through one of the downstairs windows.

The mob erupted with a bellowing, almost feral roar. As it rose to a deafening wave of noise, I saw the fence rails bulge toward us as the men farther back in the mass pressed forward, driving those in the front rank toward the line of bayonets.

Lieutenant Hanks shouted an order to his men. They raised their rifles to the sky and fired a ragged volley. In its wake the tumultuous roar slowly subsided to a dull clamor.

"Are you going to try to parley with them, Colonel?" asked Hanks.

"There is no one to parley with," said Val, surveying the crowd. "They are no longer men."

With one last intimidating glare, he pivoted on his heel and strode toward the front door of the cottage. As soon as we were inside, a guard barred the door behind us. Mr. Beecham was standing with his son in the doorway to the parlor. He took hold of my arm as I went past.

"They will be coming soon," I said, trying to avoid his eyes. I did not want him to see the utter hopelessness I felt at what was about to happen.

"I know that," he responded, his voice strained. "Captain, I do not care what happens to me . . . but Daniel . . . he has never known . . . he has had no chance to live."

His black eyes gazed into mine, completely bottomless.

"We will try," I said.

I followed Val up the stairs to the second floor. The large rear window in the center hall gave us a good view of the terrain at the back of the house. A large vegetable garden, its evenly furrowed rows still crowded with the detritus of the fall season, filled the expanse directly behind the cottage. It was bordered on each side by parallel mounds of small field stones that had been cleared from the garden patch.

The cultivated area extended away from the house about twenty yards toward a long, trellised rose arbor that bordered another farm lane. Beyond the lane a large rocky field led off to a copse of mature elm and maple trees. From off to the right, our coach came slowly into view and stopped in the middle of the muddy lane. A half-dozen soldiers quickly surrounded it.

By then there were about two hundred men behind the house. Most of them were clustered near the back door. The rest were standing near the lines of boxwoods so that they could keep track of what was happening in the front.

Val pointed to the stationary coach.

"That is our only chance of getting them out of here," he said, "but not where it is now. The men down there would overwhelm us as soon as we headed for it."

As we watched the soldiers around the coach began drifting back toward the cottage. One of them stayed behind. He climbed up on the box with the teamster and began shouting.

"I want you to take the coach across the field and into that tree line," said Val, pointing at the elm and maple stand a hundred yards across the field. "Once you're into those trees, stop there and wait for us. Don't draw any attention to yourself or attempt to come back toward the house. You must wait for us to bring them to you."

I nodded.

"In the meantime, I'll try to create a diversion in the front. Hopefully, it will draw some of the men away from the garden before we bring them out. If we can make it to the open field, we'll have a chance."

We were walking back toward the front stairs when several rifle shots rang out in quick succession. The guard covering the hall window spun backward and dropped heavily to the floor in front of us. As Val knelt beside him, I looked through the shattered window frame.

The rage of the mob became a living thing.

With a roar that filled my ears like a buffeting wind, it surged forward in a monstrous wave, smashing the post-and-rail fence and flooding into the yard.

The line of men commanded by Lieutenant Hanks never moved from their positions. I saw one of them thrust his bayonet into the chest of a man at the head of the mob. They were both swallowed up an instant later. Another guard wildly swung the butt of his rifle before he too, disappeared.

Lieutenant Hanks stood alone before them. Although it was useless to resist, he raised his pistol at the oncoming mass and fired twice before being dragged backward in the crush. He was still striking out at the men swarming around him when his blond head vanished into the maelstrom.

The house actually shuddered as the blue tide slammed into the front wall of the building. I watched as a raw log, maybe ten feet long and a foot wide, was passed above the crowd to the soldiers nearest the front door. There was a great thudding sound as it pounded into the oak frame.

Pulling out my pistol, I fired into the mass of men around the log. One of them dropped from sight but was immediately replaced by another. Then Val was pulling me toward the back of the house.

"Before I bring the Beechams out, I will have our men fire a volley from the rear windows to scatter them right and left," he said, swinging open a casement window that faced onto the garden. "That will hopefully clear a path for us. Once they are with you in the coach, head for Sam's headquarters."

I nodded and shook his hand.

"Good luck," I said, forcing myself to smile.

"And to you, my son," he said, grasping my elbow.

Feet first, I dropped from the second-story window to the ground below. Several of the men in the garden took up a shout, but the others must have decided I was no more than a rat deserting the sinking ship. They didn't interfere with me.

I ran to the coach. The teamster had disappeared, but he had left the reins tied around the whipstock. Climbing onto the box, I urged the horses forward, and the crowd of men ringing the garden parted to let me through. I kept going until I arrived at the stand of elms and then continued ten feet inside the tree line before reining up.

As I turned to look back at the cottage, a volley of shots rang out from the rear windows. Just as Val had surmised, the men in the garden scattered toward the protection offered by the mounds of cleared field stones that bordered it.

A few seconds later, the rear door burst open and soldiers started pouring out of the house, their rifles at port arms. There were six of them and they formed up in two lines of three. Val came next with the Beechams right behind him. Moving in a rough square, they began to come on at a run across the garden. Sitting helpless in the wagon, I could feel the brutal pounding of my heart.

A great clamor went up from the men at the back of the cottage, and within seconds, the horde still in front began smashing through the boxwood shrubs to join in the pursuit.

"You're too late, you bastards!" I screamed, seeing the start that Val and the others had already achieved.

What he hadn't counted on were the loose field stones that bordered the garden. The men who had taken shelter behind the mounds immediately started hurling them like missiles at the fleeing figures, and their flight through the garden became a bloody gauntlet. Two of the guards went down in the first hail of rocks, dropping like deadweight. Another staggered and fell as the group reached the end of the garden.

A line of soldiers stood waiting for the fleeing men at the edge of the farm lane. Val headed straight for the center of the line, sending two of them flying and clearing a space for the Beechams to break through behind him. As Mr. Beecham knocked down one of the soldiers with his fists, I could hear him shouting at Daniel to run ahead. Even then nothing could have stopped the boy from reaching me, but he refused to leave his father. Together they started toward me on the run as Val and the three remaining guards continued to battle the men at the lane. I watched as the monstrous blue tide swept over them.

Mr. Beecham and Daniel were now only fifty yards away from me, but the fastest of the pursuers in the mob had closed the gap behind them to less than twenty feet. I could see from the angle of pursuit that it would be a close call. The reins were taut in my right hand, and I held the whip in my left, ready to lash the horses forward as soon as they were safely in the coach.

Daniel could run very fast. He would race ahead of his father, turn to see him lagging behind, and then slow down to wait for him to catch up. With each yard Mr. Beecham labored harder, his chest heaving as he tried to keep his legs plunging forward. With only ten yards to go, he looked up and saw me waiting in the coach just inside the tree line.

"You can make it!" I yelled. Gritting his teeth, he nodded and came on again, lunging through the snow. Daniel was already at the tree line when Mr. Beecham lost his footing for the last time and went down.

Daniel gazed up at me in the coach and then back at his father.

"No!" I cried as he started running back. Reaching his father in three steps, he leant down and helped him to his knees.

"Run, baby!" I heard Mr. Beecham cry. "Oh, God, run!"

He tried to shove the boy toward the wagon, but by then, the fastest pursuers had caught up. I saw Daniel embrace his father just as the rest of the pack engulfed them.

Leaping from the coach, I pulled my pistol from its holster and ran toward the writhing mass of bodies. They had already dragged Daniel to his feet and were raising him aloft like a sack of grain, the upstretched arms of the mob passing him forward toward the stand of elm trees.

"Let him go!" I shouted, cocking my pistol and aiming it at the man who was holding his leg. Out of the corner of my eye, I saw someone coming up on my right. A sudden blossom of pain exploded at my right temple, and I felt myself falling forward.

I was on my knees and holding onto the man's waist with both hands when something struck me in the back of my neck and I slid down to the ground. Although I did not fully lose consciousness, I could no longer move. I was vaguely aware of men stepping on my legs and back as the mob surged around me.

I felt a sickening pain on the right side of my head, although the icy ground was soothing where my cheek lay flush against it. Legs and boots continued to flail in front of me, and I heard inarticulate shouting followed by the wild, frantic trumpeting of a horse. The sounds all seemed to echo down to me through a long tunnel.

The cataract of noise ended abruptly. There was a moment of silence followed by a long roar of exultation. It ended when a shot rang out, quickly followed by another. Suddenly, there was a tumult of slashing feet and legs. I was kicked again, and someone fell sprawling over me. More shots were fired. I could hear the mob running.

The pounding of their boots slowly ebbed away.

Raising my cheek from the frozen ground, I saw a mounted squadron of cavalry slowly riding toward me from the direction of the cottage. The rider in front was carrying a carbine across his saddle.

I slowly rolled over on my back.

Daniel and his father remained as close together in death as they had been in life, side by side. They were hanging from the same limb of the largest elm tree. A thin stream of blood was flowing out of Daniel's eyes and nose.

Two dead soldiers lay spread-eagled on the ground beneath them. The face of the one closest to me was canted in my direction. There was a small black-and-blue hole over his right eye where a bullet had entered.

"You got two of them, Frank," I heard one of the cavalrymen call out as they dismounted.

"Evens the score some," came the gravelly reply.

They cut the bodies down from the tree and dropped them on the ground.

When the dizziness finally passed, I regained my feet and slowly walked back to the cottage. The ground around the building looked like a battlefield that had been raked by artillery fire. All the windows in the cottage were smashed. The front door lay shattered inside its torn-off frame.

I looked for Lieutenant Hanks among the dead men in the front yard, but he wasn't there.

I found Val lying on his back on the glass-littered floor of the front parlor. A surgeon was dressing a terrible gash on his forehead. His shirt linen was soaked in blood, and he appeared to be unconscious.

"Val?" I whispered, gently. His eyes fluttered, and came open.

"Don't blame yourself," I said, putting my hand on his shoulder.

He stared straight up, unseeing.

CHAPTER TWELVE

DEATH IS NOTHING MORE than a word. I had seen it in many forms since the war began, but those deaths did not begin to prepare me for what I had witnessed in the field behind the overseer's cottage. More than anything, I was left with a sense of deep disgust at the knowledge that I wore the same uniform as the base and cowardly men who had murdered Thomas and Daniel Beecham. The act was nothing less than an abomination of the soul, and the reasons why the war had originally seemed worth fighting now seemed irrelevant to me.

I spent the rest of that day and most of the evening writing a report for General Hathaway of everything that had occurred after the discovery of the girl's body. With all the news correspondents in camp, the provost marshal general was publicly vowing to undertake a complete investigation of the incident, in which five soldiers had also been killed. Eighteen more were recovering from wounds or injuries. Of the incomparably brave Lieutenant Hanks, there was no word at all.

After delivering my report, I felt near physical collapse and returned to my tent. Lying on my cot, I relived the hideous events at the overseer's cottage over and over in my mind. Some time after midnight, I finally fell into a troubled sleep, awaking shortly after dawn with a dull, pounding headache. I got up and went to the wash tent, where I examined myself in a small hand mirror. Aside from the knot on the side of my head and some badly bruised ribs, I had no lingering injuries.

Val was not so lucky. He had been unable to move his legs after regaining consciousness, and the doctors who examined him feared that in addition to the head wounds he had sustained in the fight near the farm lane, he had also suffered a broken neck.

I tried to visit him twice the next day, but on both occasions he was under sedation and unconscious. For an hour I sat by his cot, praying that he was not paralyzed. The thought that he might lose his mental faculties was something I refused to even contemplate.

From the number of staff officers and generals who were constantly coming and going at the different headquarters, it was clear that the final preparations for Burnside's attack were underway. I happened to be standing in the front hall of the mansion house waiting to meet with Sam Hathaway when General Hooker arrived for one of the conferences followed by all his division commanders. He was very angry and looked neither left nor right as he stalked down the corridor.

There had been a new development in our investigation of the defective gun carriages. It was not good news. Based on the information he had learned from Major Duval, Sam had wired Val's deputy, Ted Connell, with instructions on how and where to find the shipping manifests we needed from the file repository in the Quartermaster General's Office at the War Department in Washington. Ted had sent a wire back several hours later to say that the War Department had refused him access to any of the files without specific authorization from General Nevins.

In the meantime, a colonel on General Nevins's staff had arrived at Sam's headquarters with an order demanding the release of Major Duval to his custody. Sam refused to comply with the order.

"I don't care if Secretary Stanton himself demands his release," he said, "I will resign first."

From Sam's window, we could see the Confederate battle flag flying from the tops of several buildings across the river in Fredericksburg. On the heights beyond the town, all activity appeared to have ceased.

"They have everything in place over there," said Sam, scanning the heights through his binoculars. "They're just waiting for us to come across and be slaughtered."

Placing the binoculars in his lap, he furiously wheeled himself back to his desk.

"Sometime in the next thirty-six hours this army will attempt to cross that river," he said, "and our attacking force will need all the artillery support they can get. We must know which carriages are defective."

"I'm convinced that when Duval thought he was facing his own extinction, he told you the truth, Sam," I said.

"I agree," he said. "But as soon as he is released, the weasel will tell his friends what we have learned, and they will wire Washington to move or destroy the files."

"If I leave for Washington immediately, I could be there by late tonight," I said, looking at my watch.

Sam's mind was already working in the same direction.

"I will find a way to hold off releasing Duval for another twelve hours. By then you will hopefully have the shipping manifests and be on your way back."

"I will get them, Sam," I said, with an air of confidence I did not truly feel.

"There will be a packet boat waiting for you at Aquia Creek in two hours. It should get you to the navy yard by about eleven tonight. The packet boat will wait there with its boilers banked until you return with the files. That is our only hope."

As I prepared to leave, he said, "Take Billy with you. He has a way of proving useful in difficult situations."

Sergeant Osceola and I agreed to meet at the packet boat.

Before going back to my tent to pick up my bag, I walked over to the hospital encampment. Val's doctor had just completed his examination when I arrived.

"It is still too early to tell whether his neck is broken, but as a precaution I have immobilized the entire area around his head," he told me.

"May I talk to him now?" I asked.

He looked at me with obvious relief.

"I would be very grateful if you would. Colonel Burdette seems to think he is ready to return to duty. But if he doesn't remain immobilized, he might well do permanent injury to himself. I regret to say we were forced to use confining straps on him."

They had sequestered him in his own tent, which had a planked hardwood floor. Around the head of his cot, the doctors had erected a metal cage, its iron ribs bolted to the floor and extending upward to a point several feet above Val's upper body. He was lying on his back, his arms and torso encased in a tightly wound linen jacket that was bound with leather straps. Another metal contraption was fitted around his head, holding it rigidly against his shoulders in a rectangular nest of rods and wires. They had trimmed his hair and beard in order to stitch his head wounds. He actually looked quite distinguished.

"Get me out of this thing, Kit," he growled, as soon as he saw me.

The sight of him reminded me of Gulliver when he was first trapped by the Lilliputians, and I couldn't help but laugh. That only made him angrier.

"These idiots are convinced I have a broken neck. The only way I can prove it isn't broken is for you to release me from this cage."

"I had to learn how to follow the doctor's orders. Now it's your turn."

"This is ridiculous," he said, straining at the bonds that immobilized his upper body.

"Look, I only have a few minutes before I have to leave for Washington," I said. "Will you listen to me, or are you just going to enjoy your tantrum?"

He stopped straining and slowly relaxed.

"Go ahead," he said, closing his eyes.

I told him what had occurred when Ted Connell tried to get the documents in Washington without arousing suspicion, as well as our new plan. He agreed that it represented our only chance.

"Time is running out," he said. "Hundreds, maybe thousands of lives, are riding on the success of your mission. I have but one change to propose. If you are able to retrieve the manifests, send them back with Billy on the packet boat. Then there is one more thing I want you to do while you are up there."

From the depths of his metal cage, he fixed his slate gray eyes on me.

"I believe that the murder of that young woman intersects with our corruption investigation. From my experience, corruption goes hand in hand with prostitution and blackmail. The young woman may well have been a pawn in the larger game. . . . But even if she wasn't, we are honor bound to try to find her murderer. The Beechams died for a crime they did not commit. If they hadn't chosen to help, the two of them would still be alive. God help us, their blood is on our hands."

The rage in his eyes was palpable. With his beard shorn, I could see the veins bulging out on his massive neck.

"The first thing you must do is find the young woman who was with the dead girl at the party. She holds the key to this mystery."

The idea of finding the sad-eyed girl seemed ludicrous on its face. I remembered him saying to President Lincoln that there were more whores in Washington than Baptists. How did he expect me to locate one prostitute out of thousands?

Regardless of his head injuries, he still retained the capacity to read my mind.

"You're thinking that it is a daunting task. Well, I can narrow the chase for you. After Billy is safely on his way back here with the gun carriage files, you go straight to the asylum and track down Tim Mahoney. He has an office down the hall from mine and is in charge of rating the whorehouses."

I wasn't sure I had heard him right.

"Don't look at me like I'm an idiot," he said. "To protect the health of our soldiers, the provost marshal surveys the quality of every bawdy house in the city. Get that list and then cross off all the houses in Murder Bay and Hooker's Division."

"Hooker's Division?"

"Yes. The whorehouse district is named after your favorite general. They named it for him a few months after his brigade arrived in the capital last year. His boys were quite prolific in their appetites. But you won't find our girl there. Those places are for men without the financial means to afford better."

I pulled out my calendar book and began taking notes.

"As you know, I examined the dead girl quite carefully. From the piercing of the flesh around her genitals to the atrophic state of her annular muscle, there is no doubt that she was willing to engage in highly specialized forms of sexual gratification. Almost certainly, it would have been in a house that caters to men with expensive tastes."

"How do you know she was German?" I asked.

"I am by no means certain," he said, "but based on the fillings in her teeth, she is definitely foreign born. Her facial structure, complexion, and interpupilary cleft suggest either Germanic or Scandinavian origin. After the Irish, the second highest percentage of foreign-born prostitutes in Washington are German. So it's a fair assumption."

"What if the other girl never left here?"

"On the afternoon of General Hooker's party, Burnside issued an order for all wives and family members to return to Washington. Two steam frigates were scheduled to escort them back the following day. Assuming that occurred, the chance that she is still here is very slim . . . unless she is dead. But if you can find her, Kit, we will learn who invited them down to Falmouth and what happened to them while they were here."

Something nudged my brain at that moment, something that I had recently seen or heard, but I was unable to remember what it might be. He saw the look of puzzlement on my face and asked what I was thinking.

"It's probably nothing," I said. "Anyway, I cannot recall it now."

"You will probably find the woman we are looking for in one of the houses near Marble Alley. Mahoney maintains a full report on each of them, including a description of the services they provide. Now untie these goddamn straps."

"I would do anything for you, but not that," I said, "not until the doctors know it's safe."

He must have seen the resolution in my eyes because all he said then was, "Her life is probably in danger, Kit . . . yours as well. Be vigilant."

"I will," I said. "See you tomorrow."

Walking back to pick up my bag, I saw that my uniform was ripped in one place and stained with blood. I stripped off all my clothes, gave myself a field bath, and put on my other uniform.

An idea struck me as I was leaving. After finding out where the newspaper correspondents' tent was located, I headed over there. It was empty except for a private who was sitting behind a sawhorse-and-lumber table, idly picking at his teeth with a pocket knife. I asked him for the billet location of Philip Larrabee of the Boston *Examiner*. The boy ran down the handwritten list with his finger and said, "The stables . . . if he ain't sleeping it off somewhere's else."

Phil was playing poker in one of the training stalls.

"I need your help," I said. "It's important."

"It would have to be now," he complained, "I've just started getting some decent cards."

He reluctantly followed me across the paddock to the icehouse. Inside, I lifted the sheet from the dead girl's face and said, "Could you sketch her as if she were alive?"

"Why don't you just ask me to bring her to life while I'm at it," he said, discomfited.

"We are trying to find the man who murdered her, Phil," I said.

He stared down again at her face.

"You'll have to open her eyes for me," he said with a grimace.

It took him less than five minutes. When he was finished, I looked down at his sketch. He had indeed brought her back to life, at least on paper.

"This is really good, Phil," I said to him. "Thank you."

As I was walking away, he called after me, "Too bad you're going to miss the last great battle of the war, Kit."

"Hope it is," I said.

I met Billy Osceola at the wharf along Aquia Creek. He stood apart from the crowd of soldiers milling near the gangplank of the packet boat. Unlike the others, all of whom were wearing heavy winter coats, Billy wore only his thin uniform blouse. The dark sky was threatening rain, and he was carrying a rolled up rubber poncho over his shoulder. A Remington revolver hung from a handmade leather holster on his hip.

"You travel light," I said.

The obsidian eyes stared up at me intently, and he nodded once. In the gloom of the day, his roughcast, coppery face was lost in shadow. A few minutes after we boarded the packet boat, it began slowly chugging out past the ship traffic that clogged the shallows near the wharf.

At least a hundred passengers were crowded into the salon, which smelled of burnt grease and unwashed bodies. A red-hot coal stove sat in the center of the cabin, surrounded by a brass railing. Much of the cabin space was taken up by soldiers who were ill with camp fever and dysentery, most of them lying on stretchers. They gave off the familiar putrid odor of the sick ward.

There were many civilians aboard, from well-heeled contractors with gold fobs hanging from their waistcoats to teamsters, blacksmiths, and carpenters on their way back to Washington after finishing their jobs for the army. Although it was only four o'clock in the afternoon, many of them were already asleep.

I went outside and took a turn around the narrow promenade of the lower deck. On the leeward side of the packet boat, a cold gloom of icy fog covered the surface of the water, making it seem as if we were crossing the Styx.

As soon as the boat cleared the barge and transport traffic heading into Aquia Creek, two stewards set up a serving table in the forward corner of the salon and put out a big crock of steaming soup, surrounded by platters of soft bread, sliced meat, pickles, and hard-boiled eggs.

I made myself a sandwich, joining Billy on a long bench that was anchored to the deck facing the stern. Before I had taken the second bite of my sandwich, Billy had finished everything on his plate. He looked up and caught my eyes on him.

"You never know how much time you'll have for a meal in the army," he said, with a shy smile.

"You're right," I agreed.

An hour later we were far out on the Potomac. I watched the oil lamps in their tin holders begin swinging from the ceiling hooks as the boat slowly rolled from port to starboard and then back again in the rough swells. As the wind came up, a squall began spitting rain against the windows.

The boat continued to pitch and roll as the stewards cleared the serving table, and people settled in around the stove rails to stay warm. Without warning, a fat man in a yellow gabardine suit leaned forward and threw up in the direction of the stove, his vomit hissing and popping as it came into contact with the red-hot metal. Like a contagion, the sickness spread to every part of the cabin, and within minutes most of the others were throwing up, too. The awful reek drove me outside.

Billy was standing next to the brass deck railing, oblivious to the wind and rain. I watched as he pulled a clay pipe out of his blouse and with practiced ease filled it with tobacco from a beaded leather sack. Scratching the head of a sulphur match with the nail of his index finger, he waited for it to burst into flame before smoothly cupping the match in his good hand and lighting his tobacco. Like many other soldiers I knew, he had developed the trick of smoking his pipe with the bowl upside down. Even with his mutilated hand, he managed it all with a smooth economy of motion.

When the squall passed over, I joined him at the rail. Together, we watched the dark Virginia shoreline slide by. At one point I saw the flickering lights of an isolated cottage and imagined a mother sitting inside by the fire wondering where her son was at that very moment.

"How many battles have you been in?" Billy asked, after several minutes of silence.

"Just one," I said.

"You wounded?"

"Yes," I said.

"You in a hospital?"

"Nine months."

"I hate hospitals," he said.

"Me, too, Billy."

"Where were you wounded?" I asked him.

"Gaines Mill and then Second Bull Run."

I remembered General Hooker telling us about him saving General Hathaway's life and asked if it was true.

He nodded.

"General Hathaway saved my life at Gaines Mill. I had a chance to do the same for him," he said.

After a pause, he added, "I'm not sure he was glad I did."

"You're a Seminole?"

He nodded again. I wondered then whether there was mixed blood in his ancestry. Apart from the bronze skin and coal black eyes, his features were more Saxon than Native American.

"Does your family still live down in Florida?"

He shook his head.

"My father and mother died fighting the army in the Third Seminole War," he said. "The rest of my family was forced to go West."

"And you joined the army after that?"

"I was put in the Jesuit School of Tallahassee when I was fourteen years old. It was run by Spanish priests," he said, as if that somehow explained it.

He tapped out his pipe on the deck railing and walked back into the salon.

A set of iron steps led to the upper deck. I went up and found a dry place between the wheelhouse and the smokestack funnel. Alone there in the lee of the wind, I began to think through everything we needed to do after reaching the capital. As I pictured the two of us attempting to gain admittance to the War Department in the middle of the night, a wave of doubt swept over me. Knowing the vast power of the conspirators arrayed against us in Washington, it suddenly seemed ridiculous that Billy and I could possibly be successful in securing the critical documents.

Truly, I didn't fear for myself; I only feared failure. And I felt increasingly sure we were doomed to fail, that the whole effort was a futile and hopeless quest. As the certainty of it crowded my brain, my spirit dipped toward complete despair. If I had been carrying a bottle of laudanum, I would have drunk it without a moment's hesitation.

Sunk in gloom, I found myself contemplating why God had allowed me to survive the kind of disemboweling wound that had killed virtually every man, Union or Confederate, who had sustained one in the war. And what had I done after receiving that miraculous gift aside from wallowing in self-pity while awash in laudanum? Gazing at the dark Virginia shoreline, my thoughts drifted to Harlan Colfax, whose body now rested forever beneath the nearby swamps at Fair Oaks.

I stared up into the night. He was there, somewhere . . . he and Johnny Harpswell, the two men who had saved my life . . . both now gone forever. Perhaps this was my chance to do something that would serve as repayment for their sacrifice—to save innocent men's lives in the same cause they had died for. It would be a point of honor now, I finally decided, pledging to do my best to make their sacrifice count.

Sitting on the deck, I tried to think through every variable we might possibly encounter while trying to gain entry to the Quartermaster General's Office, and what I could do in each case to make sure we were able to penetrate the security and retrieve the files. From all my visits to the building, I also tried to remember which offices were located on each floor. Several ideas eventually came to mind. I pulled out an order pad and began writing. When I was finished, I put the pages inside my blouse and leaned back against the warm stack.

Hoping to get some rest before we arrived at the capital, I tried to will myself to sleep. Release would not come, however. In my mind's eye, I saw the clock ticking relentlessly closer to the moment when our army would launch its attack at Fredericksburg.

I offered a silent prayer up to the black sky that we would somehow succeed. At that moment a slew of bright orange cinders belched out of the smokestack and swirled around for several seconds before blowing away on the wind. I took it as a good omen and again lay back against the warm metal of the funnel. This time, sleep finally took me.

I awoke to the shriek of a steam whistle. It took me a few moments to realize that the boat was no longer in motion. Standing up, I saw that we were anchored in the lee of a small island. I rushed to the captain's cabin only to learn that the stern wheel had become fouled in floating debris, and that two of his crew were over the side attempting to clear it.

I went looking for Billy and found him in the salon. While we waited, I took the time to again go over every detail that we had learned from Major Duval, including the exact location of the shipping manifests within the document repository in the Quartermaster General's Office.

An hour later we were moving again. For the remainder of the trip, I stood at the rail, attempting to will the boat to move faster. When we finally began edging in toward the wharf at the Washington Navy Yard, I looked at my watch. It was almost eleven-thirty, and we were already behind schedule. Sam would be releasing Major Duval in just over thirty minutes.

Chapter Thirteen

THE MAGNITUDE OF our task became evident as soon as the boat had nestled up to the wharf. A company of armed infantrymen was deployed at the foot of the arrival ramp, and an officer was checking the orders of each passenger before he was allowed to disembark. In case they were looking specifically for me, I sent Billy along the passageway to try to find out what was happening. We met back in the main passenger salon.

"They are detaining anyone with a pass signed by General Hathaway or the provost marshal general," he said.

"Good. Well we know they are expecting us," I said.

Motioning for him to follow me across the salon to the passageway on the outer side of the boat deck, I leaned over the railing. A small freight barge stacked with stove wood and coal was inching toward the loading bay of the packet boat to replenish its fuel stocks before the return run down to Aquia.

As the barge came alongside, Billy and I climbed over the railing and dropped down to the top of the woodpile. A greasy-haired man with a walrus mustache was standing in the wheelhouse, his boozy countenance reflected in the oil lamp that swung from the overhead. An open bottle of whiskey rested securely in his right hand.

Without preliminaries, I told him that I was absent without leave and hoped to avoid the soldiers on the wharf. He demanded ten dollars, which

I immediately paid him. Five minutes later he deposited us on an unlit pier near the navy drydock.

Washington had received a major cloudburst shortly before our arrival. Runnels of water were still sluicing off buildings and wooden sidewalks into the streets, transforming them into muddy trenches. It made for slow going in the hansom cab we commandeered outside one of the waterfront saloons.

We emerged onto Pennsylvania Avenue just east of the Capitol Building and headed slowly down the hill toward the War Department. The avenue was filled with vehicles of every description, and most of them were having trouble navigating through the flooded roadways. Even with the hour approaching midnight, however, people were still crowded along the sidewalks in front of the brightly lit hotels and restaurants.

Hearing the thunderous sound of galloping horses and clattering sabers, I looked up to see two cavalry squadrons in bird's-egg blue uniforms charging up the avenue as if the fate of the Republic depended on their mission. The horses' hooves kicked up great clods of mud that flew in every direction, splattering the clothes and finery of the people crowded onto the sidewalk.

The president's mansion was almost completely dark as we rode by, and I wondered whether President Lincoln was still working up in his private office. The thought of him actually being there gave me another idea as we pulled up at the side entrance to the War Department building on Seventeenth Street.

As Billy and I got out of the carriage, I stared up at the hundreds of windows in the massive building and saw that only a handful were lit. If we were lucky, there might only be a few guards on duty inside.

Five sentries stood at attention in front of the massive oak entrance doors. A sixth soldier, the sergeant in command, stood behind them smoking a thin cigar.

"State your business," he demanded.

"Captain McKittredge reporting to General Halleck with dispatches from Falmouth," I said, handing him one of the orders that I had drafted myself on the packet boat and signed in the commanding general's name.

He carried it to the gas lamp that was mounted on the brick sidewall of the portico. After reading the forged order, he handed it back to me.

"General Halleck left the building several hours ago," he said. "There ain't no one up on that floor right now besides the night clerks in the Quartermaster General's Office."

"I was ordered to wait outside General Halleck's suite until someone arrives to receive the dispatches," I said. "Believe me, I would much rather be over at the National right now, enjoying a drink with my girl. If you would just initial the back of these orders to show that you denied me entry to the building, Sergeant, I would be very grateful."

"I ain't gonna sign that," he said, taking a step back.

I shook my head as if his decision was most unwelcome.

"Why all the security?" I asked.

"Earlier tonight we were put on alert to detain anyone bearing orders from the Provost Marshal General's Office," he said. "I ain't got no idea why."

I held out the forged papers again.

"Well, as I told you, Sergeant, it would make me very happy if you would just sign . . ."

"Wait upstairs like you was ordered," he interrupted me, before standing aside to let us pass.

Major Duval had said that all the procurement files were stored in a well-guarded document repository on the fourth floor of the building. In order to gain access to it, he said, one had to go through several outer offices. Even the stairwell was guarded, he had told Sam.

Only the telegraph office remained open on the first floor. As we headed up the broad staircase, I saw two operators seated at paper-strewn desks taking down a stream of messages from the clacking telegraph receivers.

The next two floors were dark. When we reached the fourth floor, a pair of guards stood with their rifles at port arms, flanking the empty stairwell. Two more stood at attention at the doorway to the outer office of the Quartermaster General's headquarters.

I squared my shoulders and marched straight in between them, with

Billy just behind me. Inside the office, a high counter blocked further passage. On the other side of it, a group of clerks were working at long oak tables. One of them looked up from his ledger and said, "May I be of assistance, Captain?"

Through the open door behind him, I could see another hallway leading to other rooms and offices. Another sentry stood guard at the entrance to the rear corridor.

"I'm here with an urgent information request," I said.

"You'll have to talk with Major Broo about that," he said in a timorous voice, as if Major Broo sat at the right hand of God.

"Well, go get him," I said imperiously. "I haven't got all night."

Apparently, the clerk was used to obeying orders in that tone. He practically vaulted out of his chair and disappeared through the open door that led back to the other offices. He returned in less than thirty seconds.

"Major Broo will be out in a moment," he said, regaining his place at the table.

Fully ten minutes passed before I saw an officer coming slowly toward us down the corridor, adjusting his uniform coat as he came.

Major Broo was almost winsomely plump, with a nose the size of a large grape, and prominent jowls that gave him the look of a bear that has fattened himself up for the winter. He exuded an air of self-importance, and his uniform had enough gold braid on it for a navy admiral.

"Yes?" he asked, in a bored voice from the other side of the counter.

I had already rehearsed what I planned to say.

"Captain Nevins," I said with a frown, adding, "and I don't like to be kept waiting."

"This department is officially closed," he said, as if he had done me a favor by deigning to come out of his office. "Mr. Gimpel said you had an urgent request."

"I need these documents immediately," I said, placing my gloved hand inside my uniform coat and removing one of the sheets of paper I had drawn up on the packet boat. It consisted of a dozen requests for files related to personnel records in the departments of Ohio and Kentucky.

He took the paper from me, quickly scanned it, and chuckled derisively.

"You call this an urgent request?" he said, dropping the paper onto the counter as if it was soiled.

"You can come back tomorrow," he said, looking disdainfully at my rumpled uniform. "Of course, we will need this request in triplicate, and you must have the necessary written approvals from the Adjutant General's Offices of Kentucky and Ohio before we begin. From that point, it should take about three weeks."

"This happens to be a special request," I said.

"They are all special," he said right back, with a supercilious smile.

"Very good, Major Broo," I said, picking up the document and putting it back inside my blouse. "I will go back now and inform the president of your decision."

Removing a small writing pad from my blouse, I held my pencil over it.

"What is your full name, Major?" I demanded, in the tone of a Spanish inquisitor.

"The president?" he said, his haughtiness gone in an instant.

"Yes, the president," I said. "I just left him in his private office along with my father, General Nevins. Perhaps you are aware that he commands the military-procurement section of this department. I want your full name before I inform them of your response to their request."

"General Nevins is your father?" he said, seemingly awestruck.

Giving him a contemptuous glare, I turned on my heel and began stalking toward the door.

"No . . . wait," he said in a pleading voice. "Which documents were they again?"

I handed him back the list.

"It would take most of the night to assemble these files unless I use all my available staff," he said.

"Well, get them started, then," I said. "I will provide the services of my sergeant to assist them."

Major Broo hurriedly assembled his battalion of clerks and began reading aloud the list of personnel records I had requested. When he was finished, he led them down the corridor to the document repository. It was as large as a college gymnasium, and filled with row upon row of floor-to-ceiling stack shelves, each crammed with hundreds of files. I was glad that Billy and I had gone over the exact location of the shipping manifests again on the packet boat. Putting my arm around the major's shoulder, I steered him toward the door of his office.

"While the menials are engaged in this unpleasant task, I would like to get your views on procurement reform, Major Broo. The president said he was keen to learn what those on the front lines really think about my father's current purchasing procedures."

"They are perfect in every respect, Captain Nevins," he said earnestly, as I escorted him back to his office.

A few minutes later, Billy emerged from the repository with a six-inch-thick set of file folders under his arm. He motioned me to come out in the corridor. I saw Major Broo start to get up from his chair.

"I'll take care of this," I said peremptorily, and he sat back down.

With our backs to him, I briefly scanned the first file folder. It was page after page of routing manifests for gun carriages. They included the names of each manufacturer as well as the artillery units to which each gun carriage was shipped, and on what date. Most important, there were notations from inspectors identifying those manufacturers whose carriages had not passed initial inspection. All Sam would have to do was contact the batteries that had received the defective carriages and make sure all of them were replaced before the attack.

"I think you know what you have to do now, Sergeant," I said, giving him back the folders along with a private wink.

Billy grinned at me and began walking toward the outer office door. We had already agreed that if he was successful in locating the files, he was to head straight for the waiting packet boat at the navy yard.

"What does he have to do? Where is he going?" whined Major Broo, suddenly alarmed.

I gave him an icy stare.

"You may have read about the sergeant's exploits at Antietam," I said, beginning to enjoy myself, "when he single-handedly killed five Rebels with his bare hands. He just told me that he needed to relieve himself. Do you have a problem with it?"

"No," replied the major in a small voice.

I waited five minutes to make sure that Billy was clear of the building and then pulled my watch from my pocket.

"I didn't expect it to take this long," I said. "I need to go back over to the mansion to tell them the information is on the way. As soon as you have completed things here, bring the files to the president's private office on the second floor.

He gave me an apologetic frown.

"What is it now?" I said.

"I don't have authorization to enter the mansion," he said meekly.

"I'll take care of that right now. Hand me your order book."

In the order book I wrote, "Captain Nevins hereby authorizes Major Broo of the Quartermaster Corps to forthwith present himself to the president."

I ripped the order form out of the book and handed it to him.

"I will see you shortly, Major," I said, standing up.

"Yes, sir," he said.

Walking down the stairs, I felt like giving out with a Rebel yell. In my mind's eye, I saw Major Broo arriving at the mansion with the Ohio and Kentucky personnel records at around four that morning and demanding to see the president. Emerging at the side entrance, I glanced up and down Seventeenth Street. Billy was gone. The manifests were on their way back to Falmouth.

The black sky was clear of rain as I started toward Pennsylvania Avenue. I decided to walk to Mrs. Warden's, get a good night's sleep, and then begin my search for the girl in the morning.

I was crossing the avenue when a large black brougham bore down on me and stopped in the middle of the roadway, blocking my path. The passenger door swung open, and a man stepped down. In the murky darkness, I saw that he had an Asiatic face.

"Get in, please," he said, holding the door open for me. He was short and squat but very powerful looking.

It was too much of a coincidence, considering where I had just been. I looked toward the president's mansion, where I knew that sentries were still standing guard along the sidewalk. A second later I felt pressure against my ribs. Looking down, I saw a small-caliber revolver in his hand.

"Get in, please," he said again.

The interior of the brougham was lit with two small side lamps. It had tufted leather seats and thick carpeting on the floor. An enormous man with a milky right eye was sitting in the seat facing backward. Opposite him was a man dressed in formal evening clothes. I immediately recognized him as the leonine stranger who had threatened me at the Silbernagel trial. In the pallid light of the coach lamps, his amber eyes and chalk white skin lent him the aspect of a living corpse.

As I sat down next to the man with the milky eye, the Asian closed the door behind me and then began loping toward the side entrance of the War Office. The man in evening clothes tapped his knuckles loudly against the mahogany-paneled ceiling, and the brougham swung around on the avenue, before moving slowly back in the direction I had just come.

"I suppose I should introduce myself," he said. "My name is Laird Hawkinshield."

Even I had heard of him. Everyone in Washington had. He was a congressman from Ohio and a powerful member of the Committee on the Conduct of the War. Harold Tubshawe thought he walked on water.

"Where are those shipping manifests?" he asked me politely.

I looked back at him but said nothing as the brougham came to a halt in front of the War Department at almost precisely the same place that our carriage had stopped just thirty minutes earlier.

"You should know that when Major Duval was released from custody, he immediately informed General Nevins that someone would be coming for the files," he said. "I must now assume you already have them."

Through the coach window, I saw the Asian returning on the run from the entrance to the War Office. Major Broo lagged behind him, desperately trying to keep up. He ran with his legs wide apart, as if his crotch was sore.

The Asian leapt agilely up to the box with the driver. Major Broo came straight to the open door. As soon as he spotted Laird Hawkinshield in the back, he began groveling.

"Congressman, I tried to tell your man that no procurement files have gone out of the office since I came in tonight," he said, wringing his hands. "I'm fully aware of General Nevins's orders."

When he looked over and saw me in the other seat, his face relaxed into a relieved smile.

"Why, Captain Nevins here can tell you. He was right in the office with me part of the time."

"You're a stupid imbecile," said Hawkinshield, narrowly missing the major's face as he slammed the door shut. He tapped the ceiling with his knuckles again, and the brougham moved off, leaving Major Broo on the sidewalk.

"I must assume that someone is already on his way back to Falmouth with the files," he said, as the coach gathered speed. "Well, setbacks are inevitable. It just means that I will have to schedule a public hearing tomorrow to expose the corrupt manufacturers of the gun carriages myself."

"A true man of the people," I said.

"I would like you to join me for a nightcap back at the Willard Hotel, Captain McKittredge," he said.

"I don't drink," I said.

"Oh . . . that's right. You're an opium eater, aren't you? Don't worry . . . I can accommodate your tastes."

I was unable to conceal my surprise.

"We know more about you than you think," he said.

A few minutes later, we rolled up to the carriage park at the rear of the Willard Hotel. The man with the milky eye swung the door open and motioned me to step down. The Asian was already waiting for me on the sidewalk. Together they led me inside the vestibule. Laird Hawkinshield followed, keeping ten feet of distance between us.

The hotel was lavishly decorated for the Christmas holidays, and its corridors were festooned with aromatic wreaths of evergreens and lifesize papier mâché religious figures. A crowd of people in formal dress emerged from one of the ballrooms and drifted toward us down the corridor. I was immediately alert to the possibility of using their presence to effect an escape. Again I felt the pressure of the pistol in my ribs.

As soon as the party goers saw Hawkinshield coming along behind us, they became as animated as children, whispering to one another as if a conquering hero was suddenly in their midst. He doffed his top hat to them as he went by, all the while smiling and murmuring inanities such as, "It's an honor," and, "A vast pleasure, I'm sure," as their faces lit up in admiration.

His suite was on the seventh floor and faced onto Pennsylvania Avenue. Hawkinshield put down his top hat and gloves on a marble top stand in the foyer and led me inside. The sitting room was filled with rosewood furniture. Two gaslit crystal chandeliers illuminated a collection of old oil paintings. Thick Persian carpets covered the polished hardwood floors. Comfortable armchairs and couches were grouped together underneath the tall windows.

A tall blonde woman was standing next to one of the windows, looking down at the avenue below. She looked like she had just come from church and had on a silk gown of sapphire blue, with an overdress of pale pink. It rose up to her neck in a prim lace collar, which was set off by a small gold locket. Her hair was adorned with a garland of tiny red roses.

"Captain McKittredge, I would like you to meet Miss Ginevra Hale," said Hawkinshield. "Ginevra, Captain McKittredge is one of your father's constituents. He comes from a small island off the coast, I believe."

I immediately recognized her name, too. She was the daughter of our senator, Charles Hale, and widely considered to be the most beautiful and elegant young woman in Washington society.

She held out her white-gloved hand and said, "It is always a pleasure to meet a fellow down-easter here in the capital."

She had a fragile smile and lovely violet eyes.

"Ginevra, I wonder if you would make me a whiskey and soda," said Hawkinshield. "I don't believe the captain imbibes spirits . . . perhaps a glass of laudanum would be more to his taste."

"Nothing for me, thank you," I said.

Appearing to take no notice of his sarcasm, she walked over to a sideboard against the far wall and poured his drink from an array of bottles that stood in formation on a silver tray.

He waved me into a chair and sat down in the one opposite.

"I would like to retain your services, Kit," he said, using my family name as if he had known me all my life.

"I already have a job," I said.

"Yes, I know," he said, giving me a pained expression. "You work for the

great wooly mammoth or mastodon or whatever it is he was called back in
Illinois. Personally, I see him as more of a porcupine. . . . At any rate, he
has proved quite nettlesome, which is why I would like to retain you."

"I'm not interested."

"Not for a thousand dollars a month? That would seem generous for a
twenty-one-year-old captain."

I stared at him, stunned.

"How about two thousand?" he asked.

"Not for any amount of money."

"Really . . . well, I'm not surprised," he said, with an amused grin.

Ginevra Hale brought his drink across the room.

"I could also be a very good friend to you, you know," he said next,
cocking his leonine head to catch himself in the mirror on the wall behind
me. "Loyalty goes both ways with me."

"It sounds like you should have been born a dog," I said.

Miss Hale was standing directly behind him. He did not see her smile.

"Since money seems to hold no allure, and you apparently don't need
friends, what is your pleasure?" he said.

"Just what is it you do, Congressman," I asked, "when you're not serving the people?"

"Quite candidly, I am interested in anything that makes a profit," he
said. "Today it is this blessed war. Tomorrow it may be cotton or ship-
building."

"You sound like you want the war to go on."

"I can't deny that it has been good for business," he said. "However,
your Colonel Burdette has *not* been good for business. I need to have a
better idea of what he learns and when he learns it. That's why I need you."

I shook my head. "No," I said.

"Now as for your opium addiction," he said next. "I can arrange a lifetime supply of the finest quality . . . Or how about a promotion? Perhaps
you would you like to be a colonel next month . . . a general if the war goes
on for another year."

I glanced up at Miss Hale. She was looking at me with the sympathy
one feels for a helpless victim. What could possibly be her connection to
him? I wondered.

"I would wager that your mother would be very excited to see you come home wearing a colonel's uniform," he went on. "Or perhaps, your sweetheart . . . oh, that's right . . . you have no sweetheart. Well, that can be arranged, too."

"Your constituents must love you," I said.

"In fact, they do," he said. "So what is your answer?"

"No," I repeated.

Glancing out one of the windows into the darkness, I imagined the army preparing for its attack at Fredericksburg, an attack that could end in disaster because of the greed and manipulations of men like Hawkinshield. I thought of the dead he had already left in his wake and the many more who might meet the same fate. As Hawkinshield stood there grinning down at me, I felt the familiar anger rising inside me like an old friend.

"Methinks, you are about to mount your charger, sir knight," he said, caustically. "That's your problem, you know. You suffer from a permanent case of white knight's disease."

"I'm no white knight."

"Then, perhaps, you don't even know it," he said. "Have you ever read the fable of the white knight rescuing the beautiful damsel in distress?"

I turned around in my chair. The man with the milky eye had his back against the door to the suite. The Asian was standing a few steps behind me.

"Did you ever read about the damsel in distress, Kit?" he repeated.

I ignored the question, staring straight ahead, and waiting for a chance to strike back at him.

"Well, here she is," he said, with a wave of his hand at Miss Hale. "Aren't you, Ginevra?"

She said nothing in response.

"You know, in just two weeks Ginevra is to marry one of my most distinguished congressional colleagues," said Hawkinshield. "It will be the society event of the season."

He turned back to face me.

"Kit, I bet you're the kind of knight who puts every young woman on a pedestal. Well, let me tell you something about women. . . . They are not made out of marble. Are you, Ginevra?"

I had no idea what game he was playing, but it was now obvious she was a reluctant partner in it, just as I was.

"Do you think Ginevra is beautiful?"

She was starting to look as uncomfortable as I felt.

"Surely, you can answer that question," said Hawkinshield, his voice rising. "Is she beautiful? Yes or no?"

I felt the Asian move up behind my chair.

"Well, of course she is," said Hawkinshield, without waiting for my answer.

Her hands were touching the back of the ornate armchair next to his. I saw her fingers begin to coil around its carved walnut fretwork.

"You'll find that I'm quite good at plumbing the weaknesses in the human soul, Kit . . . that and fulfilling people's desires," he added. "I fully expect to discover your own. . . . Now, let me give you a case in point. During my first term in the House of Representatives, back when I possessed the same noble personality you have now, I partook of that charming Washington society custom called open house. In case you are not familiar with the ritual, there is one day each year when the important denizens of Washington society deign to open their houses to the great unwashed . . . when the lesser lights are permitted to make a courtesy call on them. It occurs on New Year's Day."

He paused to give her a seemingly affectionate smile.

"So, hearing about the lovely Miss Hale, I decided to call on her at the home of her father, the august Senator Hale. It was then that the lovely creature now standing before you chose to treat me as if I had just crawled out of the noisome Washington canal."

He got up from his chair and stepped to her side.

"Didn't you, Ginevra?" he said.

"After the things you said you wanted to do with me . . ."

"Didn't you, Ginevra?" he said, interrupting her.

"Yes," she said, turning away.

"Well, Kit, just as I know there is a way to discover your own deepest needs and desires, I set about finding those of Miss Hale."

He walked slowly around her, his face just inches from her's.

"And I did. . . . And now, here you are, Kit, with those noble brown eyes . . . the perfect white knight."

He reached for the garland of tiny red roses that circled the crown of her hair and tossed it to the floor. Loosening her hair at the back, he pulled it free. The blonde curls fell in waves from the natural part in her hair.

"Ginevra has a weakness for noble brown eyes, don't you?" he said to her then, taking her arm in his hand.

This time she did not reply.

"You know, Kit, everyone has a breaking point," he said next. "You believe that, don't you?"

From behind her back, he began to unfasten the top button of her dress. I felt my stomach turn over.

"Just to prove to you that everyone has a breaking point, Kit, I want you to see Ginevra as she really is," he said.

She winced as another button came free.

Stepping away from her, he said, "Go ahead, Ginevra. Show him how beautiful you are."

She looked up at him one last time, her eyes making a silent plea.

"Captain McKittredge is waiting," he said, his voice merciless.

With a soft rustling sound, she slowly reached up and pulled the unbuttoned pink overdress above her shoulders and head. Hawkinshield walked over and took it out of her hands.

"Stop," I said. As I attempted to stand up, the Asian's powerful hands gripped my shoulders and held me in place.

"Oh, not just now," he said. "You wouldn't want to spoil her pleasure."

Without pause, she slid the blue silk gown down her chest and stomach, stepping out of it when the top of the dress reached the floor.

"Is that color I see rising in your cheeks, Kit?" he said. "I once read that resisting temptation is the true test of character. Thankfully, I have none."

"That's enough," I said, leaping to my feet.

Before I could move, the Asian's left arm circled my chest. His right hand was at my neck holding a long, thin-bladed knife.

"Ah, yes. The white knight disease, as I thought. . . . I do not think you want to test Aki's reflexes," said Hawkinshield. "And I don't want any bloodstains on this ancient Persian rug."

Miss Hale was standing as rigidly straight as a marble sculpture.

"See the arrogance in that face," he said, with a bloodless smile. "Ten generations of fine breeding put it there. It took just one Hawkinshield to wipe it off."

As I watched, tears began streaming down her cheeks. One by one, they slowly dropped from her chin to her bodice. With trembling hands she loosened her petticoats and let them fall to the floor. Her eyes were now glassy and unfocused, her cheeks red with humiliation.

As I strained to break free from the Asian's powerful arms, I felt the blade of his knife puncture my neck. The man with the milky eye joined him behind me, pinioning my wrists.

"Well, go ahead, Kit," said Hawkinshield. "You can have her if you want. And if Ginevra isn't your type, I would be happy to offer you one of the birds of paradise. My gentleman's club appeals to the most refined tastes . . . whatever they are."

"You'll have to kill me first," I said, still writhing to get free.

"Oh . . . that's very dramatic, Kit, but I don't think it will be necessary. Just remember . . . everyone has their breaking point, even you."

Hawkinshield motioned with his right hand to the Asian. Keeping the knife to my throat, he and the other man propelled me to the door of the suite. The big man opened it wide, and they shoved me out into the hallway. As the door closed behind me, I turned and saw Ginevra Hale for the last time, her blonde head still held high above the cream shoulders, her beautiful clothes scattered on the floor.

CHAPTER FOURTEEN

UNABLE TO SLEEP after returning to my room at Mrs. Warden's, I sat down and drafted an account of the evening's events for Val and Sam. Knowing that Billy would soon be arriving in Falmouth with the shipping manifests, I focused the report on my subsequent encounter with Laird Hawkinshield and his admission of complicity in the gun carriage affair. I did not mention Ginevra Hale or what he had made her do.

It was very hard to put words to paper. My mind kept returning to that last image of her, and I couldn't stop berating myself for leaving her there. As I had stood in that hotel hallway, it had been all I could do not to break down the door, regardless of the consequences. But I had also remembered Hawkinshield ridiculing me as a white knight and wondered if he was not fully expecting me to charge back into the suite. When I had put my ear to the door, I couldn't hear anything, no sounds of a struggle, no cries. It occurred to me that she could also have been acting for my benefit. The alternative was that she had somehow become ensnared in one of his many webs and was paying a terrible price for it. If so, it was not the first time he had bent her to his will. That did not lessen my feelings of guilt.

Dawn was still an hour away when I completed my account. I took it over to the dispatch office and added the envelope to other important mail that was slated to go down to the army on the next packet boat.

On my way back to Mrs. Warden's, I recalled Hawkinshield's words about his gentleman's club, as well as his offer of one of the "birds of paradise." In our last meeting at his bedside, Val had suggested that there might well be a connection between the murder of the prostitute and our corruption investigation. What if the dead girl had been one of his birds of paradise? Perhaps both investigations were leading to the same place.

It was shortly after five when I got back to Mrs. Warden's. She was already up by then and about to remove a batch of breakfast pastries from the brick oven. The fragrant aroma drew me straight into the kitchen, and she poured me a large mug of freshly roasted coffee. With little urging, I ate an apple fritter, still warm from the oven, which she had just dusted with confectioner's sugar.

By eight o'clock I was standing outside the office of the man Val had told me was responsible for monitoring the health standards of Washington's whorehouses. A paper nameplate read: LIEUTENANT TIMOTHY MAHONEY, REGULATION. Someone had handwritten the words, "King Bung" at the bottom of it.

There was no response when I knocked on the door, and I assumed that he had not yet arrived for work. An aged clerk came through the open door of the next office down the hall and peered toward me.

"Oh, he's in there," he said, with a curious smile.

I began knocking harder, stopping only when some low, guttural, snarling sounds came from behind the door. A minute passed without further sign of activity, so I began pounding again, this time making the door literally shake in its frame. By then a whole group of clerks had come out of their offices to witness the spectacle.

"Away you rampallian troglodytes," came a loud choleric voice, followed by a long stream of profanities.

The tirade slowly faded to silence.

I waited ten seconds and began hammering again. There was a sound of something falling heavily to the floor, followed by a bout of tubercular coughing. Finally, a key moved in the lock, and the door cracked open a few inches.

I could see nothing. The room was as dark as pitch and reeked of whiskey.

"Valentine Burdette said you could help me," I spoke into the void.

As soon as Val's name was out of my mouth, the door swung open to reveal a tiny, unshaven old man with a bulbous, blue-veined nose. Barefoot, he was wearing an unbuttoned officer's blouse over long, filthy underwear. With his tangled white hair and barbarous smell, the man reminded me of a miniature version of Val. He had to be the oldest lieutenant in the army.

Looking past me, he saw the small crowd gathered in the corridor.

"I'll tickle your catastrophes, by God!" he bellowed, his rheumy eyes arched in contempt. Laughing as they went, the clerks swarmed back into their offices.

"Burdette sent you?" he asked, breathing a cloud of whiskey in my face. I nodded.

"I work nights," he replied, as I followed him back into his lair.

He opened the heavy black curtains that covered the window, letting enough light into the room for me to see that it served as both bedchamber and office.

"Has Burnside gotten off his ass yet?" were his next words.

"No."

"I'm not surprised," he said, motioning me toward a chair next to his cluttered desk. "During my thirty years at the Priory School, he was the most dim-witted boy it was ever my misfortune to have in the classroom. I don't know how Lincoln could have elevated him to the top job. How can I help?"

Picking up his pants and socks from the chair, I sat down.

"I am searching for a young woman who could be an important witness in the murder of this prostitute," I said, showing him the rendering of the dead girl.

I told him what Val had concluded about her sexual practices after examining the body. He shook his head laconically.

"She could have worked in any of a hundred places," he said. "Hell, there is one that caters to deviants right across the street from the War Department. I rated it poor and tried to close it down, but General Halleck fancies one of the girls in there."

"Val suggested that I start with the more expensive houses that cater to men with unusual sexual tastes. He mentioned a place called Marble Alley."

"You could start there," he said, "but your dead girl sounds like some-one who might have performed in one of the private shows. . . . Don't ask me where to find them. The locations tend to move quickly. There is a siz-able group of wealthy perverts here in the capital who enjoy watching women perform with different species. I'm told it can cost a hundred dol-lars or more to attend one."

"Are there any houses that specialize in German girls?" I asked next.

He laughed at that.

"German, Irish, African, Chinese, Creole, Greek, Turkish . . . They say America has become the great melting pot of the world. When it comes to the flesh trade, that is definitely the case. Our whorehouses offer the purest form of democracy you can find."

When he opened the top drawer of his desk, I heard two bottles roll together with a loud clink. Pulling one of them out, he set it on the table.

"You partial to this?" he said, pouring himself a generous glass of whiskey.

"No, thanks," I said.

He reached into another drawer, removed a file folder, and tossed it to my side of the desk.

"Those are paid advertisements from the *Evening Star*," he said. "They describe the virtues of those houses that have the money to advertise their wares."

I opened the folder. The first advertisement in the batch read,

Maude Shively
187 B Street South

For the truly discriminating taste,
Miss Shively has surrounded herself
with twenty-eight famous beauties to assist her
in the entertainment of her callers.
She has used rare judgment in selecting
them, not only for their beauty in face
and form, but also for their intellectual
and social attainments, conspicuous

among them being that far-famed
Creole beauty, Hallie DuShane.

Lieutenant Mahoney had come around to peer over my shoulder as I read.

"Creole means she is a black girl," he said before taking a swallow of his whiskey. "Most of them are contrabands."

The folder was filled with dozens of advertisements just like the first one, including "Mary Hall's," "Cottage by the Sea," "Madame Russell's Bake Oven," "Fort Sumter," and "The Ironclad." The difficulty of finding the sad-eyed companion of the dead girl became ever more apparent.

"Are these places open now?" I asked.

"They're like churches, son," he said. "They are never closed to those seeking release from the cares of daily life."

He drained his glass and put the bottle back in the drawer. Picking through the clutter on top of his desk, he found another set of papers and handed them to me.

"You can take these reports with you," he said. "They are the product of six months' honest endeavor on my part . . . the rating for every bordello in the city with more than five girls. As you can see, they range in quality from 'best' to 'very low.' "

"What does 'very low' signify?" I said.

"Very low means you will almost certainly contract diseases that have yet to be discovered in the equatorial jungles."

The list was single-spaced and ran seven pages long.

"Have you ever heard of a house called, 'The Birds of Paradise'?" I asked him.

"Good name, actually," he said, after a few moments thought. "No . . . I would have remembered it."

"What about a gentleman's club run by Congressman Laird Hawkinshield?" I asked next.

"You can find a congressman in just about every house in the city," he said with a chuckle. "If he owns one, I've never heard of it."

"I'll start with Marble Alley," I said.

"Val could be right," he said. "You may very well find her there. Start

with Julia Dean's at the beginning of the street and work your way down to
Sal Austin's. There are about forty houses between Pennsylvania and Missouri Avenues in a three-square-block area that cater to officers and
wealthier types. Someone should recognize the girl and hopefully steer
you to her friend."

He picked up the drawing of her and stared at it again before handing
the paper back to me.

"With a face like that, it's hard to believe she was selling herself," he
said. "But then I was propositioned a few nights ago by a girl of eleven," he
said, finishing his glass. "She had been working in the trade for more than
a year."

After leaving him, I walked downstairs to my old office. In my
absence, Harold Tubshawe had covered the top of my desk with his case
files. He wasn't in yet, and I took the liberty to examine the docket folder
on the Silbernagel case. Based on his latest handwritten notes, the attorney for Mr. Silbernagel was to begin presenting his defense case that
morning. Harold had prepared a complete dossier on each of the witnesses
the attorney planned to call, as well as a detailed set of questions for his
cross-examination.

There were also handwritten notes in the docket folder indicating that
Harold had engaged in secret conversations with the officers judging the
case, and that two were already prepared to find Silbernagel guilty. If this
was true, Harold had acted both unethically and illegally. To balance the
books a little, I took his case folder with me when I left, dumping it in the
incinerator near the back entrance to the building.

At nine o'clock that morning, I started my search for the sad-eyed
young woman. Marble Alley looked like the kind of prosperous residential
street one might find on Beacon Hill in Boston. The buildings were
mostly brick, with impressive facades, stone staircases, and high windows.

At the first address on Mahoney's list, an iron rail fence enclosed the
front yard. Just inside the gate stood a lifesize statue of a forest nymph. A
young boy was sitting on the stoop at the top of the front steps. He was
dressed in brightly colored pantaloons out of the Arabian Nights. Someone had powdered his face and painted his lips with red gloss. The powder

was streaked with tears. He looked up morosely as I went through the front door.

The house smelled of cinnamon and stale cigar smoke. There were potted palm trees flanking the main hall, and two front parlors, both of which were empty. I walked down the hall until I came to a third parlor, which was decorated with heavy Empire couches and chairs. Burgundy drapes covered the windows. A piano stood in the far corner.

A lush-figured girl was coming out of the room as I went in. Following behind her was a federal officer, his tongue protruding out of his mouth like a lolling dog. A second girl was sitting on one of the red-tufted couches in the parlor. She smiled and stood up when I came in. I asked her if I could speak to Julia Dean on an urgent matter. She left without saying a word.

A gigantic painting on the far wall caught my attention. It was a poorly executed oil rendition of *The Rape of the Sabine Women*. Unlike the original classic, all the physical couplings were graphically portrayed. I heard a noise behind me and turned to see another woman entering the room. Around fifty, she had a coarse, weathered face and big ursine body. She was dressed in a loose-fitting muslin robe and smoking a thin cigar.

"I am Julia Dean," she said.

I removed the drawing of the girl from my uniform blouse and handed it to her.

"Do you know this young woman?"

I waited for a sign of recognition in her eyes. There was none.

"Is she your wife?" she asked, looking up at me.

"No."

"You would like to meet her, is that it?"

"No. Actually, she's dead."

"I think I understand," she said, with sympathy in her voice. "Well, I have a girl who could be her twin sister coming in here at about four, if you would like to come back then."

When I told her it was a police matter, her manner abruptly changed.

"What police?" she demanded, her voice suddenly becoming combative. "I know every man assigned to the Alley on the Metropolitan force, and I already have an arrangement with the army."

It was obvious she thought I was there to demand a bribe.

"I'm with the Provost Marshal's Department," I said, taking back the drawing. "We are investigating the murder of this young woman."

"Well, I have no idea who she is."

"I haven't suggested you do. I am merely looking to find someone who might have known her."

"General Meagher happens to be a good friend of this establishment," she said, unable to control her anger. "I have a good mind to tell him about the badger game you boys keep playing with the honest business people of this city. I don't think fighting soldiers would take kindly to it."

"Have you ever heard of a house or club called the Birds of Paradise?" I asked next. She shook her head no.

A minute later I was back on the street and working my way down the long list of houses on Tim Mahoney's list. For the next seven hours, I showed the drawing of the dead girl to madams, prostitutes, street peddlers, procurers, hostlers, cab drivers, and anyone else who might conceivably have seen her or met her in the previous days and weeks.

At the end of that time, I had learned several interesting facts. Parrots were the birds of choice in at least half the whorehouses in Marble Alley. General Meagher and a number of other senior officers seemed to be regular patrons of many of them. Every house had a piano or pipe organ for entertaining their customers, and most, if not all of them, were paying bribes to both the Metropolitan Police and the U.S. Army. No one, however, recognized the dead girl in the drawing, and no one had ever heard of a club called the Birds of Paradise.

As darkness fell, I stopped at one of the restaurants near Missouri Avenue. Sitting at a table near the front window, I ate a bowl of mushroom soup and watched the flood of humanity going in and out of the bawdy houses. Something continued to gnaw at the back of my mind, an amorphous fragment of memory that I knew was important but simply could not remember. Several times it drifted close to the edge of consciousness like a wary fish, but each time darted away.

It was dark when I emerged back on the street. The air hung heavy with acrid smoke from the city's thousands of wood and coal fires. A man came down the block lighting the street lamps with a long match pole. As I again scanned the list Mahoney had given me, two uniformed policemen converged on a beggar across the street. Using their truncheons, they beat his shoulders and back until he scuttled off toward the blighted neighborhood beyond Missouri Avenue.

My wound began to ache as the air got colder, and I thought more than once of giving up and going back to Mrs. Warden's. At one point I also found myself longing for the sweet release of laudanum. I could almost taste the earthy bite of it and feel the grain alcohol warming me inside. Val's last words about finding the girl's killer, however, kept me going through the long night. I continued to work my way through the neighborhood, stopping at each house to ask my questions.

It was approaching eleven o'clock when I crossed off the name of the last house on Mahoney's list. I had spoken to the madam, and she had failed to recognize the girl's likeness. Beyond Missouri Avenue, I could see the dingy buildings, weed-filled open lots, decrepit rooming houses, and saloons that were part of the area known as Murder Bay.

I was ready to admit defeat, but before heading back to Mrs. Warden's, I went into a small corner tavern to rest my feet. Workmen in coveralls stood with their pints at a long bar. Even at that hour, the tables were filled with local families, including a number of small children.

The light was very dim, the smoky air hot and stale. I sat down on one of the rough wooden benches along the wall, and ordered a glass of hot cider. Someone across the room was playing a mournful dirge on a lap organ, and it complemented my mood. I closed my eyes and tried to figure out what to do the next morning. Once more the fleeting memory I was trying to recall rose to the edge of consciousness and then receded.

At that moment I felt someone sit down next to me on the bench. A shoulder moved close to mine, and I smelled the strong scent of rosewater and an unwashed body. Opening my eyes, I took in the face of a young woman. Her warm breath exhaled into my ear.

"You not happy?" she said.

I gave her an exhausted smile and shook my head. She would have been pretty except for the badly misshapen front teeth.

"Hilde . . . *Deutsche*," she said, pointing at herself and smiling.

"*Deutsche?*" I repeated.

"*Ja,*" she said. "Hilde . . . German."

Almost as a reflex, I removed the drawing of the dead girl from my blouse and showed it to her. She unfolded the cream-colored paper like it was a surprise gift. When she saw what it contained, her face lit up in a smile.

"Anya," she said.

"What?" I said, not believing it was possible that she actually recognized the dead girl.

Pointing at the girl's likeness, she said, "Das ist Anya."

"German?" I said . . . "*Deutsche?*"

She nodded her head.

"Anya Hagel."

I shook my head in wonder at the remarkable coincidence that had placed this girl next to me.

"Where does Anya live?" I said.

A bewildered look came into her eyes.

I tried to pretend I was sleeping by putting the palms of my hands together next to my check.

"Where does Anya sleep?"

Confused, the girl got up and walked to the bar, returning with a heavyset older woman who looked like Benjamin Franklin.

"She *spreache Englische*," said the young girl, pointing at her.

I told the older woman that Anya had been murdered. I'm not sure what reaction I expected, but she did not seem surprised. She told me that Anya had come to the United States a year earlier from Germany with a large group of girls who were promised work in Washington as domestics and house servants. Anya had drifted into prostitution.

I then asked them about the raven-haired girl, describing her from memory. Neither of them showed any recognition. However, Hilde thought she knew where Anya lived, having seen her come out of a house several times. I offered her two dollars to show me the place. She happily agreed.

It was only a few blocks from the tavern, just inside the district known as Murder Bay. There were no gas lamps in the neighborhood, and the houses were old, ramshackle wooden structures built side by side along the narrow street. As Hilde led me into a dark alley, something came at us from the darkness with a ferocious growl. I stopped short and raised my arms, waiting for it to leap on me. I was grateful to discover that the hulking dog was tethered to a stout chain.

Halfway down the alley, she pointed to a rickety set of stairs that led up to the rear entrance of a two-story building. When I arrived at the top of the stairs, the outline of a door emerged out of the murk. There was no point in knocking on the door. The lock had been broken off, and it stood wide open.

Lighting a sulfur match, I stepped inside.

The room was about ten feet square and contained a narrow bed, pine chest, and one chair. It reeked of spilled perfume. A candle was melted to the surface of the pine chest, and I put my match to it.

Someone had literally torn the room apart, obviously in search of something. The drawers of the pine chest had been turned upside down, and the contents spilled on the bed. Her powder jars and ointment bottles lay smashed at the foot of the far wall.

The floor was covered with mice droppings, and water was dripping down from a crack in the ceiling onto the bed. A film of white face powder lay over everything in one corner. Kneeling at the edge of it, I could see the clear imprint of a man's boot.

I imagined Val kneeling there beside me, having already managed to divine the man's height and weight, along with his name. I could discern nothing further. Glancing at the bed, I saw that even the padding in her quilt had been ripped apart. A pair of women's shoes lay on top of the bed, the soles torn away from the heels. As I stared at the carnage, I wondered what he could have been searching for. I wondered whether he had found it.

Looking at my watch, I saw that it was almost midnight. I was no closer to finding the sad-eyed girl and completely played out. It began snowing as I walked Hilde back to the tavern on Missouri Avenue. Perhaps I would have a new idea in the morning, I thought.

Riding in a hansom cab back to Mrs. Warden's, I leaned against the headrest and stared out at the falling snow. It was coming down in large flakes, reminding me of the night I had escorted Mavis Bannister back to her lodgings in Falmouth. And that was what finally jogged my memory. In my mind's eye, I was sitting close beside her and gazing out at the snow.

I even remembered the exact words she had whispered to me.

"Will I see you at the party?" she had asked. At the time I thought she must be confused, or perhaps there was another party scheduled for the next night. But that was impossible because General Burnside had already issued his order for dependents to return to Washington on the day following the party.

"One must be discreet," she had said next.

What if there had been another party, I wondered, a more intimate gathering that she had been invited to by General Hooker or General Sickles. Since she had seen me with General Hooker, perhaps she had thought I was going to be there, too.

"I hope to see you very soon," had been her last words.

It seemed probable that the dead girl and her raven-haired friend had been invited to the party as well. Knowing General Sickles's proclivities, my next thought was the girls could have been his inspired idea of a special birthday gift for General Hooker. But Laird Hawkinshield might also have been responsible for bringing them to Falmouth. If so, I knew there had to be a financial incentive involved. What if he was blackmailing General Hooker to buy his silence? I wondered next. Yet General Hooker had never made any secret of his scorn for "riding with God's cavalry." The whole army knew of his fondness for prostitutes.

I needed to find Mavis Bannister and yelled to the driver to turn around and head for the Provost Marshal's Office at the asylum. Although it was well past midnight, Lieutenant Mahoney was still working in his office when I knocked on the door. He put an immediate damper on the possibility of quickly tracking down Mavis Bannister.

"There are no records kept on married military dependents," he said.

"Tomorrow morning you could look up Bannister's service file at the War Department. At least his last known address will be in there."

"There is nothing I can do tonight?" I asked.

"Do you know anyone else on Hooker's staff?" he replied. "They might know where she is staying if she is here in the city."

As soon as he said, "Hooker's staff," I remembered hearing the joke muttered by one of the sentries on the night I first met General Hooker. It was right after the young prostitute had arrived at his convalescent suite.

"Leonora," I said out loud.

"And a beautiful name it is," said Mahoney, "the name of my sainted mother. How did you know?"

I didn't tell him it was also the name of one of General Hooker's whores.

"Have you ever heard of a hotel named the Carroll Arms?" I asked instead.

"It's not a hotel, son," he replied. "It's the fancy name of a mediocre whorehouse in Foggy Bottom."

"I need directions to get there," I said.

The Carroll Arms turned out to be a new, wood-framed rooming house in the middle of a narrow street filled with beer parlors. Already sagging inward from shoddy construction, it was sided with undressed lumber and painted a gaudy yellow. A saloon took up the first floor. The sound of raucous singing blared out into the street as I got out of the cab.

There was a separate entrance to the three floors above the saloon. Two women with heavily painted faces stood like sentries on either side of the open door. At the top of the stairs, an old black man was sitting in a chair that was tipped back against the wall. I removed a dollar from my coat and handed it to him.

"Leonora," I said.

"Number thirty-seven," he replied wheezily, pointing up the next flight of stairs.

The building was a rabbit warren of dark, narrow passages that smelled of urine and tobacco smoke. A low, wailing sound came to my ears from one of the rooms on the third floor. I steeled myself to ignore it, feeling guilty all the same. Using a match, I went down the corridor until I found the door marked thirty-seven. There was a crack of light under it. I knocked once.

"Go away," came a dispirited voice.

There was no lock on the door. I pushed it open and stepped inside. She was sitting on the edge of the unmade bed. I closed the door behind me.

Leonora was wearing the same red dress she had had on when she spent the night with General Hooker. Since then someone had apparently ripped it from her shoulders. It was crudely mended around both straps. There were dried sweat stains under each armpit. The side of her mouth was bruised purple and swollen on one side. Her thighs were slackly spread on the bedclothes.

The last time I had seen her, Leonora's eyes had danced with the confidence of a pretty young woman who knew she had power over men. Now they were the wary eyes of a mistreated animal.

"Just go away," she repeated. "I ain't workin' no more tonight."

"I need your help, Leonora," I said.

She stared up at me with a slack-jawed weariness that suggested her first twenty years had been enough for a lifetime. An empty liquor bottle lay on its side next to the bed.

"I know you?" she asked.

"I met you about a month ago. You came to visit General Hooker."

She thought about that for several seconds.

"Fighting Joe," she said, with the hint of a smile. "I took the fight out of him."

"You told me where you lived when I met you that night."

She nodded as if vaguely remembering, and then looked around the squalid room with a vacant stare.

"You want me?" she asked, as a big tear rolled down her face.

"I would like to pay you for some information," I said.

She was having trouble focusing her eyes, and I realized she was drunk. "How much?"

"Four dollars," I said, which left me exactly one dollar for a hansom.

"All right," she said warily. "But give it to me first."

I took the bills out of my pocket and gave them to her.

"Have you ever visited General Hooker down in Falmouth?" I asked, after she had counted it.

"Where is that?" she said.

"With the army down in Virginia."

"No . . . I been invited a'course," she said. "I don't like boats."

"Do you know this girl?" I asked, showing her the drawing of Anya Hagel.

"Anya," she said, without hesitation.

"Anya had a young friend . . . very pretty . . . tall . . . long black hair," I said, holding my breath.

"Amelie," she said after a brief pause. "They're birds of paradise."

"Birds of paradise. What is that?"

"I've had it rough," she said, bleary-eyed.

"I'm sorry."

She got up from the bed and tried to smooth out the front of her stained dress.

"I think they're going to put me in the shows," she said, with an involuntary shudder.

"The shows?"

"They make you do things you wouldn't believe."

"Have you ever thought of going back to Moline?" I asked, remembering the name of the place she had said she was from.

Leonora gave me a bitter laugh.

"I'd rather go to the shows than go back there," she said.

"What are the birds of paradise?" I asked once more.

Her eyes came into focus again.

"You know where the castle is?" she asked.

I knew she meant the new Smithsonian Museum and nodded.

"It's a private club on the road that goes south from there down to the river," she said. "The house was built in the olden times. Only five girls work there. They all have their own rooms . . . not like this."

"What is the address?"

"You'll know it when you see it," she said. "But it ain't open to the public. You have to belong."

I thanked her and turned to leave.

"You want to have me . . . just you, I mean?" she asked, desperately trying to bring an alluring smile to her bruised and swollen mouth. "I could be good for you."

I had no heart to tell her no.

"I know where you live now," I said. "Thank you."

As I walked down the stairs, I remembered Patrick Mahoney saying, "Every whore has a story to tell. . . . It's hard for most of them to keep their stories straight. The simple fact is that most of them sell themselves because it's easy and it pays well . . . or at least it does until they get shopworn. Then it's a different story. They tend to age real fast."

Leonora had gotten shopworn in less than a month.

Chapter Fifteen

It was almost two o'clock in the morning when my hansom passed the Smithsonian castle and turned south onto the cobblestoned street that led down to the Potomac River. There were street lamps every hundred feet or so, revealing a succession of large, brick government buildings and warehouses, all with their windows dark. As we approached the river, I saw what had to be the Birds of Paradise club. It was the only building in the entire neighborhood with all the downstairs windows lit.

The place was unlike any other I had seen in the city, comprising an acre of ancient trees and plantings enclosed behind a white picket fence. Built in the early colonial times, the house was a sprawling, red-painted, three-story wooden structure, with two side wings, wrapping porches, and dormer windows sticking out from under the peaked roof.

I told the hansom driver to stop at the carriage park in front. Another coach was already there. As I watched, two men in evening clothes came out of the house and made their way slowly down the front path. One of them was obviously drunk and barely able to stand up. His compatriot assisted him into their coach.

"Should I wait?" asked my driver with a leer.

"No," I said, immediately regretting it.

There would be a long walk back to Mrs. Warden's if my hunt was unrewarded. The men on the path had left the front gate unlatched. I walked up to the front door, which was flanked by two large gas lamps, along with a brass knocker in the shape of a woman's leg.

As I lifted it to knock, the door swung open to reveal a heavyset black woman. Behind her the hallway led toward a large, well-lit parlor. A wide staircase rose up into the gloom of the next floor.

"I wish to see Amelie," I said.

The woman erupted into a thick patois of words that sounded like French but somehow weren't. Whatever she was trying to tell me, it was obvious she wanted me to leave.

"Amelie," I repeated slowly. "Amelie."

The woman began to close the door in my face. When I pushed back, she started yelling in the same strange language, all the while kicking out at me with her right shoe.

A shadowy figure appeared at the top of the stairs.

"Tante Louise," came a commanding voice. The old woman went silent as the figure came slowly down the stairs.

I recognized her as soon as she came into the light, although her long black hair was bound up in a towel. She was barefoot and wearing a loose-fitting white dressing robe.

"Should I know you?" she asked. Her voice was low and vibrant, and had a lilt to it.

"We almost met in Falmouth three nights ago," I said. "I saw you at General Hooker's birthday party. You were there with Anya Hagel."

The expression on her seemingly guileless face didn't change at the mention of the dead girl's name.

"She was murdered that same night," I said. "That is why I am here."

"I did not know," she replied.

"May I ask your full name?" I said.

"My name is Amelie Devereaux," she said.

She was as lovely as I remembered, with a delicate beauty that radiated both innocence and intelligence. It seemed inconceivable to me that she could be bought and sold. The thought of it made me angry.

"I know it is late, Miss Devereaux, but I must ask you some questions about Anya Hagel's death."

"You have proper identification?"

"Of course," I said, silently berating myself for not having already shown it to her. I withdrew my identification card from my tunic and handed it to her.

"John McKittredge, Captain, United States Army," she said, reading the words aloud. "Provost Marshal General's Department."

"I am investigating her murder," I said. "Obviously, you are an important witness to her final hours."

"Yes, I understand. Please excuse me, but I have just finished my bath," she said. "Would you come with me?"

As she turned, the dressing robe parted at her right side, revealing a slim, naked thigh. At the top of the stairs, we turned left down a well-lit hallway. I could hear low voices coming from behind the first door.

At the end of the hall, we went through an open doorway into a candlelit sitting room. Going straight to an armoire against the far wall, she pulled out several articles of clothing.

"Please wait here," she said, before disappearing through the door beyond and closing it behind her.

The room extended under the slope of the back roof of the house. There was a dormer window at each end. Under the side roof, a French door led out to a little second-story porch. A coal fire was burning in the grate of the fireplace. Two inviting chairs sat in front of it.

A massive walnut sleigh bed dominated one corner. Next to the armoire was a walnut dressing table with matching mirror. There were no pictures or other adornments on the white plaster walls. Aside from a leather suitcase that lay on top of the armoire, I saw no personal objects of any kind.

It was very warm in the room. I removed my greatcoat and slung it over one of the chairs. The door to the armoire was open. Most of the space inside was empty. She had fewer than a dozen dresses and other outfits. A drawer at the base of the armoire contained an assortment of neatly folded silk undergarments. I heard the far door open and turned to see her coming toward me, her hips barely moving as she walked.

"Does my room pass your inspection, Captain McKittredge?" she asked, with the lilting French accent.

"I'm surprised at how little you seem to have," I said coldly.

Her rose-high complexion seemed to color slightly before she responded.

"It is good not to have too many things," she replied. "Then it is not so hard to leave them."

She had changed into a simple white shift. It fell from her shoulders in the style of an old Greek engraving. At her neck she wore a band of lace-trimmed ivory satin. There were two matching satin bands around her wrists, each of them fastened by mother of pearl buttons.

Her hair was still wet, and it shined like polished ebony in the candlelight.

"I'm sorry to hear about Anya," she said. "She was very greedy, but I liked her."

"I gather it runs in your profession," I said, feeling another surge of anger.

She smiled at me as if I were a disobedient child and sat down in one of the chairs near the fire.

"So you are an investigator," she said, making the last word sound important.

I nodded.

"How old are you?" she asked.

"What does that matter?" I said.

"You seem quite young to be involved in a matter of such importance."

"I'm twenty-one."

"Then you must be good at what you do," she said.

"How old are you?" I asked.

"Eighteen," she said.

"Then you must be good at what you do," I said with sarcasm.

"I am," she replied evenly.

"When was the last time you saw Miss Hagel?"

"The night of General Hooker's party," she said.

"Why were you there?" I asked, not pausing to think.

Her brown eyes searched mine with a puckish air.

"Why would you ask me that question?" she said. "You already know what I am."

I tried not to look as stupid as I felt.

"Did you leave the birthday party together?" I said.

"Yes," she replied. "When it ended, we both went to a more . . . to a smaller party."

"And then?"

"I did not see her again after we arrived."

"Did you happen to meet a woman there named Mavis Bannister?"

"There were a number of other women there. By then the guests were not exchanging last names," she said.

"Where was this second party?" I asked next.

"At a country house . . . I have no idea where."

"And you never saw Miss Hagel after you arrived at the second party?"

There was a knock at the door. The girl called out, *"Entrez,"* and the old woman came into the room, gabbling something in the same strange language. The girl nodded but said nothing. The woman left.

"Do you have a watch?" she asked then.

I removed it from the pocket of my uniform blouse.

"It is two-fifteen," I said.

"One of my responsibilities is to see that the other girls are accounted for by now. One of them appears to be missing. Hopefully, it will take no more than ten minutes to determine why. Then I would be happy to answer the rest of your questions. Is that all right?"

I nodded.

"May I wait here?" I said.

"Of course."

As she was going out the door, she looked back and said, "My hired woman spent an hour heating water for my bath. Perhaps, while you are waiting, you would like one, too?"

I had not had a bath in a week. The mere thought of it seemed like a chimerical illusion. Then an image of Val crossed my mind, the omnipotent gray eyes glaring at me from his hospital bed. I was about to say no, when she added, "It's just that I can see you are very tired."

What could be the possible harm, I thought, already regretting my sanctimonious air. Who was I to judge anyone else, considering what I had become after Ball's Bluff?

"Thank you," I said. "I would appreciate that."

"Would you like something to drink? A glass of wine, perhaps?"

I shook my head.

"Well, the tub is right there in the trunk room," she said, pointing to the door beyond. "I will be back as soon as I can."

The trunk room was nothing more than an unheated windowless alcove under the raw undressed beams of the roof. In the light of a small oil lamp, I could actually see my breath in the air. It made the still steaming bathwater even more inviting.

The burnished copper tub was large enough for two people and shaped like an inverted top hat with most of the brim cut away. Quickly unbuttoning my uniform, I laid it on the table and stepped into the bath, sinking down into the soapy water until it completely covered my head.

Surfacing, I luxuriated in the cleansing heat, feeling it soak into my sore muscles and feet. After a few minutes, I lay my head against the back of the tub and closed my eyes.

"Are you still alive?" came a voice from a long way off.

I awoke with a start. She was standing in the open doorway of her bedroom.

"I fell asleep," I said.

"The water must be quite cold by now."

"It is," I said.

Through the shift she was wearing, I could see the clear outline of her figure against the light behind her. She showed no sign of moving, and I felt a sudden stab of arousal. The bathwater hid my growing erection.

"If you'll give me a minute . . ."

She smiled and shut the door.

I vigorously toweled myself dry. When I went to the table to put my uniform back on, it was no longer there. Obviously, she or someone else had taken it while I was asleep. Feeling like a fool again, I wrapped the towel around my waist and opened the door. She was sitting at the dressing table, brushing her hair, which ran all the way down to her waist.

"Tante Louise is pressing your uniform," she said, without turning to look at me. "It is a service of the house."

"Please have her bring it now," I said.

"Of course," she replied, pulling the bell rope that hung next to her table. "In the meantime, I put a robe for you behind the door."

As she glanced at the reflection of my image in the mirror, her eyes suddenly widened. It took me a moment to realize that she was staring at the network of livid weals on my abdomen. Quickly turning to the side, I returned to the trunk room.

A silk robe was hanging behind the door. I recognized it as soon as I removed it from the hook. The robe was emblazoned with beautifully embroidered gilt dragons on a field of purple. General Hooker had been wearing it when I met him for the first time in the lavatory of the Washington Insane Asylum.

I put the robe on, belted it, and went back into her room.

"Very becoming," she said, standing up from the table and coming slowly toward me.

"Who brought you down to Falmouth?" I asked, trying to control my new bout of rage.

She saw the anger in my face, and halted in the middle of the room.

"I would prefer not to answer that," she said.

"Who brought you down to Falmouth?" I repeated.

She stood motionless, her hands at her side.

"Was it General Hooker?" I asked.

"You sound like you know him."

"Well enough to know that I'm wearing his robe."

She could not hide the surprise in her eyes.

"And what about Laird Hawkinshield?"

She reacted as if I had slapped her.

"He owns this place," she said.

"And you?"

"No one owns me," she said almost defiantly.

"Did he bring you and Anya down to Falmouth?"

"You do not understand," she said, slowly shaking her head. "This involves men of . . . great reputation."

"Maybe I don't understand," I said, "but Anya was murdered down there. That should mean something to you."

I was shocked at the intensity of my desire for her.

She must have seen it in my eyes because she came toward me again, stopping less than a foot away. The crown of her head came up to my chin, and I could smell the fragrance of honeysuckle in her hair.

I forced myself to look directly into her eyes.

"Was it Hawkinshield?"

Her uplifted face was inches from mine.

"Do you have a girl?" she whispered, her full lips barely parted.

"Yes," I lied.

She raised her lips toward mine.

"Have you ever made love to her?"

I could feel the sweet ebb and flow of each breath as she stood close to me, our mouths almost touching. Then she pressed her lips lightly against my mine. They seemed to soften before slowly parting.

Her mouth tasted like warm caramel.

I felt my nervousness disappear as a wave of pure sensation rippled down my spine. She groaned something incoherently against my lips, stepping away only when there was a light knock at the door. The old woman came into the room carrying my newly pressed uniform over her arm. As if there was some silent signal between them, she laid it on the back of one of the chairs and left. Amelie followed her and locked the door. Picking up a brass candelabrum from the dressing table, she carried it over to the stand next to the bed. Then almost shyly, she came toward me again.

When we were facing one another, she loosened her shift. I watched it fall away. Except for the silk embroidered band around her neck, and the matching bands on her wrists, she stood naked before me.

Untying the belt of General Hooker's robe, she slid it down over my shoulders. I began to run my fingers through her thick hair, kissing the tendrils, and inhaling the scent of honeysuckle as her lips caressed the nipples of my chest, and slowly began to move lower. At the same time, the tips of her fingers grazed my thighs, and I felt a violent surge of desire.

With great tenderness, she began to kiss the scars that crisscrossed my belly. For the first time since I was wounded, I felt the shame of that dis-figurement start to ebb away. A moment later she took me into her mouth.

The needles of raw sensation were so intense that I had to pull her head away, not wanting this time with her to be over too quickly. Raising Amelie to her feet, I stroked her pear-shaped breasts before picking her up and placing her on the bed. Lying together, we kissed for a long time. I had never felt so alive.

Suddenly, I was inside her. She gently wrapped her slender arms and legs around me, and our bodies began to move as one. Her fingertips seemed everywhere at once, now tracing my neck and shoulders, a moment later my inner thighs. The edge of my desire swept away every trace of reserve or control. I was falling. As I exploded within her, my cheek happened to come to rest over her breast. While my own heart was pounding like I had just run a race, hers was beating slow and constant.

It was a shock to discover that as wondrous as each moment had been for me, she had been in a different place, perhaps an unreachable place, cloistered from the raw passion she had aroused in me. At the same time, she seemed to take pleasure in the act of giving me so much joy. As our bodies parted, she cocked her head to the side in a glance of momentary appraisal. Seeing the total satiation in my face, she smiled.

Something occurred to me at that moment and I laughed out loud.

"What is it?" she asked, confused.

"This is so crazy," I said.

"What is crazy?"

"I came here to question you about the murder."

"Yes, I know," she whispered, her face solemn in front of mine. "And I am telling you the truth when I say that I do not know who killed Anya."

"I believe you," I said, wanting it to be true, but by no means sure.

Perhaps, it will sound jaded, but at that moment I was too happy to even care. I fell asleep in Amelie's arms, my fingers stroking her hair.

In my dream I was back at Ball's Bluff. It was the same hideous night-mare I had endured so many times in the year since the battle. I again saw Johnny Harpswell at the moment the Confederate bullet ruined his hand-some face, with the force of it taking him over the gunwhale of the row-

boat. Only one thing was different. When I reached out for him as he
went over, this time I was able to grab him around the shoulders and drag
him back.

"I have you, Johnny!" I screamed.

I came awake to Amelie's gentle voice crooning in my ear.

"You are with me now," she said, her warm breast soft against my
cheek.

Afterward, she brought me a glass of icy water from the trunk room.
The coal fire had gone out by then, and it was cold enough to see our
breath in the light of the candle. It wavered as she lifted the covers to
rejoin me in bed. Then she burrowed in next to me under the massive
feather tick.

"Go to sleep," she murmured quietly, and I did.

When I awoke next, it was to the moaning complaint of the wind as it
whistled through the chimney. All the candles in the room had burned
out, but there was a misty, diffused light coming from the windows. Without waking Amelie, I got out of the bed and went over to the nearest
dormer. There were several inches of snow on the windowsill, and it was
still coming hard.

I wasn't sure whether the packet boats would be running down to Falmouth in the morning, but even then I knew that I needed to take Amelie
back down there with me. I believed her when she told me she didn't know
who killed Anya Hagel. At the same time, I was certain she had information that would shed light on the murder, perhaps without even knowing
it. Fully aware of my own limitations, I knew I wasn't the person to
uncover that information or fit it into the other pieces of the puzzle. With
the feelings I had for her, I was also reluctant to probe her relationship
with Hawkinshield. My hope was that Val would have recovered enough
to take over again by the time we reached Falmouth. I silently prayed once
more that his neck wasn't broken.

Shivering with cold, I returned to the bed. Amelie was lying on her
side, her right cheek resting on the palm of her hand like a little girl.
Under the comforter, her knees were drawn up, almost touching her stomach. I felt a rush of tenderness toward her that was as intense as any emo-

tion I had ever experienced. She stirred awake when I slipped back under the covers. Her eyes were like two dark moons in the murky light.

"What would you like me to call you?" she asked.

I remembered that she had only read my name once off the identity card.

"My name is John," I said, "but Kit is the name I grew up with. That's what most people call me."

"I would like to call you by the same name you cried out in the night," she murmured softly. "Johnny."

I liked it. By then she could have called me anything, and I would have liked it. I stared into her eyes for a long time.

"I want to help you, Amelie," I said, finally.

"Help me?" she said, with a sigh of resignation, as if she had heard the line before.

"Help you leave this life."

"Don't say that. You do not understand," she said.

"I understand."

"Do not try to be noble for me," she said. "There is no point."

"I'm not trying to be noble," I said. The next words came out by themselves. "I think I love you, Amelie."

"You don't know anything about me," she said harshly.

"I already know the worst," I said.

Her eyes rose slowly toward mine and stayed there.

"I was once the kind of girl you might have fallen in love with, Johnny . . . not now. Do not pretend that I am."

"I'm not pretending," I said.

"This is not a fairy tale," she said, putting her hand to my cheek, "and the truth is all I have left. I will not lie to please you. Find another whore to play that game for you if you must."

"It is not a game. I love you, Amelie."

Her guttural laugh was filled with contempt.

"Like so many other young soldiers I've known, you are merely in love with the romantic notion of falling in love. It is a fantasy . . . a delusion."

"I loved you from the moment I first saw you," I said, knowing even then how callow the words must have sounded to her.

"Tell me why," she demanded.

"What do you mean?"

"Tell me what you feel for me . . . aside from my having given you physical gratification."

"That's part of it. . . . But it's everything else, too. . . . I've never been so happy in my whole life as I am right now. I don't want this night to ever end."

Her frown slowly disappeared. She tousled my hair with her fingers.

"You are easily impressed, Johnny."

"And everything is suddenly beautiful," I said next.

"Everything?" she repeated, arching her eyebrows as if I was a lunatic.

"Yes, everything . . . even that pile of coal over there," I said, pointing to the hod next to the fireplace.

"At the moment it looks beautiful to me, too," she said with a shiver.

"Everything will be beautiful as long as you're with me," I said.

Was it genuine pleasure I saw in her eyes then?

"So you fell in love with me the first moment you saw me," she said.

"Yes," I said.

"Perhaps you are in love then."

"All I know is . . . you're the only woman I've ever met who made me feel this way."

"How many other women have you known like this?"

"None," I said. "But that doesn't matter. I know my heart."

She lay in my arms without moving.

"I read once that if two people love one another enough they become immortal, like the wind and the stars," she said.

"Perhaps we shall not die then," I whispered, kissing her again.

We made love a second time. This time I tried very hard to do everything she had done so expertly with her mouth and delicate fingers the first time. At first she didn't seem to know how to respond. Her heartbeat remained slow and steady, her body as taut as a coiled spring. When I was kissing her lips again, she seemed to fight herself for one long moment and then returned it with an unexpected hunger.

A parade of vivid images are still etched in my mind of what came next; the rain of kisses on her eyes and mouth and throat, my fingertips stroking her nipples and lower spine, while my tongue roved to every part of her body. Finally, I savored her slick abundance, which to me had the same earthy taste as an opiate. I lost track of time.

Suddenly, I felt a tremor go through her, followed by another. Her stomach contracted, and she came alive in my arms. She seemed to offer herself totally to me, with a yearning strength that matched my own. I could feel her heart racing in time with mine until finally she cried out as if in agony.

Whether it was from pain or pleasure, I do not know, but when I raised my face from hers, Amelie was weeping. She was clinging to me so hard that her fingernails had cut deeply into my shoulders. I held her until the tears stopped.

"Tu as touché mon coeur," she whispered.

Our lips were almost touching.

"What does that mean?" I asked.

"You touched my heart, Johnny," she said, her eyes huge against my own.

Later, we slept again.

I woke to discover that dawn had crept into the room through the dormer window. When I heard the sound of hard rain drumming against the tin roof on the side porch, I knew that the packet boats would be running again later that morning down to Falmouth.

As I lay there bathed in her warmth, I thought my happiness would never end. I could still smell the juices of her body on mine. I had never felt more alive. That was when I happened to glance at her left hand, which was lying palm up on the pillow.

In the course of our lovemaking, the silk and lace band around her left wrist had come unbuttoned, and I could see the edge of what appeared to be a deeply furrowed line on the surface of the skin beneath it. When I gently slid the band free, I saw two hideous scars there, each about two inches long, both across the vein.

Trying not to wake her, I released the pearl button that held the other band in place. The right wrist had a single scar track, also across the vein. She came awake as I was staring at it. For a moment there was a look of terror in her eyes at what I had seen. She twisted away for a moment and then stopped. I felt the sting of tears at the thought that she could have done such a thing to herself. She lay without moving for several minutes.

"Do not ask about it," she said, finally.

"I haven't asked," I said. "But . . ."

"Every whore has a story, didn't you know that?" she said, her words echoing those of Lieutenant Mahoney. Of course her refusal to explain the scars on her wrists just made me want to know the reason more.

"If you ask me, Johnny, I will tell you to leave right now," she said, with iron in her voice.

"I don't want to know about the past . . . only the future," I lied.

There was a knock at the door. I got up from the bed and walked over to unlock it. The old woman came into the room again, this time with a bucket of steaming water. She poured it into Amelie's pitcher and bowl, went to the fireplace to stoke the coal fire, and left without a word. When I rejoined Amelie in the bed, she was staring straight ahead, her eyes dark and mysterious.

"Amelie . . . I love you even more now," I said, moving to embrace her.

She pulled away from me.

"Do not ever try to be noble for me. I have been a whore now for almost two years. I have done things you could not even imagine . . . unspeakable things. And I have only myself to blame. No one else."

Something pressed hard against my heart. For the first time in my short life, I began to consider what love really was. When she got up to wash, I lay there listening to the rain hammering on the tin roof, wondering what would happen to us.

Chapter Sixteen

Amelie became furious when I asked her to accompany me back to Falmouth. It took me almost an hour to convince her to go with me. I tried to explain that her life was in danger from the man who had murdered Anya . . . that he probably knew where she lived and worked, and at some point would come after her.

"I am not afraid," she replied.

I then told her that if she didn't come with me, Val Burdette would order someone else from the Provost Marshal's Office to arrest her as a material witness and bring her down anyway.

"There are important men who would find it in their interest to prevent that from happening," she said.

It was only when I told her about Thomas and Daniel Beecham, and what had been done to them after they had the courage to report the discovery of Anya's body, that she began to listen.

"I will go with you," she said, when I finished telling their story.

I sent one of her servants back to the Provost Marshal's Office with a letter for Ted Connell, Val's deputy in the Prosecution Division. It included a short message to be wired to Val, telling him that I had found our witness and would soon be on my way back. I also told Ted to arrange passage for us on the next packet boat leaving for Falmouth, adding that because of my fears for her safety, he should secure a private stateroom for us if at all possible.

We were having breakfast downstairs in the dining room when someone knocked at the front door. The old woman went to answer it, returning a minute later to whisper something to Amelie.

"It is a federal officer," she said. "He is asking for you."

I found Ted Connell waiting in the foyer. An almost lascivious smile was playing on his mouth as I came toward him.

"I envy your investigative technique, Kit," he said.

"Believe it or not, this was all in the line of duty," I replied.

"Well, whatever you've done, it has stirred up a real hornet's nest at the War Department," he said, his intelligent blue eyes almost glowing with excitement. "When I arrived this morning, there was a caravan of wagons parked along Seventeenth Street. The way they are moving records out of the Quartermaster General's Office, you would think the Rebel barbarians are at the gates."

"Not the Rebels," I said, "Val and Sam."

Ted nodded in understanding. He then told me that he had secured space for us on a boat that was taking members of the general staff down to Falmouth later that afternoon. Although every billet was taken, he had even managed to reserve a small cabin for Amelie.

"Good luck, my friend," he said, with a casual salute. "You're going to need it."

Later that morning, as I waited for the coach that would take us to the navy yard, I sat by one of the mullioned windows facing the Potomac River and thought about the extraordinary change that had just taken place in my life. Amelie's impact on me had been as elemental as air and water. Everything in the world outside that window—the color of the river and the sky, the sight and sound of the people walking along the shoreline—all of it seemed infinitely more vivid. Whatever happened, I knew that my life would never be the same.

Shortly after twelve, an army coach pulled up at the stand in front of the house. There were two enlisted men on the box and I went out to tell them to wait. When I walked back upstairs, Amelie was wearing a fitted green organdy dress that buttoned at the neck and wrists, along with a matching green cape lined with lamb's wool. As I picked up her valise, she came over and stopped in front of me. For several moments she stood gazing up at my face, as if trying to memorize it.

Then she drew my head down, kissed me on the mouth, and said, "Do not try to help me, Johnny."

At the front door she stopped to talk to the strange old woman she called Tante Louise. I carried Amelie's valise out to the coach and stowed it in the boot. I knew she was coming when I happened to look up at the soldiers on the box. Their eyes were riveted on her as she came toward us down the path.

The Amelie Devereaux who arrived at the curb acted as if we were meeting for the first time. At first I assumed it was because the soldiers' stares had made her uncomfortable. As soon as we were on our way, I took her in my arms again and kissed her. Amelie's lips were cold and lifeless. When I pulled away, she turned to look out the window, saying nothing the rest of the way to the navy yard.

We arrived at the wharf to the screams of newsboys hawking a late edition of the *Washington Evening Star*. ATTACK IMMINENT was the banner headline. "Burnside on the Move," read the first paragraph underneath it.

There was a frenzy of activity in the harbor. A dozen ships were under steam, all waiting to make their way into the channel. We waited in line to board our packet boat, which was already filled to overflowing with officers going down to join their commands. They stood along the rails, cheering excitedly at the news that we were finally going into battle again.

Gaily colored pennants were flying from the halyards above the wheelhouse. They snapped loudly in the brisk wind that greeted us at the water's edge. At the gangplank, a navy purser checked the passenger manifest after I gave him my name. When he asked Amelie if she was my wife, she lowered her eyes in embarrassment. After he gave us approval to board, I led her through the crush of officers lining the deck and down the passageway to our assigned cabin.

A few minutes later, I felt the shudder of the engines as the packet boat got underway. It was very quiet in the cabin, which contained just a single berth along with a copper washstand, pitcher and bowl, and a side chair. Amelie removed her cape and sat down in the chair.

Confused at her abrupt change toward me, I gazed out through the small porthole as an empty hospital ship headed into the channel ahead of us. The cold gray air floated past like a smoky haze, and I could hear the sound of the water lapping against the hull as we picked up speed.

As a precaution against the remote possibility that Anya's killer might somehow be on the ship, we remained inside the cabin for the first three hours of the voyage. When she needed to relieve herself, I waited outside in the passageway while she used the captain's small lavatory.

Back inside the cabin, the minutes passed very slowly because we no longer seemed to have anything to say to one another. Once or twice I tried to start a conversation, but it was obvious from her curt replies that she had no interest in talking. At one point she happened to catch me gazing at her, and a look of exasperation came over her face.

"Why are you staring at me?" she demanded crossly.

"Because you are so lovely," I said.

She shook her head angrily as if I had lost my senses. Perhaps I should have recognized just how nervous she was at the thought of what might be waiting for her in Falmouth. As darkness fell over the bay, I lit the small oil lamp that was bracketed to the cabin bulkhead.

It was well into the evening when I asked her for the third or fourth time if she wanted something to eat. Maybe it was just to humor me, but she finally said that she would enjoy a cup of tea. Stepping out of the cabin, I found a steward in the passageway, explained my situation, and asked him to bring us whatever was being served for the evening meal, along with a pot of tea.

He promised to bring back a tray for us. When almost an hour had gone by without his return, I concluded that he had been ordered somewhere else by more senior officers. Telling Amelie to lock the cabin door behind me, I started for the galley.

As I reached the end of the first passageway, someone called out, "McKittredge." A tall, gangly major was standing by the deck railing and looking straight at me. His face was vaguely familiar, but I had no idea who he was until he came toward me with an open smile, revealing a set of yellow horse teeth. It was then that I remembered him as one of General Hooker's staff officers. The last time I had seen him had been the night of the general's birthday party.

"It's Posey, old man," he said, extending his hand. "I thought it was you."

Not wanting to appear impolite, I took the time to shake his hand before continuing down the passageway toward the galley. I was irritated to discover that he was following me.

"I say . . . hold on there," he called after me, and I stopped to let him catch up.

"I have the latest news on our troop movements," he said, peering at me excitedly, as if he had just discovered the Rosetta stone. "And Fighting Joe is right in the thick of it."

I found it strange that a general staff officer would be remotely interested in briefing someone from the Provost Marshal's Office on the army's tactical maneuvers. I ascribed it to the fact that he was alone and anxious to share the excitement of the moment with someone he knew, if only vaguely.

"Sorry, but I have something important to do," I said, as we reached the galley.

I quickly filled a metal tray with the simple fare that was being offered, transferred a quart of hot tea from one of the copper pots into a tin pitcher, and turned around to head back to our cabin. I had not gone twenty feet when Posey appeared in front of me again.

"How about joining me in the wardroom for some buttered rum?" he said, exposing his teeth again in a ghastly yellow smile. "General Hooker thinks very highly of you, you know. He raises your name every time the staff fails him . . . which happens almost every day."

He had extended his arm behind my back and was trying to steer me toward the wardroom when I happened to see our steward coming toward us down the passageway. I asked him what had happened to our food.

"Why . . . your officer friend told me that he would bring it to you," he said in obvious confusion. "That was almost an hour ago."

When a knowing grin appeared on Posey's ugly face, I realized that he had been told to keep me occupied.

"You bastard," I said.

Hurling the tray of food at him, I started back to Amelie on the run.

Coming down the passageway, I could hear raised voices coming from inside the cabin. The door was locked, but the frame of the door was made of thinly milled pine. When I hurled my full weight against it, the lock shattered and the door flew open.

I recognized the man on top of her at first glance. Major Bannister's face was in profile, his broad powerful body covering hers on the single berth. The hem of her dress was up above her waist. Her torn undergarments lay on the floor. She was pleading with him to stop.

He was like a dead weight when I tried to drag him off her and completely oblivious to my actions. I grabbed my revolver from its holster and swung the barrel at his head. He was desperately grappling to kiss her as I swung, and it only grazed his temple. Bellowing in rage, he scrambled up and struck out at me with his right fist, knocking the gun from my hand.

"What the hell is wrong with you?" he yelled. "So we played a little game on you . . . so what . . . she's public property."

Amelie was trying to sit up in the berth, her legs bare to the thighs.

The blood was hammering in my ears. I clenched and unclenched my fists as he stood there in front of me.

"Ask her . . . She's had me before . . . plenty of times, and not just . . ."

I hit him with all the rage that had been building up inside me over the previous two days. It wasn't just for what they had all done to her. It was for Ginevra Hale and for Leonora, too.

My first blow split his mouth open, but it didn't put him down. He was shorter than me by several inches, but as broad as a tree. Making low, snuffling noises, he came at me like a demented bull, delivering a wild blow that battered the side of my nose. I felt the warmth running down my chin as I shoved him to the side. He fell against the copper washstand, smashing the pitcher and bowl, before slowly regaining his feet.

I was no longer aware of Amelie even being there. I saw nothing in front of me except his thick arms and immense head. It was the same blind rage I had experienced at Ball's Bluff. As he came at me again with another wild swing, I hit him flush on the side of his jaw with a right hand that had all the weight of my legs behind it. It landed with a sickening crunch, and he dropped to his knees before falling backward upon his lower legs, his arms splayed out at his sides.

My eyes came to rest on the revolver that was lying on the floor at his feet. As if in a fevered dream, I picked it up, cocked it, and calmly lowered the barrel to his left temple.

"Johnny!" I heard her scream and came back to my senses.

I slowly let the hammer slide forward, and put the revolver back in its holster. Grasping him under the shoulders, I dragged him out of the cabin and propped him against the outer bulkhead. From the crooked way his jaw was hanging, I knew it was broken.

Standing up again, I looked down the passageway. Every cabin door was open. A dozen staff officers were staring back at me from the safety of their compartments. I'm not sure what they saw in my eyes, but within a few seconds, every face had disappeared.

I found Posey in the wardroom where I had left him. He was using a rag to clean the food stains off his uniform blouse when he looked up and saw me bearing down on him. With a stab of fear in his eyes, he leaped to his feet and started for the other doorway. When I caught up and grabbed him by the shoulder, he let out a shrill, bleating noise before going limp. The other officers in the smoky wardroom looked up at us in curiosity.

"Come with me," I said hoarsely.

Although Posey outranked me, he came along as meekly as a private facing drill punishment. Back at the companionway, Bannister was crawling along the deck on his hands and knees, still disoriented. I left Posey there to help him and went back to my cabin. Amelie was sitting on the berth, staring up at me as I came in. I braced the door shut by propping the back of the chair under the knob and sat down next to her.

My stomach felt like it was full of broken glass, and I tried to ease the pain by massaging it with my fingers. Seeing the agony I was in, she gently placed her hand over mine, but I pushed it away.

For several minutes we sat there together in silence. My breathing finally returned to normal, and the pain slowly began to ease. I could again hear the regular throbbing of the steam engine below us, as well as the other familiar noises aboard ship.

There were at least five more hours to go before we reached Aquia

Creek. I went looking for the steward and found him in the next passageway. He was very apologetic about what had happened and said that he would bring us supper from the crew's wardroom. We ate in silence.

In the middle of the meal, I found that I no longer had the energy to lift the glass to my mouth. Everything I had gone through since arriving in Washington two days earlier was finally catching up to me. Completely exhausted, I lay down in the berth and turned my face to the wall.

Some time later I awoke to the gentle throb of the engines, and the reassuring surge of water under the keel. For a moment I dreamed it was long before the war, and I was in midpassage from our island over to the mainland. Then, I remembered where I was.

The bulkhead walls were so thin that I could listen to the officers in the adjoining compartments as they discussed the upcoming battle, and whether it might signal the end of the war.

Amelie had extinguished the oil lamp on the wall and covered me with a woolen blanket. The only illumination in the cabin came from the rippling reflection of the boat's running lights through the glass porthole. Although I still lay on my side facing the wall, I had the strong impression that I was alone in the room. The thought that she might actually have gone struck me like a fresh wound.

Rolling away from the wall, I turned my head to find her face just a few inches from my own, her big dark eyes gazing into mine. Then her mouth was pressing lightly against my bruised lips.

"Am I hurting you?" she whispered.

"No," I said.

Maybe it was because she pitied me. Maybe she realized how honest my feelings were for her. I don't know what was going through her mind, but when she pulled back for a moment, there was a sloe-eyed sensuality to the cast of her face. I hated it. And I desired it. I felt my passion for her flow through me again like a summer storm. She had already removed her green organdy dress and was wearing only the sheer white shift.

Then she was in my arms again, her soft kisses a prelude to a seeking, opening, reaching, and giving, before we finally came together. Her moaning became louder and louder, as if it was part of a painful and necessary release.

Suddenly I noticed that the conversation had ceased in the cabins on both sides of ours. I imagined the other officers listening to our lovemaking with their ears pressed against the bulkhead walls.

"Hush, my darling," I whispered.

Amelie seemed oblivious to my efforts to quiet her. When she arched her head back and let out a loud sob, I covered her mouth with mine to stifle her cries. Our bodies began to move in a slow, steady rhythm. For a long time she continued to come at me with a gentle strength, as if her lovemaking could help to restore my physical well-being. And it did, although something strange happened while we lay locked together in one another's arms.

At one point I found myself wondering if she was making love to me, or whether it was to another lover from the many she had known, perhaps Laird Hawkinshield or General Hooker, or even some faceless being who completed her passionate needs but could have been anyone. Then I was carried away by a rush of pure desire. It took me to a place that harbored no questions or doubts.

Chapter Seventeen

Dawn had not yet broken when the packet boat swung out of the channel and nosed in toward the docks at Aquia Creek. A bitter wind greeted us as we emerged from the passageway and gazed out onto the sprawling wharf, which was lit by hundreds of torches, lanterns, and fire-pots. In the glaring light, men were rushing in every direction like maddened ants, crisscrossing between small mountains of crated food and ammunition.

"We're across the Rappahannock!" a fat supply sergeant hollered from the dock as our bow and stern lines were heaved across the open water and we were pulled to the jetty. His words caused an immediate roar of approval from the throng of officers lining the rails of the packet boat.

"Hurrah for Burnside!" an officer shouted back. He must have been a member of Burnside's staff, because no one else took up the cry.

Next to us on the wharf, a towering crane was roosting over the hold of a freight schooner. As we watched, it slowly extracted a massive siege cannon. Suddenly, a piercing shriek rent the night sky, overriding the noise of the straining cables and shouting stevedores.

Farther down the wharf, the first in a train of hospital wagons was being unloaded alongside a hospital ship. One of its occupants was screaming in agony, accompanied by a more subdued chorus of groans and cries from those less grievously wounded. Their wailing put a damper on the excitement of the officers disembarking ahead of us. Major Bannister and his friend Posey were nowhere in sight.

I found space for Amelie and me in the back of a Pittsburgh wagon. It was loaded with ammunition and heading down to Falmouth. The canvas canopy over the freight bed gave us protection from the raw wind, and several packing blankets provided a small measure of warmth. Amelie soon fell asleep to the slow, rocking motion of the wagon.

The road was crowded with vehicles of every shape and size, all heading south. We had gone about a mile when the first hint of light illumined the eastern sky. By then, I could hear the echoing thunder of siege guns four miles farther south along the Rappahannock.

The sickly gray dawn revealed the extent of the desolation around us. In just the few days since my last visit, our army had succeeded in stripping the countryside bare. All the trees for miles around were reduced to stumps, the logs being used to corduroy the muddy roads and provide fuel and shelter to the army.

Every house, barn, and outbuilding along the road had suffered a similar fate. The army had dismantled them, leaving just the foundations and chimneys standing forlornly in the middle of the raw wasteland. The only fences still remaining were made of piled stones. Nothing alive stirred on the plain.

As we got closer to Falmouth, the road became little more than a vast wallow. Although our engineering battalions had tried to reinforce the lowest places, the constant churning of the wheels of the heavy freight wagons made it a roiling quagmire of mud and skewed logs.

When we passed the contraband camps where I had first met Mr. Beecham and his son, Daniel, Amelie stirred from sleep for the first time. The wretched encampment had grown much larger since I had last seen it. Some of the later arrivals must have been skilled carpenters because there were now several well-constructed structures interspersed with the mud hovels.

The rest of the landscape had changed, too. The small evergreen forest where the Beechams had gone to cut down fir boughs for their shelter had entirely disappeared. Like the countryside we had already passed, the terrain around the contraband camps was as bleak as the surface of the moon.

A slim, young black man was standing alongside the road as we passed the last of the blighted dwellings. He was around my age and dressed in a miserable assortment of rags, yet somehow he retained a certain dignity in the midst of the squalor surrounding him.

Amelie was watching him so intently that at first I wondered whether he might be someone she knew. The thought persisted when I realized that the young man was staring back at her with equal intensity. For a moment I thought he was actually going to run after us, but then he turned and slowly began trudging back toward one of the mud shelters.

I felt Amelie's hand come into mine.

We rode next through the vast encampments of the Army of the Potomac. For almost two miles, the seemingly endless vista of Sibley tents stood empty, the tent covers flapping pathetically in the wind. Smoke still drifted from the mud chimneys of a few, but all the men had moved up toward the fighting.

As if to remind us of where they had gone, another train of hospital wagons came bumping and jostling toward us from the direction of Fredericksburg. By then the road was choked with a succession of military caravans heading toward the battle, and the hospital wagons were forced to navigate a route through the rutted and bumpy pastures adjoining it. With each bone-jarring jolt, their human burden let out a collective refrain of the tortured cries I remembered so well.

As we approached the Rappahannock River, a cavalry squadron dressed in tunics with canary yellow trim overtook us in full gallop, their horses scattering clods of mud as they headed toward the front. When our wagon came over the next rise, I saw the first massed army formations preparing for the main attack.

The flat plain ahead of us was filled with men in blue. They blended into the featureless landscape as far as the eye could see, maybe twenty thousand of them spread out in the fields and pastures on both sides of the road. Their combined voices sounded like roaring surf as we rode past.

At the head of each brigade, a colorful pennant snapped tautly in the wind. The brigades were stripped down to their essential gear of rifles, cartridge boxes, and canteens. The men's field packs were stacked in massive piles next to the individual regiments, waiting to be picked up by army teamsters and hauled after them. I wondered whether the packs would be going south toward Richmond after the battle or back where they had come from.

Some of the men were already eating their field rations. Others lay asleep on their sides and backs on the cold ground. In some places they were so tightly packed that there was no room to sit down.

As the endless sea of faces flashed past, I noted a big difference between these soldiers and the ones I had gone into battle with more than a year earlier. Back then there were easy smiles on the men's faces as we prepared to take the high ground at Ball's Bluff. None of us knew what to expect. We thought we were invincible. But in the wake of all the military disasters that had taken place since, these men had no illusions left about what they would soon be facing. There was no banter in them. They looked hard and ready.

We were passing the seemingly endless ranks of the Second Corps when a large black brougham came up fast behind us. The man on the box was screaming a string of obscenities as he cracked his whip repeatedly over the eight-horse team. In the few seconds it took for the coach to hurtle past, I had a split-second glimpse of Gen. Dan Sickles in the rear seat next to the window. He was gesturing angrily at the man sitting next to him. It was Laird Hawkinshield. Neither looked up as the carriage raced past. Amelie was staring out at the men in the fields and never saw them.

As we neared the river, our teamster yelled back that he would soon be leaving the main road to ferry his supplies farther down the Rappahannock. I called on him to stop at the brick-columned entrance to General Hathaway's headquarters, which was the place I had last seen Val.

The soldiers of Gen. Thomas Meagher's Irish Brigade filled the parklike grounds on both sides of the gravel driveway heading up to the mansion house. The proud Gaelic cast to their faces and their green flags made them immediately recognizable. As we started through their ranks, I remembered their incomparable bravery along the sunken road at Antietam. Now, as they waited to cross the river, I saw that all the men had pinned little sprigs of evergreen on their caps.

From the moment I helped Amelie down from the back of the wagon, she drew the stares of every man within sight. The closest ones stopped whatever they were doing and grew quiet as she came past them up the drive. It was as if a silent message was being carried up the line from one face to the next.

Perhaps she reminded some of them of a sweetheart back home. For others, it might have been a wife, a sister, or a lover. All of them seemed to share an innocent longing as they took in her delicate beauty and physical grace. I knew that for many of those Irish boys, Amelie would be the last woman they would ever see.

"She's wearin' the colors!" one of them suddenly shouted out, as he noticed her dark green cape and emerald organdy dress.

"It's our lucky day," came back another.

When she smiled at them, the men erupted in a resounding cheer.

As we approached the mansion, two more brigades were forming up beyond the house to move across the river for the main attack. It struck me that somewhere in that vast crowd of officers and men, the murderer of Anya Hagel might be watching us at that very moment, perhaps fearing his discovery if Amelie was not permanently silenced.

I had to find a safe place for her right away. My first thought was to take her straight to Sam's office in the mansion, but there was a small horde of general staff officers streaming in and out of the front portico, any one of whom could also have been the murderer or an accomplice.

I thought of one place where the killer could not be and headed for the long brick stables where the newspapermen were billeted. There I hoped to find Phil Larrabee, who had sketched the likeness of Anya Hagel for me.

I found him shaving with a straight razor in the horse stall that had been assigned to him. Phil was wearing crimson long johns and standing in front of a small hand mirror that was wedged between the iron rungs of a hayrack. When he looked up and saw Amelie standing next to me, his hand jerked uncontrollably upward. For a moment I thought he had sliced off part of his nose, but it had only grazed the skin. He pressed a hand towel against the cut to stanch the bleeding.

"Your first honorable wound, Phil," I said, as he nervously grabbed his monogrammed bathrobe from the cot and wrapped it around his scrawny shoulders.

"This is Amelie Devereaux," I said.

"Yes . . . well, of course," he replied, completely flustered.

While he continued to dab at his bleeding nose, I explained that Amelie was an important witness in the murder of the girl whose picture he had sketched for me, and that she needed to remain out of sight until I could find Val Burdette.

"She is in serious danger here, Phil," I said.

He was having a problem looking at her directly for more than a second at a time.

"Of course . . . glad to help her," he said, with a besotted smile.

I pulled Amelie aside.

"Do not leave for any reason until I come back for you," I whispered, taking her hand for a moment. "Promise me that you will stay here."

"I will," she said.

As I was walking away, Phil called after me, his nose now covered by a tiny wedge of cheesecloth.

"They say the battle is going to start soon, Kit," he said, as if unsure whether that was more important than his current assignment. "Will you be back before then?"

I smiled at him and nodded.

Back outside I buttoned my greatcoat against the wind, and headed across the grounds to the field hospital. It was on the far side of the formal gardens, which were now filled with wounded. More than a hundred men were laid out on litters in uneven rows. Their uniforms were soaked, and the smell of wet wool hung over them.

I went to the tent where I had last seen Val, but he was no longer there. Three wounded officers were occupying the space where his lone cot had stood. A strange object was lying on the ground in the rear corner of the tent. It took me a moment to recognize it as the contraption that had been used to immobilize Val's neck. The metal struts appeared to be bent in half. I went looking for his doctor and found him talking to another surgeon in front of one of the surgical tents.

"Can you tell me where to find Colonel Burdette?" I asked.

A glum look of defeat came over the doctor's face, and my mind took in the possibility that Val had died or he was lying paralyzed in one of the hospital ships at Aquia Creek.

"I have no idea," he said.

"Was his neck broken?" I asked.

A streak of red flared in his cheeks.

"I wish I had broken it myself," he said, with open hostility. "The night before last he convinced a young orderly to remove his restraints. As soon as he was free, he destroyed a very expensive piece of hospital equipment. We haven't seen him since."

I walked over to General Hathaway's office in the mansion. Sam was seated in his wheelchair and writing out an order. He looked exhausted, and there was a grayish yellow pallor to his cheeks. Two deep purple half moons sagged beneath his eyes like ugly bruises. He seemed to have aged a dozen years in the short time I had known him.

"It never ends," he said, looking up from his paper, "putrefied meat, boots without heels, buckles that do not clasp. The latest outrage involves musket rounds that are too large to ram down the muzzle. The predators feed on this army like locusts."

When I told him what the doctor had said, he leaned back and gave me a rare smile.

"Val is fine," he said, taking off his rimless spectacles and rubbing his temples. "The doctors would have had him in their clutches for weeks if he hadn't escaped."

Billy Osceola came in from the hallway with a dispatch from the Provost Marshal's Office in Washington. Sam read the message and initialed it. Then he congratulated me on our successful mission to retrieve the shipping manifests.

"Thanks to you we were able to replace every defective carriage," he said. "And we are going to need all our guns today. It is a disaster in the making, I'm afraid."

I had never seen him look so defeated.

"Anyway, Kit, I put you in for another commendation. A great number of men owe you their lives."

"Billy made the difference," I said. "He was the one who actually recovered the files."

The young Seminole had gone to one of the windows facing the river and was staring into the fog. Hearing his name mentioned, he glanced over at us. Sam shook his head in a kindly way.

"Billy told me how you managed it all, and I know it could not have been easy for a combat soldier. In the last year I've learned that wars aren't just fought with rifles and cannon. With men like Congressman Hawkinshield running things back in Washington, we must learn to fight on their terms."

The rattle of federal drums echoed toward us from across the river.

"Our attack is set for eleven," he said, looking toward the mantle clock. "This fog should actually help us, but knowing Burnside, he will probably wait for it to burn off before sending the boys up to attack those heights. It wouldn't comport with his sense of fair play."

The bitterness in his voice was tangible.

"When did we finally get across?" I asked.

"He ordered the pontoon bridges to be deployed two days ago. Of course, by then they were dug in over there and waiting for us . . . Barksdale's Mississippi boys. They had a turkey shoot for most of the first day. Burnside then ordered the waterfront leveled with artillery fire. That didn't drive them off either. It took a river assault to finally dislodge them. Your old regiment was part of it."

"The Twentieth Massachusetts?" I asked.

He nodded and said, "They took heavy casualties like all the other regiments. Several hundred, at least."

I thought of the friends I still had in the Twentieth and wondered whether they had survived the assault. A wave of raw anger swept over me at the waste of so many men when the army could have crossed the river weeks earlier with no opposition at all.

"I need to find Val," I said.

"He is already across the river. We've had serious problems with looting, even with veteran soldiers. The army is turning into a mob, Kit. Many of the regiments haven't been paid in months . . . at the same time, men like Hawkinshield steal millions. On top of it all, the men know that their lives are being spent like donkeys."

I looked away from the implacable fury in his eyes.

"Is there a chance today?"

"If you are prone to believe in miracles," said Sam.

I left to look for Val, walking down to the riverbank, which was only a hundred feet below the house. Two artillery batteries were deployed in the terraced gardens, the guns aimed toward the town. Their caisson wheels had churned the flowerbeds into muddy paste.

At the foot of the hill was one of the new pontoon bridges. The boats that supported it were about twenty feet long. They had been set in position side by side across the width of the river and then covered with sections of rough planking.

The lead element of an infantry brigade was moving across the bridge in two files. The rest of it snaked all the way back up the hill past the mansion house. A brigadier general stood at the foot of the bridge, calling out to his men to keep moving. Thick fog hung over the Rappahannock, masking the other side of the river from my view.

I heard the rattle of hoofbeats on the timber planking and saw a rider cantering toward us from the other side, his horse smartly picking its way between the two files of infantry. He reined up a few feet away from the brigade commander.

"General French sends his compliments, sir," he said, raising the flat of his hand to his cap. "He asks that you move your brigade through the town as quickly as possible and form up with the rest of the division on the plain below the heights."

Without waiting for a reply, the courier saluted again and urged his big horse forward, leaping it across the bank and heading up the hill toward the mansion. I glanced at my watch. It was already nearing ten. Showing my provost marshal's identification to the officer controlling the bridge, I started across toward Fredericksburg.

What remained of the waterfront buildings on the other side of the Rappahannock began to materialize out of the mist when I was halfway across. Our guns had done a remarkable job of battering what had once been imposing brick dwellings built during the earliest colonial times into piles of rubble.

A steep, slippery bank awaited me on the other side of the river. Army engineers had strung ropes down to the edge of the pontoon bridge so that the troops could pull themselves up to higher ground, and I used one to gain purchase. From the fog-shrouded plain off to the left, I heard the familiar metallic snap and locking noises of men fixing bayonets to the barrels of their rifles. In the distance a Confederate bugle sounded, sharp and clear.

A cobblestoned street led toward the city, and I followed it into the mist. The first buildings I passed had all been hit hard by our guns across the river. In the business district, the buildings were still intact, but every door had been smashed in and most of the windows were gone.

A little farther on, I was brought up short by what appeared to be a small mountain rising from the middle of the street. It extended fully ten feet into the air and boasted half the colors of the rainbow. The swirling mist dissipated long enough for me to see that the mountain was made up of household objects, including beds and tables, gilt-framed oil paintings, clocks, chairs, mirrors, and great heaps of clothing of every hue and description. A grand piano with elephant-sized legs was resting on its back along the nearest edge.

"All looters are to be arrested on sight, Lieutenant," came a familiar voice through the mist on the other side.

"How will we know which ones they are?" echoed a younger voice, plaintively.

"If a soldier is carrying a Chippendale chair in his arms and is wearing women's undergarments over his uniform like this man, he qualifies."

"Yes, sir," conceded the younger voice.

I stepped around the edge of the little mountain to see a detachment of provost guards surrounding several dozen disarmed infantrymen. One of them was wearing a woman's brassiere over his uniform blouse. The one next to him had on a fur coat and a feathered hat. They were both help-lessly drunk.

Towering above them all was the vast bulk of Val Burdette, his tangled mane of ash-colored hair giving him a visage akin to the Gorgon Medusa. A lieutenant stood next to him, watching as one of the arrested soldiers relieved himself in the street. Hearing my boots on the shattered paving stones, Val looked up and saw me. For a second I thought his face revealed a look of relief or even pleasure. If so, it was gone a moment later.

"Take over here, Lieutenant," he said.

"Yes, sir," said the young officer.

"So your neck . . ." I began as he came toward me.

"Is still connected to my head, no thanks to you," he said coldly. "I was incarcerated in that torture harness for eighteen hours."

"But the doctor said . . ."

"The doctor is a fraud. He knows as much about the medical arts as you do about love," he said without a pause.

"Love?"

"Yes, you have fallen, I see. Its fatuity is stamped on your face."

I had no response.

"Where is she?" he asked.

"I left her with a friend of mine . . . one of the journalists billeted in the stables."

"At least that was intelligent. Does anyone else know she is here?"

"Not officially," I said, as we began walking back across the pontoon bridge. "But she draws notice wherever she goes."

A squadron of cavalry came clattering across the bridge from the opposite direction, making the rough planking under our feet rock back and forth like a floating cork. The riders stared incredulously at Val as they rumbled past us.

"Just as you do," I added, as he scowled back at me.

"You did a good job in Washington, Kit," he said next. "Just continue to think with your head instead of that brain between your legs."

"That is not a brain," I said.

"We shall see."

On the way back to the stables, I brought him up to date on everything I had learned in Washington, including the fact that Congressman Hawkinshield owned the club where Anya Hagel had worked.

"So the investigations do intersect," he said, after I told him of having seen Hawkinshield in the coach with General Sickles, and that Sickles had appeared terribly angry with him.

"Friends in feast, enemies in famine," he added, as we passed through the oncoming ranks of Meagher's Irish Brigade. They were marching in parade step, as if heading up Broadway in the middle of the Independence Day parade.

"Sam has made an important breakthrough in the corruption investigation," said Val. "After we took Major Duval, two colonels in the Quartermaster General's Corps began to cooperate. They have directly implicated Hawkinshield in three fraudulent schemes, including the one involving your friend Simon Silbernagel. If Hawkinshield is still here, we will arrest him."

When we arrived at the stable block, Phil Larrabee was standing guard in front of his stall, his nose encased in a white plaster patch. Seeing Val coming toward him out of the shadows, he pulled a derringer from his greatcoat pocket and pointed it at him.

"It's me, Phil," I said, coming up behind.

"You have to cock that weapon before you can fire it, young man," said Val, stepping past him into the horse stall.

Amelie was sitting on Phil's cot with one of his books open on her lap. She smiled when she saw me coming in after Val. He stared down at her for several seconds without saying a word. In the six months I had worked for him, I had seen powerful men wilt under that stare. Amelie returned it in kind, her large brown eyes unwavering. Finally, he sat down on the stool next to the bed.

"This is no time for formalities," he said, speaking so softly that I could barely hear his words. "You were brought down here three nights ago to attend a party. Who made the arrangements for your . . . services?"

Her eyes strayed from Val's to mine. I could feel someone breathing on the back of my neck, and turned to find Phil peering over my shoulder, his eyes filled with curiosity.

"Perhaps you gentlemen would allow Miss Devereaux and me a few minutes alone," said Val, with a glare.

Phil and I walked outside to the rumble of more ammunition wagons coming up the drive. We watched as they tore up the formal gardens on their way to the artillery emplacements that ringed the estate. In the apple grove behind the stables, a cooking tent had been set up next to the field hospital. Soldiers in white aprons were boiling coffee in vats over open fires. Off to our right, another of Hooker's infantry divisions slowly inched its way across the grounds toward the pontoon bridge below the mansion house.

When Phil removed a cigar from the leather case in his coat, I saw that his hand was shaking in barely suppressed excitement. Taking care not to dislodge the plaster on his nose, he carefully lit the cigar and took a long puff.

"She is the most wonderful girl I've ever met, Kit," he suddenly blurted, the words pouring out in a rushing stream. "And certainly the loveliest. I have to assume she went to finishing school in Paris, her French is impeccable. Is she eligible?"

Phil Larrabee was the scion of a prominent Boston family. One of his ancestors had supposedly drafted the Magna Carta. The first question he always asked after meeting a woman who captured his imagination was about her bloodlines—whether she was blue-blooded enough to measure up to becoming a Larrabee. Of course, her finishing school pedigree was important, too.

I wondered what his reaction would be if I had told him then that her finishing school was a Washington whorehouse. But knowing the generosity of his spirit, I concluded that he might have taken her home to meet his mother anyway.

Before I could reply, an errant shell from one of the Confederate batteries on the heights across the river came whining over and smashed with a great explosion in the grove of apple trees behind the stable. Phil took no notice of it.

"Well . . . is she spoken for?" he asked.

When I turned to look at him, I saw that he was waiting on my next words as if his future happiness depended on them.

"No," I said. "Not by me."

"Well, wish me luck, Kit," he replied, with an ebullient grin.

.   .   .

VAL AND AMELIE emerged out of the shadows through the stable door behind us, his massive body dwarfing hers.

"We're going to see your favorite general," he said to me.

From the look on Amelie's face, it was clear she wasn't thrilled at the prospect. Phil looked devastated at the thought of even temporarily parting from her.

"I hope to see you again very soon, Miss Devereaux," he said, extending his hand. "Guarding you has been an honor."

"Thank you, Mr. Larrabee," she said, accepting it in her gloved one.

Val shook his head disdainfully before calling out to one of the grooms to bring a coach around. By then it was almost ten-thirty, and the pale, watery sun was finally burning off the morning fog that swirled across the Virginia plain.

The three of us remained silent during the ten-minute carriage ride to General Hooker's headquarters. We rolled to a stop behind a caravan of other vehicles that crowded the lane in front of the three-story white mansion house. The cold wind cut through me as I helped Amelie down from the coach.

As we approached the front door, it swung open and a young woman dressed in pink taffeta came out onto the veranda. She appeared very tired and looked neither right nor left as a young sergeant escorted her to a waiting coach. The hint of a smile appeared on Amelie's lips as it rolled away down the lane.

Inside, the center hall was large and lofty. Its wainscotted walls were covered with paintings of family ancestors. The beautiful parquet floors were tracked with mud. In the dining room, four members of General Hooker's staff were sitting under a massive cut-glass chandelier, logging in messages from an unending stream of couriers. They stopped to stare at Amelie as we went past them down the hall. Val intercepted an officer who was limping toward us with a dispatch case in his hands and asked where we could find General Hooker's chief of staff.

"Colonel Sloat is along there at the end," he replied, pointing down a dark corridor.

The room at the end of the hall had formerly been the plantation office. Floor-to-ceiling bookshelves were filled with agricultural tomes on

livestock breeding and soil replenishment. A harried captain was standing
in front of a slant-top desk, reading out the disposition of a reserve division
to two lieutenants, who were laboriously hand copying the required orders.

"Colonel Burdette to see General Hooker," said Val.

"I'm afraid that is impossible," said the captain, without looking up
from his sheaf of dispatches.

"Impossible or not, I will see him immediately," replied Val.

The two lieutenants looked up for the first time. Their gaze first went
to Val before shifting briefly to me, and finally resting on Amelie. One of
them appeared to recognize her. He poked his comrade and whispered
something into his ear as another officer stepped out of the adjoining
room and came toward us.

Like Val, he was a full colonel, but the similarity ended there. About
half Val's height, he had wide bovine hips that gave him the physical
appearance of a pear. His eyes were sharp and calculating.

"I am Colonel Sloat," he declared in a smooth baritone. "What is this
all about?"

"We need to see General Hooker on a confidential matter," said Val.

The lieutenant who had appeared to recognize Amelie gave his friend
a leering grin. I was tempted to go over and remove it with the back of
my hand.

"Whose command are you attached to, Colonel?" asked Sloat.
Although he was facing Val, his eyes had come to rest on Amelie, too.
There was mutual recognition in her eyes before she averted them to the
floor.

"I report directly to Marsena Patrick, provost marshal general," said
Val.

Sloat's eyes conveyed a flicker of surprise before he said, "Whatever
the matter involves, I'm sure it can wait until after the battle. We are
expecting to begin the major bombardment any minute now."

"It cannot," came back Val. "General Hooker will want to see us
immediately."

Colonel Sloat removed a watch from his breast pocket and briefly
glanced at it before raising himself to his full height.

"Perhaps you are not aware that General Hooker is commanding the army's center. I can assure you that he has no time for disciplinary issues right now. Let me make you a promise," he said, with a smug grin. "I will personally make time to see you after the battle is won . . . perhaps in a day or two."

"Thank you for your kind offer," interrupted Val, "but it will be General Hooker, and it will be now."

The muscles in Colonel Sloat's face contracted.

"This interview is over," he said. "If you don't leave immediately, I will have you arrested."

Val gave him a condescending stare and said, "A sagacious decision, I'm sure, but please inform our beloved Fighting Joe that I will be swearing out an order for his own arrest as soon as I return to my office, that action to be carried out immediately."

"On what charge?" demanded Colonel Sloat.

Val glanced at the two lieutenants, and then picked up one of the dispatches from the desk. Turning it over, he wrote one word on the paper before handing it back to Colonel Sloat, who stared at it for several seconds.

"Leave us," he said to the two young officers.

"You cannot be serious," he said, when the door closed behind them.

"Of course I am. Ignore this at your own peril."

In the ensuing silence, I wondered which man would buckle first.

"Time is running out," said Val. "I would suggest you give General Hooker the opportunity to decide for himself whether he wants to face a court-martial on that charge."

The little colonel stared up at Val for fully ten seconds.

"Wait here," he said, finally.

We heard the sound of his boots going up the servant's stairs. He was back a minute later.

"The general will see you," said Colonel Sloat with a venomous glare.

Chapter Eighteen

He was admiring himself in front of a carved walnut-framed mirror in one of the bedrooms on the second floor. Bare chested, he wore only a tightly fitted pair of navy blue uniform pants over polished calf-length cavalry boots. Without removing his eyes from his own reflected image, he drew a starched white linen shirt over his strapping shoulders and began to button it from neck to waist.

Not a hair on his flaxen head was out of place, and the wide-set blue eyes looked stern and commanding as he continued to appraise himself in the mirror. They softened when he looked up and saw the reflection of Amelie in the glass.

"I've missed you, little one," he said, turning to face her. "I regret that I wasn't told you were here last night."

"She wasn't here last night," I said coldly.

His eyes took me in as Amelie sat down at a chair next to the fire.

"Well, Kit, I understand you are here to arrest me," he said, with a sardonic grin.

"That comes within my purview," said Val, his eyes scanning the room.

"The notorious Colonel Burdette," said General Hooker. "I gather every desk general in Washington quakes upon hearing that name. Your reputation is fearsome, sir."

"Justly earned, I can assure you," replied Val.

"Well, Sam Hathaway thinks you walk on water, and that is good enough for me," said General Hooker, as he deftly tied a black silk cravat around the linen collar of his shirt. Retrieving a carefully pressed uniform coat from the bed, he aimed another jaunty smile at us.

"So you have concluded that I am guilty of murder," he said. "Well, in truth I soon will be. In another hour you will have good reason to arrest the entire general staff for capital murder. I'm to say that we are about to witness the greatest corpse making of the entire war. General Burnside's stupidity is only exceeded by his stubbornness."

He looked up at the loudly ticking clock on the marble mantle piece above the fire.

"General Hooker, I am here solely to investigate the murder of a young woman who attended a birthday party in your honor three nights ago. As you are fully aware, she was a prostitute brought down here from the capital."

"Yes, well as Kit knows, I do not ride with God's cavalry, Colonel Burdette. If you have a moral dilemma with that, I regret it. However, I am an unmarried soldier, and can do as I please. Enjoying female comfort has been the custom of soldiers since the days of Scipio. I prefer the company of whores, principally because one doesn't have to make false promises to enjoy their favors."

He paused to smile at Amelie.

"I have no moral qualms about your sexual preferences, General, regardless of where they may lead you," said Val. "Our legal forbearance, however, stops at murder."

"I only pleasure them, Colonel," replied General Hooker, "I don't murder them. That would be a waste of the good ones. Wouldn't you agree, little one?"

Amelie sat motionless by the fire in her chaste organdy dress and said nothing. Behind her, my eyes took in a canopied bed, its sheets and blankets in complete disarray, as if a hand-to-hand skirmish had been fought upon them. A drop-leaf walnut table stood next to the bed. The carcass of a baked chicken lay in the center of it surrounded by several serving dishes. There were two place settings at the table. I remembered the girl who was leaving just as we arrived.

"The prostitute's name was Anya Hagel," said Val.

General Hooker put on his uniform coat and began to fasten its two matching rows of gilt buttons. From outside the window, I heard the drumbeat of horses clattering up the lane toward the mansion house.

"I do not recognize that name," he said, picking up a half-full bottle of whiskey from the table and pouring two inches into a pewter field mug. "That does not mean I didn't know her, of course. I have enjoyed the company of many women without ever discovering their names."

I removed the drawing of Anya Hagel from my uniform blouse. Crossing the room, I handed it to him. The odor of his cologne did not mask the scent of a strong perfume that hung in the air next to him. He stared down at the sketch with the appraising eye of a horse breeder at a Thoroughbred auction.

"I assume that Amelie has already given you a full account of everything that took place that night," he said, before taking a swallow of the whiskey. His high-bridged hawkish nose was already pink, his cheeks almost red.

"To the contrary," said Val. "She refused to tell me anything about that night or any of the people who were there."

As the general continued staring at Anya's face in the portrait, his eyelids seemed to become heavier, making him appear almost drowsy.

"I do appreciate your sense of loyalty, little one, but I have nothing to hide," he said, finally looking up from the portrait. "In any event nothing occurred that night that didn't take place at a hundred other affairs I have attended. When my admirers in Washington tell me I should run for president, I remind them that I already have a district full of whorehouses in the nation's capital named in honor of me. That cools their ardor rather quickly."

"Do you recognize her, General?" asked Val.

"I never knew her name," he said, finishing his whiskey. "But yes, I had her that night. A very energetic girl . . . she thrashed around like a rabbit in a snare."

He emerged from his reverie long enough to add, "Of course, I had Amelie that night, too. You are the best my child . . . absolutely the best I've ever had."

She stared back at him without emotion, still looking prim and virginal. I knew that she hadn't even known me when she had made love to him, but it didn't matter. The thought of her in his arms, enjoying his body the same way she had seemingly enjoyed mine, made me almost crazy with jealousy. I actually hated her then. I hated her with the same level of passion that I loved her.

"You touched my heart, Johnny," she had whispered to me when we were lying together. But General Hooker had touched every other part of her, along with dozens if not hundreds of other men. Through a black cloud of anger, I heard Val's voice again.

"When did you last see Anya Hagel?"

"I believe she was performing with some of the other guests on the balcony. Isn't that right, Amelie? Although I was somewhat the worse for spirits by that point, I seem to recall that you and I were heading upstairs to your room."

Val glanced in her direction. Amelie nodded.

"I have no idea who might have killed her or why," added General Hooker. "But I hope you discover who did, Colonel, and that he is punished accordingly."

"You might be interested to know that Miss Hagel was syphillitic," said Val.

General Hooker was pouring himself another whiskey. He took a hefty pull on it and said, "Well, that is sad. But it is not at all uncommon in her profession, I can assure you."

Going to his field chest next to the canopied bed, he removed a small article wrapped in waxed paper from the top drawer and tossed it to Val.

"I always use the lamb myself, he said. "It cuts down on the pleasure but is always safer in the long run. You can keep that."

Val shook his head disbelievingly and said, "Who supplied these women to you?"

General Hooker again paused before answering.

"I don't see the harm in telling," he said. "There was certainly nothing illegal in it . . . simply a favor from a friend. It was Laird Hawkinshield. He told Dan Sickles that the girls were a birthday present for me."

"Are you aware that we have solid evidence implicating Congressman Hawkinshield in the supplying of substandard equipment to the army, including the defective gun carriages?" said Val.

"If that proves to be true, I will have him shot myself!" General Hooker came back hotly.

"That won't be necessary, General. We will be arresting him shortly. Was he a guest at the party?"

"There were several esteemed members of the House and Senate there that night," he said, with a facetious grin. "Laird was one of them."

"Where was the party held, General?"

"I cannot tell you that with any specificity. I remember that the house overlooked a pond. That is all I can remember about it."

"We need to know the exact location, General. The girl may have been murdered there."

"Of course. Well, Major Bannister can certainly tell you . . . he arranged the details . . . no, he can't, I'm afraid," he said. "Seems he accidentally broke his jaw on the way down here . . . You can ask Sloat. He was there, too."

The thought of the toadlike little staff colonel enjoying Amelie's body filled me with a another rush of anger. As I struggled to control it, the windows suddenly began vibrating in their frames, and I felt the floor tremble under my feet. A moment later we heard the first tremendous roar of a massive artillery barrage, followed by a succession of detonations farther south. The door to the hallway swung open, and Colonel Sloat strode into the room.

"We're attacking, sir," he called out over the din.

"And so it begins," said General Hooker.

"A wire from General Halleck in Washington," said Sloat, handing him an envelope.

General Hooker tore it open and looked at the telegraphed message before crumpling it in disgust.

"The battle hasn't even been fought yet, and Old Brains Halleck is already maneuvering to escape responsibility for the impending disaster."

He stopped to pick up a pair of leather gauntlets from his field chest and started toward the door.

"Please forgive those ramblings of mine, Colonel Burdette," he said, over the cannonade. "I don't mean to sound callous to the matter you're investigating, but a few hours from now thousands of young men will lie dead across that river and most of them will be wearing blue. If I had been allowed to cross the Rappahannock three weeks ago, we might very well have been in Richmond by now. The fortunes of war, perhaps, but a terrible waste nevertheless."

Amelie stood up from her chair, and he headed straight for her.

"I wish I had time for you now, little one," he said, "but I have to go and kill some Rebels first."

As he leaned over to kiss her on the mouth, she turned her head, and the kiss landed awkwardly on her cheek. Her arms remained rigidly straight.

Stepping away, the general began pulling on his gauntlets. As he passed me on his way to the door, he seemed to remember something, and stopped. In the manner of a kindly father dispensing advice to his son, he leaned close and whispered, "If you get a chance, you should try her, Kit. I meant what I said. She is the best I've ever had."

I swung at him then, the blow glancing off the side of his handsome jaw. It sent him staggering back against the upholstered settee. Out of the corner of my eye, I saw Colonel Sloat grab his service revolver from its holster. Before he could bring it to bear, Val had plucked the gun out of his hand as if it were a toy.

"I will have you court-martialed!" Sloat screamed at me.

As General Hooker rubbed his jaw with his gauntleted hand, a look of sudden revelation registered in his eyes.

"No, you won't, Tom," he said, grinning ruefully at me. "The young man just happens to be in love."

Val handed Colonel Sloat his revolver back.

"Remember what I once told you, Kit," said the general, as he disappeared through the door. "Be a Michelangelo."

Val slowly shook his head at me.

"Brilliant," he said.

CHAPTER NINETEEN

THE HOUSE SAT on a tree-covered knoll overlooking a small brackish pond filled with water lilies and marsh grass. It was modeled after an English manor home; with mock battlements, Gothic windows, and a low-pitched slate roof. Three stories high, its exterior brick walls were covered with denuded vines of Virginia creeper.

It had taken us almost an hour to find it. Hundreds of army vehicles were clogging the roads leading to the river, and Val was forced to use a maze of unmarked farm lanes to follow the directions Colonel Sloat had reluctantly provided to him. Through the long ride, I would look up and see Amelie staring at me, her eyes reflecting continued awe at the thought that I had actually thrown a punch at one of the commanding generals of the army.

At one point, we were stopped at a small country crossroads while the driver asked directions of a local farmer. Out of Amelie's earshot, Val whispered, "Our primary mission must continue to be the gathering of evidence against Hawkinshield and his manifold conspiracies. Solving this murder will almost certainly help to accomplish that task. If we're fortunate, there will be something to aid our cause in the place of their drunken bacchanal."

The furious cannonade from both Union and Confederate guns continued unabated as we slowly threaded our way through the federal positions. By then the fog had lifted, and whenever we traveled across a patch of higher ground, I could look across the river and see a vast pall of black smoke rising high in the sky over Fredericksburg. Sunk in gloom over my conflicted feelings toward Amelie, I only knew that we had arrived at the party house when Val poked me in the ribs and growled, "Look there."

Our open carriage was winding up a narrow drive toward a knoll dotted with evergreens. As we emerged at the top, I saw that the front door of the house was yawing open at an odd angle. From the dark aperture, two federal soldiers came scuttling out with an immense grandfather clock between their outstretched arms. Seeing us coming, they began running toward the closest line of trees, the clock making loud clanging noises with each step they took.

"We are too late," said Val.

I fired my revolver into the air, and two more deserters came slithering out through one of the downstairs windows. They ran toward the far side of the knoll and down toward the pond.

Approaching the open doorway, I could see that most of the windows had been smashed out from the inside. Family possessions, including furniture and clothing, lay strewn on the ground beneath the shattered frames.

Inside, the house was a scene of wanton destruction. The marauding soldiers had not been content with stealing everything of value. They had enjoyed ransacking it too. The acrid smell of urine assailed my nostrils as soon as we stepped into the high-ceilinged great hall that took up most of the first floor. A stone fireplace dominated the room, and flames were licking out from the burning furniture that had been stuffed into its enormous hearth.

A wide staircase led up to an intricately carved balcony that overlooked the great hall. It also opened onto the second-floor bedrooms. A smaller set of stairs led to more rooms on the third level. Amelie gazed at the debris covering the floor and shuddered. Wrapping her cloak more tightly around her shoulders, she moved closer to the fire.

Muttering a string of imprecations, Val began to systematically crisscross the room like a huge mastiff searching for a lost scent. He spent less than ten minutes in the great hall, before slowly heading up the staircase to the balcony. An Oriental carpet runner extended across its entire length. His attention was briefly focused on some stains he found beneath the edge of the railing. From there, he moved into the second-floor bedrooms, apparently finding nothing that aroused his interest.

It was only when he entered one of the smaller rooms on the third floor that he became visibly excited. To me it appeared no different from the rooms we had already searched. Most of the furniture had been tossed out through the smashed window. A clutter of broken debris covered the floor, including a cracked chamber pot and the head of a bisque doll.

Val went straight to the window and began minutely scrutinizing its shattered frame. From there, he moved onto the sill, and then the floor beneath it. Standing up, he leaned so far out the window that simple gravity should have caused him to fall the twenty feet to the ground.

When I took hold of his uniform coat, however, he shook me off. With an agility I did not suspect he had, Val lowered himself out of the window, and then crawled slowly down the creeper vines until he reached the ground. After rooting among the rhododendron bushes that grew at the base of the wall, he meandered across the lawn toward the tree line. A few minutes later, he was back in the room with Amelie in tow.

"This was Miss Hagel's room, wasn't it?" he said, as if already knowing it to be fact.

"Yes," she replied. "We were each given a room to change into our party clothes and then later . . . to entertain the guests. This was hers."

Her eyes found mine for a moment, and then returned to the floor.

"She was murdered here," said Val, without further preamble.

After six months of serving under him, I no longer showed my amazement at his startling deductions. To relieve my own growing tension, I looked at him diffidently and said, "My own conclusions, precisely."

Ignoring me, he said, "The murderer was not a guest at the party. And he also has the strength of a circus acrobat."

"How could you know these things?" she said.

"Because he didn't enter the house through the front door. He came through this window, and he left the same way," Val replied. "From the dried pool of bile at the base of the windowsill, I know that she was strangled to death in this room. The angle of the scraped indentations of his boots on the husks of the vines confirms that he was carrying her on his way down."

"Why did no one notice her disappearance?" I asked.

"I can only assume that it occurred at a point in the festivities when no one cared," he said, already heading through the door and down the hall.

"This part of the investigation will have to wait," he said, when we were back in the carriage. "I must go back and issue the warrant for Congressman Hawkinshield's arrest before he discovers that some of his rats have deserted ship."

By the time we again approached General Hathaway's headquarters, the army's attack had been underway for more than an hour. Our artillery was still maintaining a constant barrage against its targets across the river. I was wondering if our troops had broken through when Amelie suddenly leaned forward and exclaimed, "Les cartes de visites."

I looked at Val. His confusion was as evident as my own. She had to repeat the words twice before we grasped what she was trying to say.

"Cartes de visites," or photographic calling cards, had been the rage of Washington since early in the war. People had flocked to the studios of photographers like Matthew Brady to have their images taken and then have them printed on the backs of calling cards. Soldiers would send them to their loved ones at home. I had my own image taken shortly before Ball's Bluff.

"What about them?" said Val.

"Anya collected cartes de visites," replied Amelie. "She asked for one from every man she slept with. She always carried them with her to impress her friends."

"Where did she keep the cards?" I asked.

"In her traveling valise."

Our carriage was just coming through the entrance columns to Sam's headquarters. Val turned to me and said, "It is probably a fruitless quest, but I would like you and Miss Devereaux to go back to that house. If you can find the cards, one of them might provide us with information that will strengthen our case against Hawkinshield, particularly if he is black-mailing federal officers to help accomplish his purposes. In the meantime, Sam and I will arrest him if he hasn't already left for Washington."

We dropped Val at the entrance to the mansion and headed back to the party house. On the way I tried to focus on what he had told us about Anya's killer. Perhaps, it was my own jealousy, but the first person I thought of who met the physical requirements was Major Bannister. He was certainly strong enough to have carried her down the vines. The theory fell apart, however, with the recognition that since he was a guest at the party, there was no reason for him to have entered the house through the window.

As we rode back, it became obvious that the battle wasn't going according to plan. Far over on the left of the Union line, we came to a crossroads that was clogged with troops trying to move in three different directions at once. To my astonishment, the largest body of soldiers, two full divisions of ten thousand men in four columns, was marching away from the river. A staff colonel galloped up on a white horse and sat fuming as the endless line of soldiers trooped by.

"Franklin's got twenty thousand men over here still waiting to cross, and no one knows which way they are supposed to go!" he railed in exasperation.

The ransacked house was deserted when we arrived the second time. The fire in the great hall had burned down to ashes. Standing amidst the wreckage, I tried to imagine the house as it was on the night of the party, with a roaring fire illuminating the faces of the guests. I felt surrounded by their ghosts—spectral images of General Hooker, Mavis Bannister, Dan Sickles, Colonel Sloat, Hawkinshield, and all the others, including Anya Hagel. An image of Amelie, a vision of loveliness in her party dress, came into my mind. She was standing in the great hall, surrounded by male suitors. Unbidden, an obscene tableau invaded my brain. I fought to dispel it.

"How many cards did Anya have?" I asked over the wailing of the wind.

"I don't know," said Amelie. "But she kept them wrapped in a red silk ribbon."

I asked her to describe the travel valise that Anya had brought with her on the night of the party, and we made a careful search for it, room by room. Amelie finally found the bag lying amidst a jumble of other objects on the floor of the dining room. It had been slashed open with a knife and was empty. We went upstairs to Anya's room and went through all the articles that littered the floor. Amelie couldn't identify any of them as having belonged to her.

"She was very good at hiding things," said Amelie. "Sometimes the men she slept with gave her jewelry or other small gifts. Anya would always find a safe place to put them until she left."

In part to take my mind off the lurid images that kept tormenting me, I began a thorough search of the room, first examining the floor on my hands and knees to see if a loose board might conceal a hiding place. There wasn't one. A Franklin stove sat against the far wall, and I carefully sifted the ashes in its firebox, as well as the tin vent pipe that connected it to the chimney. I covered every inch of the plaster walls looking for cracks or fissures.

There was a small closet in the corner. It was the last place left to search.

Again starting at the floorboards, I slowly worked my way up the plaster walls. In the shadowy light, I could see that the height of the ceiling in the closet appeared to be the same as that of the bedroom. But when I fully extended my right arm up into the darkness, I was surprised to discover that there was no ceiling at all. The narrow opening was apparently a crawl space up into the attic.

It was inconceivable that the diminutive Anya could have reached the opening above me. However, there was a side chair with a broken back in the bedroom, and I went to get it. Standing on the chair, I was able to easily extend my hand into the space above the wall. A few inches beyond the nearest edge, my fingertips came into contact with a soft mass resting on top of the loose plaster.

Bringing it into the light, I saw that it was a cheesecloth sack, tied at the neck with string. I handed the sack to Amelie, who looked at it without a hint of recognition before untying the string and reaching inside. When she withdrew her hand, it held a sheaf of currency and a three-inch-thick stack of cartes de visites wrapped in a red silk ribbon.

"Mon Dieu," she murmured.

There was a side table in the hallway where we were able to examine the cards out of the wind. Amelie untied the ribbon, and we went through them one at a time. There were fifty-three photographs in all, among them many of the most famous men in the country. I recognized five senators, several members of the president's cabinet, a publisher, and twelve members of Congress.

The generals had their own section, consisting of fourteen cards. Three of them commanded departments in the Quartermaster Corps. Another was General Patrick's deputy in the Provost Marshal's Office. One of them presided over the military court system.

"Were all of these men guests at the Birds of Paradise?" I asked, without looking at her.

"Most of them, yes," was her swift reply.

It was one of the last cards that produced the biggest surprise. The photograph was of a young man in an ill-fitting suit. I didn't recognize him at first and put it down on the table with the others.

"Don't you know who that is?" asked Amelie.

I picked up the card again, and looked at it more closely. It must have been taken at the start of the war. He looked no more than eighteen. Of course, combat had aged him, as it had all of us. His hair was longer in the photograph, and he wasn't in uniform.

"Billy," I said, as Amelie smiled down at his image.

"Yes. He is the only one Anya said she ever loved."

"Billy Osceola," I said, still amazed to find his card there.

"I never knew his last name," she said.

"Do you know how she met him?"

"I believe they met in Washington."

"Did he know her occupation?"

"She tried to keep it a secret for a few months, but I know she told him at some point. It did not seem to matter to him."

"Do you remember seeing us together at General Hooker's party?"

"Yes," she said.

The trace of a smile came to her lips.

"I was hoping that you would come over and introduce yourself," she said.

We rewrapped the cards, and left the house for the last time. On the way back to Sam's headquarters, I tried to discern what it all meant. Certainly, a number of the generals and senior officers could have easily become blackmail targets for Hawkinshield. Unlike General Hooker, most of them did purport to ride with God's cavalry. If he was blackmailing them, it might explain the influence he had over so many branches of the War Department. I was sure that Val could put the information to good use.

At the same time, I found myself wondering why Billy had not been honest with me on the night of General Hooker's party. Right after my first glimpse of Amelie and Anya, I remembered him saying that the girls appeared to recognize me, when it was actually him they both knew. Why hadn't he told me the truth?

Perhaps it was because he was embarrassed to find himself in love with a whore, I thought. I knew the feeling myself, and could fully understand it. But I also remembered that he had not shown the slightest emotion when Val had given Sam his brutally candid report after examining Anya's body.

CHAPTER TWENTY

I TOLD THE TEAMSTER to take us directly to the stables behind the mansion house. If there was even a remote possibility that Billy was the murderer, there was no point in taking the chance of endangering Amelie's life by letting him know she was there. I needed to find Val and tell him what we had learned at the house.

A handful of grooms were lounging on straw bales in front of the stable block. Otherwise, it was deserted. I took her back to Phil's stall and asked her to stay there again until I returned.

"Johnny," she said softly as I started to leave.

"Yes?"

Her lovely face tilted up toward mine. I felt her breath on my cheek.

"I am so sorry," she said. "I know what you must think of me. And it is true."

Her eyes contained secrets I would never know.

"I'm not sure what to think anymore."

"Will you . . . just hold me?" she said.

Part of me was outside myself again. As my arms circled her back, I stood as rigidly as a statue. It was only when I began to unconsciously stroke her hair that she pressed closer to me, and my heart was flooded with both sadness and joy.

I guess it was the realization that although she had known more degradation in her eighteen years than I would ever know in my lifetime, she was still only a girl. How and why it had happened to her, I did not know. Perhaps, I never would. But all the physical debasement she had endured had not broken her spirit. Somehow she had surmounted it all and survived. I kissed her, and she returned it with a gentle sweetness that for a few moments took me far away from that place.

The foyer of the mansion house was swarming with staff officers just arrived from Washington, all of them enjoying the excited humor of a great lark. From the bravado of their words, it was obvious that none of them had seen active service in the field. Their uniforms were newly pressed and immaculate.

The rest of the mansion was practically empty. When I reached the library, the only person there was a provost clerk who was copying dispatches into the master order book. A crystal chandelier gently tinkled above his head in company with our long-range siege guns on Stafford Heights. I asked for Colonel Burdette, and the clerk told me that he thought both Val and Sam had gone across the river to view the outcome of the battle from the courthouse bell tower.

Not sure whether to wait for his return, I went out onto the porch overlooking the river. Most of the staff officers I had seen in the foyer had drifted out there, too. They were passing a bottle of whiskey back and forth, and laughing over the plight of a fellow officer who had suffered the misfortune of having his presentation sword stolen on the boat coming down from Washington.

"What's the score?" demanded another new arrival, strolling out of the house. Like the others, he seemed to treat what was happening across the river as an exciting spectator event.

"They say we're still going after those heights across there," said the officer holding the bottle. "But I don't think our boys are showing very much fight."

"Hey, fellas," came another voice from the lawn beyond the porch.

A captain was hunched over an astronomer's telescope that was trained across the river. He lifted his head away from the eyepiece and shouted, "I can see some Rebel gals over there!"

Their mindless stupidity was enough to convince me to head across the river to find Val, and I walked down through the terraced gardens to the pontoon bridge. The cannons that had been deployed there in the morning were now silent. None of them was powerful enough to reach the Confederate positions on the heights beyond the city without endangering our own troops. The exhausted artillerymen were sleeping next to their guns.

On the bridge a steady stream of walking wounded was slowly making its way back across the river from the besieged city. As their smoke-blackened faces passed by, I heard one of them say, "We're licked again, boys . . . sure as hell, we're licked again."

Shells were still dropping randomly in and around the ancient center, exploding with billowing clouds of smoke and flame. Fires had broken out in most of the city's streets. Driven by the raw December wind, the acrid smoke stung my eyes and nose.

Everywhere I looked there were signs of chaos and disorganization. Upwards of forty thousand men had gone across by then, and most of them seemed to be waiting for someone to tell them what to do. On each corner bewildered groups of soldiers milled about trying to find their units. Down one street I saw an entire train of untended pack mules wandering through the debris of a burned-out building, braying mournfully as they searched for fodder and water.

A squadron of mounted soldiers was clustered in front of the courthouse. One of the officers wore the insignia of a major general on his shoulders. When his horse shied toward me, I saw that it was Dan Sickles. He was gazing down at a map on the pommel of his saddle and calling out orders to the aides alongside him.

The reeking black smoke was causing several of the horses to plunge and rear. A dismounted soldier had their reins in his hands and was making an attempt to calm them. General Sickles was putting a long cigar in his mouth when I suddenly heard the familiar whine of a shell coming over. From the pitch of its thin, wailing scream, I knew that it was close and dove to the pavement.

A moment later it exploded above the cobblestoned street about fifty feet away from us, and the earth seemed to rupture under my body. The stink of gunpowder filled my nose as pebbled dust and stone fragments came raining down in its wake. The cloud was just beginning to clear when a crazed horse raced past me, its belly trailing a blue rope of entrails as it disappeared down the street.

The soldier who had been holding the reins of the horses was lying next to me on the cobblestones, his chest pierced by a foot-long wooden splinter. A greasy pack of obscene photographs had fallen out of his pants and lay face up on the paving stones. Oblivious to it all, General Sickles calmly sat his horse as if the explosion had no more lethal force than a gnat. He calmly lit his cigar and took a contented puff before turning to the nervous aide sitting on the horse next to him.

"The shell hasn't been made, son," he said, with a wolfish grin.

Inside the courthouse a young officer told me that only General Couch was in the bell tower, along with most of his staff.

"I think there is another general up in that Episcopal Church on the next corner," he said. I thanked him and headed over there. A sergeant was sitting at the foot of the staircase leading up to the steeple.

"I don't know Colonel Burdette," he said, when I asked for Val, "but General Hathaway is up in the clock tower with a couple of other officers."

"How did he get up there?" I asked.

"That Indian sergeant carried him up."

The staircase was narrow and steep. It had to be at least 120 feet to the top. With each step I was reminded of what Val had said about the killer having the strength of an acrobat.

There was a small circular landing at the top of the staircase. Open to the elements, it was enclosed with a three-foot-high wooden railing. The interior works of a huge clock were suspended from the steeple housing that rose another ten feet above the landing. A cruel, buffeting wind was raging through the spaces around the clock.

Four men were crowded onto the opposite side of the platform, which faced the heights beyond the city. General Hathaway was seated on a plain wooden bench, his hips strapped to the top of it with a wide canvas belt. His elbows rested on the edge of the railing, and he was staring through his binoculars at the battle taking place in the distance. Billy Osceola was standing to his right. Two other officers were on his left. One was a major, and the other a lieutenant.

They hadn't noticed my arrival, and I took the opportunity to observe

Billy's guileless face. At that moment he was gazing down at Sam with such evident devotion that it was hard for me to believe he was capable of murdering a defenseless young woman in cold blood. But he had lied to me about knowing her, and I needed to find out why.

As I stepped onto the landing, he glanced up and gave me a welcoming nod. If he was guilty of murder, it didn't appear that he suspected I knew anything about it. He nudged Sam's shoulder, and the general turned to face me along with the other two officers.

I recognized the lieutenant immediately. The last time I had seen him, he was being engulfed by the mob intent on murdering the Beechams at the overseer's cottage. His corn-colored hair and striking blue eyes were seared into my memory.

"I believe you've met Lieutenant Hanks," said Sam.

"I was hoping you had made it," I said.

He gave me the familiar cocky grin.

"We both survived to fight another day," he replied.

"And this is Major Frank Donovan," said Sam. "Frank was my best company commander, all the way from Manassas to the Seven Days."

"And still alive to boast about it," said Donovan. The major's face was horribly disfigured. A shell or bullet had turned his nose into a scarred pulp and left his mouth permanently curled into a grotesque parody of a smile. The clarion call of a trumpet caused us all to look back toward the plain beyond the city.

"It is as I feared, Kit," said Sam, his gaunt, wind-bitten face creased with sorrow. He pointed toward the plain as Billy handed me a pair of binoculars. I pressed them to my eyes.

I could see it all then, the whole terrible panorama of it.

A broad plain extended out from the confines of the city. The place that General Burnside had chosen for the attack led up a long, steep slope to where row upon row of Confederate riflemen waited behind a stone wall that ran along the heights as far as I could see. Rebel flags dotted their rifle pits, and a huge red battle flag was flying from a brick mansion that sat near the center of the line.

Atop the heights was the Confederate artillery. From the constant muzzle flashes, I could see that their batteries ringed the hills from one end of the horizon to the other and were in a position to rake every inch of the ground below. It was maybe four hundred yards from the foot of the plain to the stone wall, and our men were exposed to Confederate fire all the way.

Under the sodden gray clouds, the color of the plain was a soft, liquid brown. From the base of the slope to within fifty yards of the stone wall, it was already stained blue with our dead and wounded.

"That was French's division," said Sam, pointing toward the crest. "They went up first."

A hundred yards below the wall, I could see two of our regimental flags waving from a dip in the ground. Surrounding the flags was a large blotch of solid blue. From there, the blue stain meandered all the way back down to the foot of the plain, all that was left of almost five thousand men.

As I watched a brigade began forming up at the base of the slope for another attack. They moved slowly onto the plain from the outskirts of the city, a pulsing, arterial flood of blue. Through the binoculars, they looked irresistibly strong.

"That's the Irish Brigade going in," called out Major Donovan, excitedly.

"Into the mouth of Hell," added Lieutenant Hanks impassively.

General Meagher was riding along the line in front of his men on a big bay horse, resplendent in a dark green overcoat. Just beyond the place where they had formed up, a deep ditch ran across the length of the plain. Through the binoculars, I saw that it was a canal full of still black water. There were bodies floating in it. Although the water didn't look deep, its banks were almost vertical on both sides. There were only two small footbridges in place to cross over, and the Irishmen were forced to line up in narrow files to reach the other side to commence their attack. That is where the Confederate batteries began concentrating on them.

"Didn't anyone scout this ground?" I asked incredulously, as the shells began to open large pockets between the ranks of the brigade. Almost every shell landed with telling effect.

On the far side of the ditch, the brigade moved quickly to reform into two long battle lines. With elegant precision, they began heading up the slope, closing ranks as each shell exploded above and around them.

Lieutenant Hanks turned to Sam and said, "Can't we suppress those batteries, sir?"

"They have had weeks to dig in," said General Hathaway with a grimace. "The only guns that can reach them are up on Stafford Heights, and they are firing in the blind."

On the wings of the wind, we heard the Irishmen give out with a rousing cheer, although when it reached our ears, their voices were as thin as bat's cries. They slowly passed through the wreckage of the four brigades that had preceded them. The remains of men and horses lay in their path like so much bloody spoor across the vast killing ground. Cannon flashes now seemed to come from every foot along the heights above the stone wall.

"It's our lucky day," I remembered one of the Irishmen shouting when he had seen Amelie in her green dress.

I was shocked to see an officer, still mounted on horseback, at least twenty or thirty yards ahead of the first rank of Irishmen. Through the binoculars, he looked like a toy soldier wearing a gaudy yellow scarf around his neck.

The mounted officer was definitely within firing range of the Confederate line because I could already see men in the ranks behind him dropping to the ground. There was no way he could have survived unless the Rebels so admired his bravery that they were refusing to fire at him.

"I trained that regiment," said Sam, with undeniable pride in his voice.

At that moment a shaft of weak December sunlight found a crack in the gray clouds and bathed the Irishmen in a golden aureole. It was as if the heavens were somehow protecting them from the hail of lead waiting behind the stone wall. It seemed to follow them up the slope a little way.

When they were within seventy-five yards of the stone wall, both federal lines stopped long enough to fire thin, ragged volleys at the waiting Rebels. Then I saw the officer on horseback turn in the saddle to wave them forward again.

As if in response, the Confederate rifle pits erupted in a solid sheet of yellow flame. A plume of silver smoke poured out along the length of the stone wall, and a second later the sound of their volley reached our ears.

As the smoke drifted away in the frosty air, a riderless horse came galloping back down the slope. It ran hard for almost ten seconds before collapsing to the ground. It didn't move again. Where the lines of the Irish Brigade had been, a handful of the fifteen hundred men who had started the attack were stumbling back toward the two regimental flags that still waved proudly below the wall.

For a moment the only sound was the wail of the wind through the clock tower. Then we heard the ragged peal of a bugle from somewhere along the heights. It cut through the noise of the wind with piercing clarity.

The trumpeter wasn't issuing a military call to arms. There was nothing military about it at all. The sound rose and fell as the bugler drew breath—an odd, crazy peal of triumph, a rallying cry of savage exultation. As it finally died away, I thought I heard the notes of a musical tune.

"They're singing," said Major Donovan, horror struck. "The bastards are singing."

My eyes were drawn back down to the base of the slope, where another brigade was beginning to form up. The ground around them was now thick with blue bodies, and they had to step carefully to avoid them. As they started to file across the black water canal, the Confederate artillerymen began raining shells down over their exposed position, exactly as they had done with the Irish Brigade. Reaching the other side of the ditch, the men began to dress their lines before they started up the slope.

"Where is General Franklin?" burst out Sam in impotent rage. "He has two corps over on the left to turn their flank. Why doesn't he attack?"

"A lot of them still haven't crossed the river," I said, remembering the confusion at the crossroads near the party house. "No one seems to know what they are supposed to do."

"I cannot believe that Burnside keeps sending them in piecemeal like this," said Major Donovan. "It is criminal, Sam. Just plain butchery. We need to do something once and for all."

"It's time to act, General," said Lieutenant Hanks.

Sam glanced back toward me to see if I had heard their words. I said nothing, putting the binoculars back to my eyes as the Rebel artillery began to tear big holes in the ranks of the attackers. We watched them go slowly up the slope through that killing ground, only to disintegrate like the Irish brigade in front of the stone wall. The raw wind tore through the belfry, bringing with it the faint agonized cries of the men lying wounded along the path they had just taken.

Together, we witnessed three more attacks, all of which suffered the same fate. By then I could have walked up the entire length of the slope on the backs of the fallen. The afternoon light was fading fast when Sam finally looked up at Billy and said, "Take me back."

Billy unstrapped the canvas belt from the bench and gently lifted him up. Sam put his arms around Billy's shoulders, while the young Seminole gripped his back with one hand and his withered legs in the other. As they descended the staircase, tears began streaming down Sam's ravaged face.

"Those boys," he said, his face a mask of misery, "those poor boys."

CHAPTER TWENTY-ONE

IN THE GATHERING DARKNESS we made our way back across the burning city. Billy was still carrying Sam on his shoulders. He never missed a step as he picked his way through the rubble that littered the pulverized streets. I could not help but again ponder Val's description of Anya's killer as a man with an acrobat's strength.

At the foot of the swaying pontoon bridge, the survivors of a broken regiment were staggering down the muddy embankment, their hollow-eyed faces streaked with dirt and powder smoke. They were carrying their wounded comrades on makeshift litters. We went across the river among them.

On the far side of the bridge, a group of mounted officers was shouting encouragement to the returning men as they came off the bridge and headed up the muddy bank.

"Sam . . . Sam Hathaway," one of them called out. Looking up, I saw that it was General Burnside himself. With his ludicrous mutton chop whiskers and beefy face, he looked more like a circus barker than the commander of the army.

"No man can know what this has cost me, Sam!" he cried out in an anguished voice.

General Hathaway appeared to take no notice of him. I could see his face clearly over Billy's shoulder. Like a man enduring a nightmare, his eyes were pressed tightly shut behind the rimless spectacles.

"We are going to drive them off those heights tomorrow!" shouted General Burnside. "I'm going to lead the boys up myself!"

My hands were shaking as I struggled to contain my rage at the thought of so many lives being squandered through one man's stupidity. A crazy idea went through my head of saving the men he planned to kill in tomorrow's attack by pulling out my revolver and putting a bullet between his cowlike eyes. Instead, I just followed Billy up the hill toward the mansion.

Flickering lanterns illuminated a scene from Hell as we passed through the terraced gardens. The grounds of the estate were still teeming with men in blue, but they were no longer part of the elite regiments that had assembled there that morning. They weren't part of anything now except that select band of brothers who had come through the unholy fire and paid a frightful price for it. A thousand or more lay shoulder to shoulder on the ground, most still in shock, but others already writhing and squirming in torment.

Farther on lay the dead. They were lying in neat rows as far as the light allowed me to see. Billy made his way carefully through the mass of bodies until he reached the front porch of the mansion and headed inside.

At the door to Sam's office, two sentries stood at attention, their rifles at port arms. Through the open door, I was relieved to see Val standing with his back to the fire. He was staring down at someone seated in one of the high-backed easy chairs facing the hearth. As we came through the door, the man stood up to face us. It was Laird Hawkinshield.

"You're here at last, General Hathaway," he said, as Billy gently lowered Sam into the seat of his wheelchair and covered his legs with a lap blanket. "Colonel Burdette is apparently suffering from the delusion that I am to be placed under arrest."

"You are already under arrest," said Val.

"General, I am here on official business for the Committee on the Conduct of the War," replied Hawkinshield, "of which I am the ranking member. As you know, that places me under full immunity from all civil and military laws. I might add that if this idiocy goes any further I will have to inform the president of these outrageous actions. I'm afraid it would go hard on you, Colonel Burdette."

He began shaking his leonine head sadly, as if the idea of Val being punished for detaining him was too terrible to bear.

"I'll risk it, Congressman," said Val.

Sam was staring into the fire, seemingly oblivious to what was happening around him. I realized that his mind was still with the men lying beneath the stone wall across the river.

"You have been arrested on evidence provided by two senior officers in the Quartermaster General's Corps," said Val. "Both have written and signed confessions admitting their guilt in three separate military procurement schemes orchestrated by you."

"I have no idea what you are talking about," said Hawkinshield, with an insouciant smile. "Honestly."

"Honestly," replied Val, with a harsh laugh.

"These charges are nothing more than lies spread by my political enemies," said Hawkinshield.

"With your cannibalistic approach to the democratic process, I have no doubt you've left a legion of political enemies in your wake," said Val. "In this case, however, we have already seized the records that reflect payments made directly to you by the contractors involved in the procurement frauds. We also have copies of two remarkably incriminating letters from General Nevins, in which he asks for your instructions in how to set up the fraudulent bids."

"Good help is hard to find," said Hawkinshield.

I was pondering a way to take Val aside long enough to report what Amelie and I had learned at the party house when our long-range siege guns suddenly stopped firing for the first time in almost six hours. Except for the agonized wailing from the hundreds of wounded men lying around the house, it became deathly still in the room.

From the porch we could hear muffled shouting. A few seconds later, an officer stuck his head into the room and said, "Burnside has ordered a halt to the attacks, Sam. It's over."

With those words Sam seemed to waken from his trancelike state. He rolled his chair over to the windows facing the river and gazed out into the darkness.

"All those men up there," he said, his words almost a whisper. "No food or water . . . and no way to reach them."

"It will be a long night for the ones who survive," I said, remembering my own ordeal on Harrison's Island.

The door to the corridor opened, and Lieutenant Hanks and Major Donovan came into the room. As if previously summoned, they moved without a word to take seats in the chairs behind me.

Hawkinshield removed a thin silver flask from his suit coat. Unscrewing the cap, he took a long swallow and recapped it. Then he sat down again in the high-backed easy chair.

"May I make a suggestion, General?" he said, waving a long, elegant finger toward the heights across the river. "I would like to share with you an idea that I have already proposed to the Committee on the Conduct of the War. Of course they are not professional military men and did not give it the serious consideration it deserves. Now that we have enjoyed another debacle like this one, however, they might come to agree with me. I would add that a word or two of encouragement from a decorated combat soldier like yourself might hasten its acceptance."

Still at the window, Sam turned his chair around to face him. Hawkinshield took it as an invitation to continue.

"Take no prisoners," he said.

Sam's eyes reflected no immediate reaction.

"No more code of chivalry . . . no more surrendering of swords after a valiant charge . . . no more exchanges of prisoners."

"I don't know what you're talking about," said Sam.

"What I am proposing is simply this," came back Hawkinshield, warming to the task with another sip of whiskey. "We would set a day certain for announcing the new policy, after which all Confederate prisoners would be executed upon capture or surrender. They would be summarily shot."

I wasn't sure that I had heard him correctly. From the looks on the other men's faces, it was clear I wasn't alone.

"It sounds extreme, but think about how many lives might be saved in the long run. Right now, Southern women are sitting in their parlors all over Dixie watching their niggers toiling in the sun and dreaming of their men coming home after the Yankee invaders have been destroyed. Just imagine the change in their attitude if they knew that their men would never be coming home . . . that from now on they would be executed without mercy as traitors. Why the war would be over in six months . . . maybe three."

"You're not serious" said Major Donovan from his chair behind me.

"Hardly," replied Hawkinshield, looking up at him, "I'm simply being pragmatic. Otherwise we can look back on today's bloodletting as a small appetizer to the bloody repast that is coming . . . which incidentally would be good for my business interests, but then I'm first and foremost a patriot."

"A man of true democratic principles," said Val. "However, you weren't brought here to discuss battlefield etiquette, Congressman. You have been charged with conspiracy to defraud the United States government for your own personal financial gain. It would behoove you to cooperate with us by revealing which other high government officials are involved with you."

Hawkinshield smiled and shook his head again.

"How far do you think these charges will carry once I am back in Washington?" he said. "I have four congressional colleagues waiting across the river for me to continue our inspection tour. So if you have no more questions . . ."

"I no longer have time for you," said Sam, rolling his chair back toward his field desk.

"Finally, a cooler head prevails," said Hawkinshield.

Opening the top drawer of his desk, Sam removed his Colt service revolver and placed it on his lap. Val and I had seen him do exactly the same thing before he successfully extracted the confession from Major Duval only a few days earlier. Apparently he was planning to try the same ploy with Hawkinshield.

As Sam started back toward him, Hawkinshield burst out laughing.

"I am already familiar with this gambit, General Hathaway," said Hawkinshield. "Major Duval informed us of just how you convinced him to reveal the whereabouts of those shipping manifests."

Sam stopped his chair a foot in front of Hawkinshield. Behind the rimless spectacles, he no longer looked like a college professor; His eyes were as cold as blue-veined ice.

"You sit here guilty of crimes that would get you hung if you weren't a powerful member of Congress. In your arrogance, you scoff at the laws you swore to obey. You do not even deny complicity in these crimes ... blithely confident that your power and your position will make it impossible for any court to convict you."

Hawkinshield sat there with the same smirk I had seen on his face while he was humiliating Ginevra Hale.

"And you may well be right," Sam added.

"What I have done has been a cherished part of the way our government has functioned since the glorious War of Independence," said Hawkinshield. "Just take a look at George Washington's expense vouchers sometime."

"Congressman, I have watched hundreds of noble young men sacrifice their lives today while bastards like you go on destroying the basic values they are fighting for."

"I'm sorry you feel that way, General," Hawkinshield said, glancing down at Sam's withered legs. "I can fully understand your frustration."

"By the powers invested in me by the provost marshal general, I sentence you to death," said Sam, raising the revolver from his lap and placing it against Hawkinshield's temple.

"This is absurd," said Hawkinshield, turning toward Val and me with another mocking smile. At the last moment, he looked back into Sam's eyes and went as pale as wood smoke.

The smile was still frozen on his arrogant face when the gun exploded in Sam's hand and blew Hawkinshield's brains out. His body convulsed once before it slid down from the chair and fell in a heap to the floor.

Sam lay the revolver back on his lap and looked up at us.

"No more code of chivalry," he said.

CHAPTER TWENTY-TWO

THE DOOR TO THE CORRIDOR burst open and the two provost guards who were posted in the hallway rushed into the library. Lieutenant Hanks quickly moved to block their view of the congressman's body on the floor.

"We have things under control here," he said calmly. Stepping forward, he herded them back out into the hallway and closed the door.

"Well, that is resolved," said Sam, rolling his wheelchair back to the field desk and putting the revolver down on top of it.

"Sam," began Val, "you didn't give the man . . ."

"He would have escaped justice," General Hathaway said without pause.

"Maybe," replied Val, his voice hoarse with emotion, "but we could have publicly exposed him in a way that . . ."

"I put him down like the rabid dog he was," interrupted Sam, as if he was late for an appointment. He removed a batch of papers from his desk and began sorting through them. One file went into an open satchel that was sitting on the floor next to his field desk. The others he threw into the fire.

"I am truly sorry, Sam," Val said, "but you know there will have to be a full inquest on this . . . execution."

Completely unruffled, Sam nodded in reply as he continued adding papers from the field desk into the fire.

"Of course," he said, "but first I have one final task to perform on behalf of those men across the river. Have you made the arrangements, Frank?"

Major Donovan nodded in reply.

"A packet boat is fueled and ready at Aquia Creek," he said. "There is a coach waiting outside."

"Very well," said Sam, placing the revolver in the kit bag and clasping the top buckle.

Without being sure exactly why, I suddenly knew that what Sam was about to do was directly related to the murder of the prostitute. Turning to Billy, I said, "Why did you kill Anya Hagel?"

Val stared at me, speechless. It was the first and only time I ever saw him at a loss for words.

Billy looked away as if struck, saying nothing in reply.

"I am solely responsible for her death, Kit," said General Hathaway. "I ordered Billy to do it. Unfortunately, she was attempting to blackmail him after he made the mistake of confiding some things to her that he should not have. Because of the importance of that information and the sensitivity of it to our plans, I could not allow her to live and possibly compromise them. Billy reluctantly obeyed my order."

"What plans, Sam?" asked Val, although by then I was confident he had already divined the answer.

"You at least deserve to know, my friend. I am leaving now for Washington. Along with some far more deserving officers and men, the president is awarding me a commendation for valor."

"And you will return that honor by killing him," said Val.

"His life to save the many," said Sam. "Like our dead congressman here, I, too, have a plan for bringing this war to an end. Mine is less complicated than his and will hopefully be more effective."

As he spoke those words, Major Donovan stepped behind me and removed my revolver from its holster. I stood dumbfounded at the implications of what Sam was saying. Even then it was impossible for me to believe that he was actually planning to kill Abraham Lincoln.

"Why the president?" said Val.

"He alone is prosecuting this war with the single-minded determination to see it through to the end, regardless of the cost," he said. "And the cost is too high. If President Lincoln is removed, then Hannibal Hamlin becomes president."

"But he is an ineffectual fool," said Val.

"Yes, exactly," replied Sam, "but my friends tell me that he is as appalled at the bloodletting as we are. We have every reason to believe that, as president, Hamlin would seek to end the war on honorable terms. Even if that isn't the case, the death of Lincoln will bring immediate recognition of the Confederacy from Great Britain. As you know, their prime minister was already prepared to do so if Lee's Maryland campaign had achieved success."

"You fought for the Union, Sam," said Val, with a deep sigh. "You paid a heavy price for doing so. What you are now planning to do will leave the nation divided, perhaps forever."

"I was never a fervent Unionist, Val," he said. "It was for the rights of the black man that I fought . . . but now that cost is too high to bear."

"But we are winning the war, Sam," said Val. "Look what Grant is doing in the West. With one or two more victories here . . ."

"One more life is too many," came back Sam, turning to stare through the window toward the heights across the river. "You didn't witness what happened over there today, Val. God knows how many more eighteen-year-old boys Burnside will kill before he is finished. And to know that while they are dying, men like Hawkinshield are profiting on their sacrifice . . . it cannot stand."

In death, Hawkinshield continued to make his presence known to us. The stench that accompanied his loss of bodily functions began to fill the room.

"But we have made progress in stopping men like him, and you are responsible for much of it."

"Pitifully small progress, I'm afraid. If Mr. Lincoln wasn't our commander-in-chief, I might think differently about this; but look what he has done . . . appointing Cameron as secreteary of war, elevating men like Banks, Baker, Pope, Fremont, and now Burnside to important commands. The list goes on and on. Incompetent men, corrupt men, feeding on the army as we fight and die. Bastards like him," he said, pointing to the heap on the floor.

I must confess that one part of me was glad Sam had shot him. I even found myself agreeing with the fundamental truth of his argument about the president's misjudgments. But having met President Lincoln, I knew that General Hathaway was underestimating his capacity to learn from his mistakes and to take control of the war. I hoped that Val could still convince him to change his mind.

"So you are not in this alone," Val said, glancing at Major Donovan and Lieutenant Hanks.

"There are a few of us who recognize that extreme measures are necessary to end the waste," said Sam, "men who are willing to sacrifice themselves to bring the insanity to an end."

He put the satchel bag in his lap and rolled his chair toward us.

"Will you and Kit give me your word that you will not attempt to prevent our plans?"

"I cannot, Sam," said Val. When Sam moved his eyes to me, I nodded in agreement.

"Of course. I completely understand," said Sam. "Lieutenant Hanks . . . please escort them to a secure place until it is done."

The younger officer nodded.

"And please see that Miss Devereaux is brought there from the stables, Billy."

"Yes, sir," he said.

Obviously, my attempts at secrecy had failed miserably. At the same time, I knew that there was no longer any reason for them to harm her.

"Val, I know that you and Kit are only doing your best in the cause we once shared," he said, heading swiftly toward the door. "I am sorry that we can no longer work for it together."

Billy opened it for him, and they went out together.

"Good luck and God speed, General," called out Major Donovan.

When he was gone, Lieutenant Hanks brought in the two guards who were standing in the hallway and told them that Val and I were under arrest for shooting Congressman Hawkinshield. Val's atrocious appearance did nothing to quell their suspicions that we were assassins, or worse. They took up positions behind us as Lieutenant Hanks headed down the hall.

"I have never shot a brother officer," Lieutenant Hanks said quietly, as we made our way across the grounds in the darkness. "But you must know that I will not hesitate to do so if you try to run or call out for help."

"I do not doubt your intrepidity, young man," said Val, "not after your heroism at the overseer's cottage. It is just unfortunate that you are so sadly misguided."

"General Hathaway is the finest man I have ever known," Hanks said, as if that was sufficient reason for him to participate in a plot to kill the president of the United States.

"Have you considered the possibility that he might have temporarily lost his sanity and needs someone like you to save him from this folly?"

"He is as sane as you or I," was the reply.

He led us through the legion of wounded that now lay everywhere around the mansion until we arrived at a row of brick-faced cottages that had once housed the plantation slaves. As we went past them, I saw the shadowy form of someone standing in one of the doorways. Glancing back, the figure disappeared into the darkness.

Just beyond the last cottage was a mound of earth built into the side of a low hill. An open door protruded from it at a forty-five-degree angle to the ground. From the acidulous smell emanating out of the dark hole, it was obviously an underground fruit cellar.

"I already put up my vegetables for the winter," said Val.

"Nevertheless, it will be your quarters until our telegraph operatives at Aquia have received word from Washington," replied Lieutenant Hanks.

As we were about to descend the stairs, Billy Osceola suddenly appeared out of the darkness. He took Lieutenant Hanks by the arm and pulled him a few feet away from us before whispering something into his ear.

"Conduct a search immediately," said the young officer.

I knew that, in a small way at least, their plans had already gone awry, and that Amelie had somehow evaded their capture. I wondered then if it was she I had seen standing in the doorway of the slave cottage. There was no way of knowing just then.

"You will have to forgive the accommodations," said Lieutenant Hanks, as he sent us down the stairs.

The massive door dropped into place behind us, and we were plunged into total darkness. It was like being buried in an ancient tomb. Reaching the bottom of the stairs, I stumbled over several low objects. Behind me, I heard a match striking one of the beams over our heads, and a moment later, its guttering flame illuminated our surroundings.

We were standing on a packed earth floor, about eight feet beneath the ground. Constructed of rough logs over a stone foundation, the fruit cellar extended almost twenty feet into the darkness. Rough-hewn ceiling beams and cross timbers braced the earth barrier above us. There were no outlets for fresh air aside from the thick oaken door that was held in its frame with heavy iron strap hinges. The overpowering smell of moldering fruit and vegetables filled the air.

Val removed an inch-long chunk of candle from his uniform blouse. After putting his match to it, he handed me the candle stub and motioned for me to follow him. For the next ten minutes, he slowly worked his way around the perimeter of the cavelike chamber, using a small spade to test the walls and ceiling joints. Most of the floor area was covered with barrels and bins of potatoes, apples, and onions, along with kegs full of pickling brine and fermenting wine.

"When we escape," Val said, as if it was already a foregone conclusion, "I will try to reach the telegraph station, although from what the lieutenant just said, the conspirators may have control over the flow of traffic there. There is no assurance that they won't try to prevent us from sending a wire to Washington or that it would even be delivered at the other end. Someone must also ride overland to the capital."

Knowing how adroitly his mind worked, I was not surprised at how quickly he was already defining our next objectives. At the same time, I knew which role would be mine.

"I will endeavour to find a winged Pegasus," I said.

"It will take Sam at least seven hours to reach the capital by packet boat . . . maybe longer with all the traffic on the Potomac," he said, removing his watch and glancing at it.

"This whole thing is simply incredible," I said. "Perhaps General Hathaway will not follow through with it. At heart, he is a gentle man."

"Yes, he is," replied Val, "but personal grief has unhinged his mind. Make no mistake that he will carry out his plan."

"How far is it overland to Washington?" I asked, as Val began to rummage through some unlabeled sacks along the wall.

"About sixty miles due north," he said. "From what I heard on the way down here, there are no regular Confederate units operating to the north of us, but there could be irregulars or cavalry. You will have to be careful. The bridges may be out. But if fortune is with you, and you are able to find a fresh mount or two, it should be possible for you to get there before him. In any event, you must try."

"I'll do my best," I said.

Returning to the staircase, he said, "Unfortunately, there is only one way out of here," he said, "and that is the door above us."

Planting the candle on the lowest step, Val slowly mounted the wooden stairs and disappeared into the gloom overhead. He was up there a minute or two before coming back down.

"They have left only one man to guard us," he said, "and he is breathing heavily from the croup. More important, there is no lock on the door. It is held in place by a heavy plank that runs through two iron elbow joints on each side of the frame."

"We are going to have to get him to open it for us then," I said.

"Perhaps. Or we will open it ourselves," he said cryptically.

A course of rough wooden shelving covered the closest wall. It held small garden tools, along with a number of small paper sacks that appeared to contain chemicals and plant fertilizers. As he began sniffing his way through them, I picked up an apple from one of the bins and bit into it.

"Yes . . . eat something," he said, grabbing three of the sacks along with a ball of twine and bringing the pile over to a small farm table near the foot of the stairs. "You are going to need all your strength in a few minutes."

Using a tin ladle, Val began dumping small portions of the powdered compounds onto the table. Then he filled the ladle with some oily liquid from one of the casks and hand mixed the substances together into a small mound of paste. Cutting a foot-long length of twine, he coated it with the mixture and set it aside. He scooped up the mound of paste in both hands, and was carrying it toward me when the low sound of voices reached me through the door.

"Listen," I said, racing up the stairs.

I was sure that I had just heard Amelie. When I placed my ear against a crack in the timbers, the pitch of her resonant French accent became unmistakable. She was talking to the guard, and there was a flirtatious lilt to her voice.

Val motioned me to back away from him. Slowly climbing the stairs, he quickly applied the paste like a poultice around the protruding bolt ends below one of the elbow joints. When he was finished, he went back to the farm table, returning immediately with the foot-long section of twine. Inserting it into the paste, he backed down the stairs and picked up the candle stub from the lowest step.

"What about Amelie?" I asked, realizing what he was about to do.

"Don't worry," was the reply, as he held the candle to the dangling end of the twine, "this is only Greek fire."

His homemade fuse sputtered into life, the flame hissing loudly as it moved rapidly toward the poultice charge. Retreating down to the foot of the stairs, Val picked up an axe handle that was leaning against the earthen wall. A few seconds later, the tongue of fire reached the charge, and it ignited with the loud flash of a signal rocket. The door seemed to shudder in place as the fire continued to burn white hot for a few moments around the iron bolts.

The timbers were still aflame when I vaulted up the stairs and drove my right shoulder into the side of the door where Val had set the charge. It gave perhaps an inch, but remained solidly in place. From outside, I could now hear the sounds of two people fighting.

When I heard the woman cry out in pain, I dropped down two steps and hurled myself upward against the door again. This time the wood around the elbow joint gave way, and the door burst open.

I came up out of the ground to find the guard grappling with a still battling, but badly outweighed Amelie. His musket was lying next to him on the ground. Picking it up, I automatically pulled back the hammer and swung the stock in a short arc at his head. He dropped like dead weight.

Behind me, Val emerged from the cellar, saying, "I have to reach the telegraph right away."

A masked lantern was lying between Amelie and the fallen guard. As she stooped to pick it up, the lamp's masking shield dropped free, and we were suddenly enveloped in a narrow cone of light. I reached down to cover the glass again, but it was too late. The sound of approaching foot-falls reached my ears, and a shot rang out from the darkness.

"Johnny," I heard Amelie groan.

She slumped backward into Val's arms.

Someone was still running toward us, firing as he came. With my rifle at waist level, I led him from the spot where I had seen his last muzzle flash and fired, seeing the white blur of his face emerge from the darkness just before he fell.

Val had already lowered Amelie to the ground. Although I couldn't see where the ball had taken her, Val quickly found the entry wound in her right leg, high on the thigh. He tried to stanch the heavy flow of blood with his right hand.

"It may have clipped an artery," he said, removing his belt with the other hand while continuing to clasp the thigh. As he strapped the belt tightly above the wound, her eyes fluttered and closed.

"Be on your way," he growled.

I stood looking down at her, unable to move.

"I will stay here with her," he said.

Still, I hesitated.

"You have to go," he commanded. "You're Lincoln's only chance."

With a silent prayer for Amelie's survival, I ran for the stables. Passing the man lying on the ground, I saw that it was Lieutenant Hanks. The life was already ebbing out of his eyes as I twisted the revolver free from his clenched fist and shoved it inside my belt. From the direction of the man-sion, I could hear more men heading toward us on the run. One of them was shouting orders, and I recognized the voice of Major Donovan.

When I looked back for the last time, Val had not moved from beside Amelie's inert form, but he was already surrounded by uniformed men. As I arrived at the entrance to the stable block, a big mottled gray stallion was being led out by one of the hostlers. He was already saddled, and a uni-formed courier was waiting at the edge of the paddock for him.

The horse was stamping his feet and furiously champing at the bit. Each time he angrily jerked back his massive head, the groom was actually lifted off his feet. At least eighteen hands tall, he looked strong enough to reach Maine. I grabbed the reins out of the hostler's hand, jammed my boot into the left stirrup, and flung myself onto his back.

"Hey . . . stop!" the boy cried, as I jabbed the horse's flanks with my boot heels, and we bolted toward the paddock gate. The courier began running toward me, frantically waving his arms. I turned the horse to avoid him, and then swung back into the narrow lane. The big gray responded to the merest touch, and a few moments later we were racing down the mansion drive at a full gallop.

Emerging onto the road, I took one look back toward Fredericksburg. Raging fires still lit up the city against the night sky. Up ahead, the road was packed with soldiers, dejectedly making their way back toward the encampments. Many of them were dropping their equipment as they went, the debris piling up along the shoulders.

Although it was necessary to slow the horse to a walk, I was grateful for the confusion and disarray that was everywhere to be seen around us. Men had already fallen out of ranks, taking rest wherever they found a place along the route. Someone trying to follow me would find it very difficult to track one man on horseback among the thousands of dazed and disoriented soldiers who choked the road.

As the human traffic slowly cleared, my mount moved naturally into a steady trot. He seemed happy to be in motion and moved surefootedly around the small pockets of men we passed along the way.

Once past the military encampments, we were on our own except for military vehicles and hospital trains. Occasionally, I would overtake men still walking north by the edge of the road; but as often as not, they would scurry into the foliage and disappear. None of them had rifles, and they were almost certainly deserters.

The night was black and a cold wind was coming up as I came to the first crossroad that led down to the wharves at Aquia Creek. For a moment, I considered heading for the telegraph station there at the boat landing; but knowing Sam had operatives in place, I decided to keep going. The only sure way to save the president was to get to Washington myself. I swung the stallion north.

About thirty minutes later, I crossed over a large wooden bridge that spanned one of the tributaries leading down to the Potomac. Slowing down to check my watch, I saw that it was nearing nine o'clock. At the rate we were traveling, I thought it possible that I could reach the president's mansion by early morning.

Once past the bridge, the road never diverted from its northerly heading. It was two lanes wide, with a solid gravel base. There were even macadamized sections within the silent hamlets that dotted the route every few miles. We passed through a succession of low hills. The big gray took even the steepest grades in full stride, never showing a hint of funk or weakness. At times the ancient forest that lined both sides of the road came together in a canopy far above us.

We rode without pause for four hours, stopping only once for me to water the gray in a dark, swollen creek that intersected the road near a sleeping village. With the exception of a baying dog and the rising wind, the landscape was as silent as a cemetery. By then I estimated that we had come close to half the distance to the capital.

Once on the move again, I realized that the temperature was falling quickly. Both the horse and I were warm from our exertions, but as the air got colder, the sweat quickly dried on my body. Without coat or scarf, the wind began to cut straight through me, causing my stomach wound to ache. The only other physical discomfort I felt was centered on my inner thighs. Not used to riding any great distances, the skin there was soon rubbed raw from the constant friction of my rough woolen uniform pants against the saddle.

In the hours that followed, my mind wandered constantly. A minute would not pass without it always returning to the incredible fact that Sam Hathaway was on his way to kill President Lincoln and that I might be the only person who could save him.

Over and over I prayed that Amelie was safe, and that Val had been able to stop the bleeding in her thigh. My thoughts strayed to the memory of her body, naked and alive in my arms, pulling me down to her with an urgency and hunger that matched my own. I tried to imagine a future for us after the war, a life we might enjoy together in a place where no one would know of her past.

It was almost two in the morning and the temperature had to be near freezing when I felt the first droplets of what soon became a hard, driving rain. As it began to soak my uniform, I remembered the revolver I had taken from Lieutenant Hanks. Knowing how important it was to keep the loads dry, I stopped under a stand of tall evergreens and removed the gun from inside my belt.

Unscrewing the top of my match safe, I lit a sulphur match and quickly examined the revolver. Lieutenant Hanks had fired four rounds, leaving only two in the cylinder. The remaining loads appeared to be dry, and the percussion caps both looked fine. Using my pocket knife, I cut a large piece of rubberized canvas from the liner of the saddle blanket, and carefully wrapped the gun inside it before placing the bulky pouch under my uniform blouse next to my abdomen.

Then it was on into the rain-filled night. Even as the roadbed turned muddy, the big stallion proved to be as indomitable a beast as I have ever ridden. Mile after mile, he slogged and splashed through the darkness, oblivious of the storm.

It was my own strength that began to flag first. By then my boots were filled with water, and my eyes stung badly from the relentless wind-driven rain. At some point it occurred to me that aside from the apple in the fruit cellar, I had eaten nothing since the previous night with Amelie on the packet boat, fully twenty-four hours earlier. As the minutes passed, my energy seemed to ebb ever lower until I slowly drowsed off in the saddle.

I came awake to the sound of the stallion pawing the ground. The timber stanchions of a bridge loomed up at me out of the darkness, but it was only when I looked closer that I saw the bridge itself had been burned. A felled tree lay across the roadway. Turning the gray around, we retraced our steps to a point where a well-worn path led down toward the bank of the stream.

The water was fast moving and as black as tar, but it didn't look deep. We were out in the middle before I realized that it was over the horse's head, and we would have to swim for it. By the time we got across, I was shivering uncontrollably.

Regaining the roadbed on the opposite side of the stream, I saw a faint light through the trees off to my right. Desperate for food and temporary warmth, I headed toward it. A logger's path led in that direction, and I turned off the trunk road to follow the track. Fifty yards in, I saw that the light was coming from the window of a small, two-story farm dwelling.

I reined up in front of the porch. As if trained to announce his arrival, the gray began trumpeting loudly toward the house. When I slid off his back, my stringy legs nearly collapsed underneath me. A painful tingling sensation presaged the circulation slowly coming back into them.

The door to the house opened, and someone came out on the porch. I looked up to see a slim woman of about forty standing in the open doorway. She was wearing a black woolen shawl over her full-length nightdress, and she came toward me carrying a small oil lamp. Her face seemed alive with emotion.

"Stephen?" she called out.

"I saw your light in the window," I said.

The excitement drained out of her eyes when she heard my voice.

"The light is for my son. Stephen is with Eppa Hunton's Brigade," she said. "He was reported missing after the second battle at Manassas."

"I'm sorry," I said.

"Perhaps he will be coming home soon."

"You should know that I am a Union officer," I said then.

She held the lantern up and gazed into my face.

"Come in out of the rain," she said, finally. "At least that is what I hope someone would say if it was my boy on such a night."

The woman told me there was forage in the little stable behind the house, and I put the stallion there out of the wet, leaving him quietly munching hay. Her darkened kitchen was still warm from a fire in the grate. She threw a small log on it and the coals burst into flame, illuminating the room. Aside from a trestle table and two chairs, it was full of potted houseplants. Long-handled pans hung from an iron rack above the kitchen table.

She poured me a mug of mulled cider from a jug that was lying on the warm hearthstones. Drinking deeply, I felt the coldness inside me begin to diminish.

"All I have are some eggs," she said, slicing me a thick slab of bread from a loaf on the table. "I hope they will do."

"Thank you," I said, "that would be very good."

The smell of the eggs frying in butter was almost enough to make me swoon. They went warm into my stomach along with another slice of bread slathered with raspberry preserves. All the while, I could hear the rain drumming on the roof. As good as it felt to be there, I began to worry that I would soon fall asleep.

"I need to be on my way," I said, the back of my clothes steaming from the heat of the fire. I tried to give her money then, but she firmly refused it.

"I hope your boy comes home safe," I said.

"Stephen is dead," she said then, her eyes filling with tears. "He is never coming home."

"I'm so sorry," were the only words I could muster, but they seemed to give her momentary comfort.

I brought out the horse and mounted him. Checking my watch, I saw that it was a little after four o'clock.

"Can you tell me how far it is to Washington from here?" I asked.

"You are ten miles from Alexandria," she said. "The federal capital is just across the river from there."

The big gray had carried me about fifty miles already, but he still looked strong. Restored by the mugs of hard cider and hot food, I was starting to feel confident that we could reach the president's mansion with time to spare. Soon we were heading north again through the dark, wet countryside.

Once more I became inured to the mindless repetition of sound and sensation—the thudding of the gray's hooves on the roadbed in their regular rhythmic cadence, the jolting pain of skin rubbed raw from my groin down to the upper thighs, and the pounding ache as my rear end met the saddle. We rode on, me chilled to the bone, my fingers numb on the reins.

I don't know when I first realized that someone was following me. In the wan glow of false dawn, I found myself constantly looking over my shoulder as if expecting to see a rider emerge from the veil of rain behind me. Ascribe it to a sixth sense, but with the passing of each minute, I became increasingly convinced that someone was back there in the darkness coming after me.

Of course, there was no way of knowing for sure, but soon the speculation hardened into a certainty. Somehow I knew that it was Billy Osceola following in my path, as dedicated to stopping me as I was to stopping General Hathaway.

That thought alone kept me driving forward at a pace I would otherwise have found impossible to maintain. It also made me think again about the revolver—whether it was sufficiently protected from the soaking rain, and whether the charges in the remaining cylinders had stayed dry. I had no other loads for it and could only hope that the gun would fire if I needed it.

Suddenly I heard the first salvo of a massive cannonade far ahead of me. At least, that is what it sounded like to my exhausted brain. I recognized it as approaching thunder when a jagged bolt of lightning lit up the sky.

I waited for the next flash to turn in the saddle and look back again. A tremor of fear went through me as I saw the mounted figure, just as I had pictured him, shrouded in a rain slicker and a broad-brimmed hat. He was coming hard, only fifty yards behind me.

I knew that the big gray was almost played out. He had already done far more than I ever could have expected of him. It was hard to believe he had anything left. But when I kicked him in the flanks, he took off like a fresh colt.

We went over the brow of a hill and down into a hollow where the foggy mist masked everything up to a height of four feet. On and on we raced between the rain-slick trees that lined the roadbed as flashes of lightning lit up the still dark sky. In the distance I could now see a faint halo of light that had to be Washington.

The stallion was running at breakneck speed when we came over another rise and I saw a covered bridge ahead of us, shrouded in the mist and fog. My fingers were frozen clawlike to the reins as I felt the great stallion leap to avoid a hidden obstruction in the roadway. Then we were inside the enclosed bridge, the clatter of his hooves echoing against the roof timbers above us.

Suddenly, the clattering stopped and I realized too late that the bridge plating was no longer below us. We were plummeting together through space, down through the beclouded air into a great void.

Having grown up by the sea, I instinctively drew in a deep breath and held it. The big gray began to trumpet in fear as we continued to fall. His scream was abruptly cut off when we hit the water.

It was like the buffeting blow of a crashing sea wave. The blackness was so complete that for several seconds, I wasn't sure if I was up or down, on my back, or on my stomach. I knew that I was still half in the saddle because I could feel the big stallion churning and twisting in his death throes, as desperate for air as I.

In that impenetrable murk, it seemed as if we had become entombed inside the skeleton of some vast primordial beast. The slimy, bonelike ribs were all around us, in every direction that I flailed my arms as I tried vainly to break free and reach the surface.

At some point I realized that the sunken object was a gigantic tree, torn by its roots from the ground, and lying at the bottom of the river. Still trapped next to my noble friend, I began to fear that he would kill me in his attempts to find passage out of the honeycomb of branches and vines. His powerful legs continued to slash wildly until they finally weakened and then became still.

Perhaps he saved me even in meeting his own death. I must have been driven beneath him because suddenly my face brushed the muddy bottom of the river. Somehow his thrashing legs had cleared a narrow path through the obstructions, and I was able to drift on through.

In spite of having tried to keep my mouth tightly closed, I had already swallowed a great deal of water. There was a pounding roar inside my brain. With my last conscious thought, I planted my feet against the bottom and drove upward.

I came out of the river into the same wind and rain we had left behind during our descent. Gagging uncontrollably, I held onto an exposed branch from the submerged tree long enough to regain a measure of my strength. The far bank was only thirty feet away, but it seemed like the breadth of an ocean. When my boots finally touched bottom at the muddy shoreline, I dragged myself out of the maelstrom, gasping from the cold.

Kneeling on the bank, I felt to make sure that I still had Lieutenant Hanks's revolver. Miraculously, it was still nestled behind my belt. The wind-driven rain was still coming at me with a violence that made it hard to see. I looked back toward the opposite bank, but it was hidden in the impenetrable fog. Even if Billy hadn't followed me across the bridge into the water, I knew that he must already be stalking me, and that I needed to find a place to defend myself. Farther down the bank of the river, I could see the dim outline of what appeared to be a broken mill wheel, along with the dark blur of another structure just beyond it.

I stumbled through the saplings and brush that lined the riverbank. An old mill, long abandoned and canted over to one side, emerged out of the gloom. The front door was gone, and the windows were missing on either side of it. That was all I saw before plunging inside.

It felt even colder inside the mill than it had been along the river. The first room was empty, and there were big sections missing from the floor. I went through the next doorway, coming out into a large, high-ceilinged open area that had probably been a storeroom for grain. I shut the door behind me. Although there was no key to lock it, the door closed into a solid frame.

Across the floor of the storeroom, I saw the outline of one more doorway etched in the darkness and headed straight for it. This last room had no windows and was empty of furniture. The open hearth of a small fireplace stood in the corner, partially collapsed in on itself.

With my back to the far wall, I dropped to the floor and pulled out the canvas-wrapped pouch from inside my uniform pants. When I removed the gun, it was wet to the touch, and droplets of water stippled the barrel. I had no way of knowing whether the loads were spoiled in the last two cylinders, but there was no other weapon to fight him with anyway. Pulling back the hammer, I set the gun on my left knee and aimed it toward the storeroom beyond.

All my senses seemed sharpened . . . the sound of the rain dripping through the holes in the roof, the odor of wet bird droppings, and my own smell, sour with stale sweat. My eyes were focused on the narrow view through the doorway when I heard what sounded like the creak of a floorboard, followed by the touch of an icy breeze on my face.

Several minutes went by. The sound was not repeated. I kept the revolver pointed toward the open doorway. Every thirty seconds or so, another lightning flash would brilliantly light up the next room. As I sat there shivering from the cold, it struck me that I still had a mission to carry out, and that the president's life might rest in my hands. I began to silently berate myself for the panicked actions that had brought me to this place.

What if I had simply imagined that it was Billy back there on the road? I had only seen his image for an instant. And even if there had been another rider on the road, what if he had just been a farmer looking for lost livestock? The more I thought about it, the more I knew it was sheer cowardice that had driven me to race off the bridge at the cost of my horse and then to this unnecessary refuge.

Standing up, I slowly walked through the door into the large storeroom, the revolver pointed ahead of me. In the first feeble glimmer of dawn, I could now see that the floor was entirely bare. There was no place for Billy to hide.

The doorway at the end of the storeroom stood open, and the path was clear to the front entrance. I was almost to the edge of the doorway when I suddenly remembered that I had closed the storeroom door behind me.

At that moment, a blast of frigid air from the shattered floor joists above my head caused me to glance up. That is what saved my life . . . seeing the shadow, that monstrous shadow, poised on top of the door.

Incredibly, Billy had somehow scaled the door itself, and was perfectly balanced along its narrow edge like a gigantic predator bird. Almost paralyzed with terror, I had no time even to aim the pistol as the massive form leapt toward me. I do not remember pulling the trigger, although a moment later the gun exploded in my hand.

As the weight of him drove me down on my back, I heard a short, fierce scream, followed by a searing pain in my chest. Then the back of my head slammed into the floor, knocking me unconscious.

CHAPTER TWENTY-THREE

I CAME ALIVE AGAIN to the sound of rain drumming on the roof, as well as a curious, repetitive whistling noise. Trying to sit up, I was jolted by the same searing pain in my chest and forced to lie back.

It was only when I turned my head that I saw the circular metal shank of a bayonet sticking out of the left side of my chest. I knew that it had gone all the way through me because I was pinned to the floor. Billy was lying face down just beyond my shoulder. The strange whistling sound was coming from him.

For a moment I just stared at the hilt of the bayonet as if I could somehow will the blade to remove itself from my chest. It stayed there. I reached over with my right hand and grasped the shank firmly in my closed fist. Then, I tried to lift my chest from the floor while pulling upward on it. All I succeeded in doing was to faint.

When I regained my senses, Billy was still making the same noise. He had not moved, and I realized there was nothing else for me to do but again try to unstick myself from the floor. Once more I took the hilt in my right hand and tried to pull it up. Maybe I had loosened the blade in my first attempt. This time it came free.

I knew from my wound at Ball's Bluff that the only reason the pain was even bearable was because I was still in shock. I also knew it would wear off before very long. My first decision was whether to remove the bayonet from my chest. In the hospital the one man I had known with a bayonet wound had assured me that it was always a mistake to remove it since that would make the wound bleed more. Instead, he recommended going straight to an army surgeon for assistance.

As far as I knew, there was no surgeon within miles of me. However, it was leaking very little blood at that point, which meant that no artery had been severed. Since it didn't affect my ability to draw breath, I also knew that the blade had not punctured my lung. The most severe pain was centered near my shoulder, and I surmised that it might have glanced off the left shoulder blade.

Not even sure I could pull it all the way out anyway, I decided to leave it where it was. Sitting up, I removed the match safe from the pocket of my uniform blouse, and unscrewed the top with my right hand.

I turned Billy over on his back, and struck a match against one of the flooring planks. The reason he was making the odd whistling noise was immediately apparent. The bullet had reduced his handsome face to a red cavernous mask. Small bubbles of blood and saliva surrounded the opening where his mouth had been. Above the shattered mess, his big onyx eyes were staring back into mine with a mute appeal.

I knew what he wanted me to do. There was only one round left in the revolver. I held the barrel next to his head and prayed it would fire. When the hammer fell uselessly on the wet gunpowder, he groaned and shut his eyes.

I STARTED TO shake again. Unlike the tremors brought on by my laudanum addiction, this was the deep shivering of a man slowly freezing to death. My soaked uniform was already stiffening, and with each breath, I produced a little trail of condensed air.

If the president's life had not been in the balance, I would have chosen a different course just then, remembering the fireplace in the next room. Instead, I told Billy that I would send back help as soon as I could.

The only thing I took from him was his rubberized cape, and that was to give me some protection from the storm. Mercifully, he drew his last breath while I was putting it on.

Back outside the first thing I heard through the relentless rain was the neighing of a horse. In my confused state, I thought for a moment that the gray stallion had somehow escaped his tomb at the bottom of the river and was, miraculously, alive. Then I realized it had to be Billy's animal.

Following the cries to a copse of trees behind the mill, I found a small mare with its forelegs hobbled. Looking her over, I could discern the impact of the animal's long, harrowing pursuit of me in her exhausted eyes and trembling legs. Nevertheless, I had no choice at that point but to see if she had anything left. Just as I would discover in myself.

Careful to avoid touching the hilt of the bayonet, I removed the rope from around her forelegs and led her up to the roadbed. My left arm was almost useless. I gripped the pommel of the saddle with my right hand. With my left foot in the stirrup I slowly pulled myself up onto her back. Turning north, we continued up the trunk road toward Alexandria in the pouring rain.

It could not have been more than five miles to the Potomac River, and Billy's horse turned out to be as gentle an animal as I could have wished for. She seemed to sense my infirmity and almost floated along on the roadway as if trying not to inflict further pain. I was content to allow her to walk at her own pace, which was slow but steady.

As we plodded along, I imagined the people of my Maine island stirring awake in the same first glint of dawn. My father lived his life by such routine that I could actually see him making the long climb to the top of lighthouse hill to extinguish the huge incandescent lamp that served as a beacon to mariners from Brunswick to Bar Harbor. In my mind's eye, my mother was preparing his breakfast of oatmeal, brown sugar, and milk in her little kitchen.

I looked up to see a crow flying over my shoulder. It was headed in the same direction we were and moving at a speed I could only envy. Closing my eyes again, I found myself daydreaming that the crow had offered me a ride, and I was arriving on his back at the president's mansion. A great lassitude came over me.

I must have passed out then, coming awake some time later to behold another chill, dismal morning. Although I was grateful to discover it had finally stopped raining, my head was swimming with nausea. I somehow became convinced that if I didn't hold tight to the horse's neck, I would drop off the edge of the world. As I leant forward, the head of the mare rose up to meet the shank of the bayonet, causing me to scream out in agony as grinding bolts of pain raced to my brain. For the next few minutes, it was all I could do to remain in the saddle.

I knew that I was still in Virginia when I looked up to see an elderly gentleman on a handsome black horse coming toward me. My cape had fallen open, and as he drew closer, his eyes widened at the sight of the bayonet protruding from my chest. I waited for him to offer me assistance, but he made no greeting of any kind. Instead, a small grin played over his lips, as if another Union soldier had gotten exactly what he deserved. That look alone was enough to give me what I needed to last another two miles.

But it was thoughts of Amelie that kept me going through the recurring paroxyms of pain and nausea until I finally reached the Potomac River. The memory of her sad eyes and sweet face would come surging into my brain like a flood tide, engulfing every other conscious thought, including the agony of my wound. I ached to feel her heart beating against mine again. Just imagining her presence beside me gave me strength. When I recalled her bravery in helping me escape at the cost of her own wounding, I vowed to make her sacrifice count.

We came over another rise, and the vista of Washington suddenly filled the landscape in the distance. At the foot of a long hill, the broad Potomac flowed sooty black against the ashen sky. Riding toward the Union fort that straddled the Aqueduct Bridge, I tried to husband my last remaining strength.

A painted sign next to the road announced that I was entering FORTRESS CORCORAN. The gaping barrels of its cannons were visible along the outer edge of the vast earthworks. No one appeared to be manning the defense lines. At the Aqueduct Bridge, a steady stream of commercial traffic was crossing the Potomac River from the Virginia side over to the capital. A teamster driving a brewery wagon waved me into the position ahead of him.

A long barrier pole lay across the entrance lane leading onto the bridge. Two soldiers were standing next to its heavily weighted base. I pulled Billy's rubberized cape closer around my shoulders to cover the hilt of the bayonet.

"You look all done in, sir," the first soldier said in a kindly fashion as he moved past me to examine the paperwork of the teamster on the brewery wagon.

"Less see yor'ders, Cap'n," said the second one, who wore corporal's stripes on his arm. Not more than eighteen years old, he was already missing his front teeth.

"I've come all the way from Fredericksburg with an important dispatch," I said, trying to keep my voice even. "I must get to the president's mansion."

"Frederissburg?" asked the corporal. "Where the big battle's goin' on?"

"Yes," I said. "It's over."

Nausea was beginning to flood my brain again. I watched as the other soldier raised the barrier pole to allow the brewery wagon to pass across.

"We whup 'em?" the little corporal demanded with a feral grin.

It was obvious that Washington had not yet heard about the defeat. Only victories generated a fast telegraph dispatch, I had learned, and they had been few and far between since the start of the war.

"I'm not at liberty to say, Corporal," I said, trying to control my dizziness.

With those words, his manner turned sullen.

"I must get this dispatch to the president," I said again.

"Where's your dispash case?" he demanded.

The teamsters in line behind us began yelling at him to hurry up.

"It is a verbal message," I said, "directly from the provost marshal general."

"I don't care ifiss from General Burnside hisself," he came back. "I got my orders here."

"Aww let him go, Lon," said the other soldier, who now had to deal with the rest of the traffic by himself.

"Grab his reins," said the corporal, "I'm gonna find Lieutenant Spoon."

Shamefacedly, the other soldier took hold of the bridle of my horse.

"I'm sorry, Captain, he said. "Lon's a peckerhead."

At that moment one of the freight wagons behind us swung out of the line. There was no traffic coming toward us from across the bridge, and he whipped his mule team into the oncoming lane to avoid the barrier.

"Hold on there!" shouted the private.

The teamster pretended he couldn't hear him. His hand was cupped next to his ear, and he was shaking his head back and forth as the wagon rolled past. The soldier dropped my bridle and started running after him.

I spurred the little mare in the flanks, and she leaped forward around the edge of the barrier. Grasping the reins with my right hand, I clamped my knees tight to the saddle to avoid falling off as she picked up speed.

We had gone twenty yards when the first frenzied shouts of the little corporal reached my ears. From the way he was screaming, one would have thought that Jeb Stuart was raiding the capital with his entire cavalry corps.

Another armed sentry was positioned in the middle of the bridge. He shouted for me to stop as I drew abreast of him and kept on going. By the time I heard the loud report of his rifle, I was approaching the far end of the bridge.

Two more soldiers were standing at the entrance to the Washington side. One of them was kneeling down with his rifle, and it was already aimed at me. The second was standing up. He, too, lifted his rifle to fire as I galloped toward them.

I never considered stopping. By then I was beyond caring. I saw the muzzle flash from the rifle of the kneeling soldier, and heard it strike with a loud clang against one of the permanent metal lighting fixtures mounted on the bridge abutment.

The second soldier stood with his mouth gaping open as I thundered toward him. My cape had parted with the force of the wind, and he was staring at the bayonet sticking out of my chest as I went by. Perhaps he thought I was some wraithlike ghost from a past battle. He never fired.

I slowed down as we plunged into the crowded streets of Georgetown. The pounding I had absorbed on the mare's back was making my wound bleed heavily. Although the temperature had risen considerably since dawn, I felt immensely colder and infinitely more weary.

The streets of the city were filled with Christmas shoppers, most of them women. Wearing plumed hats and feathered headdresses, they glided along the sidewalks in pink and gold. The stores were festooned with boughs of evergreens and colorful ribbons.

I cantered down the last few blocks of Pennsylvania Avenue and headed straight for the side entrance of the president's mansion. Pulling the horse to a stop near one of the covered guardhouses, I managed to drop from her flanks without touching the bayonet. Unfortunately, my legs wouldn't hold me any longer. I toppled to my knees. Reaching up to grab the stirrup with my right hand, I slowly dragged myself back to my feet.

Staggering like a drunken man, I reeled toward the guardhouse. Two soldiers with buck tails pinned to their caps were standing inside. They watched me coming toward them with incredulity in their eyes.

"Colonel Burdette sent me," I croaked. "I've come all the way from Fredericksburg . . . must see the president."

As I swayed back and forth, neither one of them moved or said anything. My principal fear at that point was that I would lose consciousness and be senseless to any efforts to revive me.

"Did you hear me?" I cried out hoarsely.

Continuing to pitch forward, my knees began to buckle again. I saw one of them finally coming toward me, but do not remember him ever reaching my side. I awoke to find myself lying on a couch in a large, high-ceilinged room. Its walls were painted a garish red. For a moment I thought I was back in one of the Marble Alley whorehouses. A young man was peering down at me. His face was somehow familiar.

"A doctor will be right here for you, Captain McKittredge," he said.

"John Hay," I rasped.

He nodded as I spoke his name.

"You told the soldiers outside that Valentine Burdette sent you," he said.

"Yes."

"And you want to see the president?"

A portly man with gold-rimmed spectacles and a shock of white hair appeared over his right shoulder. He put down a well-worn leather satchel on the marble-top table next to the couch.

"Is he here?" I asked, grasping Hay's arm.

"He is about to present some military commendations," he said, standing up to let the older man reach my side.

"I have . . . have to see him now," I said, gasping like a spent fish.

"Dr. Matz must treat your wound first, Captain McKittredge. You have lost a great deal of blood."

"Sam Hathaway," I said.

"Yes," said John Hay, "the general is one of those here to receive a commendation for bravery in action."

"You don't understand," I said.

The doctor was standing directly over me. He grasped the hilt of the bayonet in his pudgy fingers and gave it an exploratory tug. Hay's face swam out of view, and I felt myself dropping away.

I returned to life to find myself lying alone in the same gaudy red room. Even the far door was painted red. It was shut. Except for the faint noise of street traffic through the shuttered windows, I could hear no sound.

There was no way of knowing how long I had been unconscious, but the bayonet was no longer inside me. My uniform blouse was gone. In its place, a large white gauze bandage was strapped tightly around my naked chest and back. Someone had covered me with a woolen blanket.

I slowly raised myself to a sitting position and moved my legs to the floor. A tufted easy chair stood halfway to the red door. My first goal was to reach it. Using the arm of the couch for support, I stood up. Once on my feet, I willed myself to move one foot in front of the other, shambling forward across the room. I could not turn my body without feeling a stab of white-hot pain in my chest.

After reaching the chair, I paused to rest for a moment and then hobbled over to the red door. It opened into another empty room, this one decorated in dark blue. There was another door at the far end of it. It was painted blue. Although that door was also closed, I could now hear what sounded like a band performing in the room beyond. It was playing a slow rendition of "When Johnny Comes Marching Home Again."

As I lurched toward the blue door, it was opened from the other side. A young man wearing a white steward's jacket stepped into the room. He was carrying a silver tray full of empty glasses suspended over his right hand. Upon seeing me, he lost his balance, and the tray sailed out of his hand, crashing to the floor.

I trudged past him through the open doorway into the next room. Unlike the first two, this one was large enough to hold a Roman legion. It ran all the way from the back to the front of the mansion. Interspersed with the magnificent ten-foot-high windows were life-size oil paintings of past presidents. Gigantic crystal chandeliers hung from the high ceiling, casting a warm golden glow over the crowd assembled there for the awards ceremony.

I looked for the president and saw him immediately, his tall, spare frame towering over the others at the far end of the room. He was slowly working his way down a receiving line of men in uniform. There were about twenty of them, officers and enlisted men from every branch of the military, proudly standing side by side at attention. I looked for General Hathaway, but could not see him in his wheelchair through the crowd of onlookers.

There was no simple way to warn the president of his mortal danger. A military band in bright orange tunics was compacted into the space directly ahead of me, their backs to the corner where I was standing. Beyond the band several hundred guests were observing the ceremony. Most of the women were seated in the rows of spindle-back chairs that ran the entire width of the ballroom. A majority of the men were standing in smoke-wreathed clusters around the spittoons and ashtrays that were conveniently deployed across the open floor and along both walls.

The first challenge was to get past the band, and my strength was ebbing away with each passing second. I plunged forward through the woodwinds, knocking over two music stands, and drawing dirty looks from all the musicians in my path. To their credit they continued playing without the loss of a note, even making a smooth transition into "When This Cruel War Is Over."

The men standing near the spittoons turned to stare at me as I reeled past them across the ballroom floor. Seeing me wrapped in bandages and dressed in army trousers and boots, they may have thought I had been sent straight on from the battlefield to receive my commendation. It was too late to matter. Looking down, I saw a spreading stain of red on my chest.

President Lincoln was spending a few moments with each man before he presented him with his award. As he shook the hand of a cavalryman in a cherry-picker jacket, I could see that he was already about halfway down the receiving line. Although Sam was seated too low in his wheelchair for me to see him through the crowd, I realized that he must be the last one in line.

A narrow aisle along the side wall allowed me to bypass the rows of chairs, and I headed toward the end of the receiving line at the front of the room. Wobbling forward, I placed one boot in front of the other like a stiff-legged mechanical toy, maneuvering around the backs of the men blocking the aisle. At one point I blundered into a chair at the end of one of the rows, almost landing in the lap of an elderly man wearing a white suit.

"I believe you are wounded, sir," he said in a kindly way, as my fingers left a large blood smear on the sleeve of his coat.

Dizzy and disoriented, I felt as if the last measure of blood was spilling out of my chest. Although I willed myself to continue struggling toward the receiving line, my legs would no longer cooperate.

I froze there in the side aisle, hunched forward. Fifty feet still separated me from President Lincoln. That is when I looked to the end of the receiving line and saw Sam in his wheelchair, about halfway to the president.

He was staring straight back at me. I knew what he was thinking, even though the placid expression on his bespectacled face never changed. He was gauging whether I had the strength to reach him before he had his opportunity to shoot the president. Both of his hands were resting on his lap. A blanket covered his knees. His Colt revolver had to be under the blanket.

At first it appeared that he was effectively trapped at the end of the receiving line. The other honorees were standing with their backs no more than a foot away from the wall, and with the dense, milling crowd in front of them, it looked impossible for Sam to move his chair any closer to the president. From where he was seated, he did not yet have a clear shot at him.

The president had his back to the crowd and was talking animatedly to a naval officer when I saw Sam pivot the wheelchair toward the young private standing next to him in the receiving line. He was ordering him to do something, and a moment later, the private took a step forward. As soon as he did so, Sam moved his chair through the narrow gap along the wall until he reached the next soldier. Now, only seven honorees separated him from Mr. Lincoln.

The president had finished shaking the naval officer's hand. He moved two steps to the left until he was facing the next man in line. In that time General Hathaway had moved another man closer.

I knew that I could very well change the course of my nation's history if I could just stay conscious long enough to act. It was this immutable reality that gave me the strength to go on. Using the arms and shoulders of the men standing ahead of me for support, I forced myself to move forward once more, slowly closing the gap.

Reaching the front of the room, I swerved right to force a passage through the last cluster of guests standing next to the receiving line. By then Sam had already moved past two more of the men who had been ahead of him and was within ten feet of the president. The general swung his head around just long enough to see me closing in before pivoting back to order another soldier out of his way.

Pushing through the last group of guests, I hugged the ivory-colored wall behind the receiving line, leaving behind a chest-high stain of red as I lurched toward Sam's chair. I was no more than five feet away from him when he swung back again and saw me coming.

Smoothly wheeling the chair sideways, his right hand disappeared beneath the blanket for a second, coming right back up with the revolver. He cocked the hammer and trained it on me, all the while looking in the direction of the president. His movements were masked from the crowd by the honorees standing close beside him, both of whom were watching Mr. Lincoln as he stepped toward them.

Looking past Sam, I saw that President Lincoln was no more than five feet away. In another moment Sam would have a clear shot. As I covered the last few yards between us, he turned away from the president, and his eyes came to rest on mine. He could have killed me then and still completed his deadly mission.

Behind the spectacles his eyes seemed as tranquil as I imagined them to be when he had led his men toward the Rebel artillery at Williamsburg with an umbrella under his arm. I waited for the gun to explode in his hand, but for some reason he never pulled the trigger. I launched myself the last few feet and toppled over onto his chair.

There was no fight left in me. It was only my size and weight that kept him from acting as he wished. I tried to lock my fingers around the wrist of his shooting hand, but they possessed no strength. From three inches away, I watched as the barrel of his revolver pulled free.

The band had suddenly stopped playing. There was dead silence for a moment, and then people began shouting from all over the room. As I looked up across Sam's right shoulder, I saw the president being pulled back from the receiving line by John Hay. The young aide was frantically whispering something into his ear as he dragged him along. They were already twenty feet away and lengthening the gap with every stride.

Even then Sam could have killed me as easily as he had dispatched Laird Hawkinshield. My last coherent recollection was of the expression on his face, the haunted look of a soul from hell, as the barrel moved slowly past my eyes again and came to rest above his heart.

"God forgive me," he whispered, just before the gun exploded.

CHAPTER TWENTY-FOUR

Monhegan Island, Maine
December 24, 1920

A FROZEN CURTAIN of salt-crusted ocean spray covered my study windows like tattered lace, but there was enough rum in me to think I could almost see the coast of Ireland two thousand miles across the Atlantic.

Close to the edge of the cliff, a black-backed gull hovered motionless in the wind, screaming raucously for my attention. Above him, the darkening sky was filled with low, sodden clouds that threatened more snow. The island was already buried under three feet of it.

I hadn't moved from my easy chair in the study all day. The fire had gone out some time during the night, and I could see my breath condensing in the frosty air. As the wind growled down the chimney, I briefly considered the idea of going outside for more wood. Instead, I reached down and took another swig of dark rum.

At some point I drifted off to sleep. When I opened my bleary eyes, it was to the sight of a man furiously digging a path through the snow toward my cottage. The drifts were almost eight feet high along one stretch of the cliff path, but he began tunneling straight through it. A second figure was bringing up the rear, dragging a sled.

My first instinct was to run, but even to my rum-soaked brain, the idea that someone was still searching for me was ludicrous. I waited for what fate had in store. Ten minutes later I heard raised voices outside the kitchen window, followed by a shrieking blast of wind as the door swung open and slammed hard against the inside wall.

The first man through the opening was George Cabot. Although he was covered with snow, I recognized him by the bright red beard that protruded almost a foot beneath his yellow sou'wester. The second man was wearing a hooded leather cloak over corduroy trousers and calf-length boots. It was only when he removed the cloak that I was startled to discover he was a woman.

"Happy Christmas!" she proclaimed in a booming voice, her short, blonde hair framing the blunt face like a Viking helmet. She headed straight to my chair and proceeded to wrap me in her arms. I didn't have the energy to protest. Stepping away, she took in the bewilderment in my eyes.

"I'm Nancy Hollowell," she said. "Barbara's daughter."

Nancy Hollowell was my only living relative, the daughter of my late niece. Although I had never met her, I instinctively knew why she was there. By the time Cabot was finished hauling in the supplies, there was enough food stacked in the kitchen to feed me for a month. It included two fresh hams, a massive round brick of cheddar cheese, tinned fruits, a cask full of shortbread cookies, a mixed case of French wines, and a crate of fresh citrus. It suddenly occurred to me that she wasn't planning to leave.

"You can't stay here," I said, trying to keep my voice steady.

"Of course, I can," she replied, as if it was her own home. "I've come all the way from Washington, and I'm not about to be put out in the middle of a blizzard because someone has a false sense of modesty."

"You cannot stay here," I protested again. If I had possessed the strength, I would have hauled myself out of the chair and herded her out the door.

"I will not be bullied, Uncle."

George Cabot was carrying in a fresh supply of wood. After building a new fire, he began scuffing his boots back and forth on the study carpet, clearly anxious to be on his way. It being Christmas Eve, he wanted to be home with his family before the storm hit with full fury.

"Please wait here a moment, Mr. Cabot," she said, going back into the kitchen to retrieve one of her bags.

Cabot leaned in close to me and said, "You're not going to believe this, but that lady crossed over from Port Clyde this morning in the teeth of a force five gale. Ed Barstow refused to come across on his regular run, so she paid one of the lobstermen over there to bring her out in an old twin-masted Hampton. She was sick the whole twelve miles."

From the tone of his voice, it was clear he thought she was daft. Returning from the kitchen, she handed him fifty dollars, which on the island was a king's ransom. I'm sure it just confirmed to him that she was a lunatic. She saw him to the door, saying she would come by to make arrangements for our passage back to the mainland after the storm abated. When she came toward me again, I saw that her face was gray and sunken from vomiting.

"The little boat was leaping under our feet like a wild horse," she said, with a ghastly smile, as if her brave words could somehow blot out the memory of the dangerous passage. "I've never been on a craft that was pitching and rolling at the same time."

My dark mood must have registered plainly on my face because the next thing she said was, "It won't serve any good purpose for you to be angry with me. I am here, and here I will stay."

She went to the fire and proceeded to rub the circulation back into her arms while standing with her back to the hearth.

"Why are you here, Nancy?" I demanded.

"You know why I'm here."

"Then tell me."

"Because you're dying," she said without a pause.

"One of the island busybodies wrote you, I suppose. They have nothing better . . ."

"Dr. Boynton wired me three days ago," she said, interrupting me. "He said that you had cancer, and that it had spread to your major organs."

"You don't mince words, do you?" I said, glaring back at her.

"When was the last time you ate?" she asked.

"This morning," I lied.

"That would be quite a feat considering there was no food in the cottage. I am making you dinner."

I turned my head away in disgust.

"You might at least evidence some small sign of pleasure at the thought that I've come all this way to see you," she said.

At that moment it was all I could do not to tell her that having one living relative was far too many as far as I was concerned. But I held my tongue as her eyes wandered toward the bookshelves that covered the opposite wall. A moment later she was across the room and poring over the books that were crammed into every inch of space.

"Don't you have anything published within the last two hundred years?" she asked, without turning around.

As it happened, the study library was devoted entirely to the ancients. I wasn't about to tell her that every other room was filled with books as well. Leafing through a French edition of Plutarch's *Parallel Lives,* she looked up and smiled.

"Books can make good friends sometimes, can't they?"

In truth, they were my only friends now.

"More than half of these are written in French," she said next. "You must be very fluent."

"I'm not," I said abruptly.

With those words, I felt a hot stab of agonizing pain in the pit of my stomach. The attacks were coming more frequently now, sometimes striking like a sudden blow to the kidneys, other times like the cut of a serrated knife to the wall of my abdomen. I willed myself to remain seated in the chair, leaning forward slightly, breathing slowly in and out.

"How bad is the pain?" she said.

"What pain?"

"You're sweating like a coal passer," she said, "and it happens to be freezing in here."

I picked up the bottle of rum from the floor next to my chair and took another deep swallow.

"That's your medication?" she said.

"Better than most," I declared. "Would you like some?"

"As a matter of fact, I would," she said, reaching down to take the bottle out of my hands, and tipping it to her mouth.

"Thank you," she said.

I watched the color come back into her cheeks.

"I brought a supply of morphine with me," she said.

"I haven't enjoyed the use of opiates in sixty years," I said, "and don't plan to start again now."

That seemed to take her back a little.

"Are you hungry?" she asked.

"No," I said, truthfully.

"Well, I am," she replied. "I haven't eaten since early this morning, and I gave that back to the sea."

Through the kitchen door, I watched her carve a section of the fresh ham, putting a tidbit in her mouth now and then while she prepared the rest of the meal. Whatever other talents she might possess, she certainly knew her way around a kitchen.

I felt the pain begin to subside in my abdomen. Outside, the rising wind howled and groaned as it fought to penetrate every crack or fissure around the window frames. Although the cottage had been constructed from massive spruce logs at the turn of the eighteenth century, it had been exposed to constant buffeting from gales and hurricanes and creaked like an old ship.

While she prepared the meal, I limped up to my bedroom. It was all I could do to confront the wall mirror, but the result wasn't as bad as I expected. My color wasn't any better, but my eyes were clear, and my hand didn't shake while I shaved. I felt better after washing up and went back downstairs.

The food she had prepared smelled wonderful, and when she invited me to join her, I did so. We sat at the scarred old library table in the study and ate her meal, washing it down with half a bottle of wine. At one point I looked up to see her examining me with the same intensity that a research biologist might study an amoeba under the microscope.

"What is it?" I asked.

"I think you have a very distinguished face."

"How old are you?" I asked.

"Thirty-seven," she said.

"Do you have a husband?"

"I've had several," she responded. "None at present."

"I see," I said.

"I doubt if you do. I made the mistake of marrying men who saw me as only an appendage, someone who was supposed to stand by their side looking up at them adoringly and batting my eyelashes as if each word they uttered was a pearl of wisdom."

"And they weren't?"

"My first husband was a banker who didn't like to lend anyone money. The last was a U.S. Senator from Delaware. He had no passion for any cause aside from his own reelection."

I could see why men would find her attractive. She wasn't beautiful in the classic sense, being a very large woman with wide, child-bearing hips. But she projected a great life force inside her along with keen intelligence and an irrepressible vitality.

"What about children?" I asked.

Her face softened momentarily.

"I wasn't meant to have any, I'm afraid."

With those words, I confess that my heart went out to her.

"I want you to come back with me to Washington," she said, after a pause.

I was too shocked to react at first.

"You don't have to give me your answer now," she said. "We can head back as soon as the storm moderates."

"No," I said, although it came out louder than I intended. "No," I repeated more softly.

"You should know that I am a very wealthy woman," she said, in a tone that implied she had earned every penny the hard way. "My estate in Georgetown is larger than this island. You would be far more comfortable there. Perhaps a fine surgeon . . ."

"I'm not going."

She gave me a withering stare.

"According to Mr. Cabot, you haven't left this island for more than fifty years. It's simply incredible. You haven't witnessed a single miracle of the modern age. Why you have probably never seen an automobile, much less an airplane!"

She was right about that.

"You've never had a real adventure in your entire life, have you?"

I let that pass. Of course, young people readily assume when they look at someone my age that just because it is our curse to be housed in these ancient husks, we were never once like them.

"Are you afraid? Is it a fear of the world out there beyond the sea?"

"Yes," I said.

"I don't believe you," she answered, her eyes boring into mine. "It's something else, isn't it? But what could possibly keep you here?"

"I live life the way I choose. Besides, I don't like Washington," I said.

"When were you there last?"

"In . . . 1863," I said, finally.

"Abraham Lincoln was president then," she said, her voice tinged with admiration at her own mention of his name.

"Yes," I replied. In my mind's eye I could see his mordant smile again, the good, homely face creased with wrinkles.

"I will be entirely truthful with you, Uncle," Nancy was saying. "When my mother was dying some years ago, she expressed great concern about your welfare. I made a solemn vow to her that I would look after you in your . . ."

"Dotage? Well, I am very grateful for her concern, as well as yours, but I don't need your help."

"The truth is I was too involved in my work to even think about you until I received the wire from Dr. Boynton three days ago."

"Don't worry yourself about it. I'm sure you had more important things to think about."

"I failed in my pledge to her miserably, and I do not intend to do so another day longer. You are my only living kin."

"I do not need your help," I repeated forcefully.

"But you'll die out here alone," she said.

"I'll die the way I please," I said.

"Then I will stay here with you," she replied, with all the no-nonsense finality of the modern woman.

"You can't be serious," I said, realizing how they had finally won the right to vote.

"You will see just how serious."

"You wouldn't want to stay here, Nancy, and there are important reasons why I can't go with you back to Washington. I understand the pledge you made to your mother, but I release you from it."

"What reasons?" she asked, the cast of her jawline set in granite.

"Good reasons."

"Then tell me."

"I cannot."

"Why?"

"For one thing I swore an oath that I would never tell a living soul. It was a matter of some importance that took place when I was in the army. And there were innocent people involved."

"When did you sign this oath?" she demanded.

"In January of . . . 1863."

She burst out laughing.

"Then they are all dead," she said. "And if one of them has managed to survive this long, I doubt he can remember what he had for breakfast this morning, much less what happened all those years ago."

Another bolt of raw pain knifed through my stomach. It was as if a molten ball was growing inside me, larger with each passing day, twisting inside me like a demented fetus.

"You were speaking about an oath you took sixty years ago . . . in 1863, I believe you said."

"Yes. Well, it is a long story."

A blast of wind shook the timbers that anchored my cottage to the cliff. In the ensuing silence, windswept snow began pelting the windows.

"Neither one of us is going anywhere for a while," she said.

That was when I surrendered. She was absolutely right, of course. Who was still alive to know or care? The written record of everything that happened may still be buried in some secret archive in Washington, but the reports were probably destroyed long ago by Secretary of War Edwin Stanton. When it was over, he made me swear in a written oath that I would never reveal what had taken place. But after more than five decades, who would even care?

"Did you ever hear of a Civil War general named Joseph Hooker?" I asked, over the violence of the wind.

"Isn't he the one they named the red-light district in Washington after?" she said next.

"Yes," I said. "He's the one."

I looked at the clock on the mantlepiece. It was already approaching midnight.

"I guess it really began on the night of General Hooker's forty-eighth birthday party," I said, about to start the tale with the discovery of Anya Hagel's body near the contraband camp. Before I had concluded another sentence, Nancy interrupted me and politely demanded to know how I came to serve in the army and whether I had actually seen a battle.

So I started all over again, this time with my enlistment in the Twentieth Massachusetts. I briefly mentioned that I had, in fact, witnessed a battle at Ball's Bluff. When I attempted to move on, she interrupted again, wanting to know everything about the battle and my part in it.

With Nancy, I discovered it was impossible to skip forward to the more important events without her constantly breaking in with new questions. So I finally ended up telling her everything that had happened to me, just as it had all occurred.

As the story unfolded, she sat gazing at me in rapt attention, periodically getting up to replenish the fire or to ask for another detail about something that piqued her interest. At one point she reluctantly suggested that I should probably go up to bed, but I shook my head. The truth is that sleeping for me had become no more than a one- or two-hour exercise, usually snatched in my study chair.

When I responded by suggesting that she must be tired from her journey and ready for bed herself, she stared back at me as if I was a madman and then told me to go on. As the hours passed, the wind grew ever louder, and the pounding of the sea against the cliff below my cottage began to sound like a constant artillery barrage. I was in the middle of telling her about the execution of Laird Hawkinshield, when my voice got hoarse.

"Would you like a mug of hot tea with lemon?" she asked, seemingly alarmed that I might have to stop.

"Yes," I replied. When she brought it back, I laced it with dark rum, and it restored my voice.

Perhaps there was something therapeutic about finally telling someone the whole story because through that long night there was not one recurrence of my attacks. I had just finished telling her about my wild horseback ride to the president's mansion with Billy Osceola in full pursuit when I looked at the clock in the study and was astonished to discover it was four o'clock. I had been talking most of the night.

"You saved the life of President Lincoln," she said, beaming at me with an expression of wonderment.

"Just for two years," I said.

"Yes, but look what he accomplished during those two years . . . the Gettysburg Address, the appointment of Grant, the binding of the nation's wounds, the freeing of the slaves . . . he became our greatest president."

"So some would argue," I replied, staring into the fire.

"How were they able to keep such an incredible story a secret?"

"Of the few who knew what really happened, no one wanted a scandal of such magnitude to be made public," I said, "particularly President Lincoln, who was trying to rally the nation after our terrible defeat at Fredericksburg. It was Secretary of War Stanton who personally crafted the public statements that were issued by the War Department. Two days after the battle, it was sorrowfully reported that Congressman Hawkinshield had been shot and killed by a Confederate sniper while observing our attack from across the river. Similarly, it was announced that Sam Hathaway had committed suicide at the White House because of his despondency over the paralyzing wound he had received at Second Bull Run."

"And that was the end of it?"

"As far as my part in it, yes. Of course a dozen newspaper journalists had witnessed my struggle with Sam at the awards ceremony and were searching everywhere for me. After recuperating for two weeks at the same house where Val had taken me to cure my laudanum addiction, I was told I must disappear. This island seemed like the perfect place for me to go."

"Did General Hooker suspect what had really happened?"

"He may have harbored suspicions, but the general became quite busy right after the Battle of Fredericksburg. President Lincoln got rid of Burnside and gave Hooker command of the army," I said.

"Well, he may have been a complete rogue, but I can't help liking him. He was so honest about himself. I look forward to reading his memoirs."

"He was one of the few senior generals who never wrote one . . . but he did get married."

"I don't believe it," she said, with another explosion of laughter.

"It's true. A few months after the war ended, he married a rich woman from Cincinnati."

"And lived happily ever after?"

"Right after the ceremony, he suffered a paralyzing stroke," I said. "From then on, he had to use both hands just to hold a pen."

"How sad," said Nancy.

"She died soon after, leaving him all her money. Rumor has it that when he died in 1879, it was in the arms of a young woman. I would like to believe it's true."

"What about his friend Sickles?" she asked.

"General Sickles had his right leg blown off by a cannon shell while commanding the Third Corps at Gettysburg. When they took him off the field, he was smoking a cigar and holding his leg under his arm."

"He died?" she said, as if afraid to ask.

This time I laughed.

"Yes," I said, "thirty years later. In the meantime, he was made our ambassador to Spain and had a torrid love affair with Queen Isabella."

"Incredible," she said.

"When you are back in Washington, you can visit his right leg. He gave it to the army medical hospital there to be put on permanent display."

"I have many more questions for you," she said. "But since I was a little girl, I have always tried to save the best present for last."

"You consider my story a present?"

"A treasure," she said. "But I am going to make your breakfast now."

After making me another mug of tea, she headed back into the kitchen. Before I had taken the first sip, another paroxym of pain burned through my stomach like sulphuric acid, and I doubled over in the chair. Unlike my previous attacks, this one kept coming in constant waves, one racking spasm after another. I couldn't stop myself from crying out.

"Oh, dear God," cried Nancy, seeing me writhing in the chair.

I heard her moving in the kitchen, and looked up to see her returning with a hypodermic in her hand.

"No," I protested. "No opiates."

I was too weak to resist her. With practiced precision, she rolled up my shirtsleeve and smoothly injected the smoky liquid into my arm. Almost immediately, the raw nerve-endings below my belt began to dull to a throbbing ache.

"I'm putting you to bed," she declared a few minutes later, helping me to my feet and slowly assisting me upstairs to my room. She found a pair of clean pajamas in the chest. After I got into them, she eased me into the bed and covered me with a feather tick.

"I think the storm is moderating," she said, glancing outside into the sea glaze.

The snow clouds did appear to be finally lifting, although the wind was still gusting to at least fifty knots. The cliff below my cottage is almost two hundred feet high, and the waves were still breaking halfway up its face.

"I'm curious about something," she said, when I was settled under the covers, and she was sitting next to me. "Did you ever learn why Val Burdette came to rescue you at the hospital?"

I nodded.

"It was because of an old classmate at Harvard, Charlie Wilson. He was in the Twentieth Massachusetts with me. We were together at Ball's Bluff. Val was a friend of the Wilsons before the war. After Charlie heard about my troubles with laudanum in the hospital, he asked Val whether there was something he could do to help."

"Is Val still alive?"

I shook my head. Closing my eyes, I could see him then, just as he was when I awoke to find him standing over my bunk in the Glen Echo chicken shed. It was hard to believe that I would never see him again in this world.

"No, the great mastodon is no more. But while he was alive, he never stopped tilting at windmills. After the war it was Val who exposed the Crédit Mobilier scandal. He also broke the ring responsible for the New Orleans lottery mess. He went from one cause to another . . . most of them lost causes . . . but he never wavered. After Theodore Roosevelt became police commissioner of New York, he brought Val in to investigate the pervasive corruption behind the awarding of public contracts. One night in 1896, he supposedly disappeared on the Staten Island ferry. According to the police report, he accidentally fell overboard, and his body was swept out to sea."

"Oh," she said, covering her mouth with her right hand.

"He was murdered, of course," I said.

She didn't ask any more questions after that. I fell asleep with her watching over me like a protective lioness. When I awoke again, she was standing in front of the painting of Amelie that hangs above the mantle-piece in my bedroom. She heard me stirring in the bed and turned to face me.

"Amelie was truly lovely," she said, coming over to sit down again next to the bed.

"I wondered why you hadn't asked about her."

"I told you before," she said softly. "I always like to save the best present for last. But I must confess that I was afraid to ask."

"We were never apart for more than a day in almost sixty years," I said.

"You lived here together all that time?"

I nodded.

"What did you do?" she asked, shaking her head as if the whole idea was preposterous.

"I taught at the school."

"You have a school on this rock?"

"One of the oldest in the country. A one-room school. It's been here in one form or another since Capt. John Smith arrived here in 1614," I said, with unconcealed pride. "Of course I only taught for forty-two of them."

"And Amelie?"

"Like most of the island women, she did many things. In our first years here, she worked in the store, then as a chambermaid at the inn. She also knitted and did laundry for the summer guests."

"It sounds . . . it sounds very tame after what you both lived through."

"This is a place where life slows down to the rhythm of the tides and the ocean and the weather. It was here that I learned to share my heart

with a woman of courage and grace. No one knew who she was or what
she had been. Here she was judged solely for her own strengths and weaknesses . . . here she found peace."

"I am so very glad of that."

"Like you, she could never have children. She found joy in caring for
the island children. . . . She bloomed just like the wildflowers in summer.
And the islanders loved her back."

Nancy's eyes had filled with tears.

"No. . . . She found peace in this life . . . you can see it in that water-
color. It was done by a painter named Winslow Homer when he was
working out here some years ago."

"So your love endured," she said, as if that was something truly rare.

"I pray, if you haven't already known it, that someday you will have the
chance to love someone so fully and completely that you never feel alone
again. To always share a passion to be with that one person. . . . Amelie
and I are together even now . . . She lives within me . . . We are eternally
bound up together."

Nancy probably thought I was delirious.

"She died seven years ago," I said. "Her ashes are over there by the
window. When I am gone, we will be scattered together in the sea a few
miles from here."

I thought I saw sorrow then in Nancy's eyes.

"There is no reason for you to feel sorry for us," I said harshly.

"I don't feel sorry for you. To the contrary . . ."

She stood up from the chair and slowly walked back downstairs. A few
minutes later, I heard her pumping water out of the cistern as she began
making breakfast. It felt good to hear the familiar sounds of someone
moving about the kitchen, followed by the aroma of freshly brewed coffee
wafting up the stairs.

Now that I had told her the whole story of what had happened to us, I
felt a strange sense of release, of finally putting it all to rest. I, too, was at
peace. From the painting across the room, Amelie gazed down at me, forever captured with that sweet enigmatic smile.

I could feel her spirit with me then in the room. Her presence was so powerful that I could almost inhale the freshly washed smell of her hair and hear her voice faintly calling me over the wind.

Closing my eyes, I felt myself falling away. Perhaps it was the morphine, but in my imagination, the lupine was blooming purple against the pink heather of the meadows beneath a brilliant sun. Massive flocks of gulls were swooping overhead, their shrill cries punctuated by sudden dives to a tempestuous sea.

In my reverie I was on my way to Blackhead, the highest pinnacle, and taking the trail through the dark cathedral woods that form the mysterious heart of the island. As I emerged from the stand of evergreens that fringe the base of the summit, there was Amelie, standing with her back to me, as if waiting for some important signal from far across the sea. She turned to face me, the wind bringing tears to her eyes as she saw me climbing toward her.

Acknowledgments

First, my deep appreciation to Bob Krick, an incomparable historian, whose generosity of time, knowledge, and insight into the American Civil War is simply unparalleled in the writing lives of so many of us who are students of that conflict. Also, my gratitude to Kathy Robbins and David Halpern, whose patience, perseverance, and wise counsel enabled me to finally breathe life into this story. And for writers of fiction who have complaints about their publisher or their editor, may I recommend Peter Wolverton at Thomas Dunne Books (St. Martin's Press), whose unerringly fine instincts and judgment strongly enhanced this book.

And to William Francis "Frank" Bartlett, whose reminiscence of the Battle of Ball's Bluff helped to inspire this work, as well as to Col. Joe Alexander, who made the historical errors less egregious.

One final note that might be of interest to the reader. Major R. Snowden Andrews, a Confederate artillery officer serving under Stonewall Jackson at Cedar Mountain, actually survived a wound that was just as grievous as that suffered by the protagonist of this tale. He often spoke in later years of benefiting from the "dust therapy," and survived until 1903.